A RECKONING OF WRAITHS

A Trove Arbitrations Novel

AMANDA CREIGLOW

Waldron Lake Books

Contents

ONE

A Gift

Working with blood isn't as easy as you'd think. It clots and congeals and dries ugly, and it's impossible to get out of a four-inch, high-density foam roller.

Luckily, dried blood works just as well for summoning ghosts as fresh blood. I don't have to break out my stencil and roller to create a new magic ghost-summoning circle. Instead, I can just use the sheets of plywood that I've already written the precise, weirdly beautiful magic symbols on in cow's blood. I can't carry them on my own, but I had my friend Wilbur bring them along with us to this picturesque forest glen. That's the fun thing about having a troll as a friend—they don't mind a little grunt work now and then. I think he likes it, actually. At seven feet tall, he's well below average size for a troll, so I think he gets a kick out of how impressed I am every time he carries something that heavy.

The only problem with the system is that the exacting requirements for a human to perform magic mean that the little gaps where the plywood boards meet need to be filled in before the circle will do anything but smell slightly musty. And that's before I even get into finding any places where the lines have gotten smudged or rubbed away in the journey. Everything has to be *perfect*, or it won't work.

So here I sit in a stupidly pretty forest, full of ferns and unfamiliar trees, surrounded by a crowd of twenty-three trolls. I try to ignore the weight of their disinterested eyes on me as I fill in the gaps and clean up the edges with a tiny paintbrush dipped in a spice jar full of cow's blood.

This is perhaps not the kind of Saturday morning I would have envisioned for myself a year ago.

The birds in Australia make different noises than I'm used to. I don't know if they're intrinsically more interesting, or if there are just more of them than I'm used to because we're at a Crossroads, and Crossroads tend to be in the middle of nowhere. I wouldn't normally pop across the planet for a single task, but it's warm here in December, and it's freezing back home in my small northeastern American hometown of Springfield, so I figure it's worth it.

When the intricate pattern of the fourteen-foot-diameter summoning circle is perfect, I sit back on my knees and look up at Wilbur. He's wearing his usual layers upon layers of dated, worn-but-clean clothing and his usual gentle, barely perceptible smile of approval.

"Thanks again for doing this," I say to Wilbur, uncomfortable with the expectant silence. I wince as I remember too late that trolls traditionally don't like being thanked. Trolls are paid for their services. And while I don't understand the deep, guttural words of Trollish that come from somewhere back in the crowd, I'd recognize the tone of good-natured teasing anywhere.

Whatever. Wilbur likes being thanked. At least, he doesn't *dislike* it, and it makes me feel better.

"Everybody ready?" I ask to an answering chorus of affirmative grunts.

So here's the other thing about magic—it may be exacting and hard as fuck, but it's also surprising. The first time I summoned a ghost, I did *not* expect for the spirit to bring along a physical body when it manifested in the world of the living. My forbidden trove of wizard writings failed to mention that particular fact, which is just like wizards, really. But all surprises eventually fade to familiarity, and after over a month of summoning ghost cows to harvest for their meat, we know the drill.

Most of the trolls are standing in the circle, looking almost human but not quite with their too-big proportions and too-stubby fingers and faces. I learned pretty quickly that summoning a large animal on wooden panels on top of dirt and roots and uneven ground means that the first animal you pull through will absolutely destroy your circle, and it takes time and mental energy to reset it again. When you're summoning en masse, as I'm about to, it makes much more sense to leave the newly-not-dead animal plenty of space to freak out without destroying anything. And, most importantly, to have catchers standing by to pick the spirit-created body up and carry it out of the circle to be butchered before you move on to the next.

I can't decide if spirit-created meat is the most organic or least organic form of beef. In any case, it's carbon-neutral, which sparks my proverbial Millennial joy. Plus, a surplus of free meat that I can donate to soup kitchens across the world at zero cost to my strapped wallet cheers my little public servant's heart. I didn't pursue a career in small-town local government for the fame and fortune. So as weird as all this is, and as tired as I am from getting up in the middle of the night to drag myself out here, it also feels really good for a variety of reasons.

So there's that.

Wilbur and I have been doing this every other day for the last few weeks, and every few days for a while before that. And while the crowd of trolls he's brought in has grown each time, enough of them here today have been through this before that they know the drill, and they must have already told the newbies what to do, because there's very little background Trollish going on as they move into place. I start focusing my mind to summon the ghost cow, and a few of them step out of the circle to give four trolls enough room to grab their prey before it does any damage to the circle.

I take a few centering breaths, pushing the sounds of birdsong and muttered conversations in Trollish into the background. Time to do some magic.

You may imagine that only wizards can do magic. You'd be half right. Only wizards can do magic *easily*. The defining characteristic—the thing that sets them apart from humans—is that when they attempt to perform a spell, they find their lips and hands and maybe minds conforming to the words and forms and mental require-ments easily. Sort of like the way a magnetized screwdriver grabs onto a screwhead and aligns naturally, with only the gentlest nudging needed. For the rest of us, magic is possible—just really fucking difficult. More like trying to fish a screw out of a hard-to-reach gap in the floor with a non-magnetic screwdriver. An invisible screwdriver. And the screw is invisible, too. And the existence of both screws and screwdrivers is forbidden knowledge that would get me killed if the wrong person heard me talking about them.

So as I get into Right Mind—the emotional state needed to make this spell work, which for this spell is a state of unassuming hope—I gear myself up for the likely disappointment that, no matter how many times I've pulled this spell off before, it likely won't work the first time.

The four-line incantation rolls past my lips in a well-practiced stream, flawless to my ears. But not flawless, in fact, because it does nothing to pull a spirit from the void. But I'm an experienced failure, and I shake it off. The first one's always free, right?

The second time I run through it, my eyes flick up at the movement of the manifested cow, terrified and bucking at the opposite end of the circle. Ghosts manifest at random points within the circle, so it takes a moment for the nearest troll to reach out to grab it. Trolls are pretty fast, though, so it's a short moment.

I reach down and lift up the panel nearest to me, breaking the summoning circle. As soon as I do, the spirit inhabiting the newly created cow carcass is gone again, back to wherever ghosts exist when they're not being summoned. All that's left is a massive hunk of skin and meat and bones and fat, which the troll hoists effortlessly onto his shoulder and carries outside the summoning circle to butcher.

Another troll replaces him. I replace the panel. I begin the incantation again.

I get it right the third time. I usually do. It's easier when I get on a roll. The impossible task of harnessing the secret, unknowable powers of the universe to create something from nothing gets a little monotonous after the eighteenth time, and I flub one. But I get back on track and keep going.

There's no point in moderation. No point in stopping until the cow corpses are piled around us, and the glade looks like the impromptu slaughterhouse it is. Every troll has five cows to butcher when I finally sit back on the forest floor, rolling my neck and stretching out my arms. I blink hard a few times, coming out of the trance that performing a magic spell always puts me in.

"Good haul today." Wilbur's rumbly, affable voice comes from beside and above me. He's sitting down, but even though he's one of the smaller trolls present, he still towers over me.

"It's getting close to Christmas. You're supposed to be more generous at Christmas," I answer, like it makes sense. It doesn't really, but it's hard to know what to say. That I feel guilty if I don't do as much as I can? That if I'm going to help, I should help as much as I can reasonably manage? It's hard to know where the line of what's reasonable resides. This isn't exactly percentages of paychecks and average suggested donations territory.

"It's a good deed, Elizabeth," Wilbur says, nudging me gently with a massive elbow. "You can feel good about yourself for it."

I shrug. We don't comment, surrounded as we are, on the fact that it's also a practical deed. It gives me practice at a spell, along with proof of getting it right. And there are enough words of spell language that show up in other spells in the trove of spell books that just building up the muscle memory of saying them over and over and over is a worthwhile endeavor. Call it magical mental pushups.

And it also helps my relationship with the troll community at large. Wilbur explained this to me when I was making too many apologies about asking him if he would maybe… kind of… if he thought it was a good idea… *consider* thinking about talking to just a couple of other trolls about helping to slaughter and distribute the meat. I had thought of it as an imposition, but that's just what trolls are—what they do. They connect for a fee. And they're happy to get to connect this meat to people who need it, be it at soup kitchens or slums. And as their fee, they'll take some undisclosed portion of the skeleton.

I don't ask what the trolls do with the skeletons. I don't ask what trolls want with the parts of a cow that aren't edible, just as I don't ask how they all have such quick, prodigious slaughtering skills or such long knives. Wilbur once told me that he'd eaten humans at some unspecified time in the past. That was enough to convince me that I don't need to know anything more about troll dietary practices. All Wilbur tells me, and all I need to know, is that performing the act of exchange with a troll lets them fulfill their purpose as a species and, thus, is a bonding factor. And with the trouble I get into, being favorably looked on by as many supernatural creatures as possible is always a good idea.

"You ready to go home?" Wilbur asks, this time from farther above me than he was before. He must have stood up. And I didn't notice. My eyes also appear to be closed. Someone should really get on that.

I open my eyes and raise my hand toward his outstretched one.

"Let's walk the world together, Wilbur!" I say in an affected Mid-Atlantic accent that never fails to widen his smile.

He pulls me to my feet, makes sure he has a firm grip on my hand, and takes a step forward into the Crossroads.

TWO

A Specter

From a certain point of view, the Crossroads are the most impressive magical feat I've ever seen. But like all magic, it doesn't feel specifically "magical" to my plain human little senses. I don't feel any kind of supernatural physical sensation or rush of energy. It just feels like I'm taking a short walk hand-in-hand with Wilbur. It just so happens that every step we take carries us tens, or hundreds, or sometimes thousands of miles across the surface of the planet. It's a dizzying experience, each step bringing with it a new set of sensory inputs.

Wilbur keeps us in the southern hemisphere as long as possible. I've got a coat on, and he doesn't seem to get cold, but it's still nice to avoid the bracing chill for as long as possible. We take an eastern route, heading into the night in just a few steps. The moon is full—or at least, it looks full. The cloud cover varies greatly from one step to another as we head north, making some steps nearly pitch black and some easy to see the abandoned world around us.

It's been a mild winter, which I've attributed to a little

bit of kindness from Zosime, the newly minted Goddess of the North Wind, who apparently wants to make up for the vicious cold snap we had in September before she took over the gig. Or maybe I'm making that up, and she hasn't really been paying attention. She's got to have a lot on her mind.

I'd originally learned how to summon ghosts so that I could help her have a conversation with her dead boyfriend, a siren who was killed by her predecessor. But then I got cold feet—heh—for a variety of reasons. Partially because I would need to get more siren blood to pull it off, and I would have no way of knowing for sure which dead siren I was actually going to pull up, and partially because summoning a spirit seemed a lot less intense when I didn't know they manifested on this side of the veil complete with a body. It feels cruel and wrong, somehow, to break the summoning circle and banish a sentient ghost when it has a working body. And what would happen if I didn't banish it? Would it just… live? Would it age? Would it rot in place? This type of thing can't be resurrection, or the trove would call it that, right? There has to be a catch. But figuring out what that catch is feels like an experiment far too macabre for me to take on. So I stick to livestock these days, which feels way less morally fraught.

Still, even if Zosime is going gentle on us, the last couple of Crossroads are bracing as Wilbur steps us back up to the northeastern United States, and the moonlit wood where we finally stop is covered in knee-high snow. I absentmindedly take off the oversized, seventies-style glasses that let me see through the wizard's illusion that hides the supernatural world from humanity. If the Crossroads aren't the most impressive magic I've seen, maybe that illusion is. It transforms everything supernatural into a cross between what humans expect to see, what the supernatural element is, and what the supernatural creature is trying to be. It makes us humans less knowledgeable in that we don't see the magic. On the other hand, it gives us a leg up on interpreting the emotions and expressions of supernatural creatures, which, God help me, I need more than most.

When I take off my glasses, Wilbur visibly shrinks beside me, and his features and proportions become indistinguishable from a human's—albeit one on the large side of normal. It used to be hard to adjust every time I made that transition, but I barely notice anymore. If you do enough of it, even magic becomes commonplace.

"Still worried about the meat?" Wilbur asks. I've been preoccupied thinking through the further implications of ghosts having bodies *again*, and he must have misread it. I deliberately shake my head, trying to clear the thought away.

"No, not really." That was mostly true. My long-term boyfriend Faisal and I have been eating ghost-pork and ghost-beef for months now with no ill effects. Faisal also called in a favor with a couple of different biologist friends who worked at various universities—an advantage of his job taking him all around the world to meet with professors and doctoral students—and had every conceivable test known to man run on it. All the tests came back conclusive: it was just meat, plain and simple.

Besides, I've prayed about it more than once. *Way* more than once. Which is still a very weird thing for me to think about. I'd never been the praying type. But eight months ago, I became the high—read: *only*—priestess of the god of gamblers. And, as an unintended consequence, it turns out that he hears any hopes and wishes I put out into the universe. A weird and invasive consequence, as I can't actually *stop* him from hearing anything with enough longing behind it to count as a prayer. But if a little mental boundary breaking is what it costs for me to have my sliver of his divine good luck, I'll take it. That luck is the only thing that's kept me alive this long. The supernatural world is really fucking cool in a lot of ways, but it's not exactly human-friendly.

All that to say that if this meat were harmful, and I was eating it, Aloysius would have said something. He feeds on my worship in the form of the risks that I take. And to take those risks that sustain him, I need to be alive. Besides, he knows that if he were allowing me to accidentally harm hundreds—thousands?—of people and he had known and not warned me, I would be pissed off enough that I would throw his blessing back in his face, whether I needed it or not. He knows that because I've worked it into my prayers.

See? Every uncomfortable situation comes with a silver lining.

"Good," Wilbur says, drawing me into a great big troll hug, which is like a bear hug but less murderous. He's warm and smells of mountain springs and the forest after a fresh rain. I don't understand a lot of things about Wilbur. I mean, I can puzzle them out and recognize them, but sometimes I don't get how he can be so warm and gentle and yet still so utterly unwilling to do anything that he can't spin into being a form of connection for which he can demand payment. But in the last six months of paying for his services, I've learned to take his friendship at face value and appreciate it anyway—to accept what he can give me and not expect anything else.

"You going to be all right?" he asks, probably reading my exhaustion.

"I'm fine. You can go back."

He nods sharply and steps back into the Crossroads.

He's in the middle of performing a connection, just as the other trolls back in Australia are, and he's anxious to get back to it. I asked him once what it felt like for him to get interrupted in the middle of a connection, and he played it off. "What does it feel like when you're in the middle of something and you get pulled away?" he'd asked. But it's more than that. He's so solid and steady most of the time. Right now, or when he gets delayed by something, he's just… not.

The wave of gratitude that visibly washes over him when I release him confirms my suspicions, as it usually does. He pats my head with one giant hand, which makes me feel not unlike a golden retriever, and steps off back into the Crossroads, leaving me alone in the cold December morning.

It's around dawn, though at this time of year, that's not as early as it feels like it should be. I wanted to share the wealth a bit and hit some new time zones with this batch, so I woke up early. The pressure of having set an appointment with Wilbur and knowing all those giant, terrifying trolls were waiting for us, and then the intense focus required to complete the summoning, had propelled me onward and kept my energy levels up. Now, standing alone in the woods in the dim light, the exhaustion is starting to settle into me.

And that's real unfortunate, considering how far away from town Wilbur dropped me.

Not that that's his fault. Any supernatural creature—that is to say, everyone except for humans and wizards—can step to any of the closest eight Crossroads at any time, from any point on the Earth's surface. All they need to do is step with intention, and they'll find themselves standing at the Crossroads closest to them in the direction they stepped, accurate to eight points of the compass. Everywhere on Earth is in the catchment area for eight Crossroads that supernatural creatures can step to and then step back from to their original entry point. They can even bring along passengers if they're sufficiently begged or bullied into doing so.

Once they've stepped into the Crossroads, they have a choice to make: walk the Crossroads further and lose their original point of origin, or step right back to where they started. Since Wilbur and I walked quite a few steps since leaving home, there's no way he could have brought me back to town. There are no Crossroads in Springfield—or near most developed places. Crossroads tend to unnerve humans, so we avoid building near them.

But Wilbur and I planned ahead and parked nearby. Or, at least, as close as we could get. There's only so near you can get a car to a random point in a forest. I've got a few minutes' walk ahead of me. And because we stepped directly from where we parked into the Crossroads, I don't even have a set of footprints to guide my way. I have no idea which way to go to get to the car. Fantastic. Some better boots also would have been nice.

I load up the map on my phone—which is a brand new, fancy model with bells and whistles that I'm still adjusting to. Wilbur threw away my old one for reasons that don't bear recalling and gave me this one as an apology. After a brief moment of struggling through my mental haze, I set off in the direction the map tells me.

With my breath hanging in the air, the snow crunching beneath my shoes, and water seeping into the denim of my jeans, I make my way to my beat-up, old sedan, which is looking damned unimpressive next to Wilbur's sleek, silver BMW. The moon is enough light to walk by, which is a good thing, because my phone is almost out of battery. I make a mental note, as I usually do when I see Wilbur's car, not to be jealous. His car may be better than mine, but at least I don't live under a bridge. Sure, that's his choice, but still.

I brace myself for the smell of maple syrup that always accompanies my car's heater, mentally apologize to the general concept of being a responsible human for driving so tired, and climb into the car.

This Crossroads is about an hour from the small town of Springfield, where I live. It isn't the closest Crossroads, but it's the closest Crossroads that allows for any privacy that will help our cars be less noticeable. We already traveled together a fair amount, with him escorting me around to do my job as an impartial third party for supernatural disagreements. But what with our new infinite-meat-distribution-service gig, discretion has seemed a bit more important lately. So I'm used to the feeling of this drive. It's a commute, in a way—albeit a weird one. And a much longer one than my usual drive into the mayor's office, where I work a job I actually get paid for.

I turn on the radio to keep me from zoning out. The aux cable that is, amazingly, the only way to get my own music into this ancient car radio other than an honest-to-God CD, frayed too much to be usable a couple weeks ago, and I keep forgetting to replace it. My radio station options are slim, so I've got Christmas music in my ears as I head toward town.

The route back to my place takes me through some open fields that make the world feel so big, even as my walk with Wilbur just made it feel so impossibly small. I relax into the air that's finally warming up, sing the wrong lyrics to "Simply Having a Wonderful Christmas Time," and feel comfortably human. In another fifteen minutes, I'll hit the highway, and I'll be able to eat up the road between here and home. When I get home, I'll shed my shoes and layers and crawl into bed. I'll curl up next to Faisal, who is blessedly home through New Year's. He's almost certainly still sleeping, and I can just about feel the warmth of his body and the gentle comfort of his steady breathing. I'm so caught in that moment, more there than here, that I don't fully register the figure in the glare of my headlights until I'm already past it.

I slam on the brakes, heart pumping, and the cheerful song coming through the speakers takes on a hint of menace.

A child? In the middle of a field nearly an hour before dawn? In the cold of winter? It had been a child. It must have been.

Or I'm imagining things. Or it's supernatural. I stare, unfocused, at the steam from the engine drifting out into the night, illuminated by my headlights, at a loss for what to do. Nine months ago, before I knew the supernatural existed, the path forward would have been clear: help the kid. That's what anyone would do. But knowing there's a lot more in the world besides humans can have a terrible effect on a person's spirit of altruism.

My right hand moves automatically to where my protection amulet sits on my chest beneath my shirt. It's still there, protecting me from any action that I would interpret as harm. It's almost a nervous tick at this point, any time I feel the slightest bit threatened, to reassure myself it's there. Probably a habit I should get rid of, as it gives the little details away, and it's never a good idea to give out information about your defenses unintentionally.

My next motion is just as senseless, but a little more intentional. I put my hand in my coat pocket, feeling to make sure the glasses are still there. I debate leaving them off, as I might look a bit weird. But utility trumps embarrassment, and I slip them on. Then I put the car in reverse and back up slowly, making sure that the kid has plenty of time to get out of the way if they're walking toward me.

I don't see the kid in my rearview mirror. But that doesn't mean anything—they might just be standing outside the field of view. I crane my neck to look behind, but I still don't see them.

I imagined it. That's fine. Not a great sign for my mental health, but that's fine. It was a split second, and I'm tired and probably a little stressed out about... well... everything.

Knock, knock.

My hand flies to my amulet as I start in my seat. I turn to my window, where I see the little girl right outside.

She's so young, maybe eight or nine years old. Just a few years older than my nieces. Even through the glasses, she just looks like a human girl. She's wearing a knitted cap over long, straight, mousy brown hair. Her eyes are big, round, and brown. It's hard to tell for sure in this light, but it looks like she has freckles. She's wearing a homemade sweater with red, orange, and brown stripes underneath a puffy jacket that reminds me of the one I had as a kid.

And she looks scared and sorry for scaring me as she takes a few steps back.

I open my door, because a little girl standing in the middle of the road where a car could mow her down is more terrifying than whatever threat I'd been turning her into in my head.

"Sorry," she says, in the kind of tiny voice that only scared children can produce. "I didn't mean to scare you. You stopped."

"That's ok," I say as I get out. I don't close the door behind me, but I take a few steps toward her. She's wearing corduroy pants and puffy blue and rainbow boots that I feel like have a name. What was it? Moon boots?

She doesn't step away from me when I draw close. She doesn't seem intimidated, which she shouldn't be. I don't look like anything special. Average height, average wavy, dirty blonde hair, average face. There's probably some blood residue still on my hands, but she wouldn't be able to see it.

"Are you ok? Do you live around here?" I try to judge if she's been hurt. Faisal went through a true-crime podcast phase a few years ago, which I teased him for right up until he got me hooked, too. We both quit cold turkey for our own good after a couple of months. But the memories of all those stories shift me quickly from being afraid *of* this little girl to being afraid *for* this little girl.

She looks all right. Probably not dressed quite warm enough, but otherwise fine. If she hadn't been in the middle of a field before dawn. Unless she lives here, and she wandered out to the road because… why?

I search around me for the closest farmhouse. Maybe something bad happened in the house, and she came out to the road to try to find help? But that doesn't make any sense, either. Kids know how to use cell phones.

"No, I don't think so."

My eyes snap back to her.

"You don't think so?" I ask, trying to keep my voice as calm as possible as I flip the glasses up to examine her that way. No change. I must have failed to keep how worried she was making me out of my voice, because she looks concerned.

"No, I don't think I'm from here," she says again, but this time more uncertainly. "Am I?"

My heart breaks. She's so lost and confused, and I'm just making it worse. I let out a breath that billows between us. "It's okay. Everyone gets confused sometimes."

That must have been the right thing to say, because she

relaxes. "I'm Melissa," she says, holding out her hand as if to shake mine and then withdrawing it with a lost look. Maybe she was told not to shake strangers' hands? I can't be sure.

"Hello Melissa, it's nice to meet you. I'm Elizabeth," I say, returning her child's seriousness. "If you don't know where you live, I think we should go to the police station. Do you think that would be all right?"

And I should come up with a plausible explanation for why I was driving around narrow country roads an hour from where I live before dawn. Better think fast, I guess. I ready myself for her mistrust. They probably don't teach "stranger danger" in schools in those exact words anymore, but kids must still be taught not to get in strange cars with people they don't know. But she doesn't object. She just nods and goes around to the passenger side door and waits for me to open it for her.

I've never thought about putting protection wards on my car the way I have on my house, but at this point I wish I had. Nothing seems wrong or off about this kid. Nothing except the circumstances and her lack of knowledge. But isn't that enough?

But the alternative is, what? Leave her here in the cold? Sit in my warm car and watch her shiver and shake while waiting for the police to show up, and come up with some reason a normal human with no knowledge of the supernatural would believe for why I'm afraid of a little girl? I open the door, and she climbs in, settling into the seat and going about the motions of putting on her seatbelt with that endearing determination kids get when proving they can do something they know they're supposed to.

I tear my eyes away to look up where the closest police station is on my phone. Ten minutes. Great. Ten minutes to come up with a good story.

"Is this your scarf?" Melissa asks.

I look back at her as I put my phone in its dash holder, angling it so that I can see it. "No, that's my friend's scarf. He lent it to me a couple days ago. I've been meaning to give it back to him."

"It's really soft."

Despite the weirdness of the situation, I laugh. "He's really rich. He buys nice things. You can wear it, if you want."

"Really?"

If my kind-of friend Max minded that I was letting a little kid in distress wear his expensive cashmere scarf, he could go fuck himself.

"Go ahead," I say, putting the car in drive and starting us forward. I check the map to make sure I'm heading the right direction and search for excuses. Nothing believable is coming to mind. Geocaching? Do people still geocache? Are there any hiking trails near here that would be good to see the sunrise from the end of? Maybe I can google it from the parking lot.

"It has a lot of spells on it," comes Melissa's voice, sounding for all the world like she's telling me her favorite fact about elephants.

My blood runs cold. She *seemed* so human. I keep my eyes forward on the road to avoid reacting.

"Well, that makes sense. My friend is a wizard. What kind of spells?"

"Spying spells, mostly. You're Elizabeth, and you're human, so that means your friend is Max."

Fuck.

"How do you know my friend is Max?" I ask, fixing a pleasant smile on my face by sheer force of will and turning to look at Melissa.

She looks exactly as she did before… Except that her

hat is gone, there are sticks in her hair, and the sleeve of her puffy jacket is ripped at the shoulder. She has Max's scarf wrapped around her neck. It's soaked through and through with blood.

"Because Max is the wizard you killed," she says, still smiling and bright.

"I didn't kill Max." The smile I'm managing to keep plastered on my face must look manic, but it doesn't seem to bother her as much as my disagreeing with her. Her face scrunches up in confusion and objection.

"Yes, you did! You killed him twice!"

I open my mouth, still searching for words, when Melissa's attention shifts to the front windshield. Her shrill, desperate scream splits my ears. I turn my eyes to see what she's screaming at and glimpse a great, big hulk of a man, with something flashing in his hand in the middle of the road less than ten feet in front of us. I slam on the brakes and turn the wheel, my eyes closing and the tires squealing.

For one horrifying second, I think I must have gone too far. The car feels like it's going to flip. But I'm a lucky girl. I'm still sitting upright, with only the pain from where the seatbelt dug into me, the smell of burned rubber, and my heaving breath telling me that anything is wrong.

I search for the man outside the car, frantic and terrified. I don't see him. I don't see Melissa, either. I'm alone, my car across both lanes of the road at an angle. Terrified of nothing but my own memory, and a lingering blue vapor in the air that dissipates in seconds.

Even Max's scarf is gone.

THREE

An Imposition

It takes me a good thirty seconds of staring until I accept the essential fact that I am once more alone.

"Melissa?" I say into the too-small space of the car. When there's no answer, I say it louder. I want to roll down the window and call it out into the world outside, but now that she's no longer here and real and in need of help, she's back to being the terrifying unknown that she was when I first saw her.

And if I found her, I might find the other figure. At the thought of him, my sympathies shift back to Melissa. God, I hope she's safe. I'm guessing dead, okay, but safe. I don't care if that's a contradiction of terms.

I've been summoning ghosts—sometimes hundreds at a time—over the last few months. But none of them were sentient. That difference was already important before, but it's very, *very* important now.

I need to put some distance between me and this place. I need to get back to civilization—to get to where other people are. I need to stand in line at a coffee shop, with normal people going about their day. I need Faisal's arms around me. I need to not be alone. My hands shake as I get the car moving again. It's a little easier to breathe once I reach the cluster of buildings near the highway on-ramp, but I don't really start to relax until I'm on the highway, safe in the flow of traffic.

I want to put the radio back on, but it still doesn't feel right. I want to call Max, just to make sure he's alive. Or yell at him. Either/or. But mostly, I want to call Faisal. I don't trust myself to dial the phone right now, though. My hands are still shaking, and I'm holding onto the steering wheel too hard.

I try to reason with myself. It's not like the man with the axe or the hammer or the saw or *whatever* it was could have hurt me through my amulet. But I wasn't expecting him. And something about him probably having been human but being something else now makes him scarier than all the monsters I've seen in the last nine months. I don't know why.

I relax bit by bit over my journey as the sun comes up. When I'm almost to my exit, a call comes in from Faisal, which is weird. It's technically morning now, but he shouldn't be awake. Saturdays are supposed to be lazy. It's a law of nature. Still, I'm relieved he called me. I might not trust myself to dial, but I can press the answer button, and God, I want to hear his voice.

"Hey there, hotshot," I say, and then feel weird that I said it. That's the way I answer his calls when he's on a work trip, but he's not right now. I'm still shaken, and I'm sure he can tell from my greeting if he can't also hear it in my voice.

"Hey, Beth. Glad I caught you. You on your way back from your coffee and doughnut run?"

What the fuck? He knows where I am, and he knows I'm not returning with food. And even if I were, why would he say it like that? Normal people don't tell each other things they both already know, and Faisal especially hates saying things that don't need to be said.

Unless he's saying them for the benefit of someone else. A realization hits me.

"Ummm… I forgot what kind of coffee Mom likes?"

He had invited my mother over this morning to have breakfast with him. Is he talking to me like this for her benefit? It was an early time to invite her over, sure, but that's part of the point. Eight years ago, something called a vampiric spirit ate all the sweetness in my mother's memories, both in the past and in the future. Now to get her to remember anything good, you have to mix it with a little bitter. And she apparently liked the idea of one-on-one time to *finally* get to know Faisal so much that it took setting the time obnoxiously early to get her to remember the appointment.

"Well, it's good you haven't ordered yet. You wouldn't have gotten enough coffee and doughnuts for our other guests to share, too."

"Our guests?" My first thought is that Melissa and the tool-wielder must have somehow found their way to my home, but no… Faisal wouldn't be implying that we should give a little kid coffee. And that dude looked for all the world like he meant me harm. That was one good thing keeping me from panicking: if our "guests" were in the house, that meant they got through the wards. Nothing that means me harm gets through those wards.

"Yeah," Faisal says, his voice a surprisingly good impression of cheerful. "Your work friends stopped by from out of town. I'm so glad I'm finally getting to meet them. They seem like great people, and I'm glad we've gotten them over to visit in our house."

If he were close enough, I would kiss him. He's trying

to make this all positive enough that Mom won't remember it. And, at the same time, he's keeping me from freaking out about my worlds colliding by reminding me about the wards. I'd remembered that on my own, sure, but if I hadn't, that would have been useful.

As I take the exit into Springfield, I do my best to match his sunny tone, just for the benefit of whoever else might be able to hear the conversation. I'm not as good of an actor as Faisal is, but damn, I'm trying.

"Oh, that's great to hear. I didn't know they'd be around. I'll make a special occasion of it and pick up some goodies from our favorite place on my way back."

I don't mean my actual favorite coffee shop—I'm not heading to Jolt-a-Go-Go, which has and always will have the best coffee within a hundred miles—but he gets my meaning.

"That sounds perfect. See you soon."

The line goes dead, and I fight down the little flare of panic that rises up. Instead, I focus on the task at hand. Rather than turning left at the exit to head home the way I normally would, I take a right to head down to the Arts District. I wind my way through a few unnecessarily narrow streets until I find the Emporium, a used book-store/café/ice cream parlor/unusual antiques dealership.

The Emporium is closed at just after dawn on a Saturday morning. Inconsiderate, really. But I don't intend to allow that to stop me—not if Gigi's inside. And I *do* have a way of telling if she's inside. Glad that no one is on the street, I go to my trunk and open up a small metal case of useful objects. The case has wards around the edge like those that protect my house, which means I have to be careful to prevent Max from looking in my trunk, lest he see and remember the spell. But it means that I can carry a few enchanted objects in there without attracting any undue attention. The wards protect and also conceal magical residue. This is where my enchanted leather jacket lives when I'm not wearing it, with the key that can open any lock in the pocket and Aloysius's blessing on the lapel in the form of a jewel and enameled flower broach. It's also where I keep a lantern my father made that points toward magic. Gigi extinguished it once, but I was able to re-enchant it about a month ago. Unluckily for Gigi, since she's a purely magical creation.

After checking to be sure there's no one looking, I pull the lantern out and look at it. Through my glasses, I can see a thin green flame, tilting at an angle. Tilting toward the Emporium. I walk around the place, noting the way the flame moves as I do so as to always point into the building.

Gigi must sleep here. I'd suspected that for a while, but now it's confirmed.

After taking a moment to marvel at the sight of the successful place so eerily empty, I do my best impression of Max and pound on the sheet glass doors at the front, demanding attention with an utter disregard for whether anyone else actually wants to give me any.

"Gigi!" I say, puffs of breath freezing on the glass. "I need you!" I give it a moment, waiting for a response. None comes. More loudly, I add, "I know you're in there."

One nice side effect of dealing with legitimately dangerous circumstances all the time is that I'm no longer annoyed by silly little things like making a fool of myself in public. Well, most of the time anyway.

"I'll keep yelling until you come out and talk to me. I'll annoy all your neighbors. You know I will! My mom is in danger, and I need your help."

"In danger" might be a bit of a stretch, since whoever is in my home can't mean *me* harm, so they seem unlikely to target her. But I'm sure as hell not comfortable about it. I give it thirty seconds, and I am about to start screaming again when I see movement inside the shop.

I've still got my glasses on, so I see Gigi as she truly is, not as the wizard's illusion shows her. The polished white marble surface of her skin gleams in the low glow of the dawn, and her diamond eyes glint dangerously. She's a woman of solid stone—a living statue. She's one of a matched set that a whimsical wizard created longer ago than I like to think about. One of them can only lie, and one of them can only tell the truth. As the story goes, travelers would have one question to determine which of the gates they guarded was the good one, and which was the bad one.

I don't know what was behind either of the gates, but it doesn't matter now. Whatever it was has been wiped out by time. As was the wizard, and any human or wizard who might have known him. But when he created truthful Gigi and her deceitful sister, he made them to be indestructible —even by time. So Gigi can't lie and can't die, and she has never struck me as particularly happy about either of those things.

Although, right now, her unhappiness is much more to do with the irreverent human on her doorstep at an ungodly hour. I take off my glasses. Easier not to be intimidated that way. Without the glasses, she's just a harried woman with olive skin, black eyes, and startling crimson hair. Pretty, sure. And possessed of a certain elegance, even in her current state. But not the over-this-shit force of nature she is underneath.

"Your mother is upstairs," Gigi says without preamble. She tells the truth, sure, but only to the extent she knows it. She's constrained, not a seer.

"Nah, she's at my house. As are parties in need of arbitration. You can see the issue."

Gigi breathes a heavy sigh, entirely for my benefit.

"Do I, though? So what if she learns the truth? The only way that causes a problem with the treaty is if a non-human tells her. And that's only if any wizards find out. Your pet wizard is letting your boytoy stay in the know without collecting heads. Even your librarian. What's one more added to the party?"

Gigi has a lot of practice doing a lot of things. This includes getting under my skin. And practice, unfortunately, makes perfect. I do my best to shake off the twenty different things about those sentences that I want to protest and nitpick.

"I don't want her to know, Gigi. Her memory is tricky. Even if she took it well, she might not remember the right thing at the right time. I don't want her saying the wrong thing to the wrong person. It's dangerous."

Gigi folds her arms, slumping against the door. The warmth spilling out from inside the building is welcome, but I'm starting to feel the cold, anyway.

"You'd lose a tenant. Think of all that sweet, sweet rent money you'd miss out on if something unspeakable happened to her," I try brightly.

That coaxes a smile out of her. It's nonsense, of course —Gigi can't be hurting for money. If she were, she'd probably have had a tenant in the studio apartment on the third floor of the Emporium *before* my mother suddenly needed a place in town to live, and Gigi suddenly had a below-market-rate vacancy that was suspiciously freshly remodeled.

"You brought this on yourself, you know," I prod, eliciting a raised eyebrow.

"Did I?" she asks, clearly not looking for a real answer.

I could tell her that if she wants to be involved in the chaos I carry with me these days, this is what that looks like. But there's no need—she's straightening up.

"You want me to call her?" she asks. "Come up with some housing-based emergency to bring her back here, and then surprise her with something so pleasant that she won't remember any of it?"

"That's a slightly better plan than the one I had, so yes."

Gigi delivers an exaggerated mock bow to me, and I turn back to the car. She calls out after me, "So, your librarian is still angry with you, then?"

I don't want to give Gigi the satisfaction of seeing the look on my face at that, so I don't turn around. "She's my sister, and she's not mad at me."

"I didn't say she wasn't *also* your sister. But if she weren't mad at you, you'd have asked her for this, not me."

I turn around, losing the battle of not letting Gigi get to me. "She's *not* mad at me. But yes, she is still processing everything." The reminder pricks at me, just the way Gigi meant it to. After plenty of prodding from Faisal, I brought my sister, Olivia, into the know about the magical world. I thought she took it well at first, but she's been pretty cold to me lately. I guess it's a lot to take in.

Gigi gives me her trademarked sharp grin. "Oh, *processing.* Well, as long as she's *processing.* Now shoo. I have a call to make."

With that, Gigi disappears back into the dark cavern of the Emporium, leaving me shivering in the cool, dim light of the dawn.

FOUR

A Grievance

I take a circuitous route back home from the Emporium, so as to not run into mom heeding Gigi's call. My unexplained appearance on her path would probably be an annoying enough mystery that she would remember it somewhat, and this is one of the few times I'm actually rooting for the damage the vampiric spirit did to her mind. When I get home, my mother's car isn't there. Faisal's Jeep is the only other car in the driveway.

So whatever parties are in there looking for arbitration don't have their own wheels. Or maybe don't *need* their own wheels. That simple fact makes me feel a little more uneasy. Not that it's a bad thing, per se, but there's always something wonderfully disarming about seeing a supernatural creature driving a car. It makes them seem so much less intimidating. Sometimes I think it's because so many of them are old, and it makes them a little slow to adopt new technology, so they seem in a state of constant frustration with all of the new bells and whistles. But I think it's mostly because if they drive a car and aren't constantly getting pulled over, that means they follow the laws of the road.

Human laws. And if they submit to human laws in one thing, maybe they're not so far above me as it sometimes feels.

I slip my glasses back on as I head from the car to the front door, pausing to get as much of the snow off of my shoes and onto the welcome mat as I can.

A brief glance through the front picture window reveals that, whoever our "guests" are, they aren't sitting in the living room. Sitting around the kitchen table then, probably. I'll have a second to warm up and calm down before I see them, thank God.

But when I step through the door, I'm not greeted by an empty room. Not exactly. My heart sinks, and my pulse shoots up. Knotted, winding roots cling to the walls and the ceiling like vines of ivy, accompanied by vapor-like wisps of shifting, floating, dark earth pulsing around the roots. I can make out something like a heartbeat in their motion.

I've seen this kind of thing before, though never splayed out like this. The roots and the silky, suspended soil around them are what a graveling's body is made out of. Like the graveling who tried to curse my father and ended up destroying my mother's mind instead. Like the other graveling that I killed in trial by combat in a hidden cavern nine months ago, betting my sister and her daughters' lives on the outcome along with my own. I had to do it to save my own life, sure. And I didn't even know back then that exempting myself from the wizard/supernatural treaty would free me up to fulfill the traditional role of human arbiter to the supernatural community. But still, I got the sense that gravelings aren't supposed to die, really. And that I might not be their favorite person in the world, having killed two of them, and having made myself such a threat to their sacrosanct law and order.

And at least one of them is in my house with my very human, very vulnerable boyfriend, who is *not* technically the owner of this house, and whose well-being is therefore *not* technically linked to the wards around it.

I swallow hard and fight to keep my footsteps measured and posture unworried. I don't remove my glasses as I head back to the kitchen table. As it comes into view, I see three figures. Sort of. One of them—the graveling—is barely recognizable as a humanoid form, so enmeshed is it with the vine-like roots all over the walls and ceilings. The last time I saw gravelings, they were made of that same root-and-soil material, but it was shaped more like a person. The other two figures at the table are both Middle Eastern in origin, Faisal being Kuwaiti, and the woman being…

The woman being *something.* She's gorgeous, and the force of her beauty hits me as she turns her head to face me with a wicked smile. And this, the simple fact of her wild, absolute beauty, shocks me. Not because she's so gorgeous—I've seen a siren doing her best to lure her prey into the water—but because she remains beautiful through my glasses. I'm supposed to be seeing her as she really is, but she just looks like a normal human woman.

All except for her eyes, that is. Black eyes are pretty common, but the irises and pupils of her eyes aren't just black—they're void. Absolute nothing. It unsettles me on a deep, visceral level, even more so than the graveling infestation in my house.

As though on cue, the graveling speaks. The sound seems to come from everywhere the roots have expanded out to, deep, husky, resonant, and… French?

"I hope you don't mind. I have made myself comfortable."

I take off my glasses when I drag my eyes away from the woman to look at the graveling, as though that will help me make sense of the accent. And, surprisingly, it does. When seen through the wizard's illusion, the graveling is a spindly man, not too tall, with his legs crossed at the knee in a casual pose. He's leaning one arm on the table and has a lit, roll-up cigarette in his hand that I would object to if it were, in fact, real. He's wearing black skinny jeans and a black sport coat over a charcoal sweater, all of which look effortlessly casual on him.

He is cooler than I have ever been or ever will be, a far cry from the buttoned-up, fifties-accountant appearance of the gravelings I met this spring.

"Come far?" I ask, not letting my eyes wander back to the woman. One overwhelm at a time, thank you very much. The graveling smirks and tilts his head.

"*Oui,*" he says, hitting the accent hard in a way that can only be intentional. "The local contingent of my kind does not *like* you. Can't think why, can you?"

He takes a long drag on his illusionary cigarette. How does that work, exactly? I know I see a cigarette because that's the translation of what he's really doing that my eyes can interpret, but what is he really doing? I could pull my glasses back on and check, but that's not high on my list of priorities at the moment.

Finally, as if they've been afraid to wander there, my eyes rest on Faisal, examining his neutral expression and relaxed body for any sign of distress. He's well dressed, as far as he goes, in a pair of jeans and a flannel button-up shirt that I bought him as a joke when I ruined his last one.

"He's all right," the woman says, her voice thin and piercing, but not in an unattractive way. It reminds me of a high flute skillfully played. Her accent is pure American. "He's been keeping his hands off of spells like a good boy. No evidence of using magic at all. No reason Claude here is going to need to enforce any rules."

My eyes dart to the graveling—Claude, I guess—for a split second before the woman stands and pulls my attention back to her. She draws close and walks around me, trailing one cold, cold finger across my body as she goes. The impact is blunted by the winter coat I'm still wearing, but it chills me all the same.

"You, on the other hand, are not so squeaky clean. I can't tell you how strange it is to see a graveling sitting right there, in striking distance of a human with magic residue *all* over her, doing nothing at all. You really are exempted from the treaty."

I look at Faisal. He does seem okay. Physically, at least. It can be hard to tell for sure how he's doing emotionally, considering his effective poker face, but he gives me an almost imperceptible smile.

I sigh with nearly as much theatricality as the beautiful woman.

"That's pretty common knowledge by now, I assumed. Do you have a point? And a name?"

She draws back slightly, making me feel like I've won a victory. Claude smiles from the table.

"Ghouls don't have names," he says. "No more than they have faces of their own. It all changes, you know. Always a new face, new name. I don't keep track. Neither should you."

A shapeshifter. That makes sense, I guess—the reason why she didn't need to be altered by the illusion other than her eyes. If Claude's words bother her, she doesn't show it outwardly. She does seem vaguely bored by me now, though, which I take as a win. There are a lot of supernatural things it's good not to show fear around. Just figures ghouls would be one of them. She sits back down at the table, affecting a casual pose very much the mirror of Claude's.

"I've been using this face for fifteen hundred years. If that doesn't make it mine, I don't know what does."

I offer my best effort at casual, calm, and collected as I head to the only empty chair at the table. I'm across from Faisal, and the ghoul and the graveling are across from each other, like we're all about to play the world's weirdest bridge game.

"That's a long time," I say, sliding into character as the arbiter now that no one seems to be in immediate danger.

"Don't you know? Ghouls are demons. Demons live a long time, no?"

The woman, previously so self-possessed, shoots a look at Claude that could curdle milk. Don't call ghouls "demons" to their faces. Noted.

"Oh, don't look so unhappy. The arbiter likes demons. You didn't know that? How uninformed. How strange you want to come to an arbiter when you know nothing about her," Claude says.

I don't like demons. At least, as far as I know, I've never met one until today, and she's not making a great impression on me. But everyone who doesn't know my patron Aloysius is a god thinks he's a demon, and while he hasn't ever claimed the title, he doesn't usually correct it. The gods are supposed to be dead—wiped out by the wizards. Staying hidden is his way of keeping that false bit of common knowledge from becoming true.

I turn to the ghoul. "So you're the one who wants an arbitration?" I ask.

The ghoul hesitates for a long moment before shifting her attention back toward me. "My people do, yes. Because we are dying, and this prick and his kind could save us, but they won't. Because they would need to bend their precious rules."

I do my best to mask my initial sympathetic reaction,

but some of it must get through because the barest hint of a smile flickers across the ghoul's face.

"Tell her *why* you're dying," Claude urges, his own smile more amused than cruel.

The ghoul holds my gaze for a long moment before breaking away as she speaks. "Our food supply has been poisoned."

I have, slowly, been learning to think before I speak at these kinds of things. I do my best to remember what I've read about ghouls in the collection of papers in the trove that I've taken to calling *Wilhelm's Big Book of Monsters.* Ghouls eat…

"Bodies? Human bodies have been tainted? You think someone is getting into graveyards?"

That seems to have struck as much of a nerve as calling her a demon, but luckily her annoyance doesn't appear directed at me. She glares at Claude, her anger evident.

"They are not allowed to eat bodies buried in grave-yards," Claude says. "It's a provision of the treaty."

The ghoul leans forward, hunching over the table like she's about to fly across it at him. "No, we're not allowed to desecrate graves or step onto cemetery soil. Too likely to get caught, I suppose. That, and the wizards who made the treaty were none too fond of us. But there's nothing against us eating the bodies themselves if someone were to bring them to us without disturbing the graves or making anyone suspicious."

And there's the crux of it. Gravelings have prodigious powers with earth. They can carry bodies underground, living or dead. I should know, having once had the dubious pleasure of being carried in that way.

"You want them to feed you," I say, still doing my best to sound impartial.

"Which we do not consider to be an option," Claude

says, addressing the ghoul. "You read the treaty to say it would be allowed, and I see the argument. But it does not matter how you see the treaty. It matters how the wizards see it. They catch us doing this thing for you and violating the treaty, and it will be war, *ma chère*. Your kind is not worth risking war."

"Not necessarily," the ghoul says, desperation in her voice.

"No?" Claude asks, his tone raising just slightly. Just enough. "Because wizards are so even-handed? Because they are fair and just and will understand? If this were true, we would just ask them. We would just do everything aboveboard. But you know as well as I that this will not happen. They only want a weakness. They only want an excuse. We will not be that excuse. Not for you."

"Even though they are dying?" I can't stop myself. Claude's demeanor is so studied—so cool. It's hard not to find that infuriating. But at my words, I see the cracks in that demeanor. There's anger under pressure residing down there.

"Ask her what they are eating now. Ask her what has been tainted. See if you are still willing to risk the peace and the stability of the world to keep some demons alive."

The ghoul bristles at the word "demon" again, but she doesn't take her eyes off him. She doesn't look at me as I ask. "What are you eating now?" I think I might already know.

After a long time—too much time—the ghoul turns to me with a hard, defiant expression. "Your spares. The ones you don't care about. The ones you don't notice going missing."

We care about them. I want to say. *We notice them.* But we haven't noticed them, it seems. I need her to be a little clearer, though, unfortunately.

"You mean the homeless?" I'm making connections and trying not to. It takes everything in me not to share a knowing glance with Faisal.

The ghoul tilts her head, her eyes shining. "The poor, yes. The ones you don't take care of, *we* take care of. You've got your circle of life, and we've got our circle of death. It all goes round and round. But there's a hitch in the wheel, and it needs to be fixed. If our usual food supply is no longer safe—and it *is* no longer safe—then we'll have to branch out. Our hunts might get more noticeable."

"And that will not be allowed." Claude's body is stiff as an iron rod. I wonder if the silt through his roots is standing stock still or flowing.

The ghoul leans back, affecting something approaching her previous casual air, albeit undercut by the clear effort it takes her to do so. "You see our problem."

"How long has this been going on?"

"Three weeks ago, one body was tainted, and all who ate it fell ill. The hunting party split and reformed with others, as we do, and it spread from one ghoul to another. Through touch, we think. We have tried to isolate, but it is hard. It is against our nature to do. By the time we were able to stop the spread, nearly a hundred of us were exposed. All who were exposed died. And we mourned them."

It's brazen as hell to talk about mourning your kind's dead while sitting in front of a member of the kind you murder. Gotta give her that.

"But we moved on. We thought it was strange and sad, but it was over. Until a week ago, when it happened again. The hunting party was bigger this time. We still haven't stopped it completely. There are still some of us dying. And now everyone is afraid to eat anything. We don't know what was wrong with it, but it didn't begin until recently.

The already dead should still be safe. We need help just until we find out who has done this and can deal with them appropriately."

"You think someone has done this on purpose?" I ask.

The incredulous look the ghoul shoots me makes me wither inwardly. "Don't be taken in by my charming persona. There are some people who do not like our kind so well as we deserve to be liked."

It's easy to get drawn into feeling sorry for the ghouls with the sob story and the pain masked in sarcasm. Who can't relate to that, at least? And something in my manner must tell her that it's working, because she seems encouraged, straightening slightly. I turn to Claude.

"Can I take you being here as a sign that the gravelings agree to be held by the outcome of this arbitration?" I ask, almost pro forma at this point. There isn't *really* a set ceremony for arbitrations, but forming habits and patterns in the madness is just about the only thing that's kept me sane the last nine months.

Claude shifts uncomfortably in his chair. "Against my better judgement, I am instructed to tell you that we will. Though I tell you again that ruling in the ghouls' favor is an invitation to outright war. And more of your kind will die in this war than any other option."

War bad, got it. But bad enough to justify allowing the ghoul's centuries-long mass murder of the homeless to continue? "You're hoping I just, what, tell the ghouls they have to keep doing what they're doing and if they die, they die?"

Claude cocks his head. "If this were the case, we would not come to you for this. But as much as you are hated by my kind here, we are not immune to gossip. And from what word gets around, when given two options, you often choose to find a third. We are… hopeful for that third option."

The words drip from his lips like poison, leaving me no doubt that the *we* he is referring to does not, actually, include him.

"With one condition, of course," he adds.

For fuck's sake, no one ever comes to arbitrations with conditions and moratoriums. But no one's ever infested my house with their tendrils before, so there's a first time for everything, I guess.

"And what's that?"

"You don't involve your wizard."

And then Faisal, who has been so still and neutral for the entire conversation, lets out a strangled bark of a laugh. Claude and the ghoul's heads snap around to focus on him.

"You've clearly never met her wizard," he says, by way of explanation. And I can't tell if he's brave because he hasn't seen either of these people for what they really are, or because of his year spent living in the Casino of Lost Souls with Aloysius, being exposed to all kinds of supernatural creatures great and small. Or maybe I'm just underestimating how much better he's gotten at masking fear than I've ever been.

Claude looks askance at me, and I shrug. "I can try not to involve him. I can avoid telling him. But he's nosy as hell. Not like he's going to tell anyone, though. There are a lot of things he doesn't tell other wizards." At least for now. At least until he gets what he wants from me.

"As charmingly naïve as your belief that you can either trust or control a wizard may be," Claude says, "we are not content to share it. You will not involve the wizard in this. We have been under far too much of their scrutiny of late. And some of that is already your fault. The knowledge that your wizard has exempted you from the treaty does not seem to have spread through their community. We have no inclination of remedying that, but they know that *something* is going on."

And there it is, that fun little way of toeing the line between technically following the rules so that they can claim innocence when asked, but choosing how much of them to actively enforce. Therein lies the real power of any law enforcement. Is Claude threatening to turn me in? I don't think so. Human arbitration may seem an odd custom, but it has its use in the supernatural community in avoiding interspecies violence. I'm the first human technically exempted from the treaty in a long time and therefore eligible to arbitrate. So as long as I don't do anything too unacceptable, most species don't want to be the one that ruins that. But most species don't have two dead bodies on their hands that I'm responsible for.

"I'll do my best. That's all I can promise."

"Eh," Claude says, with an expression so stereotypically French that I wonder if the wizard's illusion has been mainlining bad movies. "And if it turns out your *best* is not good enough, we will have, as you say, a problem."

Yup, that's a threat. With that, Claude straightens, and I feel a change in the house that I can't see. It's like catching movement in your peripheral vision or sensing movement around you from air currents with your eyes shut. He must be pulling in his roots, unwinding them from the walls around us. I resist the urge to put on my glasses so that I can see it. It would only freak me out, anyway. And it would distract me from Claude's precise movements as he reaches into his coat pocket and pulls out a silver card case, from which he retrieves a thick, crisp, white, silver-embossed card.

He hands the card to me, and I'm not surprised to find

it contains only a single phone number, complete with a French country code.

"For when you have come to a solution that you wish to put forward," he says, standing up. Then he gives me a shallow, stiff bow, and turns toward the backyard. His air of effortlessly cool man of high-class mystery doesn't mesh well with the inherent awkwardness of opening the sliding glass door, especially as it squeals. But I'm glad he's headed to the backyard, where he will be out of line of sight from the street and our neighboring houses.

The wizard's illusion can do a lot, but it struggles with reality sometimes. I know he must be disappearing into the earth, his roots digging down into it like so many giant, coordinated earthworms. But the best the illusion can do is show him open a door into the earth, like a cellar has suddenly appeared there that wasn't there before. In a matter of moments, I see the stick-thin man disappear inside, and, when he's fully gone, so is the door.

"And to think there are those who call ghouls dramatic," the ghoul says from beside me, startling me. She's leaning in close, and I can't say I like it.

"I wasn't aware that was the stereotype," I manage.

She shrugs. "Who would expect you to know anything about the stereotypes of any of us? All you've got are folk tales and rumors."

I swallow, trying to refocus. With Claude gone, the ghoul feels both more and less of a threat. More, because there's no witness to whatever she might choose to do. Less, because it feels easier to deal with one vaguely humanoid figure sitting at my kitchen table without the infestation of a soldier of the embodiment of death pinging on the rough edges of my subconscious.

"What else can you tell me about the sickness?" I ask her, trying to keep on track. I don't want her here any longer than she has to be, but I also don't want to miss any information she's willing to divulge.

She frowns. "Not much. We bleed from our mouths. In some ways, it resembles what happens when we make a mistake and eat the undead. But when that's the cause, we can just shift shape to clear it, and it's gone. With this..." She looks out to the lawn, to where Claude disappeared. "Can you imagine what it is like to bleed out from your own lips? We can swallow it down, of course, but that only makes it worse. There's no stopping it. No slowing it."

The words don't sound as emotional as they should—it almost sounds like she might just be casually telling me about something that happened at the supermarket the other day. But there's a disconnect there. Her immense intensity is missing.

"And where did it happen? And when?" I ask.

At the question, the ghoul's attention snaps back to me as though I'd insulted her. "Does that matter?" she asks.

"It might. Better to know than not to know."

The intensity she was missing a minute ago has returned with interest. I feel uncomfortably pinned by her gaze as she answers. "The first one was in Barcelona on the twenty-sixth of November. The second one was in Portland, Oregon, just a few days ago. And the prey weren't undead. There were experienced hunters in both parties. The hunters would have known better. This was no mistake. It's poison."

"If it's not a mistake, do you have any specific reason to believe it was intentional?" Faisal asks. I wish he hadn't. He'd been doing so well keeping his damn mouth shut. But it does feel like a weight has lifted when the ghoul's gaze leaves me.

Faisal does an amazing job of looking politely interested and unfazed in the face of the ghoul's menace. I wish he'd teach me that trick—I've never managed it.

"You heard Claude call me a demon. Your woman aside, people don't tend to like demons. It would be a lie to say we were universally admired."

"But no one specific?" Faisal asks, smoothly and inoffensively and entirely absent of fear. Something about that seems to unbalance the ghoul. At least, the side of her mouth twitches, which hasn't happened so far in this conversation.

"No one I've been able to think of. And I *have* been thinking."

I like the way she's looking at him now even less than I liked how she was looking at me earlier. "Anything else you can tell us?" I cut in, which seems to amuse her.

"Nothing. But understand, I'm not asking for you to solve the mystery of the disease. I'm asking for you to bring the gravelings around to buy us time to solve it ourselves."

I raise an eyebrow. "And start a war? Whatever Claude may say, sitting here, do you really believe the gravelings will do that just because I tell them they should? You overestimate me."

The ghoul's amusement takes on a sharper edge. "You underestimate yourself, Arbiter. He played it off as dislike, but don't discount how odd it is that he was here instead of a local. You killed *two* of them, and you got away clean. You allied yourself with the chance demon, and you seem to have suffered no ill effects. You've kept the wizard from taking the wizard trove that we're all pretending we don't know you have. Just a young wizard, yes, but a wizard, nonetheless. You have more leverage with the gravelings than you think."

I don't agree, but I don't want to argue the point, either. "How do we get in contact with you?" I ask her, wondering if she too has a business card buried improbably in a pocket somewhere.

"You don't," she says, standing.

And, with no more than that, she takes a tiny half-step into the Crossroads. Faisal and I look at each other, and then at the silver-embossed card on the table.

FIVE

A Fire

Wilbur is still busy making his deliveries, and we can't call in Max, so that leaves us a limited number of wagons to circle. I also don't want to talk to Gigi until I'm absolutely certain that whatever she used to call my mom away is over. I don't know what I'd tell Gigi, anyway, other than to lay the cards out on the table.

Instead, Faisal and I curl up on the couch under a blanket with my feet in his lap, drinking big mugs of coffee and discussing how I may or may not have accidentally instigated an interspecies conflict.

"It could be a coincidence," I offer up, my tone betraying my lack of confidence in my own assertion.

"Sure, a coincidence that this starts just when you started feeding the poor with undead meat. Or re-dead meat? Extra-dead meat?"

"I mean, yeah, that doesn't seem great. But do the numbers even work out? I mean, what are the chances?"

Faisal raises his eyebrows. "Yeah, I don't know if we want to hang our assumptions on probability affecting you like it does normal people."

"I'm still normal people," I say, with overwrought, mock offense. Faisal nudges me under the blanket.

"You've never been normal," he says, smiling. "But I mean it. How many tens of thousands of pounds of re-dead beef have you made for the trolls to distribute over the last month? And they've been spreading it as wide as possible. That's what you paid them to do, and trolls do what they're paid to. Add to that the fact that any soup kitchens they provide with chunks of good, fresh meat are going to stretch that meat as much as possible into as many meals as possible and…" He shrugs. "We don't know how many of these 'hunting parties' the ghouls have. Maybe they got unlucky. Maybe not. But it still seems like too much of a coincidence not to be related."

Faisal buries his face in his overly large mug. He sometimes mixes packets of instant hot chocolate into the coffee when he makes it, when the extra treat seems necessary. This, I'm sure, is coffee heresy. I also don't care in the slightest. I wouldn't do it *myself*, of course, because I have too much respect for the sacred art of coffee brewing. But if he's going to do it, I won't complain. It's good to drink warm, chocolatey coffee in a warm, cozy house.

But still, it feels like something's missing.

I study Faisal's face, trying to figure out what's written there. Mostly worry, I think. It's been harder to be certain of his expressions since he got back from the year he spent in Aloysius's casino, where Aloysius was deciding whether or not he liked him, and Faisal spent his time generally being intimidated by every non-human creature this side of the sun. It feels like I got him back from the secrets I'd been keeping from him and lost a part of him at the same time.

These days, he's more often worried. His thoughts are more often closed to me. And he's jumpier. Sometimes he talks in his sleep, even, which he never used to do. It might have offered me some insight into what was going on in his head, except that he's even more on guard in his dreams than he is in his waking life. He gives one- or two-word answers that carefully reveal nothing. There's just a whole lot of "No" and "I don't think so" and "Is that what you want me to say?"

I go through waves of hating that Aloysius kept Faisal there for so long. I go through waves of anger. But I also go through waves of gratitude that it convinced Faisal that being involved in the supernatural is necessary. If anything, it activated his *noble hero* gene, which I only tease him about a little. It's a side of him I'd previously only seen when he talked about his reasons for pursuing a career in science, or when he talked about great, big, sweeping, worldwide problems and the people he'd met who might have solutions. It's maybe my favorite thing about him, and that's saying a lot. But I feel a little weird about how that instinct in him has changed its tether.

I'm staring. Whatever. Faisal is used to me staring. He drains the last of his coffee with a giant gulp and starts moving to get up. I try to hold him in place with my legs, but to no avail.

"I'm going to make a fire," he says, like it's an answer to something. An answer to my utterly rude focus on his face or his own frustration at not immediately knowing what to do about the ghoul-graveling problem, it's hard to say. But a fire sounds good, and I like watching Faisal intently completing a task. For some reason, it's sexy as all hell, and I can tell he knows I think so by the sly smile he shoots at me when he catches a change in the weight of my eyes on him.

As I sip my lazy macchiato and watch the man I love lighting a fire for us, the muscles in my body that have been tightly wound since I stepped into the Crossroads with Wilbur begin to unwind. They probably shouldn't. Everything is kind of fucked, but I let it happen anyway.

"I saw a ghost this morning," I say, when everything feels loose enough to own up to such a weird statement.

Faisal freezes for a bare second in the process of placing a medium-sized log to where the newly lit kindling might be able to catch it. It's just a halting split second, but it's a familiar struggle as his scientist's mind, steeped in decades of disbelief, rejects the supernatural and has to be reminded that we know this is real now.

"A human one?" he asks, completing the placement and reaching out for another log, not looking back at me.

"Two, actually. A little girl and some asshole with a weapon. I think he killed her. Maybe."

Faisal blinks slowly a few times as he maneuvers the second log into place, balancing it just right so that it's not going to smother the growing fire. "That seems like maybe not great timing. Were they solid? Like the cows?"

"Yeah," I say. "Or at least the girl was, I think. I gave her a scarf Max lent me, and she took it with her when she disappeared." For a half second, I consider not telling Faisal about what the ghost said about Max, which feels weird. Hiding from it myself, I guess. "Apparently it has spying spells on it, which is very on-brand for Max. She said I killed him, though. She said I killed him twice."

My voice shakes a little at the words, and my hands tighten around the mug in my hand, as though that will keep them from shaking, too.

At the timbre of my voice, Faisal turns and looks at me, concern in his face. He leaves the fire to grow as it will and maneuvers his way back in position beneath the blanket and under my legs, just a little bit closer than he was before.

"Past tense?" he asks thoughtfully.

I nod. "Yeah. Not sure what that means. Maybe I've already done something that will get him killed? Or I've done things that would get him killed twice over?"

It's not unlikely, really. Max is a wizard, and I've always gotten the impression that wizards are nearly as much of assholes to each other as they are to non-wizards. And knowing about me, exempting me from the treaty in the eyes of the gravelings and therefore the supernatural community at large, would probably put him on thin ice if they knew about it. And I know for a fact that there are things I've done that have gotten Max hurt. A memory of him bruised and broken and bloody after we fell out of the sky together three months ago comes up in my mind, the way it always does when I'm feeling guilty about the effect my general existence has had on Max.

Faisal massages my foot under the blanket, a far-off expression on his face. "Maybe..." he says.

"What?" I prompt, recognizing the look he often gets when he's thinking of something that happened in the Casino mixed with the look of trying to figure something out. A promising combination. He shifts his gaze to me, though he seems only half here.

"There was a satyr that came to visit the Casino. He stayed with us for a month, maybe? It was early on. I thought he was interesting, though he turned out to be kind of an asshole. But I spent a lot of time with him because he had this game that he played with twigs and gemstones. The rules seemed simple at first, but when you actually got into a game, they were more complicated, because when you skipped a twig over and then under a gemstone it turned out..." He catches himself about to go off on a deeply esoteric tangent and answers my fond smile with a sheepish one. "That's not relevant. Anyway, he wore this blue hat all the time. When I asked him why, he said that he did it because a prophet told him that he would have great fortune on a day where he wore a blue hat."

"Seems like a great way to make a prophecy self-fulfilling," I say, more because I know it's the kind of thing Faisal would think rather than because it's something I'd normally say. He nods, recognizing that I'm speaking for him, and reveling in the comfort of the familiarity stretching across the slight pain that always accompanies any talk of his year away.

"Yeah. But if all the other stuff is real, I figured maybe prophets could be, too, so I asked him where I could find one."

Faisal pauses for a long moment, holding me in unintentional suspense. I nudge him a little with my foot to prompt him to keep going. He does. "He said 'prophets are the dead.' I thought he meant they'd gone the way of the fae and been wiped off the face of the earth. Like they were a species or something. His English wasn't great, and he had a lot of trouble with articles and prepositions, especially. But maybe not."

I take a sip of my choco-coffee. "You mean maybe all ghosts are prophets?"

Faisal stares into the fire, growing healthily now. "Maybe. We know time magic is a thing. You said Moira did some in Max's living room. And vampiric spirits reach forward in time. And vampiric spirits are kind of cousins of ghosts."

"They're what?" I ask, more accusation finding its way into my voice than I mean it to. He hadn't told me he'd found anything out about vampiric spirits. And considering it's my mother who had gotten herself eaten by one, seems like I should have been told.

"I asked about them in the Casino," he says, not taking

his eyes off the fire. "Since you told me what happened to your mom, it seemed prudent. If I'd found anything that seemed like it could be helpful, I'd have told you."

"You should have told me anyway," I say, not liking the way his eyes still haven't returned to mine.

"Why? What good would that have done?" He feels so far away.

"Maybe it would have sparked something with something I know."

Now he looks at me, his gaze harder than usual. "Why? Do you know anything you haven't shared with me?"

I cringe inwardly. He hasn't one hundred percent forgiven me, I guess, for keeping everything from him for months. Even as much as he tries to. Even as much as he wants to. It still comes out in little moments like this. I try not to let it bother me, but it always does.

He softens at the look on my face. "I should have mentioned," he says, like an apology. "It's just a sensitive subject, and I felt bad that I couldn't find out more. But yeah, vampiric spirits have the same tie to the world of the living that ghosts do."

I squirm down a little more so that my legs are trapping him more in place on the couch and look into the fire. "I guess that makes sense with the way that they can be summoned by gravelings. It's all death, death, and more death."

Faisal laughs and rubs my ankle. "Not what you ordered for Christmas?" he asks.

Before I can answer, the front door opens, and an elegant, thoroughly unwelcome Gigi comes striding through. "Knock, knock," she says, then steps aside to allow Olivia in behind her.

SIX

A Cycle

"That's not really how knocking works," I grumble at Gigi, but she ignores me, just as I expect.

Gigi has on a light jacket, which isn't really enough for the December cold. I'd accuse her of playing it fast and loose with remaining under the radar with the whole magical indestructibility, but she's had a thousand years to calibrate how much she can get away with, so it's not exactly my job to play the magic police.

Olivia's dressed much more appropriately, with a thick wool coat and an annoyed expression. She takes off her coat and hangs it on the rack by her door, slipping out of her shoes with a comfortable familiarity.

"If anyone has any ideas on how to explain to Peter why my mother's landlord showed up early on a Saturday morning and dragged me away when we had plans to go to the Christmas market in Greenville today, I'm all ears," she says, plopping down in the armchair closest to the fire and setting her messenger bag down next to her.

My sister is a somewhat wiry woman, but she seems to be rubbing her bone-thin hands together more to give herself something to do than to get any warmth into them. Her voluminous blonde braid is messier than usual, but other than that, she could be headed to work at the library with her cardigan and well-pressed slacks.

I'm glad she's here, even if I wasn't expecting her. I haven't seen much of Olivia since I finally broke down to both her and Faisal's two-pronged assault and read her into the supernatural world. I'd be lying if I said it didn't bother me. I'd also be lying if I said I fully understood it. But Olivia's mind works very differently from mine. She, for instance, sees absolutely nothing incongruous about her annoyance at me for having kept our father's secret spell books—with all the knowledge of the world that came with them—from her, and her own steadfast decision that obviously her husband Peter should not be told about any of this.

Not that I think her decision about Peter is a bad one. The man may no longer be active in the military, but he owns entirely too many guns and is entirely too effective with them for me to want him to have any inkling of the danger that his in-laws end up in. Too likely, I think, to be unwilling to accept that the enemies we've made can't be handled with the judicious application of ammunition.

"Just tell him that you needed to keep your sister from leaving us out of all the fun bits of her new side-gig. That's close enough, isn't it?" Gigi says, lowering herself into the other armchair in the room with entirely too much grace. With a playful expression on her face like that, the woman really should plop more than she does as she descends.

Olivia's annoyance melts, reforming into steel and practicality. "So there's an arbitration happening?" she asks. "Now?"

Faisal and I exchange a look, and though it wasn't what I meant by looking at him, he stands and heads to the kitchen, bound to be making up something warm and calming for our unexpected guests. Ever the consummate host, that man—as long as hosting duties mean that I have to answer to my own secrets with my own relatives.

"I have arbitrations pretty often, actually," I say to Olivia's raised eyebrow. "But they're usually quick. Just something Wilbur takes me out for during an afternoon or something. At most, it's a couple of outings over the course of a couple of days, if it's something I really need to think about. If it's something tricky, I mean."

Olivia nods her head slowly, more of a thinking gesture than an affirmation. "Wilbur the troll?" she asks.

It's more of a rhetorical question, but it's something to answer, so I say, "Yes."

"But today they showed up at your house!" Gigi says, not oblivious to my glare but just not caring. "While your mother was here, even."

Aaaaaand there it is, the probable source of Olivia's anger at me. As though I were the one who got Mom's past and future joy eaten. But I guess since Dad isn't here to blame, and I'm the one who decided to carry on his legacy of messing in things I shouldn't, I'm the next best person to blame.

"She's fine," I say hurriedly, adjusting to sit up straighter. "They aren't allowed to tell Mom they're not human, and they wouldn't have done anything to her anyway, not if they want to curry favor with me."

"Because no one's ever threatened Mom to get you to rule their way in an arbitration?" Olivia says.

I wince inwardly at the memory of my mother's kidnapping by sirens three months ago, but I try to keep a steady look on my face.

"She can't help that. What do you want her to do

about it?" Faisal says from the kitchen over the sound of boiling water.

Olivia must think he's got a point, because she quickly drops the topic. At least for the moment. Which I'll take. Instead, her eyes dart back and forth between me and Gigi. "So, what's going on, then? What's special about this one?"

I take a deep breath and indulge in a brief moment of jealousy that Faisal escaped to the kitchen. I tell Gigi and Olivia about the visit from Claude and the ghoul. I tell them about the sickness, and about the status quo whole-sale slaughter that has been going on all this time. I tell them about the conflict to come—about the ghoul's threat of escalating visibility, and how willing she seemed to be to go through with it if necessary. Gigi chimes in about what a terrible thing that would be for the world, for the wizards to feel that the treaty and their dominance over the super-natural world was being threatened.

And that was all fine, mostly. It wasn't until Olivia asked if I had any theories as to what might be happening, having seen plainly on my face that there was something I was hesitant to share, that things really started going off the rails.

"You've been doing *what*, exactly?" Gigi says incredu-lously when I finish describing my latest side project.

"Feeding the poor. You should try it sometime. It's good for the old karma," I say, my voice more sheepish than my words.

"There's no such thing as karma. Didn't summoning ghosts by the dozen strike you as a little dangerous?"

I adjust nervously on the couch. "Well, not really. Wilbur was always there. And I had no idea that ghouls were out there killing homeless people en masse, or that this would cause a problem for that. And, to be frank, I don't know that I would have done anything different."

Would I have? I'm not sure. On the one hand, yes, the disease sounds terrifying. But building in consequences for murdering the most vulnerable can't be a bad thing, can it? Something had to change, didn't it? Even if I didn't know it at the time.

"I think she's talking about the wraiths," Olivia says, even and confident as a fencer's thrust.

Gigi looks at her with almost as much surprise as I do. She ignores Gigi and looks directly at me. "Gigi works in the service industry, as do I. We're around the public all day, every day. And I've been noticing that more and more people have been coming in asking about local legends and ghosts and historical murders in specific locations. I don't think our microfiche machine has gotten as much of a workout in a decade as it has in the past week." She turns her attention to Gigi. "That was what you were referring to, right?"

Gigi gives Olivia a sharp smile that I'm not comfortable being aimed in the direction of my sister. "That is what I meant, yes. I've overheard something like five conversations about wraith encounters over the last month or so. Seems pretty likely to be related."

"Make it six," Faisal says from beside me, a tray of four steaming mugs in his hands. "Beth ran into a couple of ghosts on the way home this morning."

Faisal hands me one of the mugs, which smells of cinnamon, apples, and wine. We've had our hot uppers, so I guess it's time for our hot downers. I'm not going to complain, and I'm sure as hell not going to refuse, even if we *just* had our coffee. Gigi and Olivia seem to feel the same, and they accept their mugs from Faisal as I give them a brief rundown of meeting Melissa this morning.

"So you didn't summon them," Olivia says. "Which makes them wraiths, not ghosts. Ghosts are summoned in circles. Wraiths are imprints of souls in an afterlife that manage to bleed through into our world. Same base creature—they're still souls—but different context."

"And how do you know that?" I say before I realize how dumb of a question it is.

"I read the trove," Olivia says, dry as the Sahara.

"Okay then, six," Gigi says, cutting off the minor squabble. "So we think…?" She lets the question hang in the air for a minute, and when no one seems to want to respond, I do.

"Summoning ghosts on purpose has led to wraiths?"

"An uptick in them, anyway," Olivia says. "The people looking for information in the library seem to be leaving both terrified and satisfied, so it seems to me that these aren't new wraiths, just more common manifestations of older ones."

"What a fun week at work," I mumble before taking a sip of the mulled wine.

"*Weeks*, plural," Olivia says, as though it's my fault. Which would be a whole lot more annoying if it in fact weren't.

Gigi catches my rare look of chagrin and capitalizes on the moment. "I knew you were going to break the world eventually, Elizabeth. I just didn't think you'd do it so quickly."

Faisal, goddamn traitor that he is, has the temerity to laugh at me. In my own home, no less. I give him a playful kick. And suddenly, I feel ridiculous. Something about Faisal and Gigi's attempts to lighten the mood makes it all hit home. Broke the world. I can't really have broken the world, can I? I didn't mean to.

Aloysius should have stopped me. If what I was doing was really so harmful—was really going to release a whole bunch of wraiths to roam the Earth—he *must* have known.

Why didn't he say? Why didn't he send me a message, tell me to stop?

I can feel the dark hole of guilt coming to swallow me up. But before it can, Olivia's voice cuts through.

"Right, so, that's why I'm here, isn't it?"

"What?" I ask. And, to her credit, Olivia gives me a patient look. It's a practiced patience—the patience that anyone who "deals with the public" and doesn't hate their job employs on a daily basis.

"You want me to help you find all the relevant information in the trove so we can get a better handle on what we're dealing with, right?"

I blink a few times. "That would be good, yes."

Clearly, no further invitation is necessary. As the rest of us watch, Olivia pulls an old laptop out of her messenger bag and starts loading it up. The thing is covered in stickers of ponies and rainbows—an unfortunate but unavoidable side effect of it residing in a house with two young girls. It makes some strained noises as it loads up, and Olivia pulls out a pen and small pad of paper from the side pocket of her messenger bag. I recognize the pen—I have one that looks much the same in the pocket of my yellow leather jacket. It's a way of getting in touch with Wilbur. The man does not have a cell phone. Not because he doesn't like technology—quite the opposite. He loves technology. One of the most useful tools for modern trolls to use to build their metaphorical bridges is the internet—though they don't love it when you say that makes them internet trolls. No, Wilbur just has far too much knowledge of what a cell phone can be used to do and thus chooses not to have one.

The routine that Olivia goes through to access the trove is familiar to me. She orients the screen so that Gigi can't see her fingers typing in the address to the super-secret server that Wilbur set electronic copies of the trove up on. After she presses the enter key, she holds Wilbur's pen to the pad of paper and waits.

"Wilbur gave *you* a pen to reach him?" Gigi asks when she cottons on to what's happening. Olivia doesn't dignify her jealousy with a response. I don't, either. If Gigi doesn't want to be mistrusted, she shouldn't do suspicious things so often. The woman is well over a thousand years old. She's had plenty of time to learn this essential fact.

After a few short moments, the pen moves in Olivia's hand. Even if I didn't know that the resulting text in no way resembled my sister's handwriting, it would be clear she wasn't the one writing it from her uneasy expression as she watches the nub of the pen run across the paper.

Is that you, Olivia? the pen writes, in its usual surreally round, even letters.

It's me, Olivia writes back in her own handwriting on the next line down.

And, with that magical two-factor authentication complete, the computer connects successfully to the trove. From here, her process differs a bit from mine. When I'm accessing the trove, I'm usually doing it to look for spells I think I'd like to learn. I also used to access the papers themselves directly. That was, up until I told Olivia that I was touching the papers with my bare hands. That just about broke her brain.

The box that the original trove papers are in now stays locked tight, and it has been moved from the attic down to the closet of the home office, where it's easier to manage climate control. Olivia has grumbled more than once that she really ought to take it into the library, where she can keep it in the rare book and document room. But of course, she understands why she can't do it.

But Olivia wants everyone to see what she's looking at, so with the expertise of someone who has spent plenty of time managing the idiosyncrasies of connecting to audiovisual equipment, she connects to the TV hanging over the fireplace.

"Right," she says, with a well-earned sense of accomplishment when we're all looking at a mirror to what she sees on her screen. "I haven't finished indexing, and of course I'm nowhere near done with a complete translation. That may take years with the precautions I have to take. But I have a solid majority of the sections tagged with their suspected subject matter. I figure if we look through for anything related to wraiths, ghosts, ghouls, gravelings, or reanimation, that's a good place to start."

I'm not comfortable with the way Gigi leans forward. Generally, Gigi knows more than I do. And once upon a time, when I'd just found the trove, I know she leafed through a bunch of it. Many of the scans of the documents that Olivia begins flipping through were originally scanned by Gigi, after all. Many more were scanned by Henry Thompson, my neighbor across the street who briefly knew about all of this before asking Max to remove the knowledge from his mind. I still get a little sad when I think about it.

But Gigi has come in clutch now and then. I couldn't have resolved that particularly tricky arbitration between the siren tribes three months ago without her help. And if she gets a little knowledge out of it, then the more the better. That should keep her self-interested ass involved and helpful. And God knows I need her to keep being helpful.

For all the hopefully temporary tension that telling Olivia about the supernatural has introduced into our sisterly relationship, Faisal was right: I was an idiot not to see how helpful her particular skill set would be. In her hands, the trove is a cohesive and well-connected whole rather than a haphazard collection of hard-to-understand writings in disparate languages from several dozen authors. Every page is an independent item, scanned with and without my father's original sticky notes, and including textual context and links to other related pages. And Olivia, it's abundantly clear, has spent enough time with these pages to know her way around them.

Honestly, I'm not sure when the woman sleeps.

Pride swells in my chest as she leads us down the rabbit hole, searching for terms that make sense in context. It's riveting, at first, this shared research. Now and then, Gigi has her own commentary to add, and Olivia dutifully transcribes it as color-coded notes in the appropriate pages. This catches Gigi off guard at first, but she accepts the free exchange of information without protest.

As the morning drags on, the novelty begins to wane. It turns out that the fuzzy edges between life and death were, unsurprisingly, a topic of great interest to the wizards who contributed to the trove. Considering they were all obsessed with finding the ritual of longevity to extend their own lives to five hundred years—a ritual all full wizards have but that no wizard who contributed to the trove ever managed to obtain—that makes sense. More than one of the sections that Olivia pulls up turns out to be ruminations on death from a wizard who was bitter about the whole thing. Only it was hard to tell that at first, at least without some assistance from Google Translate or from Gigi.

By the time Olivia pulls up an old-fashioned illustrated calendar of the seasons, our collective enthusiasm is flagging.

"This is another one I haven't gotten around to finding a good translation resource for. There were only a few pages from this particular wizard. He must not have had much time to add much to the trove before he passed it on." The implication that he probably died young and likely violently hangs in the air, unremarked upon. "From what I can tell, these few pages are in a dialect of medieval—"

"Lithuanian," Gigi says, sitting up straighter in her chair. Her movement pulls me and Faisal up a little straighter, too, and sharpens Olivia's interest.

"It seems to be talking about a curtain," Olivia says, addressing Gigi.

"It's better translated as 'veil,'" Gigi mumbles, her eyes moving over the screen. Her lips move, and her brow furrows. It looks odd on her, accustomed as I am to her studied, dispassionate air. Something she's reading bothers her. And the implication that it's enough to bother Gigi scares the hell out of me.

Just to make it worse, Gigi stands and strides up closer to the TV. The letters aren't that small, but it's almost as though she thinks if she just looks closely enough at them, they'll change their meaning. All of our eyes, however, are on the look on her face and the growing expression of horror and defeat there.

Finally, she takes a step back, no longer reading individual words but staring ashen at the image as a whole. "What day is the solstice this year?" she asks.

I grab my phone to look it up, but Faisal beats me. "The twenty-first of December," he supplies.

"And what's today?"

This one I know. "The eighteenth. Why?"

Gigi turns to us. "This is a calendar of the natural waxing and waning of the veil between life and death throughout the year. It's thicker during the summer months, and thinner during winter."

She hesitates, but I think I know where she's going with this, so I say, "And the winter solstice is the thinnest?"

She nods, but I can tell there's more. "And...?" I prompt.

Gigi looks between us, as though trying to read something on our faces and not finding it. "It's not a smooth progression. The veil gets thinner and thinner throughout the year, but then on the solstice, it spikes. Even on the best of years, the veil can be nearly transparent on that day. And there's a warning that if the veil has been *damaged* enough, then on the solstice, it could rip permanently, and not build back up when the solstice is past."

"What happens then?" Faisal's voice, much steadier than I feel, comes from beside me.

"Nothing good," Gigi mutters, her voice lower and less musical than I've ever heard it. She looks between our faces again, and then she seems to put herself back together, whipping on a business-like smile that feels like a slap in the face on the heels of such a serious moment. "But then, what would you expect? We're talking about dark and death and night and winter, here."

Her brightness feels wrong. The way we've been shut out feels wrong. "Want to share with the class?" I ask, sharper than I mean to.

"I've already told you everything on the page," she says. "What more do you want from me?"

"A little full disclosure would be nice," Faisal says, his face implacable.

Gigi looks askance at him. "If I told you *everything* I know, you'd run for the hills screaming. I don't think Elizabeth would thank me for that."

"Why don't we find out?" Faisal asks.

I'm glad, watching Faisal meet Gigi's stare and

returning it with his own, that he's never seen Gigi through the glasses. He's never asked to, and I suppose this might be why. It's easier to not be afraid of things when you don't know much about them. Ignorance may or may not be bliss, but it does enable a lot of dumb courage. Still, Gigi only just got used to the idea that Faisal is really sticking around. I'm considering interrupting them when Olivia speaks up.

"We don't need to know everything. Just enough to fully understand how much my little sister has fucked up the world this time."

As one, all three of us look at Olivia, with her straight posture and patient expression. I can count on one hand the number of times I've heard Olivia swear, and all of those were before she had her daughters. I don't think I've ever thought about it before. It seems natural for her not to sully herself with such vile language as we, the uncouth masses, use. But all affectionate joking aside, the incongruousness of her mini-outburst punctures the tension building between Faisal and Gigi, so I'm grateful for it.

"She may not have done anything at all. I don't know what does and doesn't damage the veil. Not for certain," Gigi says.

"But if I did?" I ask.

Those words, and the fact that Gigi is standing and we're all sitting staring at her, makes her feel more outnumbered than even usual. That fact settles on her, and there's a flash of her usual contrary instincts on her face. But after a moment of looking at our three useless little human faces, she sighs and sits down.

"I don't know anything concrete. But the wizard that created me was obsessed with living forever—not just the five-hundred years that full-fledged wizards get. I've always considered it one of the great ironies of my life that he accidentally created immortality for me and my sister, when he wanted it so badly for himself and didn't achieve it."

She leaves a long pause, but neither Olivia nor Faisal must have any better ideas of what to say than I do, because neither of them speaks either. I'm not sure Gigi notices how unnatural the length of the silence is—she's gone off somewhere in her head.

"I wasn't ever on good terms with my creator. You wouldn't be, either. And I used to taunt him, on the rare occasion I saw him, with the certainty of his death. The last time I saw him, not long before his five-hundred years was up, was no exception. But he didn't mind. He said he and his *brotherhood* had found a way around it. That living forever was as easy as tricking someone into tearing a veil."

Her eyes flick back up to the page still displayed on the TV. There's nothing for a long moment but the crackling of the fire. Until Gigi shakes it off and comes back to the here and now. She puts on her breezy smile, thankfully less manic than the one a minute ago. "You know, I've never talked to a wraith. Considered it, but never got around to finding one that came through in a predictable enough way that I could chat with them. But when life presents one with an opportunity, it's foolish not to take it."

As she speaks, Gigi is already heading to the door, putting on her conspicuously thin jacket. "Do you want a ride home, Olivia? Nothing we can do until tonight, anyway. Wraiths don't come out during the daytime. Everyone knows that."

Olivia and I exchange a glance, and I'm grateful that as difficult a time as she's having processing all of this, at least we can still end up on the same page. Olivia can scour the rest of the trove just as well on her own as with the rest of us—if there's even much left that's worth reading on the topic. We're starting to get to the equivalent of page four on a Google search, and everyone knows the only useful results are on the first two pages. Better to have Olivia go with Gigi now, both to get as much ingratiating face time as possible, and to feel around for anything Gigi's holding back that she may let slip with a smaller audience.

"That would be helpful, Gigi, thanks," Olivia says, already moving to disconnect the trove from the TV and pack up her things.

"None of this solves the graveling-ghoul problem," I say, feeling like my sister leaving my house is an unacceptable loss, but one I can't stop.

"Well, no, of course not," Gigi says. "But we found a *bigger* problem, so that one isn't important. It's called *perspective.*"

"I'm not sure the ghouls would agree with you," I say.

From the porch, Gigi calls back to me. "Then it's a good thing it's not my job to get them to agree with me."

SEVEN

A Failure

There's nothing quite like the nerves you get when you're about to do something gloriously dumb but not quite yet—like go intentionally seek out a wraith to talk to. You get the normal nerves, sure, but with a fun added layer of *what is wrong with me?* on top, left to sink in slowly. It's especially weird when contrasted against the sublime normality of a wintery Saturday, in a warm house in a frosted world and nowhere to be until the evening.

Faisal and I make an early lunch consisting of small portions of leftovers combined in such a way that makes me glad we don't know any foodies to be ashamed of us. Then he disappears into the office to do some reading around the internet to see what he can find in the way of real-life ghost stories.

As for me, I disappear up into the attic.

When I was growing up, the attic was my father's domain. He used to build train sets and model surroundings up here. He was passionate about it—and good at it, besides. So good at it that I didn't realize how "uncool" it made him until I was in high school, at which point it was intolerably embarrassing for me to be related to him. If no one was asking, though, my dad's attic was my favorite place to be. It was quiet except for my dad muttering to himself and the whirr of the trains on the tracks.

The attic is also where he started messing with magic once he found the trove. I still don't know where he got it, or when it started, but I know that he did it long enough to make a handful of items. And long enough to make and enchant a replica of a portion of Springfield. He'd linked it to the outside world so that the trains on it moved when their real-life equivalents did. I'm confident he thought the connection was only one way. It's easy to make mistakes when dealing with the trove. A side effect of wizards all giving themselves eidetic memories so that they never have to write anything down is that they tend to be awful at documentation. Even I've noticed as much. If I ever want to see the two most level-headed people I know get unreasonably angry, I can always mention something along those lines in front of Faisal and Olivia, both of whom have firm ideas about the importance of documenting information for their own reasons. For bonus points, I can do it when they've both got alcohol at hand and watch them whip each other up into incandescent disapproval.

At least, I'll be able to do that when Olivia and I are back on solid ground with each other again.

Max removed the magic from my dad's train set so that it isn't linked to the real world anymore, but I don't touch it anyway. I like that it's there. Instead of taking anything up here away, I've added things of my own. A couple of thrift store armchairs complete with cozy blankets. A few very necessary lamps. A great, big, hulking, solid wood desk that had to come up here in pieces and get screwed back together. An old vintage-looking roller chair to pull up to it. And, of course, a beanbag that I let Faisal convince me was deeply important, although he's the only one who sits in it, and it utterly ruins the whole old-professor-fallen-on-hard-times vibe I realized after the fact I was subconsciously going for.

All successfully enchanted objects and the original trove texts live in the warded cabinet in the office downstairs, but here I keep my in-process objects and my own copied notes. There's also an ancient laptop on the desk that I use solely for interacting with the trove.

I don't need that today, though. I can't think about the situation anymore. Olivia will find anything in the trove to be found, and Faisal will find anything on the internet. If I worry any more about what's going to happen this evening, I'll lose my mind. Better to focus on the things I can control.

Or, at least, the things I can try to control—but maybe fail.

I have about eight ongoing magical spells or objects I am attempting to master at any given time. That way, when I feel like lighting one on fire, I can just move to the next thing instead of burning the house down. I've got a few I've all but given up on in drawers, and the ones I'm more convinced I have a chance at stay spread across the tabletop.

For today, I decide to focus on the little cloth pouch that I hope to enchant and one day sew into the pocket of my yellow leather jacket. Faisal liked to jokingly call it a bag of holding, but when I looked up what that was, there were some key differences that made it better. For one, it's real, and not just an imaginary *Dungeons & Dragons* object. For another, it weighs nothing more than the cloth it's made out of. And finally, it can hold anything. Really —*anything.* As long as I can fit it through the bag's opening, it will fit inside.

When I explained all of these things to Faisal, knowing that he wasn't going to be able to stand the inaccuracy of calling it that once he knew better, he just started calling it my infinity pouch. Which is, naturally, much worse. And is also, unfortunately, now what I call it to myself in my head.

But when I've enchanted it successfully, it'll be useful enough to put with the nickname I can't pry off of it. At least, if the Nigerian wizard who wrote all of this down was documenting it correctly, and if my and Olivia's attempts at translation with all the tools available to us are accurate. Which I certainly hope they are, because I've sunk a ton of time into this thing. Sourcing the right fiber mix to make the fabric. Figuring out how to weave. Tying the knots in a very specific, maddeningly complicated way. Making each of the stitches exactly the specified length. Finding needles made of pure tin and then washing them with only the juice of acidic fruits.

In fact, this is my second try at the bag, because after I was almost finished with the first one, Olivia informed me that we'd converted the length measurements wrong. Which I didn't think was a real problem to start with, since everything is proportional, not absolute. But it turns out we'd interpreted each of the two measurements wrongly *in relation* to each other. So it was back to programming the Cricut cutter to cut out templates complete with dots for where the stitches should go.

I almost didn't mind that part of it, though. Translations and the nuts-and-bolts logistics of creating magic are the only things I can really get her to talk to me about at length these days. *Processing*, I remind myself as I get everything ready to attempt the enchantment, lighting the beeswax candles with wicks made from the same fiber blend as the bag.

And that's fair, isn't it? It's a lot to take in. And if she's going to blame me in her head for what happened to Mom because Dad isn't around anymore to be mad at, well… There's nothing I can do about that.

Besides, when I'm futzing with the difficulties of creating the object itself, I'm not contending with the impossibility of enchanting the thing. Dad wrote off spells that had a spoken element to them for a reason: as difficult as it is to do or make something based off someone else's instructions, it's exponentially more difficult to speak words in a language you've never heard. The ghost summoning I've been doing with livestock is doable mostly because the words in it can all be found in a long spell that I was able to record Max speaking, so I was able to stitch together the recording and repeat after it. But for this one, it's a lot trickier. There are only nine words in the entire page of written words that I can pull from the recording. And, granted, two of those are also in the summoning spell, so I feel pretty confident about those. But that leaves the vast majority of them unaccounted for.

It leaves me guessing for most of it. But I'm a chimpanzee, and this is my typewriter, and I'd rather do this than anything else today. So I get into the Right Mind for this particular enchantment—a state of unapologetic, insatiable greed—and set to it.

I speak the words over and over. I sprinkle in little variations, although I try to keep as close as possible to my best guesses for how the language works, based on the average of how different writers in the trove transcribe it as well as the sounds that usually appear in combination in the recorded spell I have.

In one way, it's mind-numbing work, but in another, it's completely engrossing. My leg falls asleep now and then, and I have to readjust every so often. I check the pouch after every time. Nothing, nothing, and more nothing.

Every time. It would frustrate me, but I can't let it. Frustration would hamper my Right Mind, after all.

About the only pleasant thing about this process is the Right Mind itself. Not so much the greed, per se, as the lack of apology for it. The excuse to allow myself to sit in that state and feel no remorse for it. After all, it's not my fault that I'm indulging this emotion. I'm required to. But in the moments between attempts, it gnaws at me.

Sometimes I wonder if one of the reasons that wizards are the way they are is because of the Right Mind required for different spells. Often, Right Mind for spells isn't pleasant, especially for the spells that can be used offensively. And if wizards have an inbuilt sense that guides them toward performing spells correctly, then maybe that means their minds are pulled to these states of Right Mind, too. It must feel so natural to them, to feel how they need to feel to make a spell work, however awful it is.

There was an experiment I read once about how being forced to perform different facial expressions can alter your underlying emotional state. Cause and effect don't always work in the direction we mean them to.

But there isn't much room for these thoughts. There isn't much room for anything. Only the task in front of me that I fail at, over and over and over.

It's getting dark out when Faisal's voice beside me breaks my concentration. "I brought you soup."

I jump a little. He doesn't ask me if I'm having any luck. There's no doubt I'd have told him if I had, and Faisal's not one to ask questions he knows the answers to without reason. I accept the soup and sit on the floor with it next to the beanbag chair, where he sits with his own bowl. He could have just called me down for dinner, but I think he likes being up here. I wonder if it's in somewhat of the same way I liked being up here when my dad was working on his trains. He can't participate, but he can be nearby. Sometimes it's good enough just to be nearby—to be close to the thing the person you love cares about.

"Your friends asked if you could come out and play," he says, after a few minutes of us eating in silence, with me stretching out my tired, cramped legs.

"They found a wraith for us to visit?"

Faisal nods. "Apparently there's a woman in a hotel room. She doesn't like men, and she doesn't like people sitting in her chair, but other than that, there are no local legends of her ever trying to hurt anyone. Gigi says you can just not sit in her chair and not be men, and you should be fine."

I'm glad I don't have to worry about Faisal needing to assert his own bravery by insisting he go in, too. I don't know whether it was Olivia or Gigi who decided what wraith we would visit, and I don't know if picking a man-hater had anything to do about avoiding that potential issue, but they needn't have bothered. Faisal knows I have an amulet, and as much as I have tried—and there's an entire plastic bin of attempts in the corner to show for it—he doesn't. Maybe he's dissatisfied about that deep down. If so, it's buried, and I'm not going to go looking for it.

"Sun's going down," I say.

"They said seven-thirty."

I take another few spoonfuls of soup. "Sorry for ruining your Saturday afternoon off."

"I'd be browsing Reddit, anyway. This way, I'm browsing Reddit for the good of the world! What more could I ask for?" I'm a little disconcerted at the way his voice echoes in the space that I've gotten used to being quiet and mine over the last nine months.

"It's pretty much what we thought," he continues. "The ghost stories that people were already telling have just gotten a lot more common, mostly. But people are definitely noticing and talking about the uptick. You know those ghosthunter shows? With the on-scene 'investigations' in haunted places and the bullshit talking boxes?"

"Yeah?" I ask.

"They're all on strike for better safety measures. Apparently, Brock Tragins fell from a railing and broke his arm. He says a ghost pushed him. They're getting great footage, but all of a sudden, the danger is real, and apparently that's changed the equation for them."

A smile hovers on his lips, but I feel something inside me go hollow. "Seriously, though, sorry. This is supposed to be your vacation."

He gives me an annoyed look. It makes him look less like himself the way visible emotional reactions always do, subdued as his expressions usually are. "*Seriously, though*, it's insulting for you to apologize for a choice that I've been clear with you I have made, for myself and for my own reasons. You don't get to take responsibility for my choices. That's not how this works."

I set down my spoon and raise my hands in mock defense, a playful smile on my face. "Okay, okay, don't shoot."

"Don't do that again," he says, still serious.

I lower my hands as my smile fades. Then I pick up my bowl and take another few spoonfuls. My eyes drift involuntarily toward the front of the house, and I wonder why I'm doing that before I piece together that some involuntary impulse is reminding me of Henry Thompson, my across-the-street neighbor who'd known about magic for a while and chosen to get out of it. He'd made his choice, and I wasn't happy about it. Faisal made the opposite choice, and I'm still not happy about it.

Jesus, I'm just fucking impossible to please, aren't I?

"I won't," I say, and mean it. Faisal holds me in his gaze for a long moment as though deciding whether to keep talking about it. But instead, he smiles, unendurably handsome in the low lamplight.

We eat in silence, each thinking our own thoughts. I could go back to trying to get the pouch to work before we leave, but we've only got half an hour, and there's a tension growing between us that I don't understand. If it's something going on with him I can fix, he's not telling me what it is, though.

Maybe it's me. Maybe I have a greed hangover. Maybe I'm frustrated after an entire afternoon of failure. Maybe I'm still mad as hell at Aloysius for not telling me I was fucking up the world—and feeling guilty for having relied on him.

But I don't have the heart to piece out what's bothering me most. So instead, when both of our bowls of hearty, cheesy potato soup are empty, I climb onto the oversized beanbag with Faisal. We adjust until we're wrapped around each other, my head laying against his chest. We sit that way as I hover between sleep and wakefulness, his heartbeat as steady as factory machinery, for a long time that's not long enough.

"Time to go," he says. I feel it more than hear it.

As we get up, the answer of what the funk I was in comes to me. It's fear. Fear that another big crisis has started again. And while I've gotten out of them unscathed so far, not everyone else does. And this time, whether I want them to be or not, the people I love are involved.

They've chosen to be.

EIGHT

A Consultation

It makes no sense to me that haunted hotels somehow remain hotels. One would think that having a ghost—wraith—problem would not be conducive for a business that requires onsite customers.

But then again, the general public tends to have a lot more curiosity than sense when it comes to the supernatural. Which is why we probably shouldn't have been surprised when we pulled into the parking lot of the Primrose Inn to find it completely packed. Faisal and I may have just gotten clued in to the uptick in wraith sightings going on, but apparently we're late to the party. Funny how spending all our spare time learning about the supernatural somehow made us the last people to know when something is actually happening in the supernatural world.

Faisal and I shoot each other disbelieving glances. "Moths to the flame," I mumble.

We can't find a legal parking spot, and while I'm willing to just eat the fine if there is one, Faisal points out that he's not going in anyway, so he can just idle and circle the block if he needs to.

"You gonna be my getaway driver?" I ask him, a lopsided grin on my mouth.

"You gonna need one?" he retorts.

I wink, unbuckle my seatbelt, and head toward the hotel entrance.

The Primrose Inn is a historically protected building, which is another way of saying that the owners weren't allowed to modernize to bring in the guests and instead have had to lean into the old-timey aesthetic to stay in business. It looks more than anything like a Victorian house that got hungry and ate the other Victorian houses to either side of it and is now doing its best to pretend that those rampant acts of cannibalism didn't give it indigestion. It's not very symmetrical, but it *is* very colorful, and it has porches for days that must be great to hang out on when they aren't covered in snow. Inside, the place is tastefully decorated in period-appropriate furniture. I'd always assumed that because Springfield isn't much of a tourist destination, our hotels would be struggling. But I guess this one is doing all right if they don't have to replace their furniture with whatever they can find within budget when it breaks.

At the reception desk, I see the beginning of a line forming. Then I see the back of a conspicuously Gigi-like figure and an overwhelmed front desk receptionist who, luckily for him, has apparently not had the misfortune to deal with a customer like Gigi before.

"Look, Jorje, I'm not interested in you repeating the same thing to me again. I'm interested in you giving me my key."

The poor man is still trying to figure out what to say as I approach, and on instinct, he shoots me a pleading glance. Sorry, Jorje. I am not here to make your day better.

"Is there a problem?" I ask, feeling short next to Gigi as

I put my hands on the check-in counter. Jorje is still looking at me, but the pleading look is out of his eye, replaced by a confused one.

"I'm sorry," he says. "Your friend doesn't have a reservation, and we're fully booked tonight. As I've been trying to tell her, there are still rooms available at——"

"I don't need to know where there are other rooms available," Gigi cuts him off. "I need room 228, and I need it here."

Jorje's eyes have stayed on me, which seems a little weird until the light of recognition comes across his face. "You work at the mayor's office," he says, and I realize too late that his confusion was trying to place me. "I've seen you on TV."

I don't go on TV often, and when I do it's just the local channels that, unfortunately, some small proportion of the town electorate still watches. With everything that's been going on what with the veil between life and death being damaged and all, I somehow managed to stop worrying about what might happen if I get recognized while out doing something weird in the service of the supernatural—and how that might reflect upon my boss and impact my job. I've been worrying about that for months and months with no actual incident. And then, of course, as soon as I forget about it, here we are.

"I do, yes," I say. "And I have to apologize for Gigi. She's a business owner in the Arts District, and we've been working with her on a tourism campaign. Not to put too fine a point on it, but she's got a lot of her hopes pinned on it, and spending some time in room 228 was supposed to be the end to the article." I lean in close. "We heard you guys have some kind of ghost experience rigged up in there, and the writer of the feature wants us to record what happens. Thinks it'll be a good button at the end of the thing, you know."

Jorje looks uncertain. I've thrown a lot at him, and most of it doesn't make sense. But he does recognize me, and there are enough people waiting behind us that his sense of urgency is amping up. Maybe that'll be enough for him not to think too much about it.

"We don't have anything rigged up," he says uncertainly.

"Oh, but I'm sure we've heard stories about a ghost in room 228. Sits in a chair? Smokes a pipe?" Gigi is in on it now. Maybe she enjoys being able to deceive without lying. *So glad I could give you this experience, Gigi.*

"I mean, it's not rigged. It's not an actor or special effects or anything." Jorje looks tired, and I may not face the public in my job the way Gigi or Olivia do, but I deal with it enough to feel that specific exhaustion in my bones when I see it.

Gigi leans in close. "What, do you mean to tell me that ghosts are real?" Her voice drips with something I recognize as condescension, but which might come off to the casual observer who doesn't know Gigi well as genuine curiosity.

"I didn't use to think so," Jorje says. And there we go— I officially feel sorry for him. Can't be great working in a haunted hotel when some idiot has been out here weakening the veil.

"Look," I say, trying to keep this from going on any longer than it needs to. "We don't need the room all night. Just give us fifteen minutes to do the little ritual that the internet seems to think gets her to show up, and then we get the details for the story like the writer asked. We won't touch anything or use the bathroom or dirty the room in any way. We'll be in and out and whoever booked the room for tonight still gets it. They haven't shown up yet, have they?"

Jorje looks relieved to finally have an answer to a question that I'm asking. "No, they haven't."

"Fifteen minutes," I say again, holding out my hand.

Jorje hesitates, then looks below the desk to a rack of keys, retrieves 228, and sets it in my hand.

I shoot him a smile that doesn't seem to reassure him. "Thanks," I say, and head toward the hallway to the guest rooms.

"Be careful," Jorje advises. He looks like he wants to say more, but the couple who were in line behind us have stepped up to the front counter and look none too patient for the wait. I try to decide if they're visiting relatives from out of town for Christmas and just wanted their own space, or if they're locals who, like us, have heard about what's going on at the Primrose Inn and have decided to come check it out. But I can't figure it out, and Gigi is pulling me along toward our room by my arm, so I don't have much more of a chance to try.

Room 228 is inconspicuous, though the door looks newer than the doors to the rooms around us. The key in my hand is satisfyingly large and old-fashioned, and the lock opens with a satisfying click. Inside, the small room is sparsely appointed with a bed, an antique-looking dresser that serves as a stand for a very out-of-place-looking TV, and an extremely worn chair in the corner.

"So that chair…" I trail off, staring at the chair, as Gigi steps into the room and closes the door behind me. It feels strange in here in a way I can't place. Wrong and uncomfortable. Like I've barged in somewhere I don't belong. Which, I guess, I have.

"That's the one we're not supposed to sit in, yes," Gigi says. "That's where the tobacco goes."

I don't know if the uncomfortable feeling in this room is affecting Gigi the way it's affecting me. It doesn't seem like it should be, what with her being immune to, well, pretty much everything. But I would believe it were by the way she wastes no time in retrieving a packet of tobacco from her jacket pocket and setting it on the chair. This must be the ritual she mentioned to poor, long-suffering Jorje.

I take a few more steps into the room, past the doorway to the compact bathroom, coming up next to the bed. I could sit on it, I guess, but I don't want to.

"And now?" I ask, once Gigi takes a step back to stand next to me.

"And now we wait," Gigi says.

We don't have to wait long. All the things they say about wraiths showing up are true. The temperature in the room drops noticeably. My skin prickles. As a special treat, the table lamps on the bedside tables—complete with antique lampshades—even flicker. I don't remember when either of us turned them on. Maybe they were linked to the light switch. The light switch configurations in hotel rooms never do make sense.

My eyes are locked on the chair, determined not to miss anything. After all, it's the surprise of the ghost showing up that is what scares you, right? Just seeing Melissa this morning wasn't inherently terrifying. But even staring right at it, I don't catch the moment the woman appears. She's just not there, and then the next moment, she is. I'd say in the blink of an eye, but I'm not sure I blinked. The only thing that gives away that she hasn't been there all along is a trace of bright blue vapor, the same color that lingered when Melissa disappeared this morning.

It's startling as hell, even to Gigi, which amuses the

woman. She chuckles, her voice husky and so horribly, painfully alive.

The wraith is not old. I don't know why I expected her to be old. She's late twenties or early thirties, maybe— somewhere in between my age and Olivia's. Her hair is black and smooth and neatly pulled back. I've got to assume her dress is period perfect for the Victorian era, and nothing about her says down-on-her-luck, but combined with the knowing look in her eye, all I can think of is a Wild West brothel in a bad movie.

She crosses her legs, slouches back in her chair, and eyes us with a defiant smile, as though daring us to comment on her unladylike behavior. I like her immediately, which cheers me up for a split second until I remember where I am and why she's here at all.

"Don't look so morose," the woman says as she opens the package of tobacco we brought her, which is inexplicably in her hands rather than beneath her. "I'm dead, not you."

"So you know you're dead, then?" I ask, bringing out her rightfully incredulous look.

She pulls a pipe from somewhere in her skirts and rubs it against her knee as though it needed to be any more polished. "I can't tell you the future," she says almost offhandedly.

I straighten, not sure what to say.

"I know who you are," she says as she starts packing tobacco into her pipe. "So I know you know what we are. But I can't tell you the future. I'm not allowed."

"We don't know much of anything," I say when I see Gigi open her mouth, more because I want to head off whatever bone she's going to pick with the wraith. "That's why we're here."

The woman stops in the midst of packing her pipe and

fixes me with a stare that would make my skin crawl if it weren't already crawling. "You don't, do you?" she asks, more to herself than me. "You're very young right now, aren't you?"

I open my mouth, but no words come. And still no words come when the woman sticks out her finger as though testing the wind. A sliver of blue fire erupts from the tip of it. My mouth closes, and my weight shifts forward, trying despite myself to get a better look. That can't have been a spell—wraiths must not need spells, right?—but some innate human curiosity in me still feels like there's something there that I can figure out.

The woman fixes me with a wry smile as she lights her pipe with the tip of her finger before putting out the flame by shaking it as though it were a lit match.

"So, no future. But you can tell us about the past?" I ask.

The woman looks back and forth between us as she takes a puff on her pipe. It all feels so homey that I can't help but feel ridiculous about all the fuss and worry about coming here. Still, I don't have any particular desire to get within grabbing distance.

"No reason I couldn't," the woman says, drawing out each word, stopping afterward to take another long puff on her pipe. "Other than we're not supposed to interfere. But I'm not *interfering*, am I? I'm just talking."

"Do you know what happened to make you all come through much more than you were before?" I ask.

Can you kill a wraith? Can a wraith die from choking on her pipe smoke from being made to laugh by a stupid question? I'm going to guess no, because she manages to recover, hitting me with an incongruously modern "you're kidding, right?" expression. An expression that Gigi, on-brand as ever, joins in on.

Just what I needed: two of them.

"Okay, so you were created by the necrowizards?" That's not what Gigi called her merry little master's band of death-obsessed wizards, but it seems apt, so I'm going with it.

"I wasn't created by a wizard."

"Okay, no, bad wording. Sorry. Your… new existence was engineered by them?"

Of all the questions I could have asked, I seem to have hit on a sore spot.

"The spirit world where we usually reside was brought into existence by a group of wizards, yes. I don't think they called themselves the necrowizards, but they're not here to argue."

"You don't know? I kind of thought you knew everything."

"We know the big things," she says. "We know things selectively, where we want to choose to look. Where we've had reason before now or after now to look."

Well, that squashes the sneaking hope that I might be able to get a wraith to slip me a spell or two—the big one, if I'm lucky. "So you're saying I'm going to be a big thing, then?" I ask, feeling far too clever about myself. "Isn't that telling the future?"

The ghost woman's cold demeanor melts back into something affectionate, and I can't help but like her again. "Oh, but Elizabeth, you already are, aren't you? Look at you, you're breaking the veil between life and death. Feels pretty big to me." She takes a puff on her pipe.

"You don't sound very Victorian," I say, taking my time to study the neat details of her dress and the painfully life-like cast of her skin.

"Would that set you more at ease? I've been *always*, since I died. And I died a long time ago. I've had a long time to get used to being always. Why should I make it harder for you to understand me?"

"You still dress Victorian."

She looks down at her clothes with mock offense. "You don't like this dress? I like this dress. I killed a man for this dress."

My eyes go wide. "Did you?"

Her lips stretch across her face, revealing charmingly crooked teeth in a smile that's just a little too intense. It's at this moment that I'm reminded that generally ghosts don't get made out of peaceful, happy deaths.

"Are all of you like this?" I ask.

The wraith smiles. "Like what?"

"So calm and considered. I always thought wraiths wouldn't be so…" I remember Melissa this morning. Her confusion. Her fear. "Lucid."

I don't know what the wraith is thinking of, but pity fills her face. "I was calm and lucid when I died. It was violence and pain, of course, or I wouldn't have ended up a ghost. But I was used to violence. I was used to pain. So I kept my head through it, regardless."

I want to offer condolences. To her, for her life. But it isn't my place. It feels wrong, somehow. Intrusive.

"If we could stay on topic," Gigi's voice cuts through my growing unease. If I had just met Gigi, I probably wouldn't hear the thread of worry strung through her casual words. "So you are definitely wraiths, and your current *position* in the afterlife *was* caused by the wizards, as suspected, and the breaking of the veil *is* Elizabeth's fault, and she *is* an unfortunately significant subversive element in the world at large. That's nothing we didn't already know. We brought you tobacco. You've got to give us something better than that. Something happens on the solstice, doesn't it?"

The ghost straightens, the objection forming on her lips.

"No, no, I'm not asking for the future," Gigi says before she can be stopped. "I'm not asking what *will* happen. I'm asking what the wizards *want* to happen."

The wraith settles back, not mollified but not as angry with those present as she appears to be with those not present. "They won't let us tell the future. What makes you think they'd let us tell you their plans?"

"The wizards are the ones who won't let you tell the future?"

The wraith sighs. "Of course they are. Something about cause and effect, and breaking everything, something, something, something. Threats of horrific torment to punish us when they return eternal if we dare break their rules. Of course, they don't greet us themselves when we die. It's carried in whispers through the world. The wizards aren't *always* like we are. They're sleeping in their little bubble of time in the center of our afterlife. They don't want to be always. Because once you become always, you're stuck that way. It's uncomfortable to be in the living world like that too long. That's why we never stick around." The ghost woman takes another long puff on her pipe. She looks at Gigi with a slight challenge, and then back at me with an expression I can't quite interpret. Something like sympathy, maybe? "Is that enough for the cost of tobacco? Really not sure how you can expect more, bringing the cheap stuff."

"First," Gigi says, "that's not the cheap stuff. Second—"

"Stop!" the ghost woman says to a space just to the left side of me, bolting upright to the edge of her seat. "Don't touch!"

How did I not notice the sudden coolness in the air?

The prickles on my skin? I swallow hard and follow the ghost woman's gaze.

There, with big baleful eyes and the same outfit she was wearing this morning, is Melissa. Max's borrowed scarf is gone, as is the blood that soaked it. Just as well.

"I'm sorry, I forgot," the little girl wraith says to the grown woman wraith. "And I forgot about telling the future." She looks up at me. "I need you not to tell anybody I told you about the future. I forget sometimes."

As does my mom. A pang of guilt runs through me.

"What happens if you touch her?" Gigi asks. Her voice is right beside me, but it feels distant anyway, so focused am I on the little girl.

My attention is drawn back to the wraith woman as she stands. Gone is the casual, modern-looking slouch. Gone is the relatable, expressive face. The woman who stands there now is ramrod straight, her face as set in stone as Gigi's.

"What else did you forget, Melissa?" she asks, her voice echoing in the small space of the room more than it should, considering the soft surfaces. She now reminds me nothing of a Wild West prostitute, and everything of an East Coast schoolmarm who shows her opinions of such loose women in a less-than-charitable way.

I look back to Melissa, whose already wide eyes have gone wider. "What did I forget?" she echoes, her voice hollow.

"That you're part of a pair," the Victorian woman says.

And then, exactly as unnervingly as she appeared, the wraith woman is gone. Nothing but that blue vapor remains, glowing dimly.

We don't have long to consider what that means. Melissa's shriek cuts through the room, drowning out the temperature drop and prickling feelings that I'm starting to associate with the disconcerting appearance of a wraith.

Gigi whirls around beside me, just as I sense a hulking presence there. I step forward, throwing myself behind Gigi. Maybe not the most noble of impulses, but a solid one from a logical point of view. The woman can't be killed, right?

I stop myself from grabbing onto Melissa and pulling her with me, but only just. It's unnecessary, anyway. Melissa sees my movement and follows along, hiding behind me just as I hide behind Gigi.

I recognize the man from the road this morning. In the confined space of the room—especially standing as he is between us and the door to the hallway—he looks bigger. His sallow face is contorted in a snarl. It's an axe in his hand. A rusty one, covered in blood. He stops trying to peek around Gigi to see Melissa and instead focuses on Gigi.

He smiles. It's a sick smile, way too happy to be facing someone as terrifying as Gigi. He brings his axe up, the speed of the motion betraying his comfort and habit with the weapon. It cuts through the air in a huge, smooth arch. But as he swings, Gigi steps forward instead of back like he must have been expecting. Instead of the head of the axe impacting her shoulder, the handle does.

The wooden handle is no match for Gigi's impenetrable body. With the force the man put behind it, the handle cracks, putting the axe head at a weird angle. The man's face fills with confusion, and I've never been so glad not to be able to see the look on Gigi's face as she takes another step into him.

In a dizzying sequence of precise, perfect movements, the tall, elegant woman fastens onto the man, anchoring herself to his body and getting a firm grip on his left arm.

And then, with no more hesitation or consideration than I would give to opening a bottle of milk, she pulls. The muscles and joint of the wraith's shoulder come undone.

I don't think a human arm is supposed to come apart like that. It strikes me as wrong—impossible. But Gigi pulls the appendage off and tosses it to the floor with no surprise. Like she's done it a thousand times. Which, very possibly, she has.

"Go," she says, her voice measured and even. I move toward the door, hitting my back against the entertainment center as I try to stay as far away as possible from the man. Melissa isn't touching me, but she's mirroring my movements so closely and exactly that she might as well be.

I expect rage from the man. I expect him to snarl and swear. I don't expect him to smile and look down at his arm—a perfectly functional, brand-new arm with another axe, still dripping with blood and unbroken, just as it had been when he first appeared.

Gigi mutters some obvious curse words under her breath in a language I don't understand. My legs grow unsteady but move faster. The sound of voices from the hallway draws me toward the door like I'm a fish reeled in on a line.

People. Light. Witnesses. Help. It's all anyone ever wants when they're scared, and I'm no exception. Even as the wraith lunges toward me, stopped by Gigi's sudden, unyielding grip, I scramble to the door. My hands are uncoordinated and shaking, fumbling with the doorknob, but I get it open.

The hallway that greets me looks longer and narrower than it did coming in. A few people peek out of doors with frightened expressions. One man, whose sturdy, compact build and middle age reminds me painfully of my neighbor Henry, is the only one who manages to get fully out of his room and into the hall. I may not be a ghost or have their foresight, but even so, I can see the wraith coming out of the room and taking his murderous rage out on this innocent bystander.

Suddenly, my impulse to get to other people seems not only stupid but criminally negligent.

Keep fighting him, Gigi. Keep him busy and away from us and all these people while I figure out what to do. Signatories of the treaty know better than to involve not-in-the-know humans in paranormal matters, but I don't think they got any ghosts to sign the treaty.

Thankfully, the doors in the hallway close—or at least narrow to a thin crack that the onlookers use to peer out from in relative safety. Good enough. I'm trying to figure out what to do next when I feel motion beside me. Melissa, looking so exactly like she did this morning, walks to stand in front of the terrified man.

"I'm Melissa," she says, exactly as she did this morning when she was introducing herself to me. It's eerie, watching the same stimuli affect someone else the same way it's affected you in the past. The man's defenses go down as he melts into nothing but a protector of this small wayward child, suspicion banished by concern and a natural impulse to help the helpless.

I feel an urge to warn him, conflicted by the need to believe I'm not wrong about Melissa's intentions. It makes me hesitate just long enough that I don't speak before the man puts his hands on her arms in gentle reassurance.

I don't scream "no" until it's too late—until his hands begin first to age, then to wither, and then to rot and skeletonize. I step forward, grabbing Melissa by the hood of her jacket and pulling her away from him, out of his grasp. But the affliction has already spread nearly to his elbows.

The man shrieks with the broken voice of a child,

staring at the bones of his lower arms. The bones from his hands litter the hallway floor. I let go of Melissa's jacket as quickly as I can. I trust my amulet—probably way more than I should—but that doesn't take away my fear, and my hands are tingling.

I stare at them, looking for exposed bone, but I find them unchanged. The man keeps shrieking, his back pressed hard against the wall. I feel more than hear doors up and down the hallway being slammed shut.

My eyes are stuck on my hands, looking for a cause of the strange feeling there. I can't pull them away. Even as in my peripheral vision, Melissa steps back toward the man she's just mutilated so horribly, holding her hands up in a non-threatening gesture.

"I'm sorry," she says, her voice eerily calm. "You touched me. I didn't touch you."

Her complete lack of performed remorse finally gets me to look up and away from my hands, which is how I see the man with the axe now in the hallway, readying his weapon for a swing. "No!" I scream.

Melissa turns, eyes wide as always. She sees the man with the axe.

She steps out of the way.

The axe, aiming for Melissa, buries itself instead in the man's upper thigh. For a horrible moment I think his body is about to skeletonize, but the wraith abandons the axe the moment it hits a live human. I guess he's better at following the rules than Melissa is, whatever his flaws. No touching, sure, but axes are fine.

"Melissa!" I scream, my voice hoarse. "Get out of here!"

She looks at me, her face awash in benign confusion.

"He'll follow you! Go away!"

Her face lights up when she understands my meaning,

which twists my gut somehow. I feel sick that she doesn't seem to care at all about the man behind her, whose shrieks of shock have turned to sobs and whimpers as he sinks to the floor along the wall.

But she does what I say and disappears. I look at Melissa's attacker, new bloody axe already in his hand. After the longest three seconds of my life, he too disappears.

The axe in the good Samaritan's leg does not, but he looks like he wants to pull it out. He's either trying to do so, or maybe staunch the bleeding, but he doesn't have hands anymore. I rush to his side.

"Gigi!" I try to shout. "Gigi! Get out here!"

The man's arm bones hit me, trying to push me away from him, but I don't let it deter me. I take off the crocheted scarf Olivia made for me for Christmas a few years back and press it onto the wound around the axe head that's probably the only thing keeping this man alive. There's no sign of Gigi, or her aloof, even-mannered voice.

She left. She fucking left.

"Someone call an ambulance!" I scream, pushing down as hard as I can as the man tries to talk but only manages a stream of unintelligible sobs. I try to shout again, my voice broken and breaking.

"Ambulance! Now!"

NINE

A Ringer

I don't know the Springfield Sherriff's Office very well. I've been here a few times, usually in my capacity as an all-around assistant to the mayor, but this is the first time I've seen the inside of an interrogation room. I've never given them a reason to suspect me of anything.

At least, not that they remember.

They let me wash the blood off my hands, but there's still some on my sleeves. I can't help but fixate on the spots as I cradle a now-lukewarm cup of coffee, waiting for someone to come back into the room. They're probably figuring out what to ask me—what to accuse me of. Who knows what the witnesses will say. Or what the man…

A sob chokes in my throat.

I know supernatural creatures kill humans. They do so in a way regulated by the treaty, the way Fish and Wildlife regulates hunters, but they certainly do it. I've seen the aftermath, but I've never been there when it was happening. I've never felt someone fighting to hold on. The only deaths I've seen firsthand were the men I killed, and they were gravelings, not humans.

I jump at the sound of the door opening, and then get annoyed at myself for jumping. That probably doesn't help me look like an innocent bystander in the wrong place at the wrong time. At least it's Andy who comes into the room. I know him from high school back in the day. He's not a bad guy. And he had a portion of his memory erased, so he doesn't remember the last time he came through for me and I let him make all the wrong conclusions.

I stare at him with what must be an unnerving intensity, trying to get the question I need to ask him out of my mouth. He doesn't look bothered by the way I'm looking at him, though. I guess he deals with people in various states of distress all the time. He does seem to be moving carefully as he maneuvers into a chair across the table from me. His eyes don't flick to the big one-way mirror on one wall, but mine do, before opening my mouth and trying—and failing—again to speak.

"He's alive," Andy says gently.

A rush of tension leaves my body. Everything else can be fixed. Not for the man, not entirely—no idea if there's anything that can be done for his hands. But the rest of the whole situation is fine.

My sudden relaxation seems to bother Andy more than my nerves did. "I'd like to ask you a few questions, Elizabeth."

I settle back into my seat. "That's fine. Ask me whatever you want. But I need to make a call first. Please give my phone back. I'm pretty sure you weren't supposed to take it, technically. Since I wasn't arrested."

Andy gives me a tight-lipped smile. "We didn't take it. We just asked if we could hold onto it for a bit."

Yeah, *asked*. Under the circumstances, how was I

supposed to say no? "Well, now I'm *asking* if I can have it back."

It's Andy's turn to look to the one-way glass mirror. He nods once. I sit up and lace my fingers together on the table, which seems to please Andy. He doesn't have any papers in front of him the way I see people have in TV shows or movies sometimes. But then again, Andy doesn't have much in common with TV or movie cops. He's too unassuming. Not enough inherent authority. Maybe it's just because I knew him in high school, but he feels like a kid who's just pretending to be a sheriff's deputy because that's how he thinks he can help people. But even as little as I knew him back when we were in school, I know he doesn't really belong here.

"What were you doing at the Primrose Inn?" he asks me, his voice disarming.

"What does Gigi say we were doing?" I ask, a little of my anger at her abandonment coming through.

"Gigi Montgomery wasn't at the hotel when we got there." A slight twitch of my mouth must give away my annoyance, because Andy's eyes narrow. "Was she in the hotel with you when the events occurred?"

When the events occurred. Jesus. That's a way of putting it. Sounds like they've talked to Gigi already—they'd have to be idiots not to, given the scene we made at check-in. From how keen Andy seems to get me to say something specific about her being there, it sounds like she found a way to imply she left right after check-in and never even went to the room. Maybe she got someone else to talk for her—to tell the lies she can't. That has to be damned inconvenient. But if I go down, she's determined to keep her current identity lily-white, apparently. Maybe she's fond of the name Montgomery. I wouldn't blame her—setting up documents and everything has to be getting harder and harder as time goes on, and she's got a whole business, after all.

But a man lost his hands and almost died, so I'm not feeling that charitable at the moment.

Andy's still looking at me, waiting for an answer. It probably doesn't matter what answer I give him in the end, but I have to say something.

"I don't recall."

The problem with Andy not looking like a cop is that his disappointment feels personal. It probably *is* personal. But I'm tired, and it's been a hell of a day, and he still looks like a kid to me, even though he's showing some early signs of wrinkles. Stress of the job, it must be. "Believe me," I say, "you don't want to know."

"Try me."

A bitter sob of laughter escapes me, my thoughts wandering to my sister. "Everyone says that until they know."

Okay, maybe what I say doesn't matter that much, but that was still the wrong thing to say. Like, really fucking wrong. I need to remember that fucking up and getting myself killed by the supernatural world isn't the only way to ruin my life.

Andy is working hard not to give it away, I can tell, but acting like I have a big secret that's bigger than the mysterious things that happened tonight has ignited his interest. Before he can speak again, though, the door opens.

Another sheriff's deputy—this one a pudgy woman with a very new-looking uniform—enters with my fancy new cell phone in her hand. She looks to Andy for approval, who gives her a nod, before she sets it down in front of me.

"Mind calling on speakerphone?" Andy asks.

I shrug and leave the phone sitting flat on the table. I

unlock it and scroll through my contacts until I find the name I'm looking for.

"Arrogant Asshole?" New Uniform asks, eliciting a mild look of admonishment from Andy.

"It's an inside joke," I say, which is essentially true.

"Still," Andy says with a hint of a smile. Trying to build camaraderie with me. Smart. "Quite a name to set for the person you'd choose as your one phone call."

I hit the call button. "I didn't set it for him. I just left him unsupervised with my phone for five minutes, and he set it as that himself. And besides, he's not my one phone call. For him to be my one phone call, you'd have to be arresting me. And you're not doing that, right?"

Max should pick up the phone before Andy can reply. That's how I timed it. That would have been cool and suave and smooth. But instead, the phone keeps ringing, while me, Andy, and New Uniform look awkwardly back and forth at one another. Finally, Max's voice starts up.

"This is Maxwell Jones! You have my condolences for missing me. Tell me what you're looking for, and we'll connect."

I roll my eyes. I've never heard Max's voicemail before. I would have remembered that. I would have teased him about it.

"Maxwell Jones?" New Uniform says, her already-high voice squeaking a little in surprise.

"Yes, why?" I say, ignoring the beep telling me to begin recording my message. Her having a history with Max is the last thing I need—or her or anyone else remembering the last time Max waltzed through the sheriff's office reassembling the day's memories.

In answer, New Uniform reached for the radio on her shoulder.

"Reception, this is Lisa. Do you still have a Maxwell

Jones up there?"

There's a brief burst of static from the radio, until an older female voice that I have absolutely no trouble believing belongs to a receptionist of some stripe comes onto the line. "Maxwell who?" she asks.

Lisa's face scrunches up as she answers Andy's askance glance with an apologetic, confused look of her own. "Maxwell Jones. He was just up there. You were talking to him."

"Honey, I don't know anybody like that."

"You..." Lisa turns her head to look at the radio, as though it has answers for her. On the table in front of me, my time to leave a message apparently runs out, and the call drops. Lisa looks between me and Andy. "He was there..." she says, looking like she's not sure what's going on, but she's sure she doesn't like it.

Behind her and to the left, the door opens, revealing Max's admittedly attractive figure. "My ears were burning," he says, fixing Lisa with a radiant grin. A knot in my shoulders I didn't realize was there, releases. If I weren't so damned tired and he didn't have so much work to do, I might not be able to stop myself from getting up and giving my very best frenemy a hug.

Sheriff's deputy or not, Lisa is still a human being, and as such, she responds in the only way someone can when confronted with a movie-star-caliber heartthrob out of place here in normal, everyday life. She opens and closes her mouth, fumbling for words. And it doesn't exactly help when he runs his fingers through his mid-length, sandy blonde hair and takes a step forward. She visibly blushes when he moves in to plant a kiss on her cheek.

And then, just as suddenly as her whirlwind of flustered feelings came, they disappear. She's not looking at Max anymore.

"Max?" I ask. He gives me a wink.

"Who are you talking to?" Lisa asks, dreamlike. For all Max's bravado, and all my relief at seeing him just seconds before, revulsion fills me. It's impressive what he's done to her, from an objective standpoint. Helpful, too. But even if I need him to do it—even if I was in the act of calling him to come do it mere seconds ago—it doesn't sit right with me to see it.

Andy stands, hand reaching for a gun that isn't there, alarm warring with the need to maintain calm. "Lisa, are you all right?"

Max moves quickly, sidling up close to Andy and planting one on him before he gets a chance to react to Max being a threat. For a horrible split second, Andy's arms are moving up in what look like practiced, precise movements that I don't believe for a moment Max could counter. But the moment Max's lips hit his cheek, he's in that same pleasant, unfocused state as Lisa, oblivious to the man who is still well inside his personal bubble.

My stomach turns again, and the reason why comes into clearer focus. I hate seeing Max do this because I know it's what he wants to do to me, essentially. If it weren't for my amulet, he'd be just as quick and just as unconflicted. He'd erase himself and all knowledge of magic from my mind just as he's erased his presence here this afternoon from Andy's and Lisa's. The only difference is that he'd get me to hand over the trove before he did it, and he'd have to go around visiting my friends and family afterward to tie up loose ends. Then he'd get me back under the treaty—he swears he has a way to do it. And presumably he'd use his newly stolen trove to beg and barter for a proper seat at the wizard's table. He'd become a full wizard—ritual of longevity and all. And presumably he'd live happily ever five-hundred-years after.

I wonder if he'd think of me at all. He probably would. He'd probably feel smug about it. Justified.

If Max senses my unease—which I'm pretty sure he does—he doesn't show it. He just steps over toward me with a big goofy grin on his face and light in his green eyes. "Pretty cool, right?" he asks.

I roll my eyes as he's expecting me to and turn my attention back to Andy. He holds his hand out to me for a handshake. I take it. It's weak and unconvincing.

"Thanks for coming down, Miss Baker. We apologize for the inconvenience. We must have got that witness statement wrong. They must have meant someone else."

Andy's earnestness—his intent desire to help—is gone. It's blunted by the force of Max's spell. That's just temporary, I know. If everyone Max put the whammy on stayed this way forever, we'd never stop fighting about it. But all the same, I still hate seeing this done to Andy.

I finish shaking Andy's hand and say some meaningless words that he probably won't remember, then I walk with Max out through the sheriff's office, collecting nothing from the people we pass but noncommittal smiles and the absolute least attention they seem capable of paying anyone. I take Max's arm when he offers it, if for no other reason than I feel unsteady on my feet after the hell at the Primrose and the purgatory of the interrogation room.

I take a cleansing breath when we step out of the station and the cold air hits me. I look down at the dry and drying blood on my coat and clothes as I walk with Max toward the parking lot. At least he occasionally obeys parking laws. There's something. But then, he probably doesn't have a spell to fix the paint on his expensive, electric-blue sports car. I guess pigment isn't as malleable as minds.

"Sorry about that," Max says as he reaches for the

driver's door handle of the shiny monstrosity. "I should have known you were going to get caught up in this wraith thing eventually."

It's sheer luck that he's too consumed with the business of getting into the car to catch the look of shock that crosses my face before I duck down and contort myself to get into a car that low to the ground.

"*This wraith thing?*" I say as Max pushes the button to start the car. He doesn't put on his seatbelt. Never does. But I, someone who does *not* know a healing spell or any other spells that would be likely to be particularly helpful in a car crash, do.

"Yeah." He spares a glance at me as he pulls out of the parking space. "The wraiths have been a lot worse lately. You know, the whole reason you went to the Primrose Inn in the first place?"

Okay, yeah, there's playing dumb and then there's playing willfully oblivious. My heart pounds in my chest. It's a childish hope that somehow this might be unrelated to my recent activities, but I can't help but grasp at straws to get something taken off my conscience. "I knew something was happening. What do you think is causing it?" I try to sound nonchalant and distracted as he is getting out into traffic, and tired as he seems to be from the effort of working mental mojo on the entire staff of a sheriff's department, I might just get away with it, too.

"Russian wizards, probably. That's what Kristoff thinks, anyway. Doesn't make much sense, though."

I don't react to the name of Max's male master. That might be suspicious, considering he and I have more than our fair share of bad blood for two people who have never technically met, but I can't help it. I don't have time to think about Kristoff right now.

"How doesn't it make sense?" I ask instead.

He shoots me a suspicious look, which I *think* is for me asking questions, not for me knowing more than I'm letting on. I go with it. "Hey, I could have been killed back there!" I say. "Did you see that guy's hands?"

Max holds my gaze for a second before returning his eyes to the road. "I didn't see, but I've heard about it."

This is a rare opportunity. I take advantage of it. "What causes that?" I say, letting the horror I feel into my voice.

Max grimaces while keeping his eyes on the road, a rare expression for no one's benefit but his own. "Ghosts are out of sync with time. When any part of them comes into contact with a living entity, even as a wraith, that time-lessness kind of... rubs off."

"It changes them to what they will be in the future?" I ask, trying to wrap my head around it.

"It changes them to what they are for the most time. And on average, if you look at them through the perspective of all of time since the wraith touched them onward, most people are dead for most of the time."

"Huh," I say. My hands twitch involuntarily, but luckily, Max doesn't notice. The tingling went away. After all, I barely touched the girl's jacket, not even her hands or her arms or anything. Still, technically, the man in the hallway had only come in contact with Melissa's clothing, too. But so much of magic is wishy-washy and based on intention. Maybe it's functionally different, intending to grab her arms versus intending to grab the hood of her jacket. It feels like a stretch. Then again, the man in the hallway also didn't have an amulet protecting him against harm, I reassure myself, but I don't feel as reassured as I wish I was.

"That must be why it didn't affect Gigi," I say, still mad as hell at her. "On average, Gigi is just Gigi."

Max snorts, which is a refreshingly unattractive look on

him. I look at the snow-covered night passing by my windows for the first time and frown. "This isn't the way to my house."

"We're not going to your house. We're going to the Emporium. Olivia called after everything went wrong at the Primrose. We're having a wraith chitchat!"

Second time going to Emporium in one day. Lucky me. Max, however, looks like a little kid on Christmas. Which, considering the time of year and his current age relative to a wizard's expected lifespan, I guess he kind of is.

"Excited to have an excuse to invade Gigi's stronghold?" I say, amused in spite of myself.

He grins. "I hear she serves good ice cream, and when I try to go there on my own, she throws me out."

"Throws you out?" I try to imagine Gigi going into open conflict with a wizard, however junior, and still can't.

"Eh, she threatens to make a scene. And I'd have to wipe too many minds to be worth it just for ice cream."

"You only say that because you haven't had her ice cream," I smirk, and he rolls his eyes at me with a smirk of his own.

I can't tell whether that actually bothers him, or if his amusement is genuine. Still, Gigi must be getting much more comfortable with Max if she's willing to stand up to him like that. I guess she figured their destruction is mutually assured at this point. Max could justify some of his association with me to the other wizards, if they found out, by saying that he was doing it to get my trove. That excuse even has the handy characteristic of also being true, albeit something he doesn't want to tell them. But *all* of our interactions? Gigi could probably find a way to spin it so that the other wizards felt the need to impose a little wizard justice. And Gigi is indestructible, after all. She has a healthy fear of wizards, which apparently stems from them being able to make her suffer, but they can't actually kill her.

"So why does Kristoff think the Russians did it?" I ask as casually as possible.

I must pull it off, because Max answers right away, and he doesn't see any edge to my question. I should get him exhausted before I ask him questions more often. He's always so guarded with wizard stuff. Probably also helps that he thinks I'm being negatively affected by wizard actions at the moment.

"Like I said, it makes no sense. They'd have to have summoned a ton of ghosts, in the same spot, one after another. And then repeated the process in a different place. And they'd have to have spread those summonings out to be able to get the veil as weak as it is now." Max shakes his head. "Kristoff has this theory that different Russian wizards are trying to trick ghosts into telling them different parts of the future that seem harmless enough on their own, but that they can add up into useful information. And they're summoning so many because they have to try again and again before they get one that will play ball each time. But I just don't buy it."

"Yeah, I don't either," I say. Finally, I am resigned and have accepted the truth. And every ounce of that resignation shines through in my voice.

Max's head turns on a swivel to look at me. He slams his foot on the brakes, and we go sliding a short distance before we come to a stop to a chorus of horns from the few drivers that are around us this late at night on our small road.

"Jesus fucking Christ. Elizabeth Baker, what did you do?"

I shoot him a sheepish grin. "I kind of feel like you've already figured that out."

"Why?" he asks, his eyes wild. It's kind of fun to see him this uncomposed.

"Well, obviously I didn't know it was going to cause *this*," I say back, more defensively than I want it to come out.

"Why do it at all?"

"Reasons! That don't matter!" I cross my arms and then realize I look like a petulant child. But uncrossing them would just make it worse, so I go with it and keep them crossed. "I'm not going to do it anymore, obviously," I say more quietly, like a complaint I have no right to make.

He slumps sideways, leaning against his door, shaking his head at me. The streetlight shining down through the sunroof illuminates the disbelief on his face.

"I'm surprised you didn't know about it, what with the spy spells," I say before I can stop myself, unintended venom in the words.

His eyebrows draw together. "You knew I was enchanting the jacket. If you didn't agree with me that the tracking spell I have on there is probably going to save your life one day, you wouldn't keep wearing it."

"I'm not talking about the jacket," I say, warming and feeling petty. "I'm talking about the scarf."

His mouth opens and then twists into a grin. His eyes, God help me, sparkle. "Oh," he says.

"Oh?" I ask, my petty rage feeling ridiculous.

"Yeah, that… I didn't put that spell on there."

That spell? Melissa had said there was more than one spell on the scarf, and I had said the same just now. If Max only thought there was one…

"Why would you give me something your masters gave you?" I say, scared and angry for a new reason.

He holds his hands up, the shifting headlights making

them look like they're moving even though he's holding them still. The car that was behind us has finally given up and is driving around, punctuating the decision with a quick, peeved blast of the horn. We ignore it.

"The scarf was from Moira," Max says. "The spell she put on it picks up on emotions and emotional states. She was trying to keep tabs on me, and I thought it would be funny if I gave it to you instead."

Me, who is in a happy, long-term relationship with all the associated emotions that brings. I remember the way Max's female master, Moira, kissed him the one time I saw them together—all the ownership there.

"It was a prank," he says imploringly.

I nod, holding his eyes and treating the moment lightly, both of us remembering that witnessed kiss and Max's helplessness. "You should have told me," I say, shifting my attention back out the windshield and finally letting my arms unfold.

Max gets the hint and puts his hands on the wheel, continuing the drive to the Emporium.

"You should have told me you were summoning ghosts," he mutters, head shaking in shock again at the thought now that he has the chance to circle back to it. "I didn't even know you had that spell." His eyebrow raises. "I wouldn't mind taking a look at that one."

I fix him with a grin. "You know, I'm not sure summoning ghosts is all that necessary anymore. They seem pretty willing to show up as wraiths if you just ask real nice."

He lets out a bark of laughter. But when the momentary amusement fades, he's left looking haunted. We make the rest of the short drive in silence.

TEN

An Uninvited Guest

The Emporium is closed when we arrive. This doesn't surprise me, but it does seem to surprise a few would-be customers, who are looking at the dark interior and the opening hours on the door with entitled outrage.

"Excuse me, coming through," Max says, shouldering his way past them as he pulls a keychain from his pocket. For a moment, I'm surprised Gigi gave him her key. But then I put together that if I'm able to make a key that can open any lock, then naturally Max can, too. According to the most modern book in the trove, it's one of the common beginner spells that they teach to children. Which definitely wasn't a nugget of information that filled me with rage while I was struggling to get it to work. Nope, not at all.

"You *were* invited, right?" I mutter, just loud enough to be heard as we slide into the building, closing and locking the door behind us.

Max makes a beeline for the sweeping, swooping staircase that leads to the Emporium's seldom-used second floor. I don't have time to stop and appreciate what Gigi's done with the place, in all its worn-in Art Deco glory. Which is a shame, because it would be one of my favorite places to spend time, if it didn't come with so much baggage.

"Of course! I'm the cavalry. Didn't you know?" Max responds.

Morning. Christmas. Kid. He takes the stairs two at a time, and I follow behind, hoping like hell that Faisal is up there and my mother isn't.

When I get up to the second floor, I see that I've gotten exactly one of my wishes. Faisal is there, sitting in one of the five nineties-municipal-chic chairs that have been pulled around into a big circle in the open space in the front half of the room. As is Gigi—traitor though she may be—Olivia, Wilbur… and my mother.

In theory, they're lit by hanging lights with drum-style shades. But to my eyes, the double-height industrial-looking wall of windows along the front is doing most of the heavy lifting, illumination-wise. The hanging lights do tend to pull the eye to the back half of the room, though, which is taken up with metal racks of books and artifacts. Other than the trove in my office closet, the contents of those shelves are probably the most valuable thing in Springfield. Probably more than anything in any of the surrounding towns, either. It's all a part of Gigi's collection.

Note to self: if you're going to live forever whether you want to or not, maybe don't pick up any hoarding tendencies. But then, at least Gigi does seem to have an eye for value. And from what I've heard, she's gone to great lengths in the past to acquire things that catch her eye.

But the quick admiration of Gigi's collection and the dramatic beauty of the room in the winter night is far overshadowed by the dread I feel as Max strides toward my mother with his charming, goofy grin plastered on his face.

"Mrs. Baker!" he says. "It's so great to finally meet you." He clears the distance between them in five long, easy strides, and, to my immense relief, doesn't immediately kiss my mother's hand when she stands and offers it to him.

"And who are you?" she asks. Mom's blonde hair is a little lighter than Olivia's and much lighter than mine. Her build is willowy—and has only gotten more so with age and her particular brand of infirmity.

"I'm Max," he says, keeping hold of her hand. He doesn't mean it badly, I don't think, but it's hard to tell whether my mother minds or not. "I'm a friend of Elizabeth and Olivia. I work with Elizabeth."

My mother's eyes light up the way they so often do when she's pleasantly surprised to remember something. "Oh, yes! The annoying one. Barged your way in one day and wouldn't leave despite not having any credentials."

Ah, yes, another side effect of having the positive half of all your memories eaten by a vampiric spirit: it can be hard to act in a socially acceptable manner when, as far as you can remember, everything is negative to some degree or another, and you're just relieved to have anything to say to anyone at all.

Max doesn't seem to mind. His smile, if anything, widens. "That's me. Like a lucky penny."

"The phrase is 'unlucky penny,'" Mom says, her own smile growing to meet his.

And this right here is a big part of why wizards make themselves so attractive as one of their first acts of wizardry. Human beings are dumb, dumb creatures. We like shiny things, and we trust pretty people. Even if we know we shouldn't. We might not want to acknowledge it, but the effect is real. For the first couple of months I knew Max, I looked up studies confirming as much to nurse my anger at him every time we had a disagreement, which was pretty often.

"Bad luck is a kind of luck," Max says. "Just ask your daughter." At that, he winks at me. Which is inappropriate if you don't know he's referencing the deal I made with Aloysius, and just obnoxious if you do.

"I'm not sure I know what you mean." A cool edge has slipped into my mother's voice. Her other hand rises up to sit on top of their joined hands. The gesture changes their grip to feel like she's holding him in her mercy, rather than any predatory sense that might have gone the other way around. She might not totally get what he's on about, but she got that there was something hinky being said, and that was enough for her.

Max breaks through her sudden distance with a warm, genuine smile. "Nothing treacherous," he says. "An inside joke between me and Beth. She made a friend I don't approve of, is all. Sometimes I get protective of my friends when I think they're doing something dumb. I'm working on it."

Credit where it's due—Max does know what to say to a mother to get her to like him. Even if it's complete bullshit, if for no other reason than that he said "friends," plural, yet no one but me is really willing to put up with his ass.

Except that he did call Olivia his "friend," and he didn't hesitate enough for that to be a lie. He usually takes a second to come up with lies. Suddenly, my mother isn't the only member of my family I'm nervous is close to Max.

"Anyway, I'm sorry we disturbed you," Max says, maneuvering my mother over toward the thin door that leads to the staircase that goes up to my mother's studio in the peak of the building. It's not a bad space, with its many skylights and suspiciously new kitchen and bathroom fixtures. "Elizabeth and I have a work project we roped everyone into helping us with. I wouldn't mind if you stayed, but there are nondisclosure contracts and everything involved. You understand?"

It's not a good cover, but when Mom looks over at me, I smile reassuringly—as does Olivia. That's apparently enough to make it go down easy, because she trusts us. Even though we lie to her constantly. A pang of guilt rises up, but that's a pretty regular occurrence every time I see my mother. Leave it to me to find the weirdest reason for a pretty normal feeling.

Mom opens the door to head back upstairs. And then, just when I think we've made it out of the woods, Max leans forward and gives her a kiss on the cheek goodbye.

My blood boils, but I manage to maintain my passive, positive expression. Maybe it's not so far-fetched to imagine I'll kill him one day after all. I keep my shaking hands at my sides as my mother disappears through the door, and we all listen to her footsteps up the stairs. Only when I'm sure she's gone do I close the distance between Max and me. I'm amazed Olivia isn't on him already. But from the unfocused, thoughtful look on his face, I wonder for a split second if he didn't get a little more than he bargained for when he tried to meddle with my mother's already-meddled-with brain.

"It's weird in there," he says quietly, while I'm still trying to distill my anger into something that won't make me sound stupid. "I don't know if I'm going to be able to fix it." He turns his gaze to me, his own preoccupation enough, apparently, that he isn't picking up on how angry I am—was—with him. "I mean, of course I'll try, but... I don't know. It's weird in there."

"She isn't going to remember you, you know," I say, stepping away from him and away from the conversation, suddenly very aware of Gigi, Wilbur, Faisal, and Olivia's eyes on us. I head to a row of chairs by the window to drag another one over into the circle. A flicker of hope that Max might be able to find a way to help my mom burns in my chest. But its presence doesn't completely eliminate my anger at him barging into her brain uninvited. I'm not sure if it should.

"What? Why not?" Max asks.

"You weren't rude enough," Gigi says.

I get my chair situated next to Faisal, who shoots me a "You okay?" look. I shake my head, and he reaches out to give my hand a reassuring squeeze. Max takes over the seat Mom was previously sitting in, between Olivia and Wilbur.

"You get the paperwork sorted out, Tiny? Everything going to be consistent?" Max says to Wilbur, a toned-down version of the smile he gave my mother back on his face.

Wilbur seems to weigh the pros and cons of picking a fight with a wizard over a nickname in the middle of a supernatural crisis and decides to take the loss.

"The paperwork matches the version of events you said you'd give everyone. If you went off script, that's not my fault."

Max continues to smile, undaunted. "I stayed on script. Good work, team. Gotta say, having a troll is useful."

"You don't have a troll," I say, more for the benefit of the people not as used to shrugging off Max's button-pressing as I am. "So, everyone's caught up, right? With the ghosts and the necrowizards and the end of the world?" Max's light tone in the face of dark shit seems a lot more natural on him than it does on me. I wonder how he manages that.

"Olivia gave Max the gist on the phone," Faisal says, his voice as measured and even as always. He's looking around the circle at everyone. "But just to be clear, on top of *everything*..." He launches into a detailed but easy-to-follow recap of what we collectively know about what's going on. He doesn't mention that I was the one breaking the veil, except to say that we had reason to believe the damage done to the veil was as bad as it was likely to get.

It strikes me this is the first time we've all been together in the same room. That's probably why Max is so endearingly excited—he gets to be a part of a team that isn't full of psychopaths for once. Well, as long as you don't think too hard about Gigi. The jury is out on her, sometimes. Like earlier, when she abandoned me in a dangerous situation.

Again.

My familiar simmering frustration with Gigi's particular set of self-centered priorities is interrupted by a pair of realizations: that Faisal is looking at Olivia a little bit more often and not nearly as warmly as he usually does, and that he had no reason to hide that I was the one breaking the veil from this group of people. They're the people we trust—kind of. We trust Wilbur, anyway, and have accepted the inevitability that Max is going to find things out eventually, whether I want him to or not. And as for Gigi—we've shown her the trove. That's the highest level of trust we have.

But if we trust everyone in this room, and Faisal is keeping secrets, that means that he thinks someone in this room isn't who they appear to be. And Olivia hasn't given me any of the passing momentary glares that she's been prone to lately. She hasn't contributed much to the conversation at all, come to think of it, not even when there was a wizard messing with our mother's mind.

My stomach drops. Faisal catches my eye, and he gives me a subtle nod as he catches my expression. I struggle to keep my reaction under control. If he's keeping this under wraps, he has a reason for it. Looking around the circle, no one else has picked up on it. I swallow down my feelings.

Faisal continues talking. "So it seems to me like we need to know two things. To start, we need to know if the necrowizards are planning to come back into the world through circles, the way ghosts are normally summoned."

"That seems pretty likely to me," Max says sunnily, seemingly pleased to have something to contribute. "Being a wraith isn't as steady or reliable a connection to the living world as coming over as a full-fledged ghost. They wouldn't settle for it. They probably made circles in advance and rigged them up to auto-trigger when the veil got thin enough that they didn't need the power of a summoning spell to activate."

"That's easy, then," I blurt out. "We find their circles and break them. That way they can't come through."

"*If* we knew where their circles were," Gigi chimes in.

"Which is the second thing we need to know," Faisal says, almost to himself. I can't tell if he's annoyed at being interrupted or not. I'm guessing not, but he's so locked down right now it's hard to say for sure.

"And we need to do it before the solstice," Max says.

I nod. "Because if we wait until after, we'll have to fight through them to get to their circles, and they'll definitely defend them. And there's no way we're going to make it through a whole group of war-era wizards."

Wilbur nods, as does Gigi. She looks haunted, though. Faisal didn't mention that her creator was one of the necrowizards in the course of the conversation. Not sure if that's out of sensitivity for Gigi or keeping it from "Olivia," but either way, Max just walked all over that plan.

"No, it's worse than that," Max says, crossing his arms in an uncharacteristic gesture.

"How so?" Gigi asks.

Max casts his eyes around the circle. "The necrowizards wouldn't have planned to come back with a big delete button just sitting there waiting to be pressed. Before the solstice, before they've come back through the circles, we should be able to destroy them. At least, I think so. I've got to think so."

"And after?" I prompt, when Max leaves us hanging longer than is comfortable. Max talking about wizards and their plans openly with me is hard enough. Him talking about them with this entire group? If I were kinder, I would help him understand that the girl that looks like Olivia probably isn't my sister. But Faisal isn't calling that out right now, and he must have a reason.

Max slumps down in his chair, making him look shorter. Almost haggard. "Okay, so, a little Afterlife 101. Afterlives can either be temporal or atemporal. Based on what the wraith at the Primrose told you, it sounds like the necrowizards went for a hybrid model. Wizards don't do anything without a reason. If they have their circles linked to the atemporal part of the afterlife, and they're linked to the permanent ripping of the veil, then the circles will be out of time, too. At least, that's my guess. That's what I'd do."

"That's what you'd *try* to do," Gigi mumbles under her breath, but there's no fire in it. The effects of Max's words ripple through the circle as Max keeps talking.

"So even if we did manage to get past the necrowizards to their circles, they couldn't be destroyed without using time magic. And time magic is finicky. It backfires easily. Plus, it's rare. I've never even met anyone who could do any."

With great strain, I avoid sharing a knowing glance with Faisal. I haven't told anyone else the details of what I saw when I was trapped in Max's invisible, shielded coffee table vault nine months ago. But I saw Max's master Moira use time magic to avoid a booby trap Max had set in case they ever came into his house uninvited. Max *does* know someone who meddles in time magic. He's just pretending for the moment that he doesn't. Even now, when we're talking big world-ending consequences and that information would be helpful. How very wizard of him.

"What about your chance demon?" Gigi says to me. "He dabbles in time magic, doesn't he?"

Faisal answers before I can, which would be annoying on other nights, but is more like a favor when I'm feeling as drained, angry, and hopeless as I am right now. "That's a simple one-variable time dilation trick, and it's built into the casino. He doesn't do it himself. If we all want to go hide out in the Casino, he can stretch time so that we die before the necrowizards have had time to do their worst. Or he can make the casino condense time so we can emerge when the dust settles. Neither of those things seems helpful."

"He wouldn't help me anyway," I volunteer. "Our deal isn't like that."

"Of course it isn't," Max says under his breath.

Whatever. Fuck you, Max. You don't know anything.

"So, what are our options, then?" Not-Olivia asks, the seriousness of her expression so close to my sister's—but not quite right.

"I don't see any," I say. "If we don't stop the necrowizards from coming through before the solstice, we're stuck with them. Forever. And that's on top of the wraith problem, which would only get worse."

Those sentences sour the air in the room and the expressions on the faces around me.

"A group of powerful, battle-hardened wizards who

will live forever?" Wilbur says. "Are we really pretending the wizards will accept that?"

Max lets out a long, harsh laugh. "Believe me," he says. "They won't."

"Wizards don't like anyone having power over them," I say, emboldened. "They won't like having one group over all of them. They only tolerate each other as well as they do because no one person is in charge, and they all have predefined boundaries."

"It would be war," Max says. "And everyone except the necrowizards would lose."

"All the other *wizards* would lose, you mean," Gigi says.

Max shifts just his eyes to look at her. "You think that'll work well for anyone else? We took out the gods. We banished the fae. We haven't gone to war in a millennium. You really want to see what we've all been working on over our summer vacation?"

The gravity of Max's words settles on us. I'm surprised I didn't notice him carrying the weight of the possibility of this coming war over the last few weeks or months. Looking back, I can see hints of it. A certain manic quality to his already upbeat demeanor. He's been bringing in more treats than usual. He's even been nicer to me, come to think of it, occasionally listening and abiding by boundaries I set—which should have been an immediate tipoff.

That's how you know you've got a wizard scared—they start acting like they want you to remember them well.

"You got my hair wrong." The true Olivia's voice carries over the still room from the top of the staircase from the first floor.

ELEVEN

A Corner

The thing that wears my sister's face smiles a big, toothy grin. Its back is to the staircase, so it can't see Olivia standing there. But it begins to rotate its head—just the head, not the shoulders—until it's on completely backwards. It pauses there for a long, horrifying moment.

Nausea rises up again. I'm growing accustomed to the grotesque and unusual. I'm even growing more accustomed to human-looking bodies harboring unexpected secrets. But nothing will ever make me accept looking at the body of my sister with her hands folded primly in her lap, her cardigan coordinating with the colors of the button down beneath it just as perfectly as it always does, and her big, semi-curly blonde braid cascading down over the front of her body instead of her back. Nothing could make it acceptable to hear my sister's voice with the ghoul's intonation coming out of what should be the back of her head.

"I assure you," the ghoul says, "it's quite accurate. You're just not used to looking at it from the back."

For a long moment, no one speaks. Everyone is

watching Olivia, or the ghoul, or swapping back and forth between them. I know everyone in this circle well enough to see their little stress tells as they try to stifle their immediate fear—or immediate revulsion. The tightening around Faisal's eyes. The way Max's hands go wide, as though he's readying them to twist into shape for a spell. The intense focus in Wilbur's gaze that he almost never has.

And Gigi's utter inability to sit still or avoid making herself the center of attention. I used to think it was a narcissistic impulse, but these days I think it's more a conditioned response to centuries of being the best person to draw fire in any given situation. Gigi stands up, dusts off the front of her pants as though she's ever allowed a speck of dust to accumulate in this, her haven, and strides toward the field of still-unused chairs by the window. "Well, it's a good thing I keep so many chairs up here. Never know who's going to come around these days, do I?"

She walks right through the line of sight between Olivia and the ghoul. And as she does, as though Gigi's motion is breaking a spell, the ghoul's head continues its journey. By the time Gigi has brought a new chair to the circle between Wilbur and Faisal, the ghoul's head is back where it started. Olivia's face and hair are gone, replaced by the Middle Eastern woman's visage, the one we saw this morning.

"And then there were seven," Max says, any trace of his previous sunny disposition now well and truly gone.

"Why'd you come here?" Faisal asks, looking at the ghoul. "Why trick us?"

The ghoul sits forward in her seat, crossing one long leg over another. She's wearing her previous body now, with all its elegant proportions, but she's still in Olivia's clothes, and it makes her gestures seem off.

"I knew it was only a matter of time before the arbiter

broke the rules and brought the wizard into the arbitration. She's human. That's what you *do*. When anything gets tricky, you pull in everyone you know and huddle together."

"You think she'd be so cavalier, even when she was told not to?" Faisal says.

"If she were afraid of breaking a graveling's rules, she wouldn't have killed two of them, now would she?"

And with those simple words, Max seems to come back into himself—back to life. "An arbitration involving gravelings, huh? And what are you, exactly? You looked human before, and now you're looking almost human, except for your eyes. You must be a ghoul, huh?"

Max leans back in his chair, visibly enjoying himself. He crosses his legs with the same overexaggerated elegance the ghoul had earlier, even putting the same leg on top. "An arbitration required between the ghouls and the gravelings. What an interesting thing you just told me that Elizabeth kept a perfect secret."

The ghoul's eyes shoot to mine, and I'm glad I don't have my glasses on to see the void in them. She looks at Faisal, the barest hint of a smile on her lips. "'On top of everything,' you said. I thought you meant the arbitration. You meant me to think that."

Faisal shrugs, his poker face intact.

I cut in, the pieces of Faisal's plan starting to fall into place. "I wonder what Claude would think of this. Should I give him a call? He'd probably call the whole thing off." I keep my affect as flat as possible.

"It would be your word against mine," the ghoul says.

Gigi perks up. "It would be your word against *mine*," she says. "Who do you think the gravelings would trust to tell the truth?"

The ghoul sits stock-still—more still than a human can

manage. It shatters the illusion of humanity completely. "That wouldn't get you anything."

"It would lose you something," Faisal says, his slight lean forward the only hint that he's paying any particular attention to this conversation. "And having something to lose if we're not happy means you'll do us the favor we need you to do."

The ghoul's eyes shift back and forth to the room around us, as though she's looking for a way out. "You need to know where the circles are," she says. "I don't know that. I don't know of anyone who might."

Gigi, however, sits up straighter in her chair. "But I do. The vampire king."

I can't help but look surprised. Wilbur and Olivia do, too. Max, however, has a look on his face like the pieces are coming together, but haven't snapped together quite yet.

"The vampire king knows where the circles are?" I ask.

"He might," Gigi says. "He had a thing with one of the necrowizards when they were alive."

"You're talking about Timur," Max says, horrible realization spreading across his face. "He was one of these 'necrowizards'?"

"He was," Gigi says, her tone clipped.

Max looks like he wants to ask Gigi something, but then his eyes shoot to the ghoul and he doesn't. "That's just a gross rumor. It's never been proven," he says instead, his cheeks reddening.

Gigi shrugs, the momentary tension at the mention of the name Timur dissipating as quickly as it came. "Well, you can tell I believe it's true. Anyway, the old wizard did let the vampire king drain him in the end. Kind of amazing how puritanical wizards have gotten about species-mixing in the last thousand years. It didn't use to be this way."

Yeah, I'm not going down that rabbit hole. I address the ghoul. "Most people try to find a way to bribe me when things are important. They're not usually very good at it. Count it as a blessing that I'm telling you, in no uncertain terms, exactly what I want."

The ghoul seems to shrink in her seat. Which she might literally be doing. "I don't know the vampire king."

"No, but I'll bet you can find out what someone who knows him looks like," I say, channeling the steady confidence of… really everyone in the room except for me. "Which means you could get close enough to him to find a way to tell him what we need to know."

The ghoul's eyes flick to Wilbur. "*He* knows someone who knows someone who knows the vampire king. Why not use that? He's a troll with a *connection*. That's the whole point of them, isn't it?"

I look to Wilbur, who shakes his head.

"That's not a connection I can use," he says.

That's a first. I don't think I've ever heard of a troll refusing to make a connection. I kind of get the impression, sometimes, that they *can't* refuse. But regardless, he is. I'll have to ask him about that some time. In private, though. I turn back to the ghoul, with a "See, there?" look.

"You understand this is risky for me," she says with the countenance of a worm who has quit wriggling on the hook.

"You understand what's at stake," I say.

The corner of her mouth tweaks up just a little. Just enough to catch me off guard, leaving me mesmerized as her face, body, and hair transform again into the spitting image of Olivia. If it weren't for the slightly different clothes—and the spiteful, devilish look in the false Olivia's eye—I wouldn't be able to tell them apart.

"For *you*," the ghoul says, standing. "For us, a wizard

civil war just sounds like more fresh bodies and no more wizard oversight."

"Gee, if only you knew whether or not those bodies would be safe to eat."

She tilts her head gently to one side and coolly narrows her eyes in the least Olivia-like expression I've ever seen. Does she know I know what killed her people? What could *still* kill them if they pick the wrong human to devour in some cold, snow-covered back alley? Does she suspect?

I'm not threatening her with the extinction of her species. But I could. It would take me twelve words to do it properly.

"I'll get you your information," she says, then pauses. "You know, I liked you better from farther away." She steps into the Crossroads before I can defend myself.

Just as well—I don't have a defense anyway.

TWELVE

A Favor

I really should have gotten the cell phone number of the ancient demon I extorted into doing my bidding. Or maybe she doesn't have one. When she shapeshifted into my sister and back, she didn't change her clothes. And if Wilbur is to be believed—which he usually is—ghouls can shapeshift into animals as well. I guess it's just easier not to worry about where you put your cell phone and wallet before you spend a week as a frog.

All that to say, the wait is interminable. Sunday passes as an age. Faisal does his best to distract me—distract us both, really—and he has some tried-and-true methods of doing so that I'm very fond of. But the lazy day with him home the week before Christmas just isn't nearly as idyllic as I was hoping with multiple supernatural world conflicts hanging over our heads.

We read the trove together. We go ice skating. I fall down. I check again to see if the 3D printer I think might give me a chance at successfully making an amulet is available. It's the only 3D printer in my price range that uses light-sensitive resin and lasers to achieve the level of detail I need. It's still out of stock and backordered. Figures.

I check in with Max half a dozen times to find out if his attempts to backchannel some rumors about the necrowizards and get the wizards to solve their own damn problem has borne any fruit. He tells me the same thing every time—that he's gotten the word out there as much as he can without drawing attention to himself and therefore to me and the squishy, non-amulet-wearing humans I love. No calls or texts reveal any more information than that. I don't expect them to.

I try to enchant my infinity pouch again, and when that runs out of the power to distract me, I turn my mind to the other problem on my plate. Wilbur doesn't have any ideas for any other species that might be able *and willing* to help the ghouls get untainted meat, although I do ask him if he thinks he can get a list of where all the meat went. I don't want to help the ghouls target better living people to murder, but having the information in my back pocket won't hurt. I resist the urge to ask Wilbur what it is about his connection to the vampire king that means he can't use it even if the goddamn world is at stake. This isn't the time. I'll dig into it after this is settled.

When all else fails, I enlist Faisal's help to start looking for crematoriums for sale. It's amazing how much you can find on the internet these days. Almost as amazing as the fact that some large commercial real estate companies haven't bothered to find anyone who can actually design a decent website.

Monday, I go to work. To my silly little job, with emails and copiers, and fliers and endless discussions about optics, in the middle of an actual apocalypse. The whole thing is wildly surreal, but if I stayed home, I would just keep spiraling until I drove myself crazy, Faisal crazy, or both of us crazy. Besides, I have something I need to talk to my friendly office wizard about, and I always find it's best to ask giant favors in person.

Our officemates have a lot to say about the wraiths, though they all call them ghosts or spirits. Luckily, no one says anything about the man and his hands and the incident at the Primrose Inn.

The citizens of Springfield have plenty to say about the wraith subject, too. Their calls and emails to the mayor's office run the gamut from "you need to tell everyone there are no ghosts, so they stop freaking out, oh, and also stop this crazy giant crime wave and rash of home invasions" to "tell us what the government knows about ghosts that they're hiding from the public."

It hits me for not the first time that, although I hate that this is happening, it does have a silver lining: it's preparing people in a real way for the possibility that the supernatural exists. Scary stories you tell around the campfire about a weird feeling you got one time and a door you *swore* you closed but was open in the morning is one thing. Your aunt Claire having a conversation with a dead guy about the evils of prohibition is quite another.

But then I wonder how much damage control wizards are doing in the background. How many minds are being messed with? I've seen what a wizard not skilled in mind magic can do to a person when they dig around in the brain.

A little before lunch, I grab Max's attention on my way by his cubicle. He could easily mind-mojo himself into an office if he wanted, but I think he likes being in the center of it all. "I need to talk to you about something," I say, putting a hand on his arm. I've caught him in a rare moment where he isn't distracting someone from their actual job with small talk and/or baked goods.

He's a little taken aback—probably by my intensity. But then he gives me his usual grin. "Supply closet?"

I roll my eyes, sighing melodramatically. Six weeks ago, I'd found out the hard way in a minor arbitration that an offhand comment he'd made was not technically correct. I'd cornered him in a supply closet to read him the riot act privately. Which would have been fine, except that our coworker Ryan stumbled in looking for staples and found us intently arguing, closed up close together in the small space. I'm still trying to quash the rumors. Max finds them funny enough not to help.

"Courtyard," I say and raise a hand to dismiss his protests about it being cold outside.

He's right, of course. It's fucking freezing in the court-yard. But it has the advantage of being private, as the nearby offices aren't in use anymore since the planning department outgrew them and found their own building. And we've both got coats, anyway. It's a decent enough place in summer, with the trees and cement picnic tables that have been ground down enough to expose the aggre-gate and then polished flat enough to look almost terrazzo-like. Today there are no leaves on the trees, but the lines of snow on the branches look fragile, and fragility is a kind of beauty. There's also maybe six inches of snow on the picnic tables, but I clear a space on top and sit down anyway, my feet kicking off a place to rest on the bench. Max stands closer than he normally would, as though it's going to keep either of us warmer.

"Someone die?" Max says brightly, though there's worry underneath. "Other than all our unwelcome guests, that is."

I take in a deep breath and let it out, watching the vapor billow up. I can't remember the last person I asked for money. It was probably Olivia, but it had never been this much.

"A lot of people do. All the time. And a lot of them get cremated."

"Ummm," Max says, with his best charmingly confused face. "Back up a little?"

I don't have my most cohesive conversations when I'm nervous. And I wish I weren't nervous. I wish I didn't have to ask him this big of a favor. Maybe he'll take a spell for it?

"So, the arbitration. It's because the ghouls can't eat their normal food supply." I hit the last three words harder than I mean to. I sound bitter. Hard not to be.

He freezes, his normal good-natured state suddenly looking hollow. It isn't until I realize how closely I'm watching his face, trying to read the truth behind his reactions, that I understand why I was really nervous to have this conversation.

"You gonna yell at me for rules in a treaty I didn't write?" he asks, an edge to his voice.

I scrunch up my shoulders and let them down while I let out a deep breath, purging some of the tension there. "No, that's not what I'm doing. I knew there was shit like this happening."

"Okay, so, why can't the ghouls eat their normal food supply? You need help figuring that out?"

I take a breath in, putting together the words to explain the situation, but Max cuts me off.

"Huh," he says. "This is you somehow, isn't it?"

"What makes you say that?" I ask, sitting up a little taller.

"Ghouls eat the dead, but they have some weird stuff about undead and graveling magic and all those kinds of things. And *you've* been breaking the veil, remember. What'd you do? Find out about what was going on and summon a ghost army to *defend the defenseless*?"

I'd let myself be insulted with the way he says those last three words if I didn't need something from him.

"No, I've just been feeding the poor with ghost cows. Which apparently renders them poisonous to ghouls."

Max's face screws up in disbelief and then goes wide as he lets out a deep belly laugh. And at that, it's impossible not to feel a little insulted.

"It seemed like a good idea at the time. The meat was fine. There was nothing wrong with it for the people who ate it. I ate a bunch of it, too. No one warned me about the veil. And it was free food with zero downside!"

I sound defensive as hell, but whatever. Max is still laughing. Hard. Way too hard to be polite. I do not buy that those are real tears of laughter he's wiping away. Maybe it's the cold. We'll call it that.

"I can honestly say that would never have occurred to me," he says, finally starting to calm himself.

"Yeah, I know it wouldn't," I say. The sharpness in my voice cuts at him a little, but he covers well.

"So the ghouls want *what* of the gravelings, then? For the gravelings to feed them from graveyards?"

"Basically, yeah. Until they figure out who's poisoning them, or so they say."

Max takes a little step closer to me as the wind picks up. "That can't happen. If that happens all around the world, a wizard's gonna notice. If it's the wrong wizard, they're gonna start asking questions, and eventually they'll find you. They'll take your trove."

I stifle the urge to lean away from him. He is blocking most of the wind. "And no one steals my trove but you?" I ask. "Anyway, they have the idea that the wizards will come down on them for breaking the treaty and start a war. That going to happen?"

I watch Max decide whether to lie to me. "Maybe," he says.

I lean in slightly. "But maybe not?" I ask.

"It's a bad idea. It can't happen. Find a different solution," he says, lead in his voice.

I shake off his uncharacteristic sternness. "Well, that's what I wanted to talk to you about. That's where the crematorium comes in. I figure I can buy a crematorium and figure out how to get the bodies to the ghouls. Or a chain of crematoriums, preferably. I don't know—I haven't worked out the details yet. But there are bodies that won't be missed so long as I can find similar-looking ashes. Feels like a net win to me. I just need you to share a little of your considerable wealth."

He won't miss it. Wizards have no qualms about using magic to get something from nothing. Which I can't judge, considering I just did the same thing. I just managed to fuck up everything in the process.

Max shakes his head. "No, I can't do that."

"Why not?" The anger is hot in my voice and in my cheeks. "You have the money."

"I have *access* to the money, but Moira is the one who manages it. I buy a crematorium, she's going to ask why, and her not knowing about you is the only reason you're still alive."

He's not wrong, but he's not off the hook either. "So make your own. Are you really going to claim you don't have any spells up your sleeve that could make you some money?"

Max looks at the dull gleam of the windows around us in the harsh winter sun. "Make it? Sure. Clean it? No."

"You can clean it through the crematorium," I say smugly, before I can stop myself.

He eyes me, unamused. "An entire race of demons starts coming to you for their meals like dogs, and it won't matter if you're in my territory or someone else's. Your days will be numbered. Someone will find you. I'm not getting you killed."

"You're not letting someone else steal what you want to steal."

Max shakes his head, a sharp exhalation puffing up around him. He takes a step back toward the door, which infuriates me more than it should for reasons I can't put a finger on.

"Ok, fine, then I'll find a spell in the trove to get myself the money. I'll figure it out. If the ghouls don't put the pieces together and kill me first."

"They're not going to kill you," Max says over his shoulder. He's almost at the door. "They know it would piss me off, and demons aren't smart enough to find a way around your amulet."

"Bullshit."

"Believe it's bullshit if you want. Don't do it, Beth. This isn't your problem. They can find food where they find it, and if they run into wizard problems for it, that's their own issue."

"It's my issue if they tell the wizards about me to try to get out of trouble."

Max turns and looks at me, as though the thought were only just occurring to him now. Which I guess it is. He hasn't had two-and-a-half days for the whole thing to sit oppressively at the top of his mind.

"Don't buy the crematorium," he says, turning back around.

"You have a better solution?"

"Not yet. But I'm not going to let you pursue this one," he says as he steps back inside.

"See, Max, this is why I don't tell you about my arbitrations," I mumble to the cold air of the empty courtyard.

THIRTEEN

A Spider

I wake early on Tuesday. Too early to have any excuse other than an unspeakable fear that the danger is closing in, and we're doing nothing about it. It's the solstice today. The point of no return. I slide out of bed carefully so as not to wake Faisal. He gets enough sleep disruption from his nightmares these days. Nightmares he's not ready to tell me about, but that I'm pretty sure stem from things he saw or experienced in the Casino.

I wander out into the living room. The winter so far this year may have been mild, but last night took a dip, and the furnace has a hard time keeping up when it gets that low. I feel the chill in my feet, my shoulders, and hands the most. I could go get a robe or some slippers or something, but in a way, it feels good. It feels more real after the coziness of the bed. After the last two days hiding from the catastrophe falling on our heads in slow motion, a little connection to harsh reality feels necessary.

I throw some grounds in the coffee maker, fill up the water, and push the button. Something tugs at the back of my brain. Something I saw without really seeing it in my focus to complete my task. I step back into the dining room and look out the sliding glass door.

I'm immediately faced with a huge black spider on the outside of the glass, the size of a large man's hand with fingers outstretched. It has a bulbous back section and rings of red, white, and gold along its tapered legs.

My pulse skyrockets, and my focus narrows. It's outside the house. Outside the glass. And with the wards in the basement, it can't enter if it means me harm. My pre-coffee brain runs through my memories of the descriptions of creatures in the trove, trying to think of what it has to say about supernatural spiders. It takes a solid thirty seconds for my thoughts to settle and wake up enough to recognize who this spider must really be.

I step forward, shoving down the impulse to burn my whole house down, just to be safe. I reach out a finger and tap the glass twice, about a foot away from the spider. It reacts with the jerky too-still-then-too-fast motions of a real spider, skittering down the glass and across the snow-covered back porch, coming to rest a few feet from the slider.

I step close to the glass to be sure it can see me. Would I be physically able to open the slider to talk to it if that's what it's waiting for? I need the information it has, sure, and I'd be safe if I didn't step outside even if I weren't wearing my amulet—which I always am. But at the same time, I know in the core of my being that there is no way I'm removing the pane of glass between us until the ghoul has the good manners to turn back into a human-looking creature. Or at least a friendlier-looking creature.

The massive spider lifts its two frontmost legs in a gesture reminiscent of a begging dog. A kind of wave, maybe? An acknowledgement? And then it's gone with impossible quickness, leaving me to assume it took one spider-fast step back into the Crossroads.

My mouth opens in disbelief that the ghoul was here, as needed, and then left without telling me what it was supposed to. Is this what it feels like to have a bluff called? Was I bluffing? But then the tendrils of the early dawn light glint off the frost clinging to a web that stretches eight feet across, from one porch post to another.

"It's like *Charlotte's Web*," says a voice in the kitchen. There, still in her same outfit—the non-bloody version— stands Melissa. She's stretching out her arms, struggling to get a hold of the pot of coffee.

My eyes dart around the room, looking for the other half of her pair.

"He can't get in here," Melissa says, using two hands to maneuver the coffee pot, pouring a full cup of coffee. "You made it safe here. I like it a lot."

"Funny how you show up at the same time as the spider," I manage.

Melissa shrugs, sliding the full coffee cup across the table and into her grasp with a child's care and lack of coordination. "You were scared," she says, beginning her walk toward me with the cup. "It's easier to find people when they're scared. It can be hard to find people in the right order, sometimes, but this helped."

I don't have the heart to tell her that I usually take milk and sugar in my coffee. She looks too eager to please. "Thank you, Melissa. You can set it down on the table."

Melissa's face scrunches up before she figures out that it's hard to take a hot mug from someone without risking touching them. She sets the mug down and steps away so that I have plenty of space to pick it up. When I do, I blow across the surface of the liquid to cool it, in theory, but I don't drink right away. It's a weird little bit of play-acting to cover the fact that I'm not sure I can trust myself to drink hot liquid right now without my hands shaking and me spilling it all over myself.

Together, Melissa and I stare out at the glittering frost-encrusted web and the words woven into it.

"Under Tron Theatre, Glasgow," Melissa reads, like she's proud of herself for being able to. "What does that mean?"

Her eagerness for attention and approval pricks at my heart. I want nothing so much in this moment than to set down my coffee mug, sink down to my knees, and pull her into my arms. The man from the hallway's boney wrist, and the horror in his face, fly up at me, quashing the temptation. "I wanted to know where something was," I say, instead. "The spider said it would find out for me."

"The spider could talk?" Melissa asked. "But it doesn't have any lips!"

I smile despite myself. "It's magic, Melissa."

"Oh, right," she says. "Why did the spider make a web? Why didn't it tell you?"

Because it didn't want me to threaten its species with extinction if it said the wrong thing? Guilt pricks at me. "I guess it didn't want to talk to me today. It just wanted to make sure I knew, and then it left."

Melissa nods with the overly large expressions of a child. "Okay, that makes sense," she says.

"Melissa," I start, never taking my eyes off the web. "Can I ask why you came here this morning?"

"I wanted to say I'm sorry. I forgot he'd follow me. I forget things sometimes. I forget a lot of things. I'm not very good at holding onto things. Some other ghosts are better at it than I am. I don't think kids are supposed to be ghosts."

Fucking true.

I could tell her what the Victorian wraith told me about a person's state of mind at time of death having an effect on who they are as a ghost, but that doesn't seem kind. I don't want to make her remember that. Better confused than afraid, I suppose. But either way is heartbreaking.

I take a sip of my coffee. It burns the roof of my mouth. "It's okay." I doubt the man in the hallway would agree if he were allowed to remember any of it—if he'd ever know the truth about how he lost his hands. "Just try to remember next time. Remember that if he's hurting people, you just have to get out of the place to get him to follow after you."

"Okay," Melissa says, the self-doubt in her tone as clear as the words in the web in front of us.

"Melissa, can I ask you about something you told me?" I try to say it as casually as possible and avoid looking away from the web, but Melissa's long hesitation after I speak tells me she's rightfully suspicious.

"I can't tell you anything else about the future. I'm not allowed."

I let myself look at her. She's standing up close to the glass slider, tracing hearts and stars onto the glass. I want to ask her more about the future. I want to ask her about the tingling in my hands, and if it's really to do with the amulet protecting me, or if it's something else. Maybe I could even trick her into revealing it.

"You're not allowed even if it means helping a lot of people?"

Melissa frowns. "I don't think wizards care about helping people. They're mean. Everybody says so."

She's not wrong there. "And why do you listen to the wizards? What makes the wizards in charge of you?"

Confusion floods Melissa's face. "They made us always!

They made the world we're in when we're not here. We're just there to keep it open for them."

I try not to betray that she's telling me something new —something important—but I must fail because her mouth opens wide and her hands fly up to cover it, as though she could keep the words from having come out.

"It's okay, Melissa. I already knew that. I was just trying to make you feel better," I lie. The lie doesn't really make sense, but Melissa's base state of confusion makes her easy to fool, and she buys it. And now I know that if I killed enough ghosts… Though that doesn't help me, considering I don't even know how to kill *one* ghost.

I take another drink of my too-hot coffee, and she turns back to focus on the hearts and stars. After she's finished one more star, her head whips around, looking into the dark of the hallway.

"What is it?" I ask, my pulse jumping back up.

"Someone's coming," she whispers, before disappearing in that same disconcerting way, leaving behind only the blue vapor.

I spin around, afraid despite what Melissa *just* said about my wards being effective against ghosts, expecting to see something horrific there. It's been that kind of morning. But instead, I just see Faisal, his hair a mess and his eyes crusty from sleep. He has on his grey, felted, faux-fur-lined slippers, plaid flannel pajama pants, a soft knit white T-shirt, and his thick flannel robe in a different-colored plaid.

"Were you talking to someone?" he asks, coming up behind me and engulfing me in his robe, coffee cup and all. He has a casual calmness I wouldn't believe if I hadn't grown to expect it by now.

"Melissa was here. Wanted to apologize for everything."

"Hmm," Faisal says, brushing his warm lips against the cool of my skin. Then he leans his head against mine and looks out in the direction I'm facing at the frosted spiderweb. "You think that's what we've been waiting for?"

"Yes," I say, wondering at the warmth. I didn't realize how cold I'd grown just in these few minutes.

"We should text Max. He needs to get his plane in the air if he's going to meet you and Gigi there in time," Faisal says, making no move to do so.

"Yeah," I say. "I still can't believe Gigi and Wilbur won't take him through the Crossroads. How long is it going to take them to come around?"

Faisal's soft, chiding laugh tickles my neck. "If you wait for that, you're going to be waiting awhile. Not saying they won't make a certain space for him or trust him with some things. Maybe they'll even see him as different from the other wizards, if he ever proves he is. But they're never going to bring him through the Crossroads."

"Why the fuck not?" I ask, too comfortable and loved at the moment to be as upset about it as I want to be.

Faisal draws back just slightly. "Have we really never talked about this?" he asks.

I feel his eyes on me in my peripheral vision, though I can't see any of his face other than the tip of his prominent nose.

"The gods made the Crossroads," he continues. "They let the rest of the supernatural world use them, mostly because they weren't wizards."

"Oh," I breathe. "So from Gigi and Wilbur's perspective, bringing a member of the species that exterminated the gods through the gods' own Crossroads would be a slap in the face to their memory?"

Faisal settles close against me again. "Something like that, sure. Although I always got the feeling from Aloysius that saying the wizards exterminated the gods is maybe not totally accurate. But that's beside the point. People not wanting to bring wizards through the Crossroads is more than that. Last time someone brought a wizard through the Crossroads, Muninn got mad. Destabilized the whole thing for nearly a year. Some Crossroads spontaneously started moving to empty air above cliffs, or underwater, or inside volcanoes. Eventually Muninn got over it, but…"

I let out a deep, husky laugh. "But most people don't know any gods are alive, so they think that's just what happens when you bring a wizard through the Crossroads. They think the gods built that in before they died."

Faisal kisses my still-chilled ear with his warm mouth. "That's about it, yeah. And you can claim it was Poseidon who destroyed the Seven Spires all you want, but people think the gods are dead. It's a bedrock foundation of the way the world works now. It's half the reason they're so scared of wizards, and being scared of wizards is what keeps the supernatural world going 'round."

I lean back against Faisal and regard the perfect, detailed artistry of the frosted web. "But I have proof—if I told Wilbur and Gigi about Aloysius. They'd believe that, wouldn't they? But that would be choosing Max over Aloysius. And that would be a pretty dumb move."

Faisal lets out a low chuckle. "That'd be pretty fucking dumb, yeah."

I revel in the moment, my thoughts wandering far afield. "Do you think ghouls are evil?" I ask at last.

"They commit wholesale murder of the most vulnerable humans on an ongoing basis." There's an edge in Faisal's voice that I don't hear often, and that always makes me a little uncomfortable.

"To survive. Because they have to. They're predators,

and we're their prey. When people killed the wolves in Yellowstone, it disrupted the whole ecosystem…"

"Ghouls are sentient beings. They have the capability to know that slaughtering other sentient beings is wrong."

"We slaughter livestock."

"That's not the same."

"It probably feels the same to the cows."

"And if cows were capable of having this conversation, I'd concede your point." He's not angry or harsh, exactly, but he is unyielding. This give and take with Faisal—the ability to see other points of view, and the way we can circle around to different viewpoints in the course of a single discussion—has always been a reliable source of entertainment. Even if that entertainment has the danger of one or the other of us getting a little too fired up and the whole thing turning sour for an hour or so before we find a creative and enjoyable way of burying the hatchet. But he's not doing that right now. Everything about his voice says he's not playing, and this isn't a game.

"I'm just saying that you can't judge the actions of a species on circumstances that are out of their control," I say. "And given that, I don't know if we can excuse genocide just because we don't like the actions the ghouls are being forced into right now. They need to *eat* the dead. They don't need to be the ones who made them that way."

Faisal sighs, and I can feel the tension that built over the last minute leaving his body. "I'm not saying we leave them to die. They're sentient, too. I wasn't the one who brought the word evil into it. I don't think evil is a useful word."

No, I guess he wasn't. But he's also hesitating even though I can tell he's not done talking. "But…?" I prompt.

"But I also don't think you need to find a way to think that wizards as a whole are okay just because you like Max.

You don't need to find excuses or make wizards in general *not-evil* for him to be your friend. And he doesn't even have to be your friend for him to be useful."

"That's not what this is about."

He gives me a squeeze and a quick kiss on the side of my head, just over my ear. "Isn't it, though? A little?"

I rotate around in his arms so I can look at his face. The haze of sleep is gone from it. He's sharp and bright and mine.

"It's very rude of you to know me. You realize that, right?"

He smiles wide and leans in to give me a deep, centering kiss. And then he withdraws his robe from around me, sliding my coffee cup out of my hands while he does. With it, he heads to the kitchen, where he pours his own cup and then gets out the milk and little packets of hot chocolate.

FOURTEEN

An Admission

I was afraid that the same old arguments of the last few days would come up when Gigi, Wilbur, Faisal, and I stand at the nearest wooded Crossroads to Springfield. But no, Faisal doesn't make any last-minute objection to not coming, or any attempt to convince Wilbur that he should join us. Wilbur, for his part, doesn't seem apologetic, and I guess that's fine. He isn't immune to the touch of ghosts the way Gigi is, or the way I've given everyone every reason to believe I am via my amulet. Faisal also doesn't, thankfully, repeat his ridiculous idea that *he* could always borrow the amulet and go to Scotland instead of me. But he was a bit tipsy when he had suggested it, so that's not a surprise.

Wilbur has the skintight, impermeable gloves and balaclava that we decided I should wear, just in case. He even produces another set for me to hand to Max with a minimal amount of grumbling. He hands both me and Gigi some British pounds, and cell phones with Scottish SIMs and information preloaded about Tron Theatre and Glasgow in general. It's probably nothing new, considering we've all spent the last six hours researching the place, but that's beside the point. Wilbur is doing his best to connect us with every tool and bit of information we would need. Everything other than his own active involvement, which is a bridge he's always struggled to cross. I thank him, though that's more for me than it is for him—the little payment from my bitcoin wallet to his that happens when I press a button on my phone is all he wants for it. Then I hug him, kiss Faisal, and slide my arm through Gigi's.

"Ready?" Gigi asks.

"As long as you're not going to abandon me again!" I say brightly. Faisal shoots me a look. My lack of under-standing that Gigi gonna Gigi, and that a certain amount of relaxing my expectations and forgiving her when she doesn't meet them is necessary to ensure her future help. We have had this conversation. But still.

Gigi isn't offended. If anything, she looks amused as she rolls her eyes. "So dramatic. Humans. I'm not going to abandon you."

"Then I'm ready."

A series of five steps, through forests and fields and beaches and mountains, brings us to a hilly, moonlit field about twenty feet away from a distracted Max, who appears to be playing a game on his phone. Gigi clears her throat, and he whirls around to us.

"You made it!" he says with a smile. "Welcome to Scotland!"

Gigi appraises him with her usual disdainful glare, though there's a little bit more of a smile there than I remember from when they first met. Progress, maybe?

"You say that like you've been waiting for us, instead of us essentially waiting for you all day." She walks briskly past him toward a shiny silver car that reminds me more of a bullet than of any automobile I've ever owned.

"And whose fault is that?" Max asks, his own smile never wavering. He winks at me, and then starts toward the car.

After a brief discussion, it's agreed that, for the sake of us actually making it to Glasgow to save the world instead of Max and Gigi attempting to tear each other to pieces far away from the city center, Gigi will be driving the car. I call shotgun, and Max relaxes in the back seat, sprawling across it with a determination that makes me glad I didn't have to take the slow path, however comfortable the private jet he chartered may be.

I'm also glad, as we enter the tangle of Glasgow, that Gigi is driving. "You've driven around here before, huh?" I ask as she makes her way through an intersection that I'm not a hundred percent sure I understand in terms of cars not hitting each other.

"I lived here for a few decades. Well, a few decades last time. About five years the time before that." Gigi's general demeanor is often so full of manufactured or disguised pleasure that it's always refreshing to see honest joy there. Even if it is tempered on the drive by outbursts of anger and disbelief at changes she does not approve of and cannot believe were allowed to happen.

We make our way to the Tron Theatre, and Gigi finds a place to park. Before we get out of the car, Gigi fishes in a pocket and comes out with a handful of long silver chains. She hands one to Max and one to me.

"What are these for?" I ask, marveling at the craftsmanship.

"For dealing with wraiths, however you can see fit to use them," Gigi says. "They're from your sister. Apparently, the research she's been doing on the depths of the internet leads her to believe these could be useful. Normally I'd doubt a human who thinks they've come across useful information all on their own, but your sister is a clever woman. If she thinks there's a reason for us to bring these along, she's probably right."

Blood rushes to my cheeks. "Why'd she tell you, not me?" I ask, although I know the reason. I just wasn't expecting to feel bad about that right now.

"Oh, you know," Gigi says. "*Processing.*"

I really shouldn't tell Gigi anything. Whatever I say is always going to eventually come out of her mouth mocking me, and this is too sore of a subject for me to deal with right now. So even though I should just keep my damn mouth shut, I whine, "I'm tired of her blaming me for choices I didn't make."

"Risking her and her daughters' lives unnecessarily was very much a choice you made," Max says, playing with his own chain. He sounds a little bitter about it, but not nearly as bitter as I am at hearing him say the words.

"I had to as part of the deal with Aloysius. If I hadn't, I wouldn't have had the luck to survive that fight, and I would have died. And besides, I didn't know if they would be okay. I thought the gravelings were going to kill them anyway if I died." The first part of that is true. The second part is what I tell myself now, and what I told myself at the time. "Anyway, that doesn't matter. She's not mad at me for that. She doesn't even know about that." I shove the silver chain into my pocket.

"Eh, she might."

The way Max says those words snaps my eyes to him. "She what? How?"

Max puts his own chain in his pocket and puts a hand on his door handle. "It might have come up." He opens his door and slides out of the car, starting in the direction of the theater.

I open my own door and hurry after him, leaving Gigi

to follow along in our wake. "*Come up?*" I ask in a harsh whisper, as I catch him. "You told her?"

"She deserved to know. And anyway, I didn't know it was part of the demon's deal. Also, I was mad at you."

"Mad at me?" I just about hiss. "For what?"

Max winces. "I don't even remember. It felt important at the time. But anyway, she was going to find out eventually. There were a lot of people in that room, and not all of them like you, and Olivia's a curious woman."

I don't need to be mad at Max right now. In fact, now would be a great time to *not* be mad at Max. But still. "How did it even have an opportunity to come up? Since when do you spend time with my sister?"

The harshness of my own voice is echoed in his mean grin. "We chat sometimes. Especially when she's said the wrong thing and needs me to clean up Peter."

Clean up Peter? Olivia has not only been giving Max permission to mess with her own husband's mind, but *asking* him to do it? I stop short on the sidewalk, grabbing Max by his coat sleeve to stop him with me so that I can look at him. He looks back at me, his cold expression meeting my anger. My over-large breaths billow out white in the cold air. All I can see is the anger that Faisal had when I told him Max had taken a few hours of his memories before I could stop it from happening. Olivia has been voluntarily doing that to Peter? And Max agreed to do it?

Gigi slides along past us, continuing to the theater as though nothing is wrong in the world. After a moment, Max's expression softens.

"You make choices you feel you have to that she doesn't approve of. She makes choices she feels she has to that you don't approve of. Maybe leave me out of it?"

He should have thought of that before he put himself in the middle of it. But I let go of his coat. Now isn't the time for this. And maybe he's right. Maybe I'm making more of his part in this than I should. Anyway, the list of gripes I have with Max that I need to lay aside for the purpose of using him to get what I want is already long enough. What's another item on it?

I pull out my gloves and balaclava and start putting them on as I walk after Gigi. Max does the same.

"You both look ridiculous, you know," Gigi says to us over her shoulder.

"It's what all the most stylish thieves are wearing these days," Max says, catching up to her quick pace down the sidewalk.

"You wouldn't say that if you knew any stylish thieves," Gigi says.

"I don't know… I'm pretty stylish, and I steal occasionally."

Gigi favors him with a smile disguised as a withering look.

"Hey, even Elizabeth steals. Boats, even," Max says, nudging her in her stone side with an unlucky elbow.

"Yes, she's not stylish, though." The tone of Gigi's voice can't be for anything but my benefit.

"You have me there."

"That was *one time*," I say in a stage whisper, forced to walk behind them like a little kid by the narrowness of the sidewalk and an oncoming group of college-aged pedestrians, who shoot us suspicious looks that we have thoroughly earned.

At last, we reach the Tron Theatre. I was surprised when I read online that the Tron Theatre was currently closed for the foreseeable future, and that all planned performances were canceled. And then I had been embarrassed by my own lack of intelligence when I realize that for one of the most haunted places in a reportedly haunted city, the recent spate of wraith activity has likely been somewhat disruptive. Without discussion, the three of us head to a door sheltered somewhat from view by a little, covered entryway.

"Well, go on," Gigi says to Max, who looks around us, trying to gauge how many eyes we're attracting.

I watch him intently. I can't help it. When he told us he had a spell to put up a temporary field that discouraged close examination, that sounded like just the kind of thing I want to know how to do.

"Turn around," Max says to me.

"What?" I stage-whisper again. I don't know why I'm whispering. No one else is.

Max takes me by the shoulders, physically rotating my body around to face away from him. "That's better," he says.

"Are you kidding me?" I say, sounding about twelve years old.

"Nope!" Max says. Behind me, I get a sense of movement, and I hear Max whisper words in the language of magic.

I may not be able to see his movements, but I listen as closely as possible to what I can make out of his words, hoping to hear something that sounds familiar. Hoping to have a correct pronunciation of a word I've got in one of the spells I've been working on. If I'd thought ahead, which I really should have, I'd have set my phone to record. There's been too much going on. I need to get better at anticipating these opportunities.

I slip my glasses on when Max has finished speaking, which is a little awkward to do under the balaclava. When I get them on, I don't see the golden force field that I'm, for some reason, expecting. Instead, everything within the covered entryway is colored normally, and everything outside of it looks like an old sepia photograph.

"If you would?" Max says to Gigi, strain evident on his face.

"This spell takes energy?" I ask while Gigi steps up to the door. Max and I could use our keys, sure, but that would leave the lock unscathed and would point the police at people within the theater themselves if we do any damage inside, which we intend to. And framing employees for a crime seems hardly fair—especially days before Christmas, when they're probably already worried for their jobs with the theater currently closed.

"It hurts," Max grits out.

With a sickening crunch of metal, the front doors open.

"After me!" Gigi says, stepping inside.

FIFTEEN

An Expiration

I follow Gigi inside the theater. Max is last, visibly relaxing as soon as he crosses the threshold. Outside, the world beyond the entryway returns to normal.

It's pitch black in here. I dig out my cell phone, turning on the flashlight and pointing it at the ground as much as possible. Max and Gigi follow suit.

All small talk disintegrates as we walk through the building. We keep the light from our phones on the ground. Wilbur got us blueprints of the theater, enhanced and made more readable. He even mapped out where we would most likely be able to get below the building—directly underneath the stage.

The best way to avoid being hassled, attacked, or delayed by any wraiths that might be hanging around, we reasoned, was to avoid doing anything to attract their attention. We make our way to the stage as quietly and smoothly as possible, following a route Wilbur chose for us. It leads us to a low, half-height door with a tricky hatch that looks to have been painted over and scraped off just enough to be functional.

Movement flutters around the dark theater at the corners of my vision. We are not alone. I don't look up. Melissa said that fear makes us easier to find, and there's nothing I can do about that. But if you just don't acknowledge the things that terrify you, sometimes they leave you alone. I fumble in the dark with the latch, doing my best not to let the fear of what might be out there get to me.

When the three of us make it underneath the stage and the door closes behind us, there's a palpable feeling of relief. Not because the wraiths are gone, or because the wood of the door will do anything to stop them, but the relief you get as a little kid when all your arms and legs are underneath the blanket and something in your brain tells you that somehow, for some reason, that's going to protect you.

"You lot are trying to get below, ain't you?" A high, melodious male voice with a distinct Scottish tinge to it greets us, stopping us short.

Before Gigi can speak, and doubtless say the wrong thing, I step forward. The wraith—and it's clear immediately that he *is* a wraith—is standing in the middle of the space, right next to a patch of plain flagstone floor. He's holding an intricate oil lamp and is dressed like the platonic ideal of a dandy. At least, what I imagine that to be. If it weren't for the massive, bloody gash running at an angle from his right collarbone to his left hip, I would say he was quite dashing.

"We are," I say. "We've got business to attend to there."

It's possible that he knows who we are. We're significant, after all. As for him wanting to stop us, it's a crapshoot. I didn't get the sense that the other ghosts we'd met so far were particularly fond of the necrowizards, but I can't imagine the dead are a monolith any more than the living are.

"I know just what business you're trying to attend," the man says. "And all the saints help me, but I want you to achieve it. And it's not interfering if I just don't stop you, is it? No telling the future. Not breaking the rules, am I?"

Shouldn't he know whether we do or not? Shouldn't he want to avoid changing that preordained matter? What even is the point of all this if we're fighting against a future the ghosts already know?

Maybe I shouldn't be trying to figure this out right at this fucking moment.

"Better move quick, though. There's others don't think the same as me."

Max steps forward. "Don't suppose you could tell us where to look, then?" he asks, the waver in his voice not so well hidden as he probably intends.

"Oh, I don't know," he says. "That sounds a lot like interfering to say a thing like that out loud." Then he steps aside and looks at the flagstone where he was just standing. My eyes widen. At the change in my expression, the dandy gives me a wink and disappears, taking the light from his oil lamp with him.

My eyes take a brief second to adjust to the slightly dimmer and more directional light of just our phones. The three of us huddle around the flagstone in question, and Max pulls a long, silver dagger out of an inside pocket of his coat. It gleams, even in the low light, the silver engraved with magical symbols.

A sharpknife. The trove talks about how to make one of these. And while I have no idea where Max got ahold of meteor metal, a feather from a mourning bird, or a decanted nymph's tear, just knowing that I've seen directions for how to do it makes the fact that he has one a little less impressive.

Of course, come to think of it, he probably didn't

make it. It was probably a hand-me-down from his masters. But they probably didn't think he'd be using it to work with a human and whatever Gigi is.

A sharpknife can cut through anything, if you say the right words and hold your Right Mind unwavering. The Right Mind for cutting with a sharpknife is, weirdly, joy. Simple, uncomplicated, unbounded joy. Someone who didn't know Max—who'd only met him in passing or who only knew him as the generous, humorous guy who showed up late every day to the office with treats in tow and a ready smile—might think that entering that state of Right Mind would be easy for him to do. But I've been worried since he pitched the plan of using the sharpknife that this was not going to work. And now, with the ghost's warning that there were others who would not appreciate what we were trying to do fresh in my mind, the worry grows. The only thing that stops me from bringing up that worry is the thought that the same characteristic of wizards that guides their hands and words to make it easy to execute magic spells makes it easier to get into Right Mind, too.

But I can see worry on Max's face as he readies the knife against the flagstone. Unlike outside, he takes no pains to hide the spell from me, saying the nine words that I could already have gleaned from the trove out loud slowly and carefully, as though he isn't sure he's going to get it right, even though that part of it was a given. He doesn't even notice when I surreptitiously set my phone to record his words. I doubt I'll ever be able to create a sharpknife, but the more words I have reliable recordings of, the better.

With a shaky smile, Max attempts to drive the sharpknife into the flagstone. It doesn't go. He tries again.

A sound of chains dragging somewhere in the darkness of the theater beyond the black-painted plywood of the stage draws our eyes and sets my heart racing. I crouch and reach for the knife.

"Let me," I say, my whisper balancing the need to be quiet with the need to convey authority and insistence.

"Just give me a second," Max says, drawing back. "I'll get it on the second try."

"It'll be easier for me. Give me the knife."

It's a singularly sad statement. In a less crucial moment, I would be able to say it gently—to let him know that I'm sorry that there is no simple joy in his life not mixed with some element of manipulation or domination, some brutality that I know Max can't possibly be entirely okay with being party to. I'd let him try again and again, easing him into the devastating idea.

But even if he was able to make the sharpknife work in practice leading up to this moment, I just don't believe he can do it now, in the heat of the moment, with the rattling of chains growing louder. And Max must believe the same, because he hands the sharpknife to me with a heartbreaking look of resignation.

I say the words exactly as I just heard them. Three of the words were in Max's graveyard spell that I have a recording of, so they're familiar to my mouth. I practiced for this possibility today, and I know the words well enough that hearing Max say the few unfamiliar ones once is enough to nail it on the first try.

Well, just having heard Max *and* a hell of a lot of luck.

As I say the words, I reach for Right Mind—for joy—using a handful of reliable memories to get me there. Olivia's thirteenth birthday, when she invited me to join in her party with her friends even though it wasn't the cool thing to do. My mom at a family dinner in the days when she still had her whole mind. My first kiss with Faisal, on the dock of a mountain lake, as awkward as it was passionate. My nieces using me as home base for a game of freeze tag with their friends. Faisal's face close to mine under the blankets, moments after he'd told me he loved me for the first time.

I don't reach for any memories of my father. What he did by deciding to mess with magic—the implications and collateral damage it had wrought—has made the joy too complex to use, even if I *would have* been able to tease out the joy in those memories from the grief that still clings to me. He hasn't been dead long enough. Even if he had, I don't know when I'll fully forgive him.

I don't feel relief as the sharpknife slides into the stone. I'm too full of tightly held joy to feel much of anything else. But the sound from Max makes it clear he's feeling enough relief for both of us.

"Remember to think of how long you want the knife to be," Max says in my ear. "You won't be able to feel it, but just think it."

I picture a sword about three feet long. That has to be long enough, right? A worry that I might hit something important tries to push itself into my consciousness, but I chase it away. I don't have room for anything but joy right now. I trace a four-foot-by-four-foot square. Well, something similar to a square in some respects. The angles, and lengths, and straightness of the sides all leave a lot to be desired.

Just as I complete the square, Max lets out a short "Yes!" As if in response, a sound from above our heads, like boots and chains hitting the stage, makes us all jump.

I pull the sharpknife out and let my Right Mind drop. It's just a simple, dull knife in my hands. And then it's a simple, dull knife in Max's hands as he snatches it away from me and tucks it away into his jacket. I roll my eyes despite the tension of the situation.

"Let me get my fingers under," Gigi says. In theory, now that it's cut all the way through, the stone and dirt and whatever else should be able to slide right down. But there's no guarantee that we'll fall into anything safe, even if there weren't such a thing as friction. Gigi places her fingers on the crack, readying herself to force them into the thin gap by sheer force.

"What is it you think you're doing?" A low, basso voice hits us from the darkness.

Before I can react, Gigi stands and hurls herself toward the direction of the voice. She doesn't have to tell Max and me to go with Plan B: jump on the slice of ground until it gives way. We move almost as fast as she did, scrambling onto the chunk of cut-out stone. The light from our phones dances around wildly as we do, illuminating snatches of Gigi's battle with something huge and dressed in crimson satin.

Max's hand grabs mine. As he readies himself to jump, I join him, taking comfort in the strength of his grip. The first jump does nothing, but we hadn't timed it perfectly and hit at slightly different times. The second jump is better, and there's a tremble of movement beneath us.

Our eyes snap to each other in hope and triumph, though Gigi's battle pulls my attention. She hasn't opted for arm-ripping this time, which seems like a good move. Instead, she's wrestled the man into a position on the ground with his arms back, and is wrapping a shining silver cord around his wrists.

Max's movement refocuses me as he prepares himself to jump again. I join him. The stone moves a little more. Three more jumps, and the ground beneath us gives way. The sickening feeling of falling mingles with triumph, and then a jolt of terror. We're falling far too deeply. I cling to both my phone and Max's hand with everything in me.

I manage to keep hold of my phone, but I lose Max.

We fell much farther than this once, but that time we fell together, and his grip had been my lifeline. Without it, the fear overwhelms me just as surely as the dark does. It must only take moments for us to fall, but it feels much longer than that before I come to a stop with a horrible crack, and pain shoots through me. Intense pain—nearly as bad as I've ever felt. And then no pain from below my ribs. No sensation from the bottom half of my body at all.

"Max!" The word rips out of me, harsh and panicked. "*Max!*" I'd say better words if I could find them. Something to tell him what's happened—to tell him that the fall broke me.

I wipe my eyes with the back of my hand, as though that's going to do anything but get mud made from tears and dust into them. "Max!" I say for a third time, my voice taking on a desperate whine. I try to fight down the panic, but it's not going anywhere.

"Max, Max, Max," I say. "Max."

More tears come. There's something that I should be able to use to get out of this, but I can't get there. I can't hear him. If I can't hear him—if he's not awake or alive, he can't heal me. Gigi's somewhere far away. She'll leave me. She left me before.

"Max," I get out again, blubbering.

Hands grip my shoulders, and a light shines into my eyes. "I'm here." With the light and the feel of connection —and the knowledge that everything is about to be made right—the panic clears. It's replaced by embarrassment.

I swallow hard, blinking as much to get the tears out of my eyes as to adjust to the light. It helps that it's no longer pointed directly into my eyes.

"You don't look too bad," Max's voice says. If I had the energy, I might take offense that he's mocking my panic a moment ago, but he seems more confused and over-whelmed than anything.

"I think my back is broken," I get out, as even as I can manage. Which isn't too bad, all things considered. "I can't feel my legs."

"Oh, yeah," Max says. "That'll freak you out every time."

I want to grumble something about being so glad to have his permission, but I'm not quite at the wisecracking state yet.

"I need to move you so you're in a good position to fix this. This might hurt."

It does. Max drags me a few feet to where I can lay flat. My hands are still gripped around my phone, but I don't feel able to move it around yet. It's only in the random glimpses of him that I discover he himself is drenched in blood. His own, presumably.

Max has healed me before, so him kneeling over me, speaking words of power over my broken body, isn't an altogether unfamiliar experience. But in the past, it happened in a safe environment, and I wasn't straining to make out the sounds of the ongoing struggle between Gigi and the ghosts from the little, slightly less dark rectangle far above me.

I gasp when the nerves are repaired, and the feeling in the lower half of my body returns in a rush.

"You good?" Max asks, and my embarrassment at how this unsteadied me returns, too. Without being able to see Max's face, it's hard to tell how he feels about anything. There's a weird tone to his voice, though. Probably still annoyed that I could use his knife and insisted on him letting me do it.

"I'm good," I say, already moving to sit up. I take charge of my miraculously unscathed phone, shining the light around to get a sense of the world around us. I try not to linger on Max—on his bloodied body. I don't know how badly hurt he was, but he's fine now. And it's not the first time he's had to stitch himself together.

"I think we're in the right place," Max says, shining his own light around the space. We're in a circular chamber, maybe thirty feet wide and ringed with what I can't help but think of as thrones. We've come down off-center, which is lucky, because there's a six-foot-tall stone altar in the center, and it doesn't look like the best thing to break a fall.

"What makes you say that?" I ask, feeling at my face to make sure my glasses are still unbroken and in place. "Do you see any summoning circles I don't?" I mean it as a joke, I think, but it comes out a little harsh. He doesn't press the issue.

"There are protection spells all over this place. We popped some of them when we fell in, but there are still a few in place."

I wander over to the closest throne and find familiar-looking carvings all over it. Yup, this is some wizard shit right here. "You know what this reminds me of?" I say as I walk around, shining light all over the smooth, unlined floors, looking for anything that could resemble a ghost-summoning circle.

"What?" Max asks, down to go with my plan of talking to each other while we aim to keep calm and focused in the face of potential failure. He's walking the room, shining his light and looking for circles, too.

"The room in Atlantis where Poseidon's trident was kept."

Max's light across the room stops stock still for a second before it starts moving again.

"Does it?" he asks, affecting a lack of concern—but with a nervous edge poking through.

"Yeah, it does. Is that a bad thing?"

Max keeps walking, and looking, and not answering.

"Max?" I ask, stopping and shining my light directly at him. The blood on him is worse now that I have the opportunity to see him clearly. He looks at the altar in the middle of the room.

"The chamber in Atlantis was made for a purpose," he says.

"Containing the trident?" I ask.

"Trapping a god."

My thoughts flash to Aloysius—to the unacceptable idea of him trapped by wizards. "I thought it was a battle, not a trap."

"It became a battle when the trap failed."

I follow his gaze to the altar. "This isn't where their circles are, is it?" I say, putting into words the fear that's been growing in both of us. This place was built by wizards, sure. Maybe even the necrowizards. But they had another use for it, and I don't see any circles or hallways leading to other chambers that might contain them.

"Maybe there are hidden chambers?" I ask, looking back at Max.

He doesn't look back at me. He keeps his gaze on the altar. "They wouldn't bring a god to where they had their circles. It would be like keeping food in your tent in bear country. If they tried to trap a god, and the god got free or other gods came looking, they wouldn't want the one thing linking them to the world of the living to be right there."

The words make sense, but I don't want them to.

We failed. It's the solstice—too late to pursue anything else. And we failed. Depending on where the necrowizard circles were, midnight might have passed for them already. The veil in that part of the world may already have torn. They may have already returned.

Max's movement catches my eye. He's heading for one of the thrones. I don't understand why until he yanks one of the arms of the chair towards him, and it moves with no more difficulty than if it were a wooden dining chair.

"We need to see," he says, all the usual levity gone from his voice. I head for the closest throne and attempt to do the same, but no joy. Apparently, Max is doing the magic, not the chair.

Instead, I walk to Max and follow him dumbly. He turns the chair around so that the tall back of it is right next to the altar. The throne is a bit overdone, and the back of it is nearly as tall as I am. At almost the same time, Max and I scramble up the chair, climbing onto the back of it, using the height to get us tall enough to see what's on the slab.

"Oh, fuck," Max says, seeing it before I do.

"Oh, fuck," I agree.

It's a woman. Naked. Beautiful. Fair-skinned, with blue lines drawn all over her body. They don't look like wizard spells. Maybe they're not spells at all—maybe they're just decoration. They seem to glimmer, but I can't tell whether that's my imagination or not. She has long, red, curly hair with raven feathers woven into it. Her eyes, black as a bird's, stare up toward the ceiling. Her mouth is open in a frozen, silent scream of pain.

It's not hard to see what put that look on her face. Her chest is broken open, her ribs splayed. Her left lung has been removed and set on top of her belly. Where her heart should be, there's only air, dust, and congealed blood.

I want to reach out and touch her—to wipe some of the dust off of her skin. To close her eyes, maybe. But that seems like a potentially profoundly stupid idea. Max's hand moves, telling me he has the same instinct and the same caution against it.

I can't look at her anymore. I can't bear it. Feeling numb, I climb back down the chair, startled only momentarily by a scream and a thud from Gigi's still-progressing battle.

And while I descend, I can't help but wonder why the altar is so tall in the first place. Sure, the thrones are tall, but the men themselves weren't. At least, I'm pretty sure they weren't. No one's ever mentioned anything about wizards being giants in the far-flung past. Given their vanity and eccentricity, I wouldn't put it past them to transform themselves in that way, sure, but still.

I shine my phone's light onto the altar and the intricate carvings there. More spells. Always more fucking spells with these people. "Hand me the sharpknife."

"What?" Max asks, as though my words are waking him up from a deep sleep.

"The necrowizards caught her for something. They put these spells on here for a reason. Her heart is gone. We don't know where their circles are, but I'm going to take the opportunity to fuck up whatever of theirs I can. Hand me the sharpknife."

He does. It takes longer to shove aside my anger to find joy this time, and I get the words wrong at first, anyway. But on the second try, I get the knife to sink into the altar. I slice through the carvings. It doesn't look like anything meaningful to me—nothing sparks or shimmers as I go. Until I apparently cut through the wrong thing, and the entire altar collapses in a crash of dust and force.

Max and I stagger back. But before the echo of the altar's collapse has even cleared, a new sound begins. The agonized cry of the woman on the altar shakes me to my core. I want to scream with her. To mourn for her. To pledge her my life if she asks it and avenge her suffering against those who would dare inflict it.

I know this feeling—the influence of a god reaching out to me. My hand flies to the pin on my lapel, ready to grab it hard enough to draw blood and recenter myself if necessary, the way I did a few months ago when I picked up Poseidon's trident. But whether from the woman's weakness or from my amulet doing its goddamn job, the impulse fades. It's pity, not devotion, that I feel when I approach the woman on what's left of the altar. Her limbs move erratically but weakly. As her cry breaks in order for her to swallow down more air, she spits blood.

She tries to scream again, but she's weak. One lung. No heart. She shouldn't be able to scream at all. But this is a god—the normal rules don't apply.

"Who are you?" I ask her.

Her face contorts, and for a moment, I think she's going to reach out and grab me—to pull me in and beg me to help her. But before that can happen, her eyes flick down to my lapel, where Aloysius's blessing hangs, and her desperation shifts to white-hot anger. "I was the Morrigan," she says, each word distinct.

The Morrigan. Ancient Celtic goddess of fate and death. It was right to learn the names of the gods when I found out they'd once been real. It's right that I know her name as I watch her die.

It wasn't my imagination that the blue lines on her body had glimmered. I know that now because I can see the difference the moment they stop.

"Why didn't you heal her?" I say into the oppressive silence after the goddess's death.

"She's a god," Max says, like I've just slapped him.

"So, you couldn't?"

"So I wouldn't."

I look down at the god without her heart and back up at Max. He doesn't look like himself. He looks set, and strong, and unquestionable. And angry. Holy hell, does he look angry. At me?

I must wear my disbelief on my face, because he softens. He opens his mouth to speak, but before he gets any words out, the sound of stone hitting stone and a flurry of movement from where we fell into the chamber stops our questions.

That right there is a superhero landing. And it's a crime that Gigi can't possibly appreciate the extent to which she fulfills my movie-going expectations. Not that she seems particularly interested in talking as she strides forward toward me, barely sparing a glance for the dead goddess.

"I ran out of silver," she says as another figure, this one a large man dressed in ragged turn-of-the-century clothing, falls down through the opening behind her. "We have to go."

A cluster of wraiths—more angry wraiths—comes falling down through the opening as Gigi's vice-like hand grabs my arm. I reach out to grab Max, but it's too late. She's already taken a step into the Crossroads. We're on a moonlit moor, and Max isn't with us.

Instead, there's an army. More than one.

And they don't seem overwhelmingly pleased to see us.

SIXTEEN

A Betrayal

I wrench my arm away from Gigi before she can take another step further into the Crossroads, carrying us away from the wraith battle happening around us and dooming Max entirely. If I didn't have my amulet, I wouldn't be able to. But she'd have to hurt me to hold on tight enough to stop me from wresting my arm from her grip, and she can't hurt me.

"What are you doing, Elizabeth?" A wraith arrow hits Gigi's neck, splintering. I wince despite myself at the sight.

"We have to go back and get Max."

"We can't. We're outnumbered, and I ran through all my silver."

"Max doesn't have an amulet. And he isn't you. The wraiths will touch him, and he'll be bones."

Gigi gleams in the moonlight like the work of art she is. Her eyes sparkle with anger. "I can't prevent that."

"You *can!* Just go get him! We can step right back there! Hell, don't take me—I don't care. Just go get him!" I'm so intent that I don't see the ghost warrior running at me until it's too late. Gigi plucks him up by the back of his shirt like a wayward puppy and flings him away.

"I'm not taking a wizard through the Crossroads."

"Gigi, you…"

Her stare bores through me. I could tell her right now. I could tell her about Aloysius. I could compromise his secret to save Max's life. But of all the people to have know about Aloysius's secret, a person who is incapable of telling a lie would be the worst choice.

"It's worth the risk," I say. "His life is worth the risk. We can't let him die."

This time, a ghost arrow is coming at me. I throw myself to the ground on my ass to avoid it. Gigi crouches down so that she can address me almost on my level. "Do you have any idea how many people I have had to let die? Almost every person I have ever known has died. I couldn't save a single one of them, and I can't save your wizard. But this will save him from turning into what you don't want him to be. Maybe that's a good enough death for him. We failed, anyway. Unless there were some circles down there that I didn't see, the necrowizards are back now, and a wizard civil war is on its way. It's a mercy for him to die this way. Better than what he might have suffered at the hands of his own kind."

Gigi reaches out to take my arm, doubtless to take me farther into the Crossroads with her, to make my abandonment of Max complete.

"Just because you're used to failure doesn't mean you should accept it," I say, stumbling away from her, stopping her from being able to take my arm.

"You can't save him, Elizabeth!" Gigi says, like she's been holding in the words for a long time. "You're going to get yourself killed trying. Now, take my hand and let's go."

"We have to go back for him. Just bring him through the Crossroads. Just do it, Gigi."

I want to say more. I want to say I promise it'll be all right. I want to tell her to trust me. But anything I say, she can use to find out the secret I have to keep.

Gigi reaches out for me, and I shrink away again. She straightens, her elegant posture and the stately tilt of her head a jarring contrast to the screaming, wailing men running at each other in full tilt behind her. "Are you going to come with me, or aren't you?" Gigi asks.

"I thought you liked him," I whine more than say.

"I like almost everyone, to some degree," Gigi says, looking off into the distance as though she can see the next step in the Crossroads from here. "Liking someone doesn't make the impossible possible. Liking a life doesn't make it worth saving at the expense of others."

"You've made that choice before. Don't try to claim you haven't. Just make it now. Just one more time." Maybe I can't convince her that bringing a wizard through the Crossroads won't break it in a potentially dangerous way, but maybe I don't need to.

"I've made it too many times already. It backfires so much more often than you'd think it would. And he's a wizard, Elizabeth. Baked goods and inside jokes and shows of trust aren't going to change that, no matter how much you want them to."

She sounds regal—and sad. I wonder how much she wishes she could lie to me, to tell me she was going to take me back to Max and instead take me all the way to Springfield. I wonder how many times she's wished she could do that kind of thing. Something settles in her, and I see her prepare to step off into the Crossroads—preparing to leave me. And the reality of where I am, surrounded by a raging battle and still not able to save Max without her, strikes home.

"If you leave now, you're out," I say, scrambling up.

Gigi's stone eyebrows rise, and her eyes widen, revealing more diamond to sparkle in the moonlight. "What do you mean?" she asks icily.

"I mean, you're hanging around me for a reason. You're helping for a reason. You want to be close to me as I fuck up the world so you can end up on the right side when the dust settles. That front-row seat has a cost."

I scramble up onto my feet, and then onto a large, flat rock. Between the rock and the hill, I'm almost eye-level with her.

"The cost is listening to me and helping even when you don't want to. You don't think saving Max is worth it because of the wizard you think he'll become. Okay, sure, whatever. I don't really give a fuck. But if you want the benefits of being close to me, you're going to help even when you don't feel like helping. You want to be a part of this team, then you're going to be a part of it even when it hurts. Even when it means helping more than you want to. Because that's what a team is."

Maybe I'm being too emotive because I'm still stung by her abandonment at the Primrose Inn on Saturday night, but I sound like the coach in the scene before the climax of a nineties' sports movie. My arms are shaking as I look into Gigi's pupilless eyes.

But however strong a wave may crash into the shore, the strength of the strike isn't where its power lies. And you can't stand stronger than a stone. Wordlessly, Gigi takes a step into the Crossroads, abandoning both me and Max to whatever fate the wraiths around us intend.

SEVENTEEN

A Persuasion

With Gigi gone, I'm less protected from the wraiths. Luckily, they don't seem interested in me. I'm not part of the battle they're playing out. Do they fight in the afterlife the necrowizards made for them? Are they happy that the veil is thin enough that they can come all the way through and reenact the battle where it originally happened, like the most dedicated of larpers?

The thought would be a lot more charming if their arrows weren't quite so real. Or if the few times warriors take it into their heads to attack me, the attacks weren't so blood-curdlingly realistic. But the question of whether wraiths have enough of a capacity for intention that my amulet works against them is answered when an axe swung with full power at my head feels like a kindergartener's wiffleball bouncing harmlessly off me.

After that, I become less worried about dodging the arrows, allowing them to hit me if they feel like it. More often than not, arrows that look like they're going to hit me end up missing, anyway. Whether that's my amulet coming into play or Aloysius's luck, I don't know.

I just know that I can't think out in the open like this, and I need to think. Max's life depends on it. I'm pretty sure it does, anyway. Unless he has some super-secret way of calling in his masters, which is almost worse. Maybe a little backwards, but whatever.

When I get over a little ridge and find a hollow that will hide me, I start being able to sort through my options. I can't walk the Crossroads back. I don't know anyone in Glasgow. I could call Wilbur to come here, but even if that weren't putting him in danger from the wraith battle around me, what could he do? Lend me moral support in the cab on the way into town while we wonder together if Max is dying?

I want to call Max. Tell him I'm working on his problem. Ask him if he has any ideas. But I don't know what he's doing right now—what spells he's using to keep the wraiths at bay or how delicate the Right Mind required for them is.

Or if he's even alive anymore. It's entirely possible he's a skeleton by now—a wizard interred forever with a god. Or at least until someone notices the hole we made in the floor of the Tron Theatre that we didn't worry about patching.

Think, Elizabeth. Think. I sure hope he's alive. I send the thoughts harder, though I have a feeling it's in vain. Aloysius will hear my prayer, sure. But he's hardly likely to intervene to save a wizard's life. Too bad I don't have a powerful supernatural creature hanging around to extort. That worked great last time—up until it didn't.

I have to cover my mouth to stop a rough laugh from ripping its way out and alerting all the wraiths around me to my presence. Of course.

I dig into my pocket, looking for the card that Claude gave me on Saturday. It's just as cryptic and elegant as ever.

My fingers are stiff, so used to holding my phone like a claw and using it for its light that it's hard to punch in the numbers. Probably doesn't help that my hands are shaking, too.

The phone rings five times. I'm just beginning to wonder if eternal death monsters sleep at night when Claude's voice greets me with a string of annoyed French.

"Hello," I choke out, trying to sound dignified and in control. "This is the arbiter. I have bad news and worse news for you."

There's a slight pause, which I'm sure means nothing to him, but during which I imagine Max succumbing to wraiths.

"Elizabeth," Claude says. "Have you come to a decision in our arbitration?" His accent is just as thick as I remember it being.

"No, this isn't about that. Well, it's related. So the bad news is that I got my wizard involved. You can huff about that all you want, but it was inevitable. The worse news is that he's about to get himself killed."

"And this involves me in what way?"

I should have expected that. I *did* expect that, really. Though it still annoys me. "It involves you because his master is Kristoff of Boston. And *he* knows that Max gets involved in my arbitrations sometimes. Max dies, and Kristoff is going to come looking for blood. And since I'm currently arbitrating for you, that search is going to wind up at your door. Why don't you go ask a siren what happened the last time an apprentice of Max's family line got killed by a supernatural creature."

The only French curse word I know is *merde*, but if I had a wizard's eidetic memory, I'd be learning a hell of a lot more of them right now. I jump in again before he runs out of steam. I don't have time to wait for him to calm down naturally. "You want to avoid wizards paying more attention to you, you've got to go save him. That's just how it is. You're the only one who can."

"And why should a wizard need saving? Even a baby wizard should be able to defend himself." Nope, not calm yet.

"He's fighting wraiths in a cavern underneath Tron Theatre in Glasgow. There's a ton of them there. And unless he's learned to fly in the last couple months, he has no way out. No way but you."

More cursing in French, but at least this string sounds more resigned.

"Great. I'll tell him you're coming." I hang up before he can say anything else. I hold the phone in my hands for a solid thirty seconds, waiting to see if Claude is going to call back with a protest. He doesn't.

I give in and call Max. I told Claude I'd warn him to expect a graveling, after all. No answer. I try not to take that to mean anything too significant. I wouldn't pick up the phone if I were fighting for my life, either.

Instead, I text.

Help is on the way. Go with the graveling.

And then I wait. I try to calculate the time it might take Claude to get Max out of there. He can take the Crossroads here from wherever he is, so that's barely any time at all. But how fast can gravelings travel from there? Is there a closer graveling already in Glasgow that Claude can rope into helping?

I should have asked Wilbur. Asked him if he had any connections. It's less certain he would have had any, but maybe it would have been quicker. I get out my pen and scribble some words on the pad of paper I keep in my jacket pocket for just this purpose. The response is not good. Wilbur's got nothing. It's up to Claude.

Five minutes pass. Then ten. I watch the wraiths fight. The longer I do, the less terrifying and sadder they become. It's one thing to watch a battle run its course. It's horrible, yes, but it's moving forward. With this fight, each and every slash or lunge or arrow fired is intended to do harm. And often they do—terrible harm. But no matter what, no matter how much pain they inflict or suffer, the wounded or killed wraith just stands back up, resets his wounds, and goes again. They're locked in constant warfare without even the dubious comfort of exhaustion.

I hate it. I pity them. I hate the grind and the churn and the violence. I hate the axe-man always chasing Melissa, and the battle never abandoned.

Finally, after an age of pity and regret, my phone buzzes.

One certified not-dead dirt-covered wizard at your service.

I allow myself a silent, triumphant fist shake. I try to leave it at that. But I need to hear his voice to believe it. I dial the phone, grateful again that Wilbur gave me a Scottish SIM card.

"Hello," Max says in greeting, instead of something quippy. That would be enough to tell me he's exhausted, if I couldn't also hear it so clearly in his voice.

"Hey, next time we go to the theater, let's go when it's open, okay?" I ask.

"Yeah," he says instead of the laughter, even tired laughter, that I'm expecting.

"You good?" Worry is getting to me.

"I'm alive," he says.

I want to ask a thousand things. But he doesn't want to share them. At least his hands probably aren't skeletonized if he could text and answer his phone. But there's so much daylight between good and alive.

"You need a ride back?" Max prompts, and I realize this may be the first time I've ever been on the phone with Max where I got the impression that he wanted the call to end.

"No, you can catch a cab to the airport. I'm fine."

The line disconnects with no further fanfare. I look around at the wraith battle. I kept my voice down, and I haven't attracted attention from any of the warriors. Maybe I've been here long enough to be part of the scenery—to have faded into the background.

But what do I do now? I'd told Max I was fine, but that's not true, is it? As of now, I don't have a ride home. I could call Wilbur here, sure, but would it be safe for him to come? Maybe if I tried my best to remember where the actual Crossroads was, I could stand right by it, and he could grab my hand in passing as he stepped through, to minimize the risk of us finding out just how dead trolls are on average.

I'm so distracted thinking through the potential plan that I don't notice the root and floating silt figure of the graveling until he's standing right in front of me. When I do, my adrenaline spikes, and I claw my glasses off my face with such fervor that I'm afraid I'll break them. With the glasses off, I see what I expect—the thin figure of Claude, difficult to see against the night around him, dressed as he is in his stylish black.

"The little wizard is out of his cage," Claude says, looking as casual as a smoker waiting outside a theater at intermission.

"How did you know where I was?" I ask, trying to straighten out my stiff body.

"You think you're the only one who knows a troll?"

"Well, okay, but wouldn't it have been cheaper to just call me?"

Claude is about to respond when his head snaps to the side. I may have faded into the background for the warriors, but he hasn't. An over-six-foot hulk of a man with a double-headed axe flings himself at Claude.

Gravelings aren't the hardiest of supernatural creatures in existence, but they do have their own particular set of skills. In one smooth motion, Clause pulls a spear out from the side of his body. Without my glasses, it looks like smooth black metal, but I know from experience that it's made of his own body.

I know the strength of that spear—of how right and good and just holding it feels. And I know the feeling of thrusting it into another body, the way Claude does now to the approaching wraith.

I've been seeing wraiths suffer and "die" and stand up again unscathed long enough now to notice the difference when the spear goes into this one. It doesn't stoke his rage or call forth a blood-curdling roar. Instead, the man looks at the spear through his gut like it's telling him something he's never heard before. With new, wide eyes, he looks around the battlefield, and I see the pity I've felt watching the battle reflected in the man's face. Only deeper. Truer. His eyes rest on some figure in the background—I can't tell which—and his face contorts. A weak, mournful phrase in a language I don't speak pours out his mouth.

Claude gives the spear a firm shake forward and back the way you'd shake dirt off a shovel, and the body of the man falls to the ground. I never thought the death of a goddess and the death of a man from hundreds of years ago who may well have worshipped her would be so simi-lar, but they are. He coughs, and spits up blood, and the spark of awareness he gained in his final moments of afterlife fades from him. He does not rise again to fight. He does not move.

"Because we need to discuss what you saw in that cavern, and you might have refused me. It's easier this way." Claude holds one well-manicured hand out to me, his spear disappearing back from whence it came. I take his hand and let him pull me up.

EIGHTEEN

An Exchange

Four steps through the Crossroads lead us to a stand of trees in the middle of the round part of a cloverleaf overpass. We're probably in Europe somewhere, as it's still night, and I don't think we crossed the Atlantic. I'm not entirely unused to passing through Crossroads that have ended up near something built by humans—humans avoid building near Crossroads on an instinctive level, but sometimes it can't be avoided. The wizard's illusion is strong enough, and the weight of humans' preconceptions is heavy enough that supernatural creatures blipping through these semi-inhabited spaces don't spark any interest. But generally, these Crossroads aren't used as final points of departure from the system.

"How do we…" I begin, trailing off when I see a hatch, like one that would lead to a basement, appear in the ground nearby us. My glasses are still off. The wizard's illusion is showing me exactly how Claude intends to take us further. "Oh, shit."

I could fight Claude bringing me through the earth. I could think of it as harm to myself, and my amulet would kick in, as long as I thought quick enough and caught it early enough that I didn't end up buried ten feet underground with no air. But then I would just be stuck in the middle of a highway, and I wouldn't know what Claude wants to say about what I saw in the cavern. So instead, I just keep my glasses off, and let the wizard's illusion shield me from the uncomfortable reality of being dragged through the earth—and all the terrible sensations and worse memories that come along with it.

From my view, Claude picks me up and carries me through a soviet-era-looking tunnel, complete with flickering lights, rusted-out electrical conduits, dripping pipes, and illuminated signs in Russian. The walk isn't long, and it's almost nice being carried, so long as I can ignore the constant urge to wipe the grit from my eyes, or how hard it sometimes feels to breathe.

Partway through the tunnel, it occurs to me that the last time I was carried through the earth graveling-style, I wasn't wearing my glasses, either, but the wizard's illusion didn't shield me from the reality of what was happening. I try to think of the difference between then and now, and the only thing I can think is that that time I was being transported not by a graveling, but by their… what? King? Ruling spirit? Still, good to know there's some power on Earth that defies the wizard's illusion.

At last, we come up in another stand of trees. The spaces between the snow-covered branches reveal the tall, carved stone and masonry buildings of a city much older than my country, with bright lights shining behind antique glass. We're in a park, I think, from the snatches of wrought iron fence I can see between us and the road.

"We're in France?" I ask, catching a snatch of conversation from a passerby.

"Paris," Claude says. "It is a good place for conversation, and I was just about to have my dinner. And American women all dream of Paris, do they not?"

I want to argue against being stereotyped, but I had really enjoyed the city the one time I'd been here. I feel a little bit foolish now, remembering how I'd told people afterward that I would definitely be coming back.

I feel even more foolish wandering down a Parisian street covered in dirt and with my hair a mess. Claude, naturally, doesn't look as though it would ever occur to him to touch the earth, let alone disappear into it. I at least pull off my balaclava, so that my yellow leather jacket and general ruffled look are the only things making me stick out. Oh, and the six-inch knife in my pocket, feeling uncomfortably large. I really need to find a way to get the incantation to work for the infinity pouch.

Claude leads us off the main street, down an alley, and to a little hole-in-the-wall place that technically has a sign, but not one I'd ever notice. My skin flushes immediately as we step inside, unused to the sudden warmth after so long in the oppressive cold of Scotland without a proper coat. I worry momentarily that we won't be able to find a seat, so full is the café with lively customers, all arguing incomprehensively. But, of course, Claude says a few words to a portly, amiable man, who shows us up a stairway to the second floor. Claude and I shoehorn ourselves into what could almost be considered a nook, but with enough of a window to not feel too constricted.

I'm still getting my gloves off and rubbing my face to warm it when the waiter leaves us a bottle of red wine, carrying on with what can only be one tiny segment of an ongoing conversation with Claude.

That same odd sense of movement I can't see that I felt when Claude contracted in his roots in my house hits me again. I fumble for my glasses to confirm my suspicion.

When I do, I wonder if the rough plaster of this place, with all its many cracks, isn't a big part of the reason Claude likes it here. He's stretched out already and still further unwinding over the walls, down the stairs, and around the windows. He reminds me of dying vines in winter. I put my glasses away to have any hope of reading him—and not being too overawed by the alienness of him to play my part in the conversation.

"He's bringing you a sandwich. He says you look sick," Claude tells me, once the waiter has gone again.

"I'm not sick," I say. "Just curious."

Claude tilts his head. "I am not surprised anymore that you are curious. But then, I suppose I should not have been before, knowing your history. Now… Tell me, Arbiter, what is it you think you saw in the chamber beneath the theater?"

Maybe it's my recent foray down a Russian-styled tunnel, but something about the "think you saw" in his sentence is giving me *1984*, you-didn't-see-what-you-thought-you-saw vibes. But Claude's face is open, and calm, and not the slightest bit accusatory. That same cigarette he lit up at my house is out again, and although I'm sure they *must* have anti-smoking laws inside restaurants *even* in France by now, I somehow doubt anyone is going to tell him to put it out.

"I saw a goddess die," I say. I mean it to come out strong and factual, but too much of my awe and terror slips out. Maybe I am still cold and shaken.

Claude nods. "Yes, and which goddess?"

"The Morrigan."

"Very good," he says, like I must have done an excellent job studying my god-spotting guide. I don't tell him I cheated. "And do you recognize the significance of that?"

Unfortunately, the Morrigan did not stay alive long

enough to get me past this part of the quiz. I shake my head.

"I thought not. The Morrigan is—was—not only a goddess. She was a death goddess."

Something about the way he says those last words makes it feel like "death goddess" means more than I'd assumed—like it's more than just what we mortals decided to associate her with, or where she gets her worship.

"A death goddess?"

"You do not know even this much? Ah—" He lets out a string of what I can only assume is affectionately insulting French. "A death god or goddess was one who could create an afterlife. Who could take advantage of that little time that a human soul clings to its body after death, and give it a new cage to live in. And so they secure their worship, without question of chance or disobedience or disbelief, forever."

Claude laughs at the look on my face as it begins to click. "You see?" he asks.

"The necrowizards caught a death goddess and found a way to use her—to use her heart—to create an afterlife of their own, for their own ends."

Claude makes a little congratulatory click of his lips and teeth and gestures to me with his not-a-cigarette. "You see there? She understands. And the Morrigan was especially useful. A death goddess who had not already managed a permanent afterlife of her own. A clever choice for them."

I slump back in my chair and pick up my wine glass. My hand is steady enough now that I stand a real chance of getting the liquid in my mouth, and I gobble it down with no sense of decorum or class. I have a spare thought that I'm on the job, and one really should not drink alcohol when one is on duty, but what is he going to do? Call HR?

"Why tell me this? Why explain?" I ask, my muscles already beginning to loosen after a few mouthfuls. "I mean, I can't say I'm not grateful, but…"

"Because searching for answers, *especially* searching for answers about wizards, is much more dangerous than simply possessing them."

"Aw, geez, Claude. I didn't know you cared." I shouldn't be so irreverent and casual, especially in the face of apparent kindness as a response to extortion, but I can't stop myself. Luckily, Claude only laughs.

"Not wanting a person to die a horrible death for no reason is hardly an extraordinary act of caring. If you believe it is, you have been spending too much time with that wizard, I think." Claude takes a drink of his own wine.

My hand moves toward my glasses. I hesitate, thinking that it would be rude to so transparently try to get a look at a being's digestive system working, but what the hell. I slip the glasses on and see his face, a knotty and gently moving but thinned out version of his illusory face. He takes another sip of his wine, presumably at least in part for the benefit of my prying eyes. The red wine disappears into his body from his mouth. The light is low, so it's hard to tell, but I think I see a red tint in his floating, shifting silt begin to flow out from where he consumes it.

I take off my glasses and try my luck. "Does it taste good?" I ask.

Claude laughs louder, beginning to rival even the shouts of the diners downstairs. "I cannot taste, Elizabeth. I do not know the difference. But it feels of earth and of rot, just the way it should. And to drink it surrounded by others who drink it feels of unity and shared purpose. I do not dislike the experience."

I raise my glass at him in a poorly executed jaunty toast. "Here's to shared purpose."

To my surprise, he clinks his glass against mine, and I can't help but let out an untamed laugh of my own. The tension from the last hour and the wine hitting my stomach are conspiring to undo me. I take another drink. *Where is that sandwich?*

"So you're taking care of it, then?" I ask, and as I hear my own words, the real reason I'm starting to relax hits me. This isn't on me. This isn't my responsibility. Someone bigger and better and stronger than me is in charge.

"Take care of what, exactly?"

I stare at him. "The situation. With the ghosts and the necrowizards. You just said it was dangerous for me to be digging into it, and you know what's going on, so…"

"So, what is it you think I am going to do?"

So much for that. "Your fucking job. Doesn't this fly in the face of everything you care about?"

"And what do we care about?"

I flounder. "The… rules. The natural order?"

Claude takes a long, unhurried sip of his wine. "There is nothing natural about order. Rules, yes, we care about. And the wizards have the strength to make the rules. So we will enforce the rules as they have been made. But the necrowizards, as you call them, are wizards, too. This is an internal affair. It is no business of ours."

How is he so calm? So rooted and strong in the face of being so infuriatingly fucking wrong? "But people… everyone. So many people are going to die."

"I think perhaps, *ma chère*, you have forgotten who you are drinking with."

I set my wine glass down and try to regather my thoughts. The momentary reprieve from the weight of my failure bearing down on me was a trick—I just feel more lost now. And worse.

"You know a lot about death gods."

"We do."

"Did they give you your vampiric spirits?" I spit the words out with the hatred they deserve. But Claude knows why. And he's capable of understanding human emotion, even if he's incapable of feeling it.

"They did."

Something is clicking together in my head, but I'm not sure what yet. Something about the way Claude had given that ghost on the battlefield true death.

"Have you come to a decision in the matter of the arbitration?" Claude says, with all the intensity of a question about the price of gas in another state. I start.

"I… have not come to a decision yet, no." I'm going to have to figure out how to get the money and how to avoid Max shutting me down from the only option I have, but there's bigger fish to fry at the moment.

"You put a lot of things off, Elizabeth Baker. You are a procrastinator. If you are not careful, you will forget even to die."

A memory of the tingle of my hands when I grabbed Melissa's hood rises in my mind. "Do you know something that I don't?"

Claude smiles endearingly, genuinely amused. "I know many things you don't, but about you? No. It is only a saying. If you want to know about your future, perhaps you should capture one of these wraiths. Torture it into telling you, no?"

"I think they're being tortured enough, don't you?"

Claude nods solemnly, as though he really feels it. But that's a trick and an illusion, just like everything, isn't it? "I do," he says. And I could really believe him if I tried.

"Of course, I'd need something to torture them with," I say.

Claude's eyebrow raises. "Ah, so we come to that."

He got here before I did, maybe, but I don't really care. "We come to that. I want a spear. Or a knife, if you can manage it. Easier to carry. You say you don't want me to die a horrific death, then give me a fighting chance. You might think it's an internal wizard matter, but I don't. And I'm not breaking the rules by getting involved, am I? No rules that you can punish me for?"

A smile hovers around Claude's lips. "No rules, no. But what will you give me?"

I'm an idiot. An attractive, mysterious Frenchman whisked me away to Paris, plied me with wine, whispered secrets to me, and I somehow didn't see it coming that he wants something. Maybe I am the cliché of the naïve American woman. "What is it you want?"

"I want a guarantee that you will not, in your ruling, attempt to force the gravelings to feed the ghouls from our graveyards."

A lot of creatures try to bribe me to rule their way in an arbitration. Some of them have even tried to threaten me. One of the siren tribes kidnapped my mother, for God's sake. But none of them have ever been so brutally effective at it. And Claude doesn't even have the common decency to look smug.

If I make this promise, it takes away what is probably my best option. Maybe the only option that avoids passive genocide, if Max really isn't going to let me pursue my crematorium plan. Either passive genocide, or the knowledge that ghouls are going to start killing live humans again.

And maybe that's not a huge disruption from the status quo—not if I give them the information from Wilbur about where the meat from the ghost-cows was delivered. But can I really be party to mass murderers better selecting their victims?

But if I don't, they'll just attack people who are better off. If they do, then there's a chance their deaths will be noticed, in which case we're going to start the big wizard treaty-breaking crackdown the arbitration was trying to avoid in the first place.

Of course, the wizards can't do that at all if they're embroiled in a civil war with likely much higher human casualties. And my chances of finding a way to stop *that* go way up if I have a weapon that stands a chance of actually working against the necrowizards.

And then there's the chance that the weapon, given its origin and the origin of vampiric spirits, might in some way be able to help my mother's condition. But is it morally right to stack my own personal family issues up against genocide or world-ending conflicts? Don't their lives mean as much as hers to their own children? And my mom isn't *dead*, after all. Would she want me to make the wrong choice for the world if it's the right choice for her?

Okay. Fuck. I should not have had the wine.

"You are worried about your reputation as arbiter. Do not be. This deal comes with a presupposition of secrecy."

Presupposition, huh? I guess when you live forever, there's no reason not to be perfect at any language you try your hand at. That accent's just for fun, isn't it?

"You'll really give me your spear?"

"No. But you have a knife in your pocket. Show me."

I pull out the sharpknife and lay it on the table. The dark of the theater and the battlefield didn't do it justice. In the warm incandescent light of the café, the thing gleams, the carvings seemingly coming alive with every slight rock on the table.

"I can imbue that. Give it some of myself."

I nod. Maybe it's not the morally right choice. But it's the *strategically* right choice. I'll carry the weight on my soul later if I need to. Claude requires no more encouragement. He sets down his wine glass and reaches out a slender, lazy finger. He runs it along the blade of the knife. I realize partway through that I should be wearing my glasses for this and shove them on. Through them, I see silt from his body, ever so slightly tinted red from the wine, writhing over the blade. Flowing into the etching. Disappearing into the leather-wrapped hilt. After a time, the knife can absorb no more, and Claude removes his hand. I push my glasses back up onto my head. To my normal eyes, the knife looks no different, but it smells faintly of red wine.

"Put that away. Luc is coming with your sandwich."

I do, remembering just in time that, reasonably dull or not, I should be careful putting away a knife. Luc and Claude chat loudly and amiably, with no apparent regard for the ravenous way I'm staring at the sandwich in his hand. Almost as an afterthought, he eventually sets the plate down in front of me. He says a few words to Claude and disappears again.

When he's gone, I feel more sick than hungry. "I'd rather eat alone, if you don't mind," I say.

Claude holds me in a long, appraising stare. After a few moments, I get that same sense of unseen feeling around me, telling me he's going to acquiesce to my wishes before he gives me a nod. "As you like."

I suppose I shouldn't be surprised. He got what he wanted from me, after all.

And hopefully, I got what I needed.

NINETEEN

A Grudge

Claude paid for my sandwich. Least he could do, considering he corrupted my not-so-sacred duty as Arbiter. When I finish, I pull out my pen to ask Wilbur how I should get to a Crossroads so he can come get me. Instead, he sends me to the other side of Paris, where I meet up with another troll friend of his named Heinrich. I figure it's fine, just as long as I remember to pay him. Paying Wilbur has gotten to be such a habit that it's almost automatic. Sometimes, it even is.

But when I run through my payment options, Heinrich looks at me like I just suggested we jump in the Seine.

"I'm not going to give you a way to pay me through technology without my participation," he says. "I don't even know you. And you're not just a human."

This day has been way too long for this. "I *am* a human."

"Yes, I know. But not an unknowing human. What if you took advantage? You could pay me ahead of time and put me in your service without my consent. I trust Wilbur.

He's a good man. But that doesn't mean that I'm going to give you that power over me."

Just when I think I'm beginning to understand this world, or at *least* the one species in it that I have the most to do with, I discover how truly lost I really am. I guess if you pay a troll, that obligates them to connect you to something before they've agreed to? That isn't something Wilbur has ever mentioned. But it's fine—I find an ATM nearby and pull out some euros. Heinrich accepts ten of them and walks me through the Crossroads to just outside Springfield, where Faisal is waiting with the car to take me home.

I bathe. I cry a little. I emotionally dump the entire thing on Faisal, who listens with the patience of a saint and the face of a statue. I let him know right at the beginning that we failed—that the circles weren't where we were expecting, and that there turned out to be nothing we could do about it.

I tell him about the Morrigan's last breaths and the rage that seeing Aloysius's blessing called out in her. I tell him about Gigi's betrayal, and Claude's leveraging of my desperation into forcing my hand on the arbitration.

But I also tell him about the knife. About the way the wraith on the battlefield died. About my conviction that it isn't over—that it can't be over. Not now. Not yet. I fall asleep in Faisal's arms, where I belong, with the sharpknife under the mattress.

We spend the morning scanning news reports, looking for any sign of the necrowizards coming into their own. I figure I'll let Max get some sleep after what must have been a worse day for him than it was for me. The news remains blessedly free of mass murders or anything I can divine as evil wizardry. At least it hasn't started yet. At least there's that. For now, the cone of silence about the supernatural is holding.

The news does have a lot to say about the crazy rise in wraith behavior, though. Various articles treat the reports of paranormal activity with arms-length disbelief. Most of the journalists seem more interested in talking about how the growing belief that there is something legitimately supernatural going on is another sign of the failure of our education system, or the widespread prevalence of misinformation networks. In the better-researched ones, however, they talk about the variety in the education level and social networks of the people who have been "drawn in" by this information—and the lack of a political affiliation.

There's a kind of brooding suspicion underlying so many of these reports, though they never come out and say they believe something strange is going on. And much of the internet seems devoted to sharing and laughing about videos of newscasters getting caught out live on the air—which I always forget is still a thing—revealing that they think the ghost sightings are legitimate. The comment sections of these videos are always filled with a mix of people saying that it's hilarious that people are getting drawn in, and people talking about their anecdotal experiences that support the idea there's something more going on than anyone official wants to admit.

Well, I wanted the world to believe in the supernatural. I guess this is where we start. Kind of weird to be standing on the side of the conspiracy theorists, but I'm starting to get used to it.

I consider calling Olivia, but Faisal tells me he already filled her in. We don't discuss how angry she is at me, or how she has a right to be, in light of knowing about me risking the lives of her daughters to save my own skin. I don't need to know that Faisal, although he's happy with the results of the decision I made in the cave this spring, would never have done the same.

All in all, it's almost normal enough of a day that I start feeling guilty for calling in sick to work. Up until there's a knock at the front door, and I open it to reveal Wilbur's awkward bulk.

"Has it started?" I ask, which is maybe not the best way of putting it, and I can't blame Wilbur for the confusion that crosses his face.

"I don't think so. But Gigi called me. Max is at the Emporium."

My heart drops. That was not the vector I thought the damage would begin from. "What's he doing?"

Somehow, in all my anger at Gigi, I had overlooked the foregone conclusion that Max would be considerably more pissed off.

"Nothing, I think," Wilbur says, clearly uncomfortable. "He's just sitting there. But Gigi told him to leave, or she'd cause a scene, and he called her bluff and refused."

Times like this, it seems even weirder and less convenient to me that Wilbur doesn't have a phone. I guess he could have emailed the info. But to be honest, I'm glad he's here in person. I don't mind a little backup in going to talk to Max.

"Should we go talk to him?" Faisal says beside me, laying a hand on the small of my back.

"Wilbur and I will," I say.

Faisal hesitates, as though he's going to object, but he picks his battles and seems content to accept that this isn't one to push. I may be overprotective at times, but I have good reason. And if I could figure out how to make another fucking amulet, I wouldn't *need* to be so overprotective.

But I digress.

Wilbur and I pile into his impressive, expensive marvel of German engineering and head to the Emporium. The Arts District, I have the time to recognize in full daylight, is decorated for the holidays. Wreaths, sprigs of fake evergreen boughs, draping strings of lights. It's all very tasteful and beautiful, and the absurdity that *this* is how we're all choosing to spend our time when the world is crashing down around our shoulders suddenly hits me. I laugh for a solid two minutes, tears in my eyes, and don't stop until Wilbur finds a parking spot close to the Emporium. To his credit, he says nothing about my mini-breakdown.

It's a weekday afternoon, so the place isn't too busy, but it's a popular enough spot that even now it's not empty. The current clientele is mostly young people—teenagers and college students on break from their respective institutions. Singles and little groups of them litter the stacks, and a few chat at tables. Gigi is behind the counter with a rigid, disapproving look on her face. And at one of the front tables, right by the glass, reading an honest-to-God paper newspaper, is Max.

I'm used to seeing Max's face with a casual cheerfulness on it. It's not always real, sure, but it's convincing enough if you don't know better. I've even seen just enough of him playing at the intimidating wizard not to be taken aback by it. But the tension in his jaw and the stiffness of his muscles makes him feel like a stranger.

Holy shit, he's mad. No wonder even Gigi, unflappable as she usually is, felt the need to get in touch with Wilbur— though I'm not sure how she did it, exactly. Email? It would have been easier for her just to call me. It would have made more sense. But in a moment of anger and in a dumb, dumb bluff yesterday, I'd kicked her out of the gang, I remember. Because I'm an idiot who's in over my head, and I should have known better than to try to strong-arm someone with provably super-strong arms.

I slide into the chair across the little table from Max. "Whatcha reading? Anything interesting?"

"Oh, you know, the usual. Fiddling while Rome burns."

I'm glad I got my manic laughter at that very thought out of my system in the car. "You want to put the newspaper down and look at me?"

"Why? You planning on doing something interesting?"

"Are you?"

Max pauses for a moment before he answers. "I haven't decided yet."

I glance around the little café area, trying to gauge how likely we are to be overheard. The closest customers to us are a couple of teenage girls who seem very interested in what they're doing—at first glance. But given the effect Max's looks have on most women, I'm not so sure.

I lean in and lower my voice. "Look, we all knew we were heading into a dangerous situation. Gigi is certain she can't bring you through the Crossroads for whatever reason. She made the call in the moment to save the person she thought she was capable of saving. And in the end, you got out fine. All's well that ends well."

Max turns a page, doubtless for dramatic effect. "It could easily have gone differently."

I reach up and pull the newspaper down so that I can see his face. And immediately wish I hadn't. Christ, he's furious. "But it didn't. And if it had, you would have been avenged."

"By you?" There's amusement in his smile, but I don't like the shade of it.

"I wouldn't need to, would I? But you know whose wrath Gigi was risking when she left you behind. Do you really think she would have done that, knowing the consequences, if she'd had any other option?"

He holds me in an intense stare, considering. "She could have stayed."

"And let me probably die when she knew she could save me?"

"And your life is more important than mine? You're immune, anyway, with what you have."

"Well, I am and I'm not. And we didn't know to what extent I was, then, anyway."

It's subtle, but I catch the first sign of a crack in his furious tension. "How so? How are you not?" He looks down at my hands, as if to reassure himself that they are, in fact, still living flesh.

This line of conversation may be working, but I don't really want to continue it. "Nothing. I just... I don't feel *nothing* when they touch me."

"A bad 'not nothing'?"

I slouch. "Honestly, I don't know. Maybe it's fine. Just weird."

He visibly relaxes. Just a little. Just enough. "I'm not working with her. I don't trust her."

I shrug. The fire has gone out of his voice. "Like you ever did? Like she ever trusted you? And anyway, you don't have to. I kicked her off the team."

He examines me, like he's trying to decide whether to believe me or not. Out of the corner of my eye, I see Gigi's motions stop stock still for just a moment before continuing. "When she wouldn't go back for you, I told her she was out. That's why Wilbur's here. She didn't call me. He did."

Does Max know how childlike he looks, trying to decide whether he will allow himself to be consoled? He glances at Wilbur, as though to confirm that he is, in fact, standing there. Although to me, and to all the other humans in here, it looks like he's gazing into the air above Wilbur's head. It seems to be enough. He believes me. And hopefully that'll be enough for him to keep playing nice until I figure out how to fix this.

"What were you going to do, anyway?" I give him a smile. "What do you think you could do that wouldn't hurt everyone else more than it would her? And out in the open like this. Not very characteristic of your kind, is it?"

"I don't know," Max says, some semblance of his good nature returning. "Set her feathers in a flurry, I guess."

It's all I can do not to laugh at the idea of Gigi wearing feathers. I'd stake my life on it that there was a time in her life she was accustomed to the casual application of feather boas. "Well, mission accomplished. You want to come over?"

Max winces. Maybe it wasn't the smartest time to emphasize his inability to get through the wards surrounding my house.

"Oh, come on, I haven't forgotten. I've got a surprise for you."

With that, I stand and head for the door. For one horrible moment, I think Max isn't going to follow. But then he does, and I feel like I can breathe again.

Crisis averted. For now. Now I just have to figure out how to take out the temporary splint I put in place to keep us limping forward. That is, if we survive resolving this current crisis without Gigi at all.

TWENTY

An Invitation

"You have to be kidding," Max says as he stands on the porch, looking up at me through the trapdoor I put in the place where the attic hangs over the front porch —the only portion of the house that is indoors but still outside of the perimeter of wards that I put around the foundation in the basement.

"I put in a wizard door, just for you. Merry Christmas."

Max smirks. "You put it in?"

"Okay, Henry put it in. But I asked him to." Saying the name of my across-the-street-neighbor to Max feels wrong. For a moment, a pang of old grief and betrayal over Henry's choice flares up before I push it away.

"This is humiliating," Max says.

"Someone is going to see you if you keep standing there," Faisal chimes in from farther back in the attic, lounging on his beanbag. Wilbur is sitting nearby on the floor and doesn't seem interested in joining the conversation, engaged as he is in devouring every detail of the space. I'm amazed we got him up here, but trolls are more agile than they look. It comes from centuries of learning to climb the underside of bridges. Ever seen a climber without grace, whatever their size?

With a melodramatic sigh, Max climbs the folding ladder. I step back away from the space, going behind my desk to pull out my chair. Max fumbles with the ladder, getting it pulled up from the hatch and set beside him. He seems to examine the wood of the hatch carefully as he gets the rug back into place over it, and for a moment I'm afraid I didn't scrub it well enough to remove the circle from the first time I summoned a ghost. But the hatch is brand-new plywood. I relax.

I'm half expecting Max to test his boundaries—to try to get past the line of the wards between his little overhang and the rest of the attic. It's too easy to imagine him banging his fists against an invisible wall. But the wards don't work like that.

Their first line of defense isn't a physical boundary— although they will physically stop someone or something that means me harm from getting through. But before it even gets that far, they stop anyone from intending to try to step over the boundary. Max doesn't try to test the boundary formed by the wards around my basement because he can't form the intention to try.

"I texted Olivia from the road," Max says, still a little grumbly, like he can't believe he agreed to this.

"She's coming?" I ask.

"You really shouldn't text and drive," Wilbur says, fiddling with an aborted attempt at a magical floatation device he found in the corner.

"I use voice dictation," Max says. "And yes. I told her it was important."

Max was so bothered by Gigi at the Emporium, and then so bothered by the audacity of me putting him in a corner of my attic that I'd missed it so far, but there's something off in the way he's talking. He's not himself. Something's wrong. Something is very, very wrong.

"Max, what happened?" I say, in my best impression of my mother in the years before her mind was destroyed.

"I'll explain when Olivia gets here," he says, his grim expression doing nothing to allay my worry.

At which point, we are four people sitting in an attic without, to be frank, a ton in common other than the thing we can't talk about until our fifth person gets here. It's a very special kind of awkward.

"So, did you have a nice flight?" Faisal asks, leaning back in his beanbag.

Max seems almost unbalanced by the question, innocuous though it may be. He looks like he's searching for the barb buried in it. But that isn't like Faisal, and from what I can tell, Max comes to that conclusion too.

"It was fine. I got a hotel in Glasgow for the rest of the night, though. I was kind of… tired."

Faisal nods and lets out a little huff of laughter. "I'll bet."

The look on Max's face is hard to read. Like he's not sure what to do with Faisal's words. Like he's looking for some insult or ulterior motive. But Faisal's easy, friendly smile doesn't leave much room for any of that. Max rubs his chin. "Yeah," he says.

So that's how you get Max to quit quipping. Good to know.

At the sound of a car—Olivia's presumably—pulling into the drive, Max gets a little of his mischievous magic back. He moves aside the carpet and listens for the sounds of Olivia climbing the porch steps. When she knocks, he swings open the hatch.

"We're in the attic," he says into the open space below him. "Come on up!"

I can't see Olivia's face, but I can hear her laugh, and an unflattering rush of jealousy runs through me that he can make her laugh, and I can't anymore. Max gets resettled on his rug as the rest of us listen to Olivia's movements. Opening the door. Walking through the hallway below us. Climbing up the still-open attic hatch from *inside* the house.

"Why are you sitting over there?" she asks when her head pops above floor level, addressing Max with a casual familiarity that sets me further on edge.

"This is my time-out corner for daring to have goals."

That's a really funny way to say "for wanting to erase the memory of the owner of the house."

"Hey, any time you want to cross over the line and join us, you're welcome to," I say.

Olivia is dressed neatly in a skirt suit, and presumably not looking to sit on the floor. Instead, she selects a dusty armchair that Faisal and I found at a thrift shop.

"Hi Olivia, glad you were free," I say, fumbling for something to get her to talk to me the way she's talking to Max.

"I wasn't," she says with a flat affect. So much for sisterly affection. Still pissed at me. I don't know why I expected differently. I didn't have any reason to. Except maybe that we're family, and it's Christmas—and maybe the end of the world.

I've never been that skilled at keeping my feelings out of my expression—not, at least, from the point of view of those who know me. Faisal pipes up to redirect the conversation. "Max was just about to tell us something important."

All eyes except for Wilbur's turn to Max, whose temporarily returned good cheer is already withering. Wilbur, for his part, is too engrossed in my magical castoffs to seem to be paying attention, even if I'm sure he's taking it all in.

"Right. So." He interlaces his fingers and locks in a knee with his hands. "I stayed in Glasgow last night and flew back here early this morning. When I got home, I noticed that the, ah, intruder alarms I leave set in my house had gone off."

"By which you mean boobytraps," I say, remembering the little metal insect-like devices that I watched momentarily take down his masters. They would have killed them, in fact, if Moira hadn't survived long enough to rewind time a minute and try that entrance again armed with the foreknowledge that they were coming.

"By which I mean security measures," Max says. "But when I called Kristoff and Moira to yell at them for coming into my space uninvited, they were just relieved to hear from me. I guess they'd been calling. I lost my phone below the theater. They said they'd gotten a wizard's invitation to a celebration of peace."

At those words, Wilbur's massive body shifts. The failed spell attempt he had been fiddling with forgotten and his whole body rigid, he looks at Max as though he'd never seen him before.

"A traditional wizard's invitation?" Wilbur asks.

Max nods, the pain of the admission evident on his face.

"What does that mean?" I ask Wilbur, not feeling cruel enough to want to ask Max directly.

Wilbur looks away from Max as he answers. "Back before the treaty settled things down for everyone, wizards used to get into conflicts more than they do now. More than was good for anyone. And by tradition, when one wizard defeated another, they would send the defeated wizard an invitation to a party. Usually a lavish one."

Wilbur pauses. I don't interrupt, no matter how much I want to. "They send the invitation by sending the defeated wizard the head of their apprentice. Or, failing that, the apprentice of another wizard that they know or who owes them… not *fealty* exactly, but a kind of wizard recognition of superior status. The time and place of the surrender party would be written on a piece of cloth, stuffed in the mouth of the apprentice's head."

What I'm taking away from this is that our little field trip—and even Gigi's betrayal—basically saved Max's life. And I'm not going to say that right now, because it's sure as fuck not the time, but eventually, Max is going to realize this. Faisal shoots me a quizzical look, seeing me relax just slightly at such gruesome news. I give him a little shake of my head. We'll discuss it later.

"Did you know the apprentice they used to send the invitation to Kristoff and Moira in your place?" I ask, and immediately regret it. If we were alone, maybe he could show some emotion over the gruesome act. Maybe he could even do that in front of Faisal and Olivia, human as they are. But in front of a troll? No chance.

"I never met her, but I'd heard of her," he says, face stone.

"When's the party?" I ask.

"Christmas Eve," Max says, still in his funk, but starting to look a little relieved somehow. A burden shared is a burden lightened and all that, maybe. "A Yule ball. At a castle in Lithuania. Google says the castle is in ruins, but I guess that was just temporary while they were away."

"Glasgow wasn't even close," Faisal says.

"Nope!" Max agrees, a manic glint in his eye.

"So we're going, obviously," I say.

Every head in the room whips around to face me. "Come again?" Olivia says.

I face Max. "You have an invitation, right? Did every wizard get invited?"

Max lets out a bark of manic laughter. "Every wizard in the world wouldn't fit in one ballroom. But yeah. I could go. They sent out *invitations* to the fifty or so most powerful wizards in the world, and Kristoff's on that list. As his apprentice, I could show up. If I were dumb enough."

"What are the chances they're not just throwing that party to get all the most powerful wizards in the same place so that they can kill them?" Faisal asks.

"I honestly don't know. It's possible. There's also a chance that it's just intimidation. That's what Kristoff and Moira think. But there's also the chance the wizards invited will take the opportunity to kill the necrowizards before they've had a chance to settle into the modern world. Personally, I think there's a high probability things are going to go to hell at this party."

"So everyone's going to be distracted," I say.

"I'm not comfortable with how excited you look right now," Wilbur says, while Olivia rests her head in a hand, disbelief written on her face.

"I'm not excited. I'm just…" I rub my face, trying to slow my thoughts down enough to get them out. "Look, we couldn't have asked for better. This is good luck. *Really* good luck for us." Suspiciously good luck. *Thank you, Aloysius*. I make a note to try and track him down and run this plan by him in person after I'm done convincing all the people who actually care about me first. "Their circles have to be at that castle, right? If it's their new home base? And they are voluntarily letting people into that castle. *And* they're high on their victory. They probably think that their circles are invulnerable, because it's after the solstice, and they've come all the way through, so their circles are atemporal, right? I bet the conqueror's paranoia hasn't even set in yet."

"They *think* their newly atemporal circles are invulnerable, because they *are*," Olivia says.

"I'm getting to that. There's going to be a party with complicated politicking going on that will be distracting everyone. Max shows up, smuggles me in somehow. I find the circles and destroy them. At that point, the wizards won't be ghosts anymore. The spirits will go out of their bodies, just like with the cows. Maybe they'll come back through as wraiths, but wraiths are less reliable. Less consistent. Are you really going to tell me the fifty most powerful, pissed-off wizards in the world can't handle some wraiths?"

The shock from those around the circle is fading, but I haven't won them over yet. Olivia looks worried. Wilbur looks his version of scared. Max looks angry, for some reason. And Faisal... Faisal looks frozen.

"Even if that were a good idea, which I'm not saying it is, how do you think you could accomplish it?" Olivia says.

I stand up and head to my desk drawer. Probably shouldn't show Max that this is where I've been keeping the sharpknife, but whatever. I can always move it later. "With this," I say, showing off like a schoolkid with a fully completed Lego castle.

"What did you do to my knife?" Max does not seem suitably impressed.

"I *upgraded* it. And you should be glad I did."

"For those of us in the room without wizardvision?" Olivia asks.

I don't want to go too in-depth about what I did to get this to happen. What I gave up. I don't even really want to think about it. "I got a graveling to imbue it. It can kill ghosts now—even atemporal ones. And if it can do that, and it could already cut anything else, I'm betting it can destroy the necrowizards' circles."

Or, at least, the Morrigan's heart that they've used to create the afterlife. Or enough ghosts that the afterlife collapses. However things end up going down, it can only help. But I'm going to keep it simple for now. Come up with the plan that will go to hell later.

Even not indulging the hypotheticals, no one in the attic seems to see what extraordinarily good luck this is.

"That's a hell of a bet," Faisal says, and Olivia winces.

"She'll take it," Olivia says, her body too stiff.

Faisal notices what he blundered into a moment too late—not that I'd be able to tell if I hadn't lived with him for so long. He doubles down. "And she'll be right to. But I think we need to try to make the chances better."

Ok, so I've got Faisal. One down. The only other person I *need* to agree is Max, though I wouldn't mind if Olivia and Wilbur did, too.

"How?" Max asks.

"Time magic," Faisal says, to Max's answering eyeroll.

"That's great. Know any? Have anything in the trove you're willing to lend me? Time magic is tricky. And dangerous. There's no way I believe that any of the apprentices that have contributed to the trove knew any. I'm sorry, but they just didn't."

I pick up on what Faisal's putting down. "No, but we don't need to be the ones doing it. We get Moira to do it."

"Moira doesn't know any time magic," Max says.

I purse my lips. "There's no point in trying to keep that a secret now. I know you don't want to share things, but this isn't the time to hold out."

"I'm not keeping any secret. Moira doesn't know any time magic." Max holds his hands up, exasperation cutting through his weird anger.

"Oh, shit, you actually don't know." I don't think there's anything I could have said that would have unsettled him more. I keep my forward momentum. "When I was in the box in your living room, I saw her reset time by a minute. Easy as breathing. Kristoff knows she does it, too." The words come out like an apology.

The gears click in Max's head. He shakes it slowly.

"You all right, there?" Faisal asks, with no edge whatsoever in his voice.

"Just putting together why I've never won an argument with Moira. Not that I've ever tried to *argue* with her exactly, just…"

That kiss she gave him. Her position in his life. It's fucked.

Max's eyebrows knit together. "Resets time by a minute? She knows *that* one?"

"Yeah," I say as gently as I can. "She knows that one."

His eyebrows go up, and he clasps his hands, weaving his fingers together on his lap. "That could work, actually. That spell… it works by folding the timeline. It's supposed to be lost because it's dangerous—it weakens the timeline wherever you do it. You fold the timeline over itself too many times in the same place, and it can mess with cause and effect. It's a long shot, but we're trying to destroy something that's drawing its strength from being bound to time. Doing it when the timeline is already folded over on itself and weakened sounds like a good idea."

Which is more or less what Faisal said, just with more certainty. I sneak an instinctive glance at Faisal to see if he minds the way Max is saying it like it's his own idea. He doesn't seem to care.

"If we can get her to do it at the right time," I say, leading.

"That's easy," Olivia chimes in, with her usual brutal, if well-meaning, efficiency. "Max just said he knows she uses it to gain an upper hand over him in arguments. That means he can get her to do it again when you're in position."

Is she on board? Have I won them over? Everyone but Wilbur, who would never agree, but he isn't going to argue with me about it anymore. He's given up on me making what he considers good decisions at this point. I love him for it.

"Right, so do you cut the circles before the reset, or after?" Faisal asks. "Either way would put you within the folded minute."

"We'll do both," I say. "To be safe."

"Which you'll know how, exactly?" Olivia says. "Max is a wizard and even *he* couldn't detect she was doing it."

"Same way she did in my living room nine months ago," Max chimes in. His anger isn't gone, exactly, but it seems to have dimmed. Buried under the revelation about what Moira's been keeping from him as he gets into the nuts and bolts of the plan. "Seals herself in an invisible vault. That'll make her cut off from everything magic— even time magic. If she leaves a clock outside to watch, she should be able to tell when time outside the vault goes back a minute."

The thought of being trapped in Max's *invisible vault*, even by choice, sends a bolt of panic up my spine. I try to ignore it, though Faisal's hand on my knee tells me he noticed.

"I doubt I can sneak in your coffee table," I say. "I mean, I can be sneaky, but not that sneaky."

"No one thinks you can be sneaky," Wilbur says affectionately.

"She can when she wants to be," Olivia says. The

words sting, but there's no real fire in them, and she said it quietly enough that it seemed mostly to herself.

"And how are you going to sneak in the knife, anyway?" Max asks. "Or your amulet, for that matter? They'll see the magic on you, even if you could somehow conceal them in a formal dress."

"I wasn't planning on anyone seeing me at all."

"Oh, because you're suddenly a trained cat burglar? No. If you're getting in there, you're getting in there disguised as my escort."

Wilbur laughs. I do not laugh. Nor do Faisal and Olivia.

"Your what?" Faisal asks in a warning tone. His casual pose in his beanbag has taken on a tension.

"I'm saying escort because it sounds better than slave. Every wizard there will be bringing along someone to tend and serve them on the journey and show off to other wizards on arrival. You can pretend to be mine. Just practice looking dead inside, and I'm pretty sure we can pull that part of it off. *If* we can find a way for you to carry things in. If you trust me to carry your amulet for you, I can give it back to you once we're inside."

"Not happening," Faisal says.

I'm already standing, getting ready to walk to my desk. Once there, I open the drawer and pull out the infinity pouch. "Will this hide the magical signature or whatever?"

Max's mouth goes slack. "You have an endless purse?"

Okay, yes, because that's a much less silly thing to call it. Unfortunately, nothing is going to change the nickname I have for it in my head now.

"Almost. I've created it, but I haven't been able to say the enchantment correctly to activate it. I bet you could, though."

Max's gorgeous green eyes flash with predatory zeal. "I bet I could," he says.

"Great!" I say. "I'll grab the candles."

"No need. I'll take it home with me."

Of course. It was all going just a little too easily. "Why not do it here?" I ask, the tone of my voice making it clear I already know the answer.

"Where you can record me? No, thank you."

"You'd be getting a spell, too. You do it here, let me record you, and I'll even show you the page of the trove that the spell is on. You'd be able to make your own."

Max's body adjusts in tiny movements. Not much is different than it was moments before, but it gives me the impression that he's about to go into battle. I don't like this side of him. I see it so rarely that I sometimes forget it's there. But I don't like it all the same.

"I told you three months ago, I'm not trading you a spell for a spell. That was a one-time thing."

For a long moment, I stand behind my desk, and he sits, trapped in the corner on the floor but still somehow entirely in control.

I put the pouch back in the desk drawer and close it. "Then we'll enchant it at your place. That way, you know I can't record it. And I'll watch you do it, so I know you aren't going to take it apart and put it back together somehow to see how it's made." We don't quibble about how I know that recordings don't work in his house. He knows I've tried and failed to do so.

Max gives me a half-smile. "Done."

With the deal struck, the tension fades. The five of us spend the rest of the afternoon and late into the evening discussing the details and what-ifs of the plan. I eventually relent to Max's complaints and fetch him several pillows and even a blanket. He makes more jokes about it being his playpen or dog kennel, and we all carefully sidestep what exactly is holding him there. It's easy to ignore the elephant in the room if everyone present cooperates.

When even we can recognize that our questions and answers are becoming nonsensical, and Olivia quite rightly points out that we have another day to work out the finer details, Max, Wilbur, and Olivia all head out. I can't shake the feeling that Faisal and I have just thrown our first dinner party since we attempted to be sophisticated during college, and then decided that sophistication was not nearly as fun as being casual and finding things outside of the house to do with our friends.

I enjoy the sheer extravagance of getting to go to bed with Faisal, knowing that he's not going to be sent away on work until well after I am.

"You don't like this plan, do you?" I whisper into the dark.

"I don't have to like it," he says. "I just have to believe it'll work."

"Do you believe it will work?"

In lieu of an answer, he pulls me in closer.

TWENTY-ONE

A Snake

O ne day.

I've got one day between when we make the plan and when I'm going to go kill myself in a futile attempt to save the world.

I wish I had less. I wish it were all as in-the-moment and urgent as it was when I found the trove after Dad died, or when the sirens called me up. Most of my other arbitrations, too, have been nonstop occasions. Maybe they end up being longer than expected, sure, but there was never this waiting. Never this thinking. Never this wondering if I should call a lawyer and have a will made up.

Really, I should have done that months ago. But it felt like a self-fulfilling prophecy. And anyway, what lawyer would I get to help a reasonably healthy twenty-eight-year-old woman to fill out an emergency will two days before Christmas without requiring a ton of money and/or asking some uncomfortable questions I can't answer?

The most valuable thing I have, anyway, is the trove, and that can't exactly go into legal documents. While it would be tempting to make sure that ownership of the house passes correctly to ensure the protection of the wards continues to work right, in all honesty, I don't know how probate would affect the protections on it. In the time between when I die and when the will is adjudicated, who would own the house, and therefore who would the wards be keyed to? I don't think there's much of a chance that the magic will transfer seamlessly.

No—if I die, Max will end up getting the trove. He'll wipe Olivia and Faisal's minds of all knowledge of magic. There'll be a lot of confusion on their parts of what has been taking up so much of their time lately, but they'll be as safe as Max can make them. As safe as any human is in the world with the way it is.

Or the world as it would be once plunged into an eventual wizard civil war. A civil war that wouldn't be inevitable, except that wizards are wizards and don't do well with big changes to the careful balance of power that keeps them from being as destructive to each other as they are to any humans that come into their lives.

I want to think there's something I can do to keep my loved ones safe other than the big dumb thing I'm doing anyway. But there isn't.

Except, perhaps, for calling in a favor that I couldn't in front of everyone the other day.

Over magic pen, Wilbur agrees to meet me at one of the field Crossroads closest to Springfield around ten a.m. I tell him that I want to go consult with the chance demon to ask about the probability of success of our upcoming venture, and I think he believes me. In a way, it's not entirely wrong. He offers to drive me from Skyway Park, where his bridge is, but I decline. I want the drive to the Crossroads in order to center myself. To just have some space to breathe and consider—and yes, intentionally pray a little so that Aloysius knows I'm coming and isn't surprised to see me.

Even though it's day, I still can't help but search the world around me for wraiths. They'd only showed up during the night before, but with the veil ripped, all bets are off. The fields I drive through remind me of when I first saw Melissa, and my heart breaks for her again. If I can't manage to change things, my heart will be breaking for her a little bit for the rest of my life.

Which, at least, probably won't be very long.

I get to the Crossroads early. I don't know if there's some wizard illusion help in making sure that the farmer who technically owns this land doesn't notice that people pull over and park in one of the fields. I think it's a big corporation, anyway, and there's no actual building in easy sight, windbreak trees getting in the way as they do. But still. At this point, I know more or less where the point of the Crossroads itself is, and I start heading that way.

Snow crunches beneath my feet. It's thin on the ground here, thankfully, and I'm dressed properly for the weather.

What is not dressed properly for the weather, however, is the massive red-, white-, and yellow-banded snake. It's bigger than I've ever seen, up to and including at the zoo. Easily over thirty feet long and a foot in diameter along its length.

It shouldn't be able to survive here in the snow. It should be frozen solid. But then, the spider shouldn't have been able to survive outside on my back porch, either. I stop short of it when I see it, maybe thirty feet away. I want to run, but it's sitting on the Crossroads, and I told Wilbur I would meet him here.

Does the ghoul know I called in help from the graveling? Can she possibly have known what I agreed to in the little Parisian café? My hand goes to my amulet by instinct as I imagine her changing into a flea or something, coming along for the ride on me unnoticed. I don't know why it didn't occur to me before this would be possible. Would she have been noticed by anyone?

Although that would mean she'd have voluntarily tagged along on a trip that involved not-insignificant danger, and she doesn't strike me as the kind to do that unnecessarily.

The snake has noticed me. It winds its way toward me over the snow with breathtaking quickness, the movement of its dark body against the white reminding me of oil sliding over water. I force myself to release my amulet. It's going to do its job. I have to trust that.

My feet are anchored to the ground as the snake circles around me. I fight the almost irresistible panic from some deep mammalian part of my brain. I already gave into panic once in the last few days, and the embarrassment of that moment is still fresh, even if only Max saw it. I clench my teeth and take deep breaths, doing my best to remember the many terrifying encounters of the last nine months that all ended in me surviving unscathed. Or, at least, only temporarily scathed.

I can't help but feel that I passed some test when the snake stops churning. I'm just beginning to wonder how we're supposed to have a conversation when it's currently incapable of speech when it begins to display the first signs of uncharacteristic snake behavior—other than being out in the middle of winter in a cold climate, that is.

It winds around on top of itself, assembling its bulk into a person-like column. It's hard to say how it manages not to fall over, other than the sheer strength of the muscles along its length and, presumably, a certain amount of practice balancing. Oh, and movement. Constant, churning movement as it gathers its long length away from the earth and into a single figure.

With an eerie suddenness, the movement stops. The snake, gathered up as it is, is perfectly still. I half expect to look around me and see time itself stopped—the way I know Aloysius can do inside his casino—but a plume of smoke in the distance continues to rise, and the sporadic snow flurries around me continue to fall.

It takes nearly a full minute for the snake in front of me to transform into a woman. The changes seem gradual, but also so profound. The rounds of the snake change color gradually to the same skin tone of the woman I saw in my kitchen a few days ago, knitting together and smoothing out, like clay molding itself into a new shape slowly and by its own volition. The face is the worst. The snake's head spreads and takes on the ghoul's habitual human face with a horrifying steadiness—spending too long in the chasm between natural shapes.

Does it hurt? How could it not?

When I can see no trace of the former snake, the naked woman before me tilts her head just slightly.

"That was quite a show to put on for me," I say.

"Snakes are good at waiting. Humans are good at speaking."

If it's at all strange to find your voice again after reforming your vocal cords, the ghoul doesn't show it.

"How did you know I'd be here?"

"This is the closest Crossroads to Springfield," she says. "And it's where you met your demon. I took a guess."

"Didn't want to hang around town?"

The ghoul snarls. "Not now that your wizard is involved. I've lived a long time, and I didn't do it by taking stupid chances."

"But you wanted to talk to me?"

How is she not freezing in this weather? And, while we're at it, where the fuck is Wilbur? It should be easier to deal with a woman than a snake, but the ghoul's presence is still unnerving.

"We have business. Have you accepted yet that there's no other option but to tell the gravelings what they must do?"

Right. Great. Because this is what I need right now.

"Can this conversation wait a day? There's kind of a lot going on at the moment." *Please say yes.*

The ghoul fixes me with a quizzical look. "A lot going on? With your side project?"

Since when is saving the world a side project? "I can talk to you about this, and I will. I know I need to. But there are some things I need to research. I have some ideas. I… I will get you fed."

I could swear she was still a snake from the cold-blooded look she gives me. And I feel like I deserve it for what I'm doing. There's no guarantee that my cremato-rium will work. Guaranteeing her kind food might mean helping mass murderers select their victims. Even if it was going on long before I was born, and I could maybe find a way to minimize the harm done, that thought won't ever sit right with me.

Of course, I could lie. I could take the list from Wilbur of the cities the trolls have delivered meat to. I could tell them those are the cities that are safe to feed in, rather than the cities that are dangerous. Which would be sentencing ghouls to a slow, painful death.

Save human lives, but intentionally destroy the lives of sentient beings that live much longer. Which brings me back to the question I asked Faisal, the one that he doesn't think is useful: Are they evil?

This is a moral dilemma I can't deal with right now.

We're not dealing in right and wrong. We're dealing in what gets us through the day and doesn't blow up the world before humanity has enough leverage to come out the other side in a better position.

"We're starving," the ghoul says. "We need food *soon*. We can live for millennia *if we're fed*. Dying is unacceptable." She takes a step toward me, the goosebumps all over her skin and an involuntary shiver from the cold unnerve me more than her words. I'd thought she was just immune to the cold somehow, but that body doesn't look immune. She just doesn't care.

"I'm not going to try to force the gravelings into tempting fate by betraying the treaty. That's too big a risk."

"You'd rather risk us exposing ourselves? Kill the humans your kind actually cares about, and risk the wizard's wrath at the same time? Why?"

Lie, Elizabeth. Lie like your life depends on it. "One species betraying the wizards is less of a risk to stability than two conspiring together. Especially the gravelings. And that's even if they would abide by my ruling if I tried to strong-arm them, which I'm not sure they would. And besides—I told you, I'm working on another solution. I just need to deal with this thing first. I'll get to you."

She takes another step closer to me. I resist the urge to throw my winter coat over her, the one I've got on over my yellow leather jacket. I need it.

"This is important, but you're distracted. What is it that's happening? Did you not find the wizard circles where the vampire king said they would be? Tell me."

"She doesn't have to tell you anything." A voice with a heavy Indian accent cuts across the flat, open field. It comes from a man I don't recognize. Heavyset, only an inch taller than me. Indian, with salt-and-pepper hair and a wide, kind face beset with pockmarks. He's wearing a thick, charcoal, woolen coat that reminds me of the military uniforms you see in Napoleonic movies. His boots, certainly, are better constructed than anything you see on modern-day shelves.

He walks toward us with an easy gait and a crooked but genuine smile, despite the growing tension hanging in the air between the ghoul and me.

"Who are you?" I ask. Although I think I know the true answer, and I think he's going to lie.

"I am Arjun. You have seen me before. I serve the chance demon you've bargained with."

Two lies for the price of one. Both that Aloysius is a demon, and that this man is a servant of him.

"You come here to interrupt?" the ghoul asks, though it sounds more like a statement than a question.

"My lady. You are a demon. I serve a demon. Should we not be charitable with each other?"

Lies, lies, more lies.

"You mean to intimidate me?" She draws herself up to the full height of her current form. What could she change into? I know she can get considerably smaller—the spider told me that. How much bigger could she get? A tiger? A woolly mammoth? A dinosaur? A creature of her own creation?

"I mean to mollify you," Arjun says. "To reassure you that the arbiter will be made to keep her word. That you have my master's stake on it that your arbitration will be settled by the end of the week, one way or another. Your wishes have been made known. She has informed you the matter is still in progress on her end. Thus reassured, you may depart."

Arjun comes to a stop a mere four feet from the ghoul, practically in striking distance.

"And if I don't?" she asks.

Arjun's friendly smile takes on an edge of menace. "My master gets his due from his dealings. And he's not your kind. He cannot extract value from a corpse. He will take it very personally if his best interests are countermanded."

For a long, long moment, the ghoul stands stock still. "I've heard stories of your master," she says slowly, so quietly that I have to strain to hear even on as still and quiet a day as this one.

"Some of them are true, and some are not," Arjun says. "Would you like to take your chances on which are and which aren't?" The glimmer in his eye is nothing but Aloysius. Which makes sense.

And just like that, the tension snaps. The ghoul gives Arjun a deep, melodramatic bow and spares a passing sneer for me before stepping into the Crossroads. We see her appear and disappear where Arjun had appeared before she's gone entirely. Hopefully to warmer climes. Or, at least, somewhere she can find some clothing.

I watch the Crossroads as though afraid she'll reappear. When she doesn't after twenty seconds, my shoulders relax. I take a look back toward my car, just to be certain that Wilbur hasn't driven up while I was otherwise occupied. Sure, I probably would have heard if he did, but better safe than sorry.

I step toward Arjun, feeling suddenly awkward. I haven't seen Aloysius since the thing with the sirens three months ago, though I'm aware he's been hearing my thoughts, and he's never been far from them. But I thought the next time I saw him, he would look more like himself.

"Hello, Aloysius," I say, looking at the man. He's not right. He doesn't have his usual intensity or pleased affection. He has a congenial outlook, sure, but it's not the same.

"That's not what you should call me," he says. "I am Arjun."

"Right, that's the name you just gave the ghoul. But you're an acolyte. You're a piece of Aloysius that he broke off to run his errands and do his bidding."

Arjun nods. "Your lover has been telling you all our secrets."

"Was he not supposed to?"

Arjun gives me a little noncommittal head wobble. "All the same, I am an acolyte. I have my life and my purpose in my master, yes, but I am myself as long as I exist."

I step close and walk around him, looking him up and down like the headmistress at a boarding school in a movie. He looks so much more realistic than I would have thought. There's more difference between him and Aloysius. Too much detail to be the cardboard cutout I'd imagined when Faisal told me about acolytes. But then, leave it to gods to go big on creation, however temporary.

"Do I pass inspection?" Arjun asks, clearly amused, when I'm standing back in front of him and looking at his face.

"Did you used to be someone?" I ask.

"I *am* someone. Intermittently."

He may not have all of Aloysius's personality at the moment, but he's got his talent for exasperating responses, regardless.

"I mean, you're based on someone. Someone who was real."

I regret the words as soon as they come out of my mouth for the sadness they bring. I don't know if it's regret that he's not *real*, as I put it, or simply nostalgia. Ancient grief, maybe.

"Memories make it easier for Himself to build, that's so."

I was the one who took us down this *Let's talk about who you are!* road, but I wish I hadn't. Luckily, there's plenty of ground to cover. Even if it doesn't feel right to yell at Arjun for Aloysius's decision to knowingly allow me to keep breaking the veil between life and the necrowizards' afterlife. "Thanks for interrupting that. I didn't know how to get her to leave," I say.

Arjun gives me that little head wobble again. "You are most welcome. But that isn't what I'm here for."

"It isn't?"

"No." His magnanimous expression melts to something more serious. Something regretful. "You were preparing to make a journey. To go have a talk with Himself. I've come to tell you not to bother."

Not to bother? Maybe it's the whirlwind of confusion and heightened emotions that the last few days have held, but I'm suddenly furious. "He's not even going to talk to me?"

"What is there to talk about?"

The rumbling of a car in the background draws Arjun's eyes and tries to pull my attention. I won't let it. We have limited moments before Wilbur shows up.

"What is there to *talk about*? This whole thing is to do with gods. It's god power. And it's threatening the balance of the world. What, is *Himself* just going to sit by and do nothing? He's not going to give me any help? Any clues? Any assistance?"

Arjun's voice carries a weird mix of indulgence and the warning end of patience. "Is the bargain you made unclear to you? I am under the impression this was discussed in Chios."

"Discussed, yes, but not…" I flounder for words. "He said he wouldn't help, I know. It would taint his precious worship from me. But surely this *has* to be an exception."

"Why?" Arjun asks, looking for all the world like he's legitimately curious.

The slam of a car door in the distance again draws his eyes. I can't ignore it fully this time. I turn in time to see Wilbur take a step toward me and Arjun, but I hold up a finger in a *one minute* gesture. Wilbur hesitates, and I add on a smile and a shrug. I watch him struggle with his own natural cautiousness. This has been an issue in the past, before he gave up and accepted that being mad at me for taking risks wouldn't get us anywhere. Even centuries-old creatures can sometimes show personal growth. Wilbur folds himself back into his car and shuts the door.

"Because I'm in over my head," I say at a whisper. Trolls don't have super hearing or anything as far as I've been able to glean, but better safe than sorry. "I need *help*."

Arjun smiles. "Himself is betting you don't."

You have to be fucking kidding me. "Well, he's betting wrong. I have his luck, sure, great. And I have a dumb plan that sounded a whole lot better to me before I really thought it through. I need *more*. I need backup that isn't angry at me, super killable, or eager to wipe my brain the second they get the chance. I need Aloysius to help me."

That same maddening smile never leaves Arjun's face. "No, you don't. He believes you will be all right. Or, at least, that you will survive."

"He *believes*?" I say, my incredulity warring with my attempt to keep my voice low.

The same infuriating smile. "It is a bit of a reversal that *he* believes in *you*, I suppose. But traditions were always made to be broken when they need to be."

Who had the real Arjun been? What had he done to make Aloysius want to recreate him? How close was it to who he is now? Sorry, who he is now *intermittently*. I sputter, looking for words to tell him how unacceptable this is, but I don't have any solid ground to stand on. Arjun isn't as intimidating and impossible to argue with as Aloysius, sure, but he also doesn't work for me. If the ghoul couldn't bully him, I certainly can't. And although I have more damning information on Aloysius than I do on any of the other two ancient creatures I've blackmailed in the last week, I'm not anything like stupid enough to think that would work out the way I'd want it to.

"Do not come looking for the Casino," Arjun says when it's clear that I'm not going to come up with anything. His infuriating smile has finally melted into an expression with a little bit of Aloysius's usual sparkling seriousness in it. "You will not find it, no matter how many Crossroads you look at. And if by some stolen miracle you do, its doors will be closed to you. At least until you have concluded your business. Himself wishes you the best of his luck."

Arjun gives me a bow, short and curt and military in the same way his jacket is, before stepping into the Crossroads and leaving me alone and disappointed in the fallow, snow-covered field. I trudge back to the road, putting together how I'm going to apologize for wasting Wilbur's time.

We are, in the end, on our own.

TWENTY-TWO

A Test

It would be easier if I knew for certain that I was going to die at the necrowizards' Yule ball. Then I'd know how I would use up my final afternoon. But alas, there's no certainty either way, so the time is spent doing everything I most want—sleeping with my boyfriend, watching my favorite movie, and getting takeout from our favorite restaurant—while still being worried that there's something else I should be doing to increase my chances of success.

By the time the appointed hour arrives to head over to Max's house to enchant the infinity pouch, I can't tell whether I feel good or bad about any of it. I only know that I don't want this to be over, and that I don't share Aloysius's faith in me, and I wish he had a little less of it.

I haven't been to Max's house since the advent of the holiday season. I don't actually come here often—really just to get healed up after an arbitration goes awry and things get messy. I'm not expecting the above-and-beyond that he's gone with the Christmas decorations.

Of course, I should have. Max is exactly the kind of guy that would throw himself headfirst into the holiday.

The sun is setting, and it's just dark enough that the metric shit-ton of lights he very well may have magicked into place in the middle of the night make the whole massive Victorian sparkle, reminding me uncomfortably of the frost on the ghoul's spiderweb a few days ago. There are evergreen boughs intermingled with the lights in strategic places around the porch and on the handrail. And then there are red ribbons and holly berries in all the right places.

It's all very over the top, sure, but also tasteful. I'm not sure why, but that bothers me. Maybe because it reminds me of the general outlook of his masters, and the idea that they may come to see him at some point during the season—or even that they already have. Probably more so that he would care what they think about his decorating choices. I know Max rebels against them. I'm happy to aid and abet that rebellion. I'm uncomfortable with the idea that his rebellion has its limits. I know it must, sure, but I don't want to be reminded.

Faisal talked his way into coming, and I agreed, even as uncomfortable as I always am with Faisal and Max being in the same room without an amulet around Faisal's neck to protect his mind. Olivia, too, said that she was going to come, as did Wilbur. They both beat us here, and we have to park—gasp—on the manicured street like commoners.

Inside, the house is as thoroughly and tastefully decorated as the outside. The only concession to how I imagine Max really wants to decorate is the bright, tacky, ugly Christmas sweater he has on as he leads us into the living room.

As I always do when I enter Max's house, I fight down a moment of panic at seeing the clear coffee table that I know is actually a hiding place. I hid in there twice. The second time, I almost suffocated. And now I'm about to do it again.

"I'll show you mine if you show me yours," Max says brightly as I sit down. I get a pang of missing Gigi, though I'm not sure why. Maybe because she'd have had something to say about his innuendo. But I just give Max an *after you* gesture.

He disappears into the other room as Faisal rubs my back, not able to tell that I'm missing Gigi, sure, but able to tell that something's wrong. When Max returns, the object in his hand reminds me of a clear, plastic garment bag.

In fact, as I look closer, it *is* a clear plastic, zip-up garment bag.

"Excuse me?" I ask.

Max's face falls. "I thought we were on the same page with this. We wanted a version of my coffee table vault, but one that you could fit in the pouch once enchanted."

"I think she was hoping it wouldn't look so much like a body bag," Olivia says, though without any warmth for me.

"Body bags aren't clear." Max frowns.

"I won't even fit in that," I say, trying to keep the panic out of my voice. "Why couldn't you use something bigger?"

Max looks back and forth between the garment bag and me. "It needs to be clear or mostly clear to work. I had like a day to find something I could enchant that would fit the bill. This'll fit you, and it already has a built-in zipper."

"If you knew it was going to be a problem finding something you could enchant in the time frame, you should have asked for help," Faisal says, the anger in him only betrayed by the stiffness in his body as he sits beside me.

"This will fit. It'll be fine. And I'm going to tell you

how to get out of it, so you don't need to freak out about it."

Don't need to freak out about it. Really easy for him to say. He's not staring at the thing that he almost died in.

"Maybe we can do this in another room?" Faisal says.

A momentary hint of confusion passes across Max's face before he shrugs. "Yeah, okay. Sure."

He brings us up to a room on the second floor of the house that could, I suppose, be called a den. It has what looks like a rarely used pool table with a poker table insert made to sit on top of it. I have a hard time imagining Max playing pool, until I remember he almost certainly has a way to cheat, both in his own favor and in the favor of whoever he's playing with, and that winning isn't *not* an aphrodisiac. It's not difficult to imagine him bringing women back here and feigning amazement at their pool skills. It's a little distasteful. But then again, the room does have more space than downstairs, and I've never almost died here, and that's all that really matters.

Max lays the garment bag back down on the ground and unzips it. He wasn't wrong—I do fit, however uncomfortably.

"You should do this yourself," Max says, his hand hesitating on the zipper. I nod and put my shaking hand over his. Then he lets go, leaving me to zip myself in. I take a deep breath of the air around me, as much to steady myself as to make sure I'm entering the thing with as much air already in my lungs as possible.

Everything in me screams not to move the zipper, but I don't listen. I draw it up, scrunching my body down as much as possible. I have to stop to smooth my hair out of the way so that it won't get caught as the zipper goes up over my head. For the last inch or so, I have to pull my fingers back inside the bag and use my fingernails to nudge the zipper to the very end of the track.

I know when the bag is fully sealed off from the outside world by the reaction of the other people in the room. Faisal twitches, quickly shutting down his involuntary panic at my sudden disappearance. Wilbur raises his eyebrows in a kind of casual surprise, the way you might if you see a cat make a jump up onto a bookcase it really shouldn't be able to. Olivia's mouth drops open in transparent amazement. And Max…

Well, Max just looks sad, squatting down beside me. He reaches down in a quick, certain motion to unzip the bag. I almost hit his head with mine as I sit up the second I'm able to, my breath heaving in and out. Faisal's at my side, his hand in mine as I take a long second for my panic to subside.

"It works," I choke out.

"It works," Max says, almost regretfully. "Now to make sure you can get out of it yourself."

I nod. "*Stregur fishui*," I say, doing my best to pronounce the words he said on the phone to me last night.

Max bares his teeth in a mocking, overdramatic wince. "Ouch. That is *not* how I said it last night."

It's a devoted attempt at making me laugh, but it's off-key, considering that I'll die if I can't get it right. Max takes a few minutes to coach me on my pronunciation, making little micro-corrections with each repetition.

"That's it," he says at last. "Let's give it a try. I'll give you five seconds and then let you out. I'll count. You've got Right Mind?"

I smile. "A desire for attention. To be seen. Must be pretty easy for you."

Max rolls his eyes with an enthusiasm that would make

Gigi proud, but he seems to be glad underneath that I'm cracking a joke before I go back in.

Does Max feel as good as I do to have him instructing me again, the way he did in the siren library three months ago? How can he not? I don't know how to read the fleeting look of regret on his face.

I lay down and maneuver the zipper back up into place. As before, the reactions of the people in the room with me tell me when I've disappeared from their view, although all of their expressions are more muted this time around. All except Olivia, maybe, whose shock and amazement has changed into a laser focus—like if she can just devour every detail of what's going on, she's going to be able to see how it works. I'd read it as another manifestation of her anger at me if I didn't know her, but it's not that. Olivia's care is expressed in action—always has been. If anything, her transparent greed to understand the situation I've put myself in makes me feel loved, even strained as things are.

I take in a breath of the precious, plastic-scented air of the garment bag and shove down my panic. I have the tool to get out of here. Right Mind is easy to get into, considering how much I truly do want everyone in this room to be able to see me again. The words are a little harder, but on the third try, I get them.

I was expecting the spell to break. I wasn't expecting the zipper to shoot, with the speed of a runaway train, from the top of the bag to the second. My surprise at the movement hits against my shoved-down panic, making me shoot up out of the bag again, just as visibly shaken as I had been the last time.

Faisal's hands are on my shoulders before I can reach for him. "Well done," he says, his voice steady. Max shoots him an annoyed look.

"Looks like you got it," he says, like he's uncertain about it.

"We should do a few more times," Faisal says, with a tone that leaves no room for disagreement. "So you can troubleshoot if she runs into problems."

"A few more times" turns out to be twenty. Olivia has gone through enough higher education that she's well practiced in not looking bored, and I'm not sure if trolls are capable of boredom. Faisal is also, if I had to guess, too terrified each and every time I disappear that he is still fully engaged in the process, even though I stop needing him to talk me down after the third repetition.

Max, however, is visibly less interested in the entire thing after the fifth try and growing almost annoyed by the fifteenth. I feel pretty judgmental about it until I realize how strange and dumb it must look to him. His eidetic memory, after all, means that he's never needed to study, and his wizard sense for doing spells correctly means that *practicing* magic must be more or less foreign to him. Has he ever run up against a challenge he hasn't had some way to shortcut or avoid before in his life? Jesus, I must look like an idiot to him.

"I think you've got it," he says, when he can take no more. I'm not as certain, but I also think I could use a break between now and when I practice again, mostly to give my brain time to forget if it's going to forget, so that I can practice remembering.

"Let's move on to the pouch," I say, glad that my mental exhaustion from facing panic and escaping certain death over and over is a good cover for my excitement.

It *is* almost Christmas, after all. Only right that I should be getting the one thing I would ask Santa for if he existed.

I rifle in my bag to produce the pouch, candles, and the three-by-five notecard that I wrote the incantation on.

Getting the whole thing set up and the candles lit is a comfortingly familiar process, though it's a little weird for me to be sitting on the wrong side of all of it.

Max mouths the words on the card while I get it all set up. Is it my imagination, or does he seem more relaxed than I've seen him almost ever? In his element, I suppose. About to show off with a spell that he must know I've been struggling with. About to show me he can do something that I can't, even with instructions and endless effort.

Whatever. I shove aside the jealousy he surely wants me to feel. And even though he keeps his voice low as he's enchanting the pouch, I'm still able to hear him. I cling to each and every syllable, repeating it again and again in my head. I may not be able to record the words on my phone with the protections Max has in place in his house, but that doesn't stop me from doing my best to remember. And after all this practice, my best is getting pretty good. For a human, at least.

It takes less than a minute—mere seconds, really—for Max to complete the incantation. I see no difference. There's no magic sparkle or anything, even with my glasses on. But Max's smile tells me he *felt* something. The feel of magic working correctly. The certainty that he's done it right because the magic itself is telling him so. Something I'll never feel.

But I can feel the sense of relief as I roll up the garment bag tightly and work it into the pouch. It's a little bit of a tight fit, getting the roll into the mouth of the pouch, and there is no way the length of it should be able to go in. But it just keeps disappearing as I keep pushing it farther in, until it's completely gone. And the second I withdraw my fingertips, the pouch looks for all the world as though there's nothing in it.

I put my hand back in the pouch. Nothing but cloth.

But as I think of the garment bag, I feel the squeaky-new plastic grazing my fingers, just waiting to be seized and pulled back out.

This is going to work. Relief floods through me—right until the moment the doorbell rings.

TWENTY-THREE

A Celebration

Max's face brightens, his flashing green eyes alive and merry. "Guests are here!"

For one horrifying moment, I'm afraid he's invited wizards to come here. A whole passel of them to skin me and Faisal and Olivia alive, getting around my amulet somehow and forcing me to hand over the trove. But that doesn't make sense. If Max were willing to have Faisal or Olivia be tortured in order to force me to hand over the trove, he'd have done it already. And we *just* did some contraband magic that he shouldn't be doing where anyone can see him.

He bounds downstairs, and I follow at his heels, shoving the pouch into my purse. I can feel the bulk of the rest of our little party behind us. He heads right for the front door and swings the solid oak-and-stained-glass antique slab open.

Behind it, looking for all the world like a group of cheerful carolers in the pre-Christmas cold, is our coworker Angela, her husband, and our other coworker Jean.

"Merry Christmas!" all three of them say, joyfully

oblivious to what a very unmerry Christmas it is. They're holding up bottles of wine that I'm sure are a fraction of the cost of anything Max might buy himself.

"Merry Christmas!" Max says back, stepping away from the door to allow them entrance. "Come in, come in! You're the second to arrive after Lizzie and her people."

Lizzie and her people. Second to arrive. A wry smile finds its way to my lips. I follow the flow of people inside, noting the car that's already parking across the street, and another car that I swear I've seen in the office parking lot making its way toward us as well.

"I'm glad you made it, Lizzie," Angela says to me in the unintentional stage whisper people sometimes take at parties when they feel it's a show of some kind. "I thought you said you were going to be too busy for the office party this year?"

I offer something non-committal and let her pass by me. Don't office parties usually happen in offices? All of the past ones did, I seem to recall. But of course Max would offer his home as a venue. And of course it would be accepted. And of course I would be too distracted with everything to know when it was going to happen.

Say what you will about Max, but the man can throw a party. Turns out most of his party treats and libations were in the kitchen when we arrived, so we didn't see them, but they are extensive. And everyone at the office other than the mayor herself shows up. And I imagine the mayor would probably have shown up if she didn't think it would make it harder for the rest of us to cut loose.

I don't drink too much. Tomorrow is going to be hard enough without a hangover of any kind. Plus, whenever I get close to any red wine, I'm reminded of Claude, the dagger, and what I had to do to get it. I feel corrupt, which isn't a good feeling around all of my fellow local government people. Plus, it makes everything about this celebration—about these people and the real, normal life that they represent—just feel hollow. And that makes me feel like shit.

But if I don't think about things too much, it's good to be here. It stops me from getting too much in my head during the evening, and I need that. I need the joy and the togetherness and all the messy edges of gossip and the awkward exchanges brushed aside by genuine affection, delicate the way it always is when people are interacting with each other in a new context. It's something to fight for.

Gradually, I come around to the idea that I'm glad the party is at Max's house. Because if I want anyone to have a reason to fight for humanity, to see us as whole and interesting and interconnected and worth saving, it's him. I watch his face as he lights up in conversation with Christine from Budgeting and her husband, who used to work in Admin before he got a job elsewhere.

It warms me, right up until Max catches me looking at him and winks. Like we know something they don't, which we do. Like we're separate from all of them, which we are.

And suddenly, the whole effervescent quality of the evening falls flat. I head to the back of the house and step out the door into the well-kept garden. The cold of the night bites at me, but I need air. I need space to breathe, even if being in the garden again reminds me of the time the graveling spirit snatched Max and me from this very spot.

Everyone in that room is in danger because of me. Wizards take a burn-it-all-down approach, and when I allowed Max to become enmeshed in my life, he became enmeshed in theirs. The closer he gets to them, the more likely it is that Kristoff or whoever will kill them when they're cleaning up whatever eventually becomes of this fucked up dance we've got going on. I didn't have any more right to do that to them than to do what I did to my sister. It's right that she blames me for it.

My skin feels hot, and the air is freezing in my lungs as I take breath after calming breath, trying to clear the nausea that this wave of guilt has brought on. I don't realize I'm not alone until I feel a hand on my upper arm.

"Beth?"

At Olivia's voice, I turn to face her, trying to put away my overemotional mess. She's talking to me. I need that. I've been wanting that.

"What's wrong, Beth?"

Oh, Jesus. Not like I can really talk to Olivia, of all people, about my guilt about how I brought Max into our lives. It's all too little too late.

But hell, maybe I can try.

"I'm just thinking everyone would be better off... you know... if they didn't know me."

Now that the words hang in the air, I wish I hadn't said them. They sound like fishing for reassurance, which I didn't mean to do. Olivia takes her hand back, crossing her arms in front of her. Her usual stable of cardigans has been laid aside this evening in favor of a chunky sweater that gives her more protection against the cold than my thin long-sleeve colorblock knit shirt does, even with the scarf I threw on.

"Is there a point?"

"What?"

"Is there a point to making yourself feel sick about it? To marinating in the guilt? Would it make you make different choices?"

Her words spark anger, which is more useful than guilt but not any more pleasant. "I'm making the best choices I can," I say. I should be groveling. Apologizing. Why won't she just let me apologize?

Olivia huffs and looks around us as though appealing to a silent audience sitting somewhere in the boughs of the trees. "And they work out! So you'll keep making them. You're lucky now, and someone has to make the hard calls, so why would you do any different?"

"What the fuck do you want me to say?" I ask. "I'm sorry? I'm sorry."

"You are, but that doesn't matter. Because you'd do it again. And I don't get to say that you shouldn't, because it's the right thing for you to do, and I'm a selfish asshole if I ask you not to."

I don't want to be standing anymore. Don't want to submit my whole body to the night air. I sit down on the back porch step, trying to save some of my rapidly escaping heat by scrunching up tightly. The slight sway of Olivia's body betrays her instinct to join me, but she remains standing.

"I *am* sorry, though. I'm sorry about the way it is. I'm sorry that I could do it. I shouldn't have been able to do it."

It. Don't make me say what *it* is. Don't make me say that I decided to risk bringing you down with me at the possibility of saving myself. Don't make me say that I said the words that might have killed your daughters, with full knowledge of what I was doing. Don't make me make it plain for us both that *I'm* the one who's the selfish asshole.

"I can't forgive you," Olivia says. "I'm trying, but I can't. If it were just *my* life…"

Fair. Fucking fair. I try not to think about it, but Olivia's probably unable to stop thinking about it. God knows I would have that shit on repeat in my brain if I were her.

"Do you want me to get you out of it?" I ask. "I know Max is acting like your friend, but I'm the one who has what he wants. If I ask him to take away your memories, he will."

That gets a harsh laugh that hurts to hear and looks like it hurts her to make. She sits down beside me on the stairs, looking out at the night with me.

"I know he'd erase my brain. He already has."

My blood runs cold, followed by a wave of adrenaline. It's all I can do to stop myself from heading into the house, finding Max, and... I don't know what. "What are you saying?"

The uneasy, absent look that began to grow on Olivia's face when we started talking around the choice I'd made in the cavern becomes harder, more distinct.

"He had to try," she almost muses. "You know he did. I have access to the trove. So he gave me a kiss on the cheek before I'd really seen what he could do with one of those. And for a little while, everything he suggested seemed like a great idea. He told me to open up the trove on my computer so that he could leaf through it. I tried. But when I tried to do the two-factor authentication with Wilbur, Wilbur could tell he wasn't the only person inter-acting with my mind and refused. So Max told me to walk into your house, grab the trove, and bring it out to him. You weren't home, but I have your key. And I didn't mean you any harm. So I walked into the house. But the second I did, I recognized what Max was doing to me. His control didn't work through the wards, I guess.

"I wrote an email to myself, detailing all of this. And I don't know what happened afterward, because I don't remember, and it wasn't in the email. I imagine I must have gone back out. Maybe we fought. I'd like to think I at least yelled at him."

I'm torn between my desire to scream at Max and my desire to comfort my sister. I reach out to put a hand on her shoulder, but she flinches.

Ah, right. Because I'm a monster she can't forgive, too.

"Wilbur didn't tell me about this."

"I asked him not to. Because it would make you not trust Max, and you need to trust him. For the sake of getting anything done. And he needs to be trusted. Because there are worse things that he could do, if he decides that getting the trove is really all that matters. And the longer we keep that on the other side of his imaginary line of what he will and won't do, the better. The longer we'll have to take the option out of his hands."

She's colder than the night around us. More calculating than I've ever seen her.

"Why tell me this now?"

"Because he's about to whisk you away on a private jet to put on a beautiful gown and go to a party in a castle and save the world together. That needs to happen. But you need to keep perspective, too. Remember where your priorities are."

I don't know if I'm numb from her words or because I've sat outside for too long. "I know what my priorities are."

Olivia hugs her arms closer. Feeling the cold a little more now, I guess. "Good. I understand you making hard choices. I understand you making choices that hurt *me*." Just not her daughters. "But I wouldn't understand you making hard choices for the wrong reasons."

I'm not a big crier. Never have been. But I have to blink my eyes to keep it that way. "That's fair."

I rub my numb hands across my too-wet face. "You know, I'm not feeling much in a party mood. I think I'm going to head home."

I get up to go in the house, but before I disappear inside, Olivia speaks again. "But that's not why I came out here."

I turn, and she comes up close to me, the two of us sheltered in the relatively small space in front of the doorway.

"I've spent the last six days reading everything I can find about wraith encounters. Not just this week, but further back. Cross-referencing trends with anything I can find in the trove. And I don't think this plan is going to work."

"Olivia—"

"I know we're still going to try it. We have to. But in case it goes wrong…" She digs in her pocket and pulls out a set of ten silver coins, and another two long chains to match the one I already have left over from Scotland. "Silver is important. And coins. There's more than one account of wraiths trying to get people to give them silver coins. I don't know why. But if they're valuable to them, it seems worth it for you to have some."

"Thanks," I say, looking at the way the silver gleams in Max's over-bright LED porch light.

"I don't want you to die," she says, like it costs her something. With that, she retreats into the house. I don't follow her right away.

TWENTY-FOUR

A Flight

Flying on a private jet is an entirely different experience from flying commercial. Add to that a wizard who has no problem employing any tool in his vast magical arsenal to minimize inconvenience, and the whole experience is friction-free. If I'd slept at all last night, I might appreciate it more. Maybe I'll get some sleep on the plane. I'll need it.

In the meager predawn light, Faisal pulls up right next to the stairs that lead onto the plane. We took my sedan, and I get a weird feeling of closeness the way I always do when he drives my car. I don't think it would be so strong if it were a cleaner, newer vehicle. Old, broken-down cars mold themselves to their owners the way new cars just can't. Faisal driving my car feels like he's wearing my sweatshirt.

"You don't like this plan, do you?" I ask again, as though I haven't asked him several times before. I don't know what I keep asking him for. To give me an excuse to cop out, maybe. To have him tell me that absolutely not, under no circumstances should I go. That he wouldn't allow it. That it would be a betrayal of him and our relationship if I prioritized fixing wizard problems over staying alive to be with him. Hell, maybe he could even fly into a jealous rage about me going to a party with another man. If he did all that—said all that—I couldn't go. I could stay in Springfield and watch the world burn down around us.

And feel horrible about it for the rest of my possibly very short life.

He doesn't give me a straight answer, as he hasn't been able to the other times I've asked him. Instead, he pulls me in for a kiss across the console, the heater blasting to try to keep us warm.

"I got you a Christmas present," he says, when I can't justify extending the kiss any longer. He pulls out a little box, and for a horrible second, I have the Pavlovian *oh my God, it's a ring* response to my boyfriend pulling out something that looks like a jewelry box. But it's much too large for that, and when I open it, I find an antique watch instead.

"I know you've got your phone for time," he says. "But I thought this might come in handy, the way time's getting wrapped around everyone's fingers in this thing. And I thought you'd like it."

We don't do gifts for Christmas anymore. Haven't in years. We usually just plan something special together that uses up the money we would have each spent on presents. But, for obvious reasons, we didn't get around to planning anything this year.

"I love it," I say. I stifle the urge to tell him I didn't get him anything in return because A, that's obvious, and B, there's too high a chance he's going to say that coming home alive would be my Christmas present to him. The thought of hearing that right now feels horrible for reasons I don't want to look at too clearly.

"I wish you hadn't made me try to slap you last night," Faisal says, while I'm still putting together what I don't want to say.

"But you didn't slap me. And we had to know the amulet would work from the pouch if I'm carrying it," I say, as if he didn't know that. As if that justified asking him to do such a shitty thing.

"I know," he says. "I just hate that we did that last night."

Hates that it'll be a part of the last night we have together if I don't come back.

Oh, fuck this maudlin bullshit. "Well, if I don't come back, you won't remember it for very long," I say, bright and brash as all hell. Faisal's laughter echoes around the car and fills up something hollow in me.

"I love you," he says. I return the words and leave him, heading for the plane and trying my best not to slip on the pavement of the runway.

Max is already onboard. This plane is a good deal bigger than the last private plane we were on. It would have to be, though, since this one is crossing the world with us in it, and that one was intended for little domestic hops. This one even has a few little sleeping pods. No hostess, as far as I can see, which is for the best.

"All aboard!" Max says, his feet propped up on a footrest in front of him.

It's a skill, to swap out one feeling for another. To take anxiety and doubt and transmute it into reckless freedom. Max has had a lot of practice at that particular kind of alchemy, and he's a master of it.

I sit in a chair across the aisle from him. Comfortable as hell, naturally. "Let's get this show on the road."

I barely listen to the pilot's speech. He's got an accent, but I can't place it. Max and I wait until we get up into cruising altitude to start talking. When we do, it's him who starts us off.

"So, what do we want to do first?" he asks, his eyes bright and his smile wide. "Dress or spell?"

Fashion show at thirty thousand feet or delicate telepathy performed by someone who wants to rearrange the contents of my brain?

"Let's go with the dress," I say. At least if the communication spell goes wrong, and I'm not able to pick and choose how much of Max's influence I let into my brain as I want to, then I'll have gotten to try on all of the dresses he brought along that collectively cost as much as my house.

Max seems delighted by my choice. He slaps his armrests in a fun little rhythm. "Excellent choice, madam. Let me show you our collection."

I know Max is rich. I know Max likes to show off. I know that rich people often like to show off their riches. But I somehow didn't expect the sheer number of dresses that he prepared for me to choose from.

Because, sure, he didn't have time to find me a clear vessel larger than a garment bag, but he had time to assemble a boutique's worth of black-tie gowns.

Which means that he either just made a call and told some high-fashion store—are they even called stores at that point?—to put together a bunch of options and send them over, *or* he had them sitting around for some reason.

I'm going to choose to go with Option A.

I bite back a comment about being able to afford a crematorium or two. But I guess spending a ton of money on high-end fashion before heading to a party wouldn't raise the alarm bells that purchasing a business would.

Going for the fashion show first was a good choice. I've never been an exceptionally feminine woman, but I'm not a tomboy, either. I'm somewhere in the middle of the pack. So I can enjoy this extravagance without ever having had the motivation to make this kind of thing happen before.

And Max is an excellent fashion show audience, it must be said. He manages to compliment me convincingly without leering, which is good, because I'd hate to get in a fight with my only wizard ally in a flying airplane. He also stays mission-focused enough that we can pretend that we really *need* for me to try all of these on, and we couldn't have just picked one of the first ones that fit decently.

I end up going for a velvety little dark green number with long, slim sleeves and a full skirt. It has some strategic, asymmetrical cutaways on the top that make it feel artful and unusual to me, although I get the feeling from Max's expression that it's not the *most* fashion-forward thing he brought with him in the bunch. But I feel comfortable in it, and it miraculously already has pockets, so stitching in the pouch will be easy, and it won't look weird that I'm pulling things out of it—just so long as no one notices that the things I'm pulling out of my pocket have no business fitting in there.

"I'm glad you picked that one," he says once we're seated across from each other again, and I've finally allowed myself to be distracted enough to drink a glass of champagne.

"Why's that?" I ask.

"Because the Christmas present I have to go along with that one is one of my favorite options."

"We're not getting each other Christmas presents," I say, the champagne glass feeling less natural in my hand than it did a moment ago. "And if we were, then you know what I'd want, and you don't want to get me that."

"What you'd want?" he echoes.

"Help with literally any spell."

Max frowns. "Why are you trying to ruin me giving you a Christmas present?"

Good question. Why am I? "I don't know. Because this isn't a party, maybe."

Max smirks. "It is a party, though."

I stare at him and set down my champagne glass on a nearby little table.

"Okay, yeah, I get what you're saying," he says. "But it's *also* a party. And what we're doing is dumb and dangerous, and fuck me for trying to make things a little more pleasant, right?"

Maybe I am being unfair. I pick my champagne glass back up.

"It's part of your disguise, anyway. It's just also a present you can keep afterward. Hell, you could say the same thing about the dress if you wanted to."

I lean forward, feeling appropriately chastised. "Okay, sorry. Point taken. What's the rest of my costume?"

He smiles like he's won something and pulls a jewelry box out of his bag. I barely have time to remark to myself that this is the *second* one of these I've gotten tonight before Max opens it to reveal a pair of teardrop earrings with the biggest diamonds and emeralds I've ever seen. My eyes and mouth both gape.

Max beams. "Do you like them?"

"That's..."

Max seems able to tell I'm going to protest again. "Expected," he finishes for me. "You're supposed to be an ornament, and we ornament our ornaments. It's the old wizard philosophy: There's no such thing as too much of a good thing."

He holds the box out to me, and I take it. I don't agree with opulence on a philosophical level. But holy shit, does something inside me not care as I look at these things.

"I'll give these back to you as soon as we're done," I mumble as I close the box and put it away in my bag.

"You can try," Max says through a grin.

We decide to wait until after our layover in Paris to refuel the plane to prepare the communication spell. I don't think I'm going to be able to sleep at first, even tired as I am, but eventually I do, my hand clutching my amulet. Faisal and I did a little experimenting to confirm it last night, and it turns out the trove is right: Objects placed in the infinity pouch can only be brought to the surface to be removed by the thoughts of the person who put them in there in the first place. All that to say: I'm not scared that Max is going to steal my stuff while I sleep.

God, I should get better allies. For the entirety of the time we're sitting on the runway in Paris, I think about Claude, and the meeting we had in a little café not so far away from here—relatively speaking. I knew he wasn't to be trusted. He got me to let my guard down by letting me use him for my own purposes. And then he used that vulnerability to get what he wanted. Is that a pattern? Do I have a recurring point of failure?

When we're back in the air after Paris, the real test of trust begins. We sit on the floor of the plane, legs crossed, facing each other.

"I've got to draw something on you. It'll stay on for as long as the spell is active. Wizards will be able to see it if they see your bare skin, but it'll be invisible to anyone else. Where do you want it?"

I'm suddenly especially glad I chose a dress with long sleeves. He draws the sigil on the inside of my upper arm. True to his word, I can't see it. I think for a moment that I'm going to have to put my glasses on to draw the sigil on him, which would be unfortunate, because the way wizards look through my glasses—like a photoshop cutout figure not blended very well into the background—isn't my favorite thing to see. But Max does it himself, lifting up his shirt to draw the sigil on—*of course*—his perfect six-pack abs.

Once that's done, Max looks at me as though we haven't said a word to each other for months and were speaking now for the first time.

"You don't have to look so scared. It's pretty much like the communication stone that we used at the siren library. Only we don't have to hold anything, and we can turn it on and off, and we can send thoughts if we want to."

"I look scared, do I?"

Max laughs. "You totally did. And now you're trying not to, but you just look like you're scared and trying not to be."

"Can you really blame me?" I ask, my anger from last night over hearing what he did to Olivia rising up to the surface. Which is unhelpful. I don't need that right now. She shouldn't have told me.

Max shrugs, his usual steady smile faltering. "You don't need to be."

I don't believe him, but I try to look like I do. And whether he buys it or not, he picks up my wrist, raises it to his lips, and kisses it.

Hello? I hear in my mind.

It's Max. I *know* it's Max. But it doesn't feel like I expected it to. I'm not hearing his voice, per se. It's more of an insistent, benevolent presence. It's careful and a little bit afraid. The feeling of the voice reminds me of hugging a golden retriever.

Okay, yeah, Olivia was right to tell me.

Hey. I try to think back. Max lets out a joyous peal of laughter.

"What?" I say out loud. I didn't think I'd feel self-conscious about my mental voice. It's a whole new frontier for self-esteem.

"You're so sad, and sweet, and serious. And sorry."

All the S words, huh? I think at him. He doesn't laugh this time. Instead, his expression melts into childlike joy.

Something like that, the eager-to-please, afraid-to-offend voice in my head says back.

That's not going to be helpful.

"So it sends feelings along with words?" I ask.

Max shakes his head. "No. The feelings are just a way of telling whose thought it is. Call it a mental signature. That's one of the problems with the spell, actually. We can't communicate anything but the words. It'll be like talking over text message."

I'm not sure if that's a good thing or a bad thing. "Try to send me your experience," I say.

He does, and I have to close my eyes at the weird double-vision of seeing the inside of the plane from two opposite angles. And from seeing myself, which is weird. I try to focus on something other than sight, trying to take in as much of his sensory input as possible. I can feel my—his—heart racing in his chest. His breath is too fast, too shallow. As much as it seems like he's trying to bring it back into normal range with deliberate breaths, he's not able to.

And then, in Max's experience, I feel something entirely alien. A sense of myself extending beyond the borders of my body. The anticipation of a coming closeness.

I'm so lost in the newness and strangeness of this feeling—and of the joy that I'm getting to experience second hand what will never be mine—that I don't realize Max has my arm again until I feel his lips on my wrist. Joined with that strange sense is a second feeling of seeking and oneness, touching so close to his mind that I can feel his own deep, earnest affection.

"Hey!" I say and think at the same time, pulling my wrist back from him.

The impact of my thought and the violence of reclaiming my hand hits him like a slap. He gives me a sheepish grin. "You can hardly blame me for trying. I never forgave myself for not doing it last time."

"Trying to take over?" I ask. "Like you did with Olivia?" The words come out almost as a snarl. I didn't mean them to. I didn't really mean for them to come out at all.

Max's face falls. "Wilbur finally told you?"

Of course he'd think it was Wilbur. Maybe that was the purpose behind him telling Olivia what I'd done in the cavern in the first place. Keep us from being close enough that we'd share info.

Or maybe I'm adding in conspiracies where there are none. When has Max ever thought that far ahead, really?

"Can you really blame me?" There are layers there. He's got his brash, cocky face on, sure. But there's a little of his general earnest puppy underneath—that feeling of his mental signature. I always knew it was there, but I hadn't realized until tonight how much more authentically him it was than any other face he wears.

And how much I want to yell at him—even completely fucking justified as it is—makes me feel like a puppy-kicker. Which really isn't fair. Can't help myself, though. I level an uncompromising gaze at him.

"So, what's the deal with Moira?"

The change in subject trips him up. "What do you mean?"

"This whole plan hinges on you being able to goad her

into turning back the clock. I'd like to know what your deal is with her."

"She's my master."

"Yeah, I got that. Thanks. What's the deal with her?"

He knows I mean the kiss. The weird energy. The sense of possession, even though she's clearly with Kristoff. And Kristoff, so far as I can tell, raised him.

She's my future.

Him saying it in my head just makes the puppy-kicking feeling worse, which he has to know, right?

"Go on," I say out loud. "Details."

"Don't be cruel."

There's a warmth at my throat that I don't feel often—only when I'm mad. "Oh, is this invasive? Is it taking things a bit too far?"

"I *had* to try!" Max stands, and his sudden height advantage over me only makes it worse that this is the first time I've heard him raise his voice this loudly. "What don't you get? I'm not being selfish. I'm not being an asshole. I'm trying to save your fucking life. And Olivia's fucking life. And, hell, your boyfriend's fucking life. Probably even Wilbur's. You disagree with how far I will go to protect my friends, fine. I don't care. If I have a chance, I'm going to take it."

I scramble to my feet, a slight burst of turbulence conspiring with Max's size advantage over me to make me feel even more ridiculous as I try to match his sudden volume, but I find my voice so much hollower than his. "I didn't ask you to! I asked you *not* to!"

"I don't care!"

"You should!"

"No, I shouldn't!"

What do I say now? Start talking about how I have the right to make my own decisions? I sound like a teenager. I don't like how that makes me feel. I can't come up with a convincing argument if he won't buy into the essential concept that other people's choices matter. Without that, there's nothing to build on.

Another burst of turbulence hits, this one a little bigger. The first one was just an appetizer, apparently. I'm too lost in my own head and thoughts to notice until too late, and I might have fallen if Max hadn't reached out with both hands on my shoulders to steady me.

He looks like he wants to say something as much as I do, but he doesn't know what to say either. It's a relief to both of us, I think, when the pilot's heavily accented voice crackles over the PA system, informing us of the turbulence and insisting we should take our seats and fasten our seatbelts until further notice. I gather up my things and take up a seat behind Max. Facing backwards, so we can't see each other.

It's the same fight. It's always the same fight. It's always going to *be* the same fight. But Olivia is right. It's good to keep perspective in my mind, especially as we head into the lion's den. Or castle, as the case may be.

TWENTY-FIVE

An Entrance

I'm ready, for certain values of ready, when the lavish car Max had waiting for us draws close to the location on the necrowizards' gruesome invitation. I've got my gown, my earrings, my communication spell, and even a pair of single-use contacts Max enchanted to act like my normal enchanted glasses. Not sure how he did that, exactly—it's not a spell in the trove. Am I grateful he made them for me? Yes. Am I really fucking jealous he *can* make them for me so easily—so casually? Also yes.

When the driver arrived, he was concerned about how well we were dressed, given that the castle we were headed to was supposed to be in ruins. But as we draw closer to the site and see a perfectly good, honest-to-God castle festooned with wreathes for the holiday, the poor man must be eating crow seasoned with confusion.

But that's fine. Not like he'll remember his embarrassment for long.

The green dress fits well and is comfortable enough. I brought my shoes with me. They're nothing to write home about, but I can run in them if I need to, and the dress is long enough to keep their relative cheapness from being noticed. The infinity pouch is sewn into the pocket and contains everything I need for the job. In theory. If it all goes well.

You know how to act? Max thinks at me.

I give him a mental feeling of affirmation, which is easier than worrying about words. Probably annoying to feel, though, as I don't enjoy the mental nudge he gives me back. Words are nicer to have someone put in your brain than concepts. Harder to confuse with your own, carrying the sender's mental signature as they do.

Docile. Mind controlled. Follow where I'm taken. Wait until I'm not being watched to figure out how to get out of where I'm going. Sure you don't have anything you can tell me about where I'll hang out while you rub elbows in the wizard-only section?

The driver pulls the car up to the curb and gets out, intending to get our doors for us, presumably.

"You need to beat him out. Get my door for me," Max says in a rush. He forgot that was something he'd need to warn me about, apparently. We're off to a great start.

I scurry around out of the car, and only have a few seconds to push away my panicked expression before other wizards might see me. I put on the blank look that I practiced with Max on the flight. And when our driver lets out a hail of flustered words, I give him no reaction.

I'm to pretend nothing exists except for Max. The only thing I care about is any order he gives me. If I had enough frustration left over after… well, after everything else, I would be pretty annoyed.

But if feigned subservience is going to keep me invisible to the wizards, so be it. Every survivor in a zombie movie who has to cover themselves in zombie guts would kill to just have to act subservient.

Max, when I let his esteemed highness out of the car,

has his rakish confidence turned up to eleven. It looks good on him in a certain kind of way, even if I can identify the rough edges to his mask—and Moira and Kristoff will be able to, as well. But to these other wizards, who hopefully don't know him as well, he might be convincing.

In any case, "apprentice to the Boston bigwigs trying to play at being a bigwig himself but failing" isn't an unconvincing look. He doesn't have to come off well. He just has to look like he belongs.

Which he does.

I've never been to the servants' room. Max answers my question. I asked him this before, on the flight and the car ride here, and he answered it before, but treading over old ground makes me feel better as we make our way through the entrance. Helps me steady my heartbeat. I need to calm the fuck down, or people are going to think Max doesn't have me under sufficient control for the event and maybe, if they aren't afraid of Kristoff and Moira enough, decide to intervene and put me under their own mental spell. And when they can't…

That line of thought isn't helping to calm me down. I focus on the back of Max's head as I walk three steps behind him and to the left. I don't focus too hard on any of the pretty people around me. If it weren't for my contacts, I would be able to tell the other arriving wizards from their human servants only by their position as they walk, which I guess is why the position is so important. Other wizards would be able to see the difference, of course, but to me they would all just look hopelessly, implausibly attractive.

And as nice as this dress is, and as much effort as I put into a chic updo in the airplane mirror on our way here, I have never felt less attractive by comparison.

I always wonder what these people used to look like, Max thinks at me.

I blink once in surprise before remembering I'm not allowed to be surprised and not supposed to have anything to be surprised at. I want to tell Max that I always wonder what *he* used to look like before his make-me-gorgeous spell, but that feels too personal somehow.

Terrible, obviously. All threes at best, I fire back. If he's trying to make me feel better, let him think he's succeeded.

And he has a little. Right up until the first three people he talks to all comment on how extraordinarily ugly his human servant is, and how he really ought to do something about that. The reasons why range from it reflecting badly on his masters—whom everyone seems to know—to how it must impair his fun with me, to how embarrassing it must be to walk around in public with me.

Max toes the line we came up with for him: He has to keep my face the same because he's selected me for my position in local politics, and it would be far too much work to change my face, since it's a small town and everyone knows what I look like. I get the sense that no one thinks this answer is very good, but in my peripheral vision, they're more looking at him with disapproval than at me in suspicion, so we're all good. If Moira and Kristoff's precious wizard reputations take a hit because their apprentice is slumming it, I'm okay with that.

When Max gets into conversation with people who don't want to speak English, I attempt to scan the room for Kristoff and Moira. It's not easy to do without moving my eyes from the neutral stare at Max's feet that they're supposed to stay in. But as far as I can tell, we've beaten them here.

The entry room where everyone is mingling and showing off their servants is about what I'd expect. Tall stone walls with tapestries hanging from them. Chandeliers with candles. Twinkling lights that could easily be LEDs, but which I imagine are magic instead. The necrowizards haven't been in the modern world long, and although they didn't miss a beat in killing fifty wizard apprentices, their interior decorating hasn't exactly caught up to the contemporary era. They seem to have grabbed a handful of touches that are new to them to incorporate into the space. Some Rococo styling here. Some mid-century modern furniture there. The result of this historical magpie approach isn't necessarily cohesive, but everything is so well executed that it works better than it has any right to. Classical music that I don't know enough about to nail down to a time period drifts to us from a staircase. Down from where the real party is taking place.

How many conversations do you have to have here before you move to the adult table? I ask, the worry that Max's masters are going to come in any second and have an issue with me hanging over my head.

I think I've done the polite thing and ogled everyone's servants enough by now. Are you ready to split off? Max's mental signature in the thought doesn't change based on his current emotional state. We covered that on the plane. Still, I can't help but project a little trepidation into the words.

I'll be a lot more comfortable the farther I am from wizards and the less likely Moira and Kristoff are to see me.

Rather than reply in words, I get a rush of the concept of affection and the concept of hope—his version of "goodbye and good luck," I guess. He directs our path toward the music. Beside the stairs stands an attractive woman with a blank enough expression to be a human, but without a wizard standing by her to fixate on.

When we reach the woman, Max turns on his heel and looks directly at me. I keep my gaze down as I'm supposed to, but it's really hard not to look at someone when they're looking at you. Didn't realize that until just now.

"Go with her, Lizzie." And the nickname I hate under the circumstances should feel just a jab, but mostly it just feels like an inside joke.

As rehearsed, I turn my attention to the woman with no further acknowledgement of Max's order. And when she begins to walk me into the depths of the castle, I follow.

Every step we take away from the reception room full of mixed wizards and their servants, I feel better. I shouldn't, because we're running out of plan, and I have no idea what the fuck I'm going to do now without raising suspicion, but I do.

The human babysitter I'm following is a good four inches taller than me, and she has the same baseline beauty everyone here but me does. Her pin-straight Asian hair is also wrapped in an elaborate style, and while she's also gone for a green dress, hers is a shade lighter, a lot shinier, and it reveals considerably more skin. With the way we must look walking next to each other, any casual observer could see that we both chose the right dress for our general levels of attractiveness.

If I didn't know she was under a mind control spell, I'd try to make small talk. Try to figure out if there was some way to get her out of here. Some way to save everyone and run away. But the only way I'm going to get through this experience without screaming, breaking my cover, and getting myself killed before I can even accomplish anything is to think of all of the other servants here as already lost— already dead—and not think too much about the fact that they aren't.

Max timed our flight and car from the airport to be sure we'd get here reasonably early, and the thirty-foot-by-forty-foot or so kiddie table room is only sparsely populated. It's natural human instinct to want to group together in this kind of open space. I'd expect people to have formed clusters and sat down facing one another, even if they wouldn't be actually speaking. But wizards don't see any reason to leave room for human instinct, and the people in the room are seated seemingly at random, and seemingly without any rhyme or reason to the direction. It gives me the eerie feeling of being in a room of hyper-realistic mannequins, and when one of them moves to rearrange themselves to avoid a leg falling asleep or fix a stray hair, it freaks me the fuck out. The mismatch between everyone's fancy evening wear and the chairs—which look to have been bought surplus from a closed eighties restaurant—makes it feel even more like we're seldom-used dolls in a dusty case.

At least there's the fact that the servants don't have orders to look anywhere and don't have the curiosity to do so. I can move my eyes slowly around the room and observe them without fear that someone's going to out me as not belonging. Max and I have a contingency plan for that—that he'll just pretend to be an incompetent apprentice, and he'll ask Kristoff to help him put me under properly. Kristoff knows my secret, so he'll have to pretend to do so to avoid revealing it to the wizard community at large. The man wants me dead, but he wants me dead *secretly*. We can use that. But it would be a thin fiction for anyone who knows Max well enough to know he's a natural at mental magic—and would almost certainly put an early end to our evening and be the death knell for our plan.

Only about a third of the people here are men, which wasn't what I expected. I'd assumed there would be an even mix of men and women. But maybe that was a bad assumption. After all, I might not understand how new little wizards come to be, but I'm given to understand it's not the natural way that humans reproduce. Maybe there's some sex selection going on from the very beginning. No wonder they're all so unhinged—single-sex communities rarely go well. I can't imagine how a wildly unbalanced species would get along.

There I go again, trying to find excuses for the wizards being the way they are. What's wrong with me? And while sitting in a room full of their victims, even. The thought throws me to my conversation with Faisal in the early morning with his robe wrapped around me. The wave of longing to be back there hits me so hard it feels like a physical force.

In the moment. Right. Focus. Being able to move my eyes to look at what I want to look at is the tiniest piece of freedom I've ever treasured, but it's also absolutely nowhere near enough. Max hadn't really known what to warn me about. I had kind of been hoping we would all be stashed in a series of small rooms, and I could use the sedatives that I'd packed for just this purpose to knock them out and go running through the castle, away on my mission. But in a room like this, that plan isn't going to work at all.

Okay, Plan B. The restrooms. There have to be restrooms. Maybe I can go use the restroom and just… not come back. Not like there's enough higher reasoning going on in this room to notice, right? It's riskier than I'd like, but it'll do.

I scan the room with a purpose, and I realize only after a few seconds that I'm looking for European-style "WC" direction signs. Which, if this castle had been maintained and modernized by human hands, might be present, but are unlikely to exist in a structure rebuilt with magic.

Shit. Nothing to do but ask, I guess. That's not going to be too suspicious? Max doesn't actually go to these kinds of things. Hasn't been to one since he was still living with Kristoff and had no choice. Which makes me feel better about him as a person but isn't helpful at the moment. Max hasn't had occasion to learn the finer points of the spell he's supposed to have put me under, because he's never been the one with a servant in tow.

Which means he didn't know and therefore couldn't tell me if there were any circumstances under which I was allowed to talk. Well, allowed or not, I'm talking.

"Excuse me, but where is the bathroom?" I ask, addressing the person closest to me. It's a man in a dashing suit with a chiseled jaw and Fabio hair.

He doesn't respond. So much for that.

You all good? Max thinks at me. I want to imagine there's fear in that question, and he's afraid for me.

A little stuck. I share my current experience with him, letting my eyes scan over the room before I cut off the feed. *Any ideas?*

There's a longer pause than I'd like before he responds.

Sorry. Conversation. Nothing I saw that gave me any ideas. You have a plan?

Well, at least he knows I'm alive.

Wait and see, I guess.

Good thing we came early.

I send him back the concept of rolling my eyes. Or, at least, I think I do.

Just saying it was an excellent idea I had, and you should give me credit for my excellent ideas more often. Without tone, his playful feigned grandiosity would be easy to read as asshole-speak. It hits me how much like the inability to communicate sarcasm over text or email this is.

Somehow, we always end up coming full circle, don't we? Anything magic can make, we'll eventually create a technological equivalent for. I stop myself from going too far down this line of thought. It usually leads to the idea that eventually we'll invent enough technology that magic won't matter anymore, so why am I rushing things? I should just give in to Max and let him have what he wants. It's an excuse, not sound logic, and it's not going to help me right now.

That was a joke, I get from Max. I guess my pause was also ripe for misinterpretation.

Ha. Ha. Ha. You're hilarious. I give it another pause. *That was also a joke.*

And just when the little ins and outs of communicating with Max this way lull me into a more relaxed mood, the metaphorical line goes dead. He's busy making small talk with people who wouldn't hesitate to kill him if they had half an inkling that he'd let a human whose mind he can't erase into his head. Wizards have very clear ideas about how much power and influence humans should be allowed to have in any given wizard's life. They maintain those rules with draconian measures. And Max, these past nine months, has been joyfully flouting all of them.

If the other servants in here won't tell me where the bathroom is, I'll just have to wait for my babysitter to return.

It's no more than a few minutes, although I'm not watching the clock, before the escort comes back. But the sight of the woman she brings in with her makes me momentarily forget my plan.

She's a tall woman with freckles, cheekbones for days, and wild red curls like the Morrigan's that spill down over her shoulders and back, almost as low as her low-cut, skin-tight black dress. She has the same flat affect as everyone else in the room, but nonetheless I want to run to her and her familiar face.

Heads up, your masters are here, I think to Max. *Phoebe just got deposited in day care.*

I let myself look directly at her, even though I know I'm not supposed to. I can hardly help it. I'm searching for any scrap of recognition there, any sign that she remembers me or the conversation we had three months ago in Boston. The information she gave me was invaluable. She helped me save the world. She should know that. But even if I told her, she'd never be allowed to remember.

Is she all right? Max asks, and for once, I'm glad the words don't carry any tone with them. I don't want to be distracted by his guilt or angry at him for the lack thereof.

Because, no, Phoebe is not all right. Her mind has been written and overwritten at Moira and Kristoff's whims too many times to have anything left to *be* her. I think I would have liked to have known her as she once was. Max is adamant that the reason she's so mentally broken is because Kristoff and Moira just don't have the knack for mental magic, and that his own spells could never have that effect unless he wanted them to. But I'm not sure if that's something that's true, or simply what he wants to believe.

As fine as anyone down here, I send back, trying to move on and not get distracted. Knowing her—knowing her name and a little of her history—makes it harder for me to ignore the plight of the people around me, and I *do* need to continue to ignore it. I tell myself that what I'm doing is saving their lives, after all. If a wizard civil war breaks out —which it will if we don't nip it in the bud now—then their life expectancy leaves much to be desired.

That gets harder to do when Phoebe, instead of choosing a seat at random in the large room, sits in the seat directly next to me. She sits *with* me.

Shock will give me away. I lock it down, though my

slight gasp is hard to cover. For a second, our babysitter notices. But aside from a bare moment of her attention, nothing comes of it.

The babysitter stays in the room for longer than I wish she would before she finally goes. I'm impatient to try to make contact with Phoebe. It feels like a risk. No—it *is* a risk. But I'm also a little bit trapped, and if she can help me out here, I have to try.

"Phoebe," I whisper, quietly enough that she can hear me but no one else should be able to. Unless their senses have been enhanced, which is possible, but also just not something I can worry about right now.

Phoebe doesn't respond in any way. Not the slightest twitch or movement of her eye. I give it a solid minute before I try again, hoping that the response is just delayed.

Okay, whispering doesn't work. How about touch? Slowly, so as not to draw any attention from my fellow occupants on the island of dolls, I move my hand over to her leg. I nudge her. Soft enough that it won't be noticed by anyone else, but hard enough that she absolutely couldn't miss it.

Again, there's no response. Whatever spark in her that I thought her choosing a seat next to me indicated, it isn't strong enough to break through. Does she remember me, really? Or is it just the lingering aftereffect of talking to me in the past that led her to sit next to me now? At least she doesn't seem inclined to rat on me or react to my unexpected behavior in a way that's going to draw attention.

Either way, she's of no use to me right now. Time to go back to the ask-for-the-bathroom plan. And if that doesn't get me anything, I'll go ahead and try my chances at just walking out, and hope that the docility spell cast on everyone else in the room is strong enough that they won't even notice. I might not have tried that before, but

Phoebe's lack of response gives me hope it might be a viable option if all else fails.

Any progress? Max's thought cuts through my plans.

Not yet. I'm thinking. You come up with anything?

There's the barest pause before Max responds. *No. But whatever you're doing, you need to do it sooner rather than later.*

What? Why?

Max doesn't reply for what feels like a long time but is probably only thirty seconds or so. *Nothing concrete. But I'm kind of catching a vibe. Something's going to happen up here.*

We thought it might.

Yeah, maybe. But I thought it would take them longer. It's fucking tense, Beth. If I think at you to run, you need to get out, okay? Leave everything and run. Try to avoid being seen, but just get out.

I steady myself, trying not to get too caught up in my head with hypotheticals and possibilities. I'm tempted to ask Max to show me the ball—and all the gorgeous people and extravagant clothes and impossible feats of magic that must be going on up there. Somewhere over my head is where real life is happening, while I'm trapped down here. I want to be where the wizards are. I want to see, want to see them dancing…

And getting ready to slaughter each other? What a great fucking metaphor for my goddamn life at large. I'm not a fan.

Beth? You still there? You haven't answered. Is that a yes?

What the fuck does he want me to say? *I'll try to get out if you tell me to get out.*

And leave the rest. They won't follow.

My eyes scan the room.

They won't follow, Beth. You know that.

I know that.

I leave it at that, and so does he. I don't know if that's because he knows arguing is worthless, and in the end I'll do what I need to, or if someone drew his attention away. Either way, I'm off the hook for now.

After what feels like an age, our babysitter comes back into the room. My heartbeat spikes as I ready myself to pipe up and ask for the bathroom. But the words die on my lips when I notice she's not accompanied by a servant. She's not here delivering another one of us to the room. Which leaves…

She scans over the silent crowd, a light of intelligence in her eyes that has been sorely lacking in this room for as long as I've been in it.

I share my vision with Max, not wanting to put my suspicions into words.

Don't do anything to make her notice you. You don't want to be picked.

Fuck. I stay stock still, following Max's direction. The babysitter, seemingly having made her decision, walks over to a man with clear blue eyes and delicate features.

"Stand up and come with me," she says, her tone neutral. The man does as he's told.

I need to not respond. I need to leave it alone. I can't get myself caught. I didn't get them into the position they're in, and it's not my responsibility to get them out of it, and even if it were, I wouldn't be able to.

All the phrases I've been telling myself. All the phrases that aren't working anymore.

Max, what is going to happen to that man? I ask, glad that Max won't be able to hear the panic and fury in those words.

Nothing good. Leave it alone, Beth. You can't do anything about it.

I can't do anything about it. Fuck him. Fuck this. Fuck all of this. My temper rises.

I didn't use to have much of a temper. I was well socialized into constructive, peaceful problem-solving. But it's been developing swiftly since I learned about the brutality of the supernatural world, and like any small child, it can be hard to predict. I have to clench my fists to keep them from shaking, and even then, I don't do a very good job.

My distress is obvious. Maybe that's a good thing. Maybe she *should* take me in the man's stead. I have an amulet, after all. That's what a truly moral person would do, right? Don't risk others. Don't allow them to get hurt just because you think that what you're doing is more important? If I were that kind of person, maybe my sister wouldn't hate me right now.

But I'd also probably be dead. I'm at war with myself, and the battle is visible. Which maybe wouldn't be a problem if our babysitter weren't going to pass right in front of me on her way back to the door with the doomed man. She's more alive and alert in her mission, and when she comes within a few feet of me, I know I've lost the battle.

She looks at me with a spark of interest. She sees me, and she knows I wouldn't be acting this way if I were properly subdued. The jig is up.

TWENTY-SIX

An Intruder

The babysitter's eyes on me don't do much to help calm my nerves, although they work wonders for my moral dilemma. The prospect of being forced to make the moral choice that I was getting down on myself for not taking suddenly pulls all of my excuses into clear relief, and reminds me that, even though they sound like excuses, they also have the unfortunate quality of being true.

The babysitter steps toward me, lighting up with more interest every second. It takes everything in me not to clench my jaw, which would be just as noticeable. I let myself look at her, which I've noticed other people under the docility spell do, but I do my best to put on the glazed stare they carry.

It's not working. The babysitter has no apparent interest in continuing her mission. I want so badly to point out to her that she was given a task and that she's being distracted from it, and isn't that bad? If only I knew enough about this goddamn spell to be certain that trying to manipulate her this way wouldn't just backfire, which it seems likely to do.

The babysitter is a few inches from my face, which is shaking despite my best efforts, when she stops.

And... winks?

The blood drains from my face as confusion riles in my abdomen. Her perfect, tiny mouth quirks up in a subtle smirk. And then her dark, soulful eyes roll up, and just keep rolling. The revulsion at the inhuman act is as hard to force down as my terror. Pupils and irises rise back up from the bottom of her eye, as though her eyes have made a full rotation, but they aren't the same black of a human eye.

They're void. The kind of void I've only seen one place.

Realization dawns over me, and the ghoul gives me a tiny nod of recognition.

"What are you doing here?" the words spill out with a breath, so quiet that I can barely hear them myself.

The ghoul's voice is just as quiet as mine when she replies, although the words are considerably better formed. "Saving my species."

A thousand questions fill my head at once. But before I can pick one, my attention and the attention of every half-alive creature in this god-forsaken room is drawn by the sound of a noise like furniture falling from somewhere down the hall.

As one, the dolls stand, turning like soldiers to orient themselves toward the sound. My concern over fitting in had started to feel a little absurd, what with the ghoul showing up and acting as she pleased. But the militant focus that suddenly lit up the faces of all the human slaves tells me I was right to assume that, even in this state, they were programmed to protect their masters as well as serve them.

I get a sinking feeling in the pit of my stomach. I can't stop myself. I look at Phoebe. The same single-minded focus is there on her face as on the others. If she truly recognized that I was a threat, she wouldn't hesitate to kill me. She would die to do it.

One by one, the servants' heads turn to face the ghoul. It makes sense, I suppose—she was the one we were all told to listen to and follow. That's how they're programmed right now. And when she snaps her head around to me, a sliver of hope slides into my heart.

"This one will go," the ghoul says, the voice that isn't hers as clear as a bell. "She will investigate and protect our masters from the threat. The rest of you will stay here."

If the wizards had seen fit to trust their servants, allowing them any space for intelligence or free will in the situation, this wouldn't have worked. So maybe it's a nice little bit of karma that it does. Not that I believe in karma. But I believe in everything else now, apparently, so why the hell not?

In a dizzying display of simultaneous movement, all of the humans in the room except for me and the doomed man sit down. The ghoul continues toward the door, and both the doomed man and I follow her. When we get to the hallway, the ghoul turns left, and the doomed man follows behind.

I'm left with a choice. I can follow the ghoul, which seems like a bad idea. Or I can head to the right, which was the direction the sound came from.

I don't actually want to investigate the sound. I have my own problems to worry about, and my own goals to achieve here tonight. It's tempting to go the whole my-enemy's-enemy-is-my-friend route, except that I've learned from painful experience that it isn't always true. I've got a two-way grudge between me and Poseidon to tell me so.

But maybe it's because of the way I just saw human curiosity suppressed in so many other people that makes me think I should find out, just to be safe. Or maybe it's because I don't know what the ghoul's overarching plan to save her species is. I'm not sure that I want to know, other than that I don't want it to end up conflicting with mine, and the only way to be sure it won't is to know what it is. Maybe there'll be another ghoul there that can help me out. Maybe a whole pack of them that will turn into mice or some other useful thing, and they'll scour the castle for the Morrigan's heart so I don't have to worry that I won't be able to find it.

Hey, a girl can dream. Still, expected friendlies or no, I draw the sharpknife. Its ability to slice through almost anything might not be helpful to me without being able to say the right words and get into Right Mind first, but it does *look* intimidating. And that's not nothing. But it's also a wizard tool, so if I'm running into a wizard, I can still play like I'm enchanted and was just following orders. Hopefully.

With steps as quiet as I can manage in these dressy shoes, and my knife at the ready, I head toward the noise. I have to go farther than I thought. The sound had been loud enough that it had seemed close, but there's no evidence of anything that could have caused it in the hallway or any of the nearby rooms.

Suddenly, I feel cool, hard stone around my shoulders and pushing against my head, forcing me to look over my shoulder. It takes me a solid two seconds of confusion to figure out where I know this feeling against my skin from.

"Gigi!" I let out a hoarse whisper. "It's me!"

The stone arms around me loosen and let me go. I step out of them and turn to face Gigi, her gleaming stone and diamond eyes somehow more at home here in these surroundings than I've ever seen them. For her part, she looks surprised to see me. I guess it wouldn't be the first time she's underestimated my ability to get myself into the thick of things.

I don't think too much about what I do next. If I had, I wouldn't have done it. But this is a shitty day, and a shitty duty, and Max is upstairs probably watching a man die horribly for the sake of entertainment—if not worse. I can't say how glad I am to have someone by my side, even if I temporarily kicked her out of my clubhouse like a petulant child with no perspective.

I step forward and hug Gigi for the first time.

She's just as firm and solidly stone as she always is. There's no possibility of her ever softening. But she does drape her stone arms around me in return, and I feel for a second like I might actually pull this off. After a perfect moment, I step back and look her up and down.

"Were you trying to snap my neck?" I ask. At some point when I don't need her so much, we should talk about acceptable collateral damage. I thought we were at least partially on the same page on that score, but I'm thinking now that maybe we aren't.

"Of course not," Gigi says with her usual crispness. "Just trying to get a look at the person who was coming to sneak up on me."

The initial shock of running into Gigi when I didn't expect to starts to fade, and I start to piece things together. "You weren't expecting me," I say. "You weren't in on any of our plans. You're not here to help me at all. You're here to kill your creator."

Gigi tilts her head and looks at me, and I wish I didn't have my glasses on so I could read her face better. "I'm not here to kill my creator," she says after a second. "I figured you were going to try to do something brave and noble and came to keep you from getting yourself killed."

I stand looking at her for a long moment. Not deciding

whether or not to believe her, of course, since Gigi can't lie. But more trying to figure out where this puts us. That's a big admission for her to make, and I'm glad she made it. But I also know that Max isn't going to be okay with her helping out on this mission.

Which is why it's probably for the best he doesn't know. I step forward and give Gigi another hug—why not double-down on the weirdness?—though only a short one.

"Thank you," I say, the words carrying everything I want them to. Gigi seems less surprised this time, but still a little off balance.

"So," she says. "What's the plan?"

It's this question, more than anything else, that makes me feel like I know what I'm doing. After all, if you have to explain something to someone else, then you must know what you're talking about.

"Right, so. The necrowizards got their ability to survive forever by harnessing the power of the still-beating heart of a death god to create a built-to-order afterlife," I say, which may be the strangest sentence ever to leave my lips. As I speak, I start pulling my yellow leather jacket, complete with Aloysius's blessing, out of my infinity pouch. Annoyed at Aloysius as I may be, I need his luck, and it's in my best interest if he keeps getting enough worship to make supplying me with his luck worth his while. Does yellow leather go with a flowing green velvet dress? No. Am I here for fashion? Also no.

"Where that heart is, their circles must be, and it's a pretty good bet it's somewhere here, since this is their new headquarters. Besides, they think the circles are indestructible, because they made their afterlife atemporal. When I broke the veil between the real world and that afterlife, the circles got activated on this side, and became atemporal. So they can't be destroyed in time."

Gigi nods. "You know the problem with that, don't you?"

"That they're right? Yeah, no. Got a plan for that, too." I hold up the dagger. No point in discussing the whole folded-time-pocket part of the plan to Gigi. It feels like a transgression to tell her about any of Max's hard-to-share wizard magic conclusions, even still. And anyway, she doesn't need to know. "If I can find the circles, I think I have a good chance of destroying them."

Gigi's smile looks softer than it normally does, even on her stone face.

"And how do you propose we find these circles?" Gigi asks.

It's my turn to smile. I dip my hand into the infinity pouch and think of the patch of net spell that Max made for me, just like the one Kristoff once made to trap me in the siren's undersea library. I feel the threads at my fingers and pull it out.

It's a beautiful thing—all knots of glimmering, spun gold. The slight horror I feel at seeing it isn't its fault.

"This spell is one of the ones that react badly to god magic. Like very badly. Glows, heats up, and even explodes if it gets close enough. And the beating heart of a god being used to maintain an atemporal afterlife while it actively collides with reality is an awful lot of god magic for it to react to. We know the circles are probably underground somewhere in this building. Probably walled in somewhere. We just have to walk around, watch this spell, and wait for it to react. That should help us narrow in on it."

"And you want me to help break down the wall when you do?" Gigi asks, sounding almost bored.

"That would be pretty helpful. I had a plan before you showed up, but chances are I'd end up making more noise if I did it my way." The next words are a little bit hard to say, although they shouldn't be. They're important, though. "I'm glad you came."

"I'm glad you found me." Gigi smiles and holds out her arm. "Shall we?"

TWENTY-SEVEN

A Break

Every now and then, when the stars align and my god looks down upon me with favor, a plan actually goes the way it's supposed to. And at least for this sliver of the plan, today is that day. Gigi and I skulk through the abandoned halls of the castle as quietly as we can. It turns out that I couldn't have done it without her. There are some areas that, despite the castle's magical restoration, are still impassible hallways. Gigi's strength is invaluable for tossing aside broken walls and getting us through them. I guess the necrowizards restored the castle mainly by adding what's missing—not so much by taking things away.

After some time, Max's net spell reacts in my hand. And by looking at it and moving it closer to and further away from certain points on the walls of the hallway, we're able to zero in on the wall that must be hiding the necrowizards' circles.

"Allow me," Gigi says, when it's clear we're in agreement about where we should break through. "I recommend you stay back while I get this wall open."

I do as I'm told, thinking of the booby traps that Max

has in his own house. His react to magic, sure, but it's less his specific traps that I'm concerned about and more wizards' known propensity for a deadly set-and-forget security system.

In theory, my amulet should keep me safe from that, as this would count as harm directed at intruders, and I'm the intruder. But there are a lot of fuzzy edges around intent. I'm still not sure if I just got lucky when I wasn't harmed by the last time I ran into a wizard booby trap in Atlantis, or if it was my amulet that kept it from hurting me.

Either way, it's a solid life strategy to let the invincible woman with centuries of experience in dealing with wizards go first when she offers.

"Are you coming?" Gigi asks, thirty seconds and a dozen unpleasant noises later. I step into the room after her, avoiding a suspicious purple puddle on the floor. There's the smell of ozone in the air, along with a few floral scents I can't put a finger on and don't want to breathe in too deeply. Some shredded metal objects lay on the floor by Gigi's feet, none of them in their original shape from the looks of it, but a few of them still moving. But it isn't the collection of sprung traps that has my attention.

"Gigi," I say, "I think we found it."

"Oh, my," Gigi says, her voice dripping with sarcasm. "Whatever makes you say that?"

As if in a trance, I step toward the center of the room.

Magic is a lot of things. Horrible, mostly. Cruel, a lot of the time. But also, unfortunately, often beautiful. The elaborate silver cage around the Morrigan's pierced and still-beating heart is all three. The silver chains with links so fine they look like water are beautiful, too, and they link the cage to twelve circles of familiar design carved into stone.

But it's the circles themselves that are entrancing. All this time summoning ghosts, the circles I've made have always reminded me mostly of landing pads. But these are more like portals. Around them is the solid stone of the castle floor, but in the middle of the circle is another world. A strange, entrancing, broken reality.

I step forward to try to see through the closest circle. Lines of blue that remind me of the silver chains and the blue lines on the Morrigan's skin in equal measure extend out through an absolute, starless void like the one in the ghoul's eyes. They connect and wrap around silver platforms, like very large silver coins, upon which stand figures in the dress of various historical periods.

Ghosts, they must be. All of the ghosts preserved in this afterlife, when they aren't out in our world wreaking havoc and skeletonizing people.

But that "when" isn't right, either. Time isn't moving right in the world through the portal. It's not that everything is frozen—if anything, it's a mess of frenetic motion. But time seems to be flowing forward and back, like the waves in the ocean, and then skipping far ahead or far behind—it's impossible to tell which.

Gigi's hand on my shoulder brings me back to the here and now.

"Do you see what I see?" I ask her.

She smiles, soft and sad. "How would you expect a temporal mind to behold eternity?"

Good point, I guess. My attention goes back to the boobytraps on the floor.

"We need to get this moving. Which means I'm going to need to talk to Max, and he's going to want to see the room. You shouldn't be here when he does. I'll fix this between you, but not now. And you're going to need to apologize for leaving him behind in Glasgow, whatever your intentions. You get that, right?"

Gigi raises an eyebrow. "I *can* apologize when I'm in the wrong."

I don't know what about that sentence bothers me the most, but I can't deal with it now. I look back toward the entrance.

Gigi catches my meaning. "I'll stand guard," she says, already in motion.

When she's gone, I feel both more alone than ever but also a little relieved. I reach into the infinity pouch and pull out the garment bag, getting it positioned on the floor not far from the circles.

Hey Max, you'll never believe what I found in the basement.

Is everything okay? I get back. Right, no sarcasm allowed. I share my experience with him, and look around the room, even taking a second to peer into one of the circles. Not long enough to get lost in it, though.

"There were some booby traps that triggered when I came in. I managed to avoid them, but I don't know if they'll have alerted the necrowizards somehow."

It feels good to know he can actually hear my voice, even if it's through my own ears. It's weird how communicating in thoughts is a less intimate way of speaking, but everything has pros and cons, I guess.

Hard to say, Max thinks back at me. *I don't know what these people know how to do. But we need to hurry. There's a group of wizards in the corner that I think are going to make a move soon. And I think the necrowizards have noticed. Stop sharing your experience. I'll go find Moira.*

I do as I'm told and ready the sharpknife. After all of the worry and panic that it took to get here, I'm now weirdly calm. I have a simple four-step process that I know how to execute. It involves spells, which are always hard, but I've practiced the fuck out of them. For the first time all day, I finally feel like I really know what I'm doing.

Cut them now and get in the bag. I'll get Moira to say something she wants to take back in less than a minute.

Does a part of me want to listen in on Max's intense, personal, drama-filled conversation with Moira? Yes. Yes, it does. But I have other priorities right now. I say the words to activate the sharpknife and get into Right Mind. Memories of Faisal, my mother, Olivia, and my nieces get me where I need to be. I think of the knife as being no longer than its physical length, and I take a quick walk around the outside of the circles, slashing each intricate circle as I go.

It doesn't destroy any of the circles, but that's all right —it was a slim chance that it would before Moira rewinds time. So far, so good. I climb into the garment bag, remembering just in time to pull my phone out of the infinity pouch, bring up a clock app I downloaded that shows time passing in seconds, and set it outside the garment bag where I'll be able to see it. Not much point in hiding from Moira's spell if I don't have a touchstone to be able to tell when she's done it.

The first tinges of panic start nipping at me as I get the bag zipped up, but I shove them down. I get the bag closed over me and feel the undeniable sense of separation from the outside world that I've gotten used to. It's not magic that I'm feeling—it can't be. My theory is that it's the sudden and complete absence of ambient noise that is registering subconsciously.

I hold my breath and stare at the face of my phone, watching the seconds tick by and keeping an eye on the minute figure at the same time. Even focused as I am, I almost miss it—the second hand is on the twenty-three, but the minute hand shifts backward by one.

I struggle into Right Mind for getting out of my figurative glass coffin. It doesn't work the first time, which freaks me out more than it normally would, given the circumstances. But I get myself back under control, try again, and succeed this time.

Once free, I shift my attention to the circles. They're still intact—still showing their portal to the other world. That's a little bit of a disappointment. Moira's fold in the timeline didn't weaken them enough that my first cut worked. But if at first you don't succeed…

Cut them now and get in the bag. I'll get Moira to say something she wants to take back in less than a minute. Max's words appear in my head.

You already did. I answer back. *Prepare to lose your argument.*

I step toward the circles and grip my knife tighter. The nerves make it a little harder to summon up Right Mind, but I manage. It's the memory of Faisal's surprised pleasure the first time I convinced him to try a bacon, mayo, pickle, and peanut butter sandwich that does it in the end.

I slash through the first circle, hoping against hope that it succeeds.

It does not.

Okay, not great. But it doesn't necessarily mean anything. They're all linked together, after all. And it would be just like wizards to plan for treachery in advance and put measures in place to ensure that no one died unless they were taking all the others down with him.

I walk around the outside of the circles, slashing each one. I try to do it in about the same place as I did before, but with the minute reset, it's impossible to tell for sure. The sense of *déjà vu* is powerful.

I don't have any excuses. There aren't any more chances for the plan that we hatched together in my little attic to work.

Beth, nothing's happening.

Shit. The plan didn't work. I step forward to the middle of the circle and start slashing at the silver chains, the cage, and the heart itself. Though my Right Mind is intact enough—somehow—that the knife passes through everything, no lasting damage appears.

How about now? I ask Max. *Anyone falling to the ground lifeless?*

Nothing, comes his answer.

I look down through one of the circles at the polished silver platforms in the artificial afterlife. They remind me strongly of the roll of silver coins from Olivia sitting in my infinity pouch.

If I can't destroy the wizard's circles from this side, I'll just have to do it from the other.

Change of plans. This isn't your fault, Max. You didn't fail.

I step over the edge of the circle and let myself fall into the netherworld beneath it.

TWENTY-EIGHT

A Damnation

I fall into the void like falling into a tree. There are silver coin platforms that I miss like branches, with the blue threads between them like vines. I want to hit them to stop my fall—need to, really, or else I'll fall forever—but the more I pick up speed, the more I dread their impact.

But I've fallen before, and much farther than this. The first time you do a thing, it's terrifying. The next time you do it, it's still terrifying, but at least it's also familiar.

I have nothing to grab onto with my normal senses, no way I could reach, but one of a wizard's first spells they learn is to grab onto an object, and that's something I learned to do a while ago.

Before I have the chance to build up any more speed, I reach out with the right contortion of my hand, call up Right Mind—a sense of desperate longing and despair—and latch onto one of the glowing blue threads connecting the platforms. For a fraction of a second, I feel the thrill of success as the force of being connected to something solid racks through my body. But then a searing pain shoots through my hand, forcing me to lose my grip and scream into the void.

Blisters mar my left hand, but I'm still falling, and I still need to do something about that. My original plan is still the only feasible one. Grabbing onto the blue threads may burn me, but there's a chance that grabbing onto the platforms won't.

I reach out, painfully contort my wounded hand, get into Right Mind, and grab the closest platform. Again, it fucking hurts, but only as much as I'd expect it to from the jolt of my sudden stop. Suddenly going from free falling to hanging on an invisible magic thread is hell on the shoulder. I swing back and forth, as the gravity of this place pulls me down to come to a stop directly under the platform.

Hanging in the air gives me a second to stop and think. Or, at least, I think it gives me a second. The disjointed sense of time that I got from peering into the necrowizards' afterlife is only worse, looking at it all around me. But I don't feel disjointed, don't feel eternal or out of time. It isn't bending my brain. I have no knowledge of the future.

I look at the watch on my left wrist that was Faisal's Christmas present to me. I half expect it to be losing its mind, going forward and back and jumping around the way everything around me is. But it seems to be frozen, the second hand settled on forty-six.

Shit. Is it better or worse if I'm trapped in a single second?

Forty-seven.

I let out a breath. Okay, I've got time. Time that's moving forward around me, albeit at a slower rate. That's got to be better. Probably helpful, even, since my thoughts and the way I'm experiencing time itself don't seem slower.

So first things first: get oriented. The silver platforms and the strings connecting them to each other make sense. They're a way of shelving away all of the different ghosts that have been populating the afterlife and keeping it open for the necrowizards all this time. There's a pulsing through the strings that doesn't connect right, because of the problems with time, but I'd bet a lot of money it's the Morrigan's heartbeat. And if the Morrigan's heartbeat is sounding through them, then that means…

I look up as best I can around the silver platform I'm hanging underneath. I can't see the portal I fell through, but I can see some of the others, splayed out in a sphere. There, in the space beyond them, I see it: a blue anatomically correct heart. As I watch, it contracts, sending a pulse through the strings that connect it to the portals.

The pulse is slow, like it's stretched out the same way my watch is. These portals are each connected to the heart by one of the glowing blue threads, and they seem to be made of the same glowing blue material. The threads then branch out to the rest of the platforms. The pulse from the heart, through the strings, to the portals looks to be in the same slowed-down, linear time as the heart and the watch. But from there, the lack of time rules applies.

There's the difference, then—that must be what the wraith was telling me back in the Primrose Inn. The necrowizards stayed inside their exploded sphere of portals where time was linear. They used those portals as the boundary between linear time and eternity. It makes a certain kind of sense if you don't think about it too hard.

Looking at how it's laid out on this side, the answer seems simple: cut the strings between the heart and the necrowizards' circles, and the whole thing will come crashing down. Or, at the very least, its connection to the outside world will be broken. Maybe I can make it through one of the portals before it does. Maybe not. But either way, it'll work. The necrowizards won't be able to manifest in the outside world as full ghosts. We won't have a wizard civil war to contend with or all the collateral damage that would entail. There will still be a wraith problem, sure. But the world has survived wraiths so far. It's not ideal, but it's survivable. And modern-day wizards may not be up to the task of fighting the necrowizards, but they can sure as hell figure out what to do with wraiths.

But my plan will only work if my graveling-infused sharpknife will work the way I want it to. And assuming I can shimmy up the heartstrings to get there. And even though time is moving slowly, it still seems like a good idea to do this in the fold in the timeline that Moira's spell created. I'm still attacking the timeline, kind of. Maybe it won't make a difference, but I'll take anything that ups my chances.

Which means I need to stop hanging here and do something. I look down, trying to gauge what would be the best platform to drop down onto. There's one maybe 30 feet below me and slightly to the left, which is longer than I really *want* to fall, sure, but I should be able to survive. I move my body to get it to swing from my invisible thread, once, twice, three times. Then, when I'm guessing the angle is about right, I let go.

The hardest thing is maneuvering my body midair so that I'll hit the platform on my jacket, which absorbs the impact and avoids me breaking my leg or something. I might have been more worried about spells working in here if I hadn't already used one to stop my fall. I sit up, awash with success and self-satisfaction.

And I look directly into the eyes of a stocky man in a leather jacket with bleach-blond hair and a gun.

He says something German-sounding that I don't understand and levels the gun at me.

I try to scramble up, but my shoes slide on the slick surface of the platform, and I can't gain purchase. No matter how long I have my amulet, it is never going to stop me from feeling fear when a weapon is pointed at me. And it's not going to stop me from flinching when a gun is fired at me. But this is the first time it hasn't stopped a weapon aimed at me from actually hurting me.

"Fuck!" The impact of the bullet punishes me hard as it hits my right shoulder on the opposite side of Aloysius's blessing. It doesn't break through my jacket, enchanted as it is, but the pain of the impact can only mean that something about this hit isn't being stopped by the amulet. Which is really fucking bad news.

The ghost sneers at the panic on my face that this realization brings. He takes a step forward and aims at me again.

I have a knife that could hurt him, but he isn't close enough. My grabby spell can latch onto people, but can't bring them to me. That only works on objects, and I'm not sure if a ghost-object counts for that or not. But considering my grabby spell worked on the platform just now, it really should work on his gun.

I give it a try and feel the tell-tale resistance to movement as the connection clicks into place between my hand and his gun. The ghost can feel it, too, judging by how he stares dumbfounded at his gun.

I shift the position of my hand and get into the Right Mind to call the gun to me. It flies through the air, straight as an arrow, to my hand, pulling the ghost after it. Just in time for impact, I maneuver my knife so that he'll fall on it.

I'll never forget this—the first time I feel a dagger in my hand sink into flesh. I'm not even using the sharpknife for its abilities, so it's just a reasonably dull blade infused with graveling magic, but that's enough. The shock of realization on the bleach-blond ghost's face is so similar to the ghost Claude killed on the Scottish battlefield that I know it can be nothing else.

He's dying. Again. I killed him. Maybe. The revulsion at the thought drives me to shove him off me. He's still got a gun on him, and he's not quite dead yet, so I push him further. He rolls over the side of the platform.

I sit on the platform, breathing hard. I look at my watch. Forty-eight. All that was one second. Moira reset time at twenty-three seconds past. I've got thirty-five seconds to get all the way up to the sphere of portals around the heart. Is that doable?

If it is, I'll need to move fast, and it won't do to be slipping and sliding all over the place. So, first things first, I take off my shoes. The silver platform feels cool and smooth and good underneath my feet.

"Why don't you want to wear shoes?"

Melissa's voice calls my attention up to where she stands a few feet away from me. She looks like she did when she died now, not the sanitized version. Her jacket is torn. There are sticks in her hair, and Max's scarf around her neck is soaked through with blood.

"I don't want to slip," I say, feeling dumb for being surprised to see her.

And then I remember what her presence here means.

"Oh, fu—" I see Melissa's shocked expression. "—uuudge."

I sense the bulk of the axe man in my peripheral vision before I see him. My cute little trick of grabbing the weapon isn't going to work, with as quickly as he's moving toward me. He swings the bloody axe at me, using his longer arms to strike at me from outside my range. I raise up the sharpknife, trying to call up Right Mind and say the right words, but I fail at both. The axe deflects the sharpknife easily, and it's all I can do to keep from dropping the weapon.

The strength of the axe man's blow hits my shoulder through my jacket, which may be the only thing that saves my life. The impact knocks the wind out of me, but as with my fall and the bullet, the enchantments Max put on it eat up much of the force and stop the weapon from breaking through. It's going to be a hell of a bruise, but I'm alive.

My survival stokes the axe man's anger. Instead of coming at me with the axe, he brings his left hand up. Faster than I can react, he grabs my neck, flooding the skin there with tingles and pulling me up off the ground with sickening strength. I go to raise the sharpknife—to plunge it into him—but before I can, the axe man twists his grip around my neck in a sharp, decisive motion.

I thought I knew pain, and horror, and panic when my back broke below the theater in Glasgow. It's nothing compared to the feeling of my own neck snapping. My cry of terror breaks off in an instant as I lose control of my lungs. Everything below my neck—except the wild tingling I can still feel there—is just gone. I only know that my absent hand has dropped the sharpknife by the sound it makes hitting the silver platform beneath me.

I want to scream—to wail, to rage—but I don't have the breath or the body to do it. The axe man sneers, bringing me closer to him. I can see his startling blue eyes, and the flecks of silver in his beard and bedraggled, brown hair. I can see the faint indents on his nose where the pads of glasses normally rest. He wore glasses, but he didn't die with them.

And then something beneath the tingles in my neck reconnects, and the feeling in my body rushes back to me. I take a shuddering, panicked breath in. The axe man's face contorts in sudden confusion.

And then I feel a tingling in my right fingers as Melissa's tiny hand places the hilt of the sharpknife in mine.

It is my right to kill this man. It was not his right to kill me. It is good, and just, and pure for me to plunge the sharpknife into his torso, forcing the dull blade to the hilt in his muscled flesh. It is fair for me to light up his face with confusion and pain as I pull the sharpknife back and drive it in again. And again. And again.

The axe man stumbles backward, dropping me as he collapses down to the cold silver surface of the platform. His eyes search around him frantically, awash with panic. He looks older with confusion painted on his features instead of anger.

His eyes settle on Melissa, and his expression shifts again. A horrible, hoarse sob of grief rips its way out of his throat. It's followed by an inhuman wail, too big to be coming from his body, but too small for the endless void around us.

I lean forward, my sore limbs trembling. I think of the perfect stillness and beauty of the frozen world through the glass of my window on one Christmas morning when I was a child and I woke before the world did. I whisper the words to give the sharpknife its bite and slash the axe man's throat.

His agony fades in an instant. Melissa and I are alone on the platform. She's looking at the man with more than her usual layer of confusion. "Did you kill him?" she asks me, tears welling up in her eyes, blood dripping from Max's saturated scarf.

Statistically, children are most likely to be killed by members of their own families. He might have been her father. He might have been her uncle.

I don't know what I am on average—what I become when a ghost touches me. But I know that whatever it is, it's nothing this little girl can hurt. I shuffle forward on my knees and pull Melissa into my arms. Wherever she touches me, my skin tingles. She sobs into my neck, and the blood soaked into Max's scarf drenches my chest, my amulet, and the front of my dress.

TWENTY-NINE

An Ascension

When Melissa quiets, too short of a time later, I pull back and look at her. She's confused again, the way she often is, but not noticeably more.

It reminds me of my mother. It reminds me of Phoebe. It's the same wound, the same cruelty.

"Why don't you want to wear shoes?" Melissa asks me, just as she had a moment ago when she first appeared on the platform, as though nothing had occurred.

"I don't want to slip on the silver," I say.

"Why are you here?" Melissa asks. "I came to you because I wanted to know. I didn't remember I would bring him with me."

She sounds sorry, but no more sorry than I am. I look up at the portals and the beating heart, and all the madness that surrounds it. "I need to get to the middle of the world. I need to cut all the heartstrings."

Melissa nods solemnly. "Okay. But you're not always. You brought a little bubble of time in with you to swim in. You can't just be everywhere you need to be like we can."

"You've got a point there." Not sure how I brought

time in with me, but the alternative would probably fry my brain or otherwise make me unfit to return to the outside world. Maybe it was a safety measure the necrowizards built in.

I can't climb the heartstrings. If grabbing one magically burns my hand, I can't imagine grabbing one with my hand directly would be any better. I could go from platform to platform, gripping them with alternate hands with my magic grabby spell like I'm climbing an invisible rope. I did something similar underwater once.

I glance down at my watch. Fifty seconds. Even if my arms were up for the climb, I don't know if I'd have enough time.

"It's too bad you don't have any coins with you."

My attention snaps to Melissa, my eyes going wide. Wordlessly, I put my hand in the infinity pocket, thinking of the coins Olivia gave me. When I pull them out, Melissa's smile lights the world around us brighter than the glowing heartstrings.

"May I have one?" she says, adorable as hell.

"Yes, you may," I say, feeling surreal.

She takes a coin and walks to the edge of the platform, not far from a heartstring that connects to it at a slightly upward angle. Melissa tosses the coin out from the edge, a giggle spilling out around her huge, toothy smile. The moment it leaves her hand, the coin starts to grow. When it hits the level of the closest heartstring, it's the same size as the platform we're standing on now. It connects to the heartstring where it intersects, and more heartstrings fly out to where they can connect with other platforms, steadying the whole thing.

Of course. In the light of this new knowledge, I look down at the platform I've been standing on. Now that I'm looking for it, I can see the outline of a profile.

"Come on!" Melissa says, giggling as she jumps onto the new platform.

I do, making the little jump to the next platform without too much trouble, and glad that I took my shoes off. I only have ten coins, but I give Melissa the second one, and she throws it out.

When we're on the second coin I brought with me, I turn back and look at the first. If I can't call it back to my hand, if I can't reuse it to make another platform before I run out of them, I'm screwed. Ten coins isn't going to get us to the heart. But I brought in this coin—it was given to me by my family to pay for my way in the land of the dead. It's fucking *mine*.

I put away the extra coins to free up a hand. Then I reach out with my grabby spell, shift my hand position, and enter Right Mind to call the coin to me. The coin Melissa and I stand on rocks slightly as the heartstrings around the coin I'm calling snap, but a new heartstring appears to balance it out. The first coin Melissa threw out returns to my possession, shrinking back to coin size as it lands in my hand.

Melissa giggles. "You did it!" she says, reaching out her hand flat, asking for the coin again with the gesture. I give it to her. After I do, she takes my now empty hand in her little hand, filling it with tingles as she pulls me along with her to the edge of the platform.

Again, she throws the coin and makes a new stepping-stone for us. Again, we jump onto it, but this time we do it hand in hand. I turn back to call the previous coin to me. But I only have two hands. To retrieve the coin, I either need to put away the knife or let go of Melissa's hand.

I put away the knife and call the coin to me, hand it to Melissa, and start the process all over again. Fifty-one. Fifty-two. Fifty-six. Fifty-nine. We jump and run and climb.

Back around past zero, to four, eight, ten. I shift which hand Melissa has in mine when the tingling gets too intense, but I don't let it drop. We get close to other occupied coins, but never close enough to step onto them. They're not bothering us. I don't know why. Maybe it's because Melissa's with me. Maybe it's because I've killed two of them already. Maybe because with the veil so thin, the angriest ones who want to meddle with the world of the living are busy back where we're from.

I'm too busy to look that particular gift horse in the mouth.

I've got ten seconds left as Melissa and I reach a coin as close as possible to the ring of portals. This close up, I can see through them to the castle beyond. The thought sends a wave of homesickness through me before I shove it down.

"This is as far as I can go. I can't go to the middle. None of us can."

I look down at Melissa, trying to find the right words to say. But I can't find them in time, and she gives my hand one final tingling squeeze, and walks off the edge of the coin and away from the bubble of protective time I brought in with me, back into the dizzying eternity beyond.

I'm alone again. I don't know how to get around the portal to reach the heart beyond, which seems like the most efficient way of cutting all the strings. If I had enough time, I could try to get close enough to the nearest portal and climb back into the world of the living. I bet if I lay down on the floor and figured out which way to go, I could cut the strings from that angle. But on that side of the veil, time would be running at normal speed, and I'd never get it done in time for my actions to lay in the fold of the timeline where they're most likely to succeed.

Hell, I'm barely going to be able to get it done on this

side, if I don't get a move on. I bring out another coin and toss it the way Melissa has been doing, just on the other side of the invisible boundary made by the portals. But tossing a coin within the peripheral sphere of portals yields a result I don't expect. Instead of expanding and springing heartstrings of its own or falling down past me into the void beneath my feet, it falls *up*. Gravity, it would seem, goes the other way past the portals.

I jump, following the coin I threw and angling my body again to hit the surface of the heart on my jacket. I miss, but it doesn't matter. The surface of the heart is soft like a body, not hard like a planet. This keeps me from hurting myself, but it's also pretty fucking disgusting.

I pull out the sharpknife and head for the first heartstring connected to a portal. I say the words and then conjure up the image of Olivia, the exhaustion and light on her face holding her first daughter in the hospital, just barely conscious enough to allow me and Faisal in to see her. Too happy to care, at least for that moment, that Mom hadn't made the trip. I slash through the heartstring for her. When I do, the portal above me, the one that this particular heartstring connected to, winks out of existence.

In a rush, it hits me. The portals are twenty feet up. I can't jump that far. I can't fly. The coins aren't sprouting more heartstrings.

To save the world, I need to cut all of the strings. And when I do. I won't have a way out.

I head to the next one and slice through it, calling up another memory of my oldest niece feeding me a cookie she had made—that Olivia's expression told me she expected me to pretend was edible. I slice through the second heartstring.

And the third. And the fourth.

I bury my grief in their joy as I run and slash and run

and slash. Until I stand at the base of the final heartstring, beneath the final portal. The room up there has so much color. So different from the silver, blue, and black that's all my world now. There are hues of brown and grey and so much solidity.

And I'm giving all of that up so that they can keep it. I grip the knife in my hand, and think of Faisal, on our first actual, official date, laughing into his curry bowl in an uncontrolled way he rarely does. I hold the sharpknife to the heartstring.

Okay, yeah, no. Absolutely not. Fuck this.

The heartstring had previously burned me, but that was before I'd run hand-in-hand with Melissa all the way up. That was before my hands were alive with pinpricks, spreading all the way up to my elbows. I'd barely realized it in the immediate violence of fighting the ghosts on the first platform, but those original burns have long since healed.

I grasp the heartstring. Nothing happens. Nothing but that continual tingling.

Good enough for me. I put the sharpknife in my mouth, the scent of red wine overwhelming. I climb hand over hand, struggling to keep my feet away from the heartstring.

Finally, I get a hand through the portal, and the stone on the other side is the most solid, perfect thing I have ever felt.

Bless you, Gigi, for teasing and shaming me into never skipping arm day. I pull myself up through the portal and spill out on the other side. The stone floor feels solid beneath me in a way the coins never could. The portals I've already severed are plain stone again, with a chunk taken out of them from before I went into the afterlife.

I dip my head back in, looking around to orient myself. I can barely tell where the heartstring connects at this angle, but based on the view I saw while I was climbing and the view I can see now, I figure it out.

Is this thing going to cut off my arm? I shimmy around the circle, finding the place where I can hold the sharp-knife against the heartstring but submerge my arm the smallest distance. If I do this right, it'll hit only my trans-formed flesh.

I think. Probably.

But the seconds are ticking by at normal speed, and I don't have any more time to hesitate. I think of my dad, working on a trainset when I was a little kid, so entirely entranced that the world could fall to pieces around him, and that would be okay.

And I cut the final heartstring.

THIRTY

An Arbitration

My arm. Fuck. My arm. I yank it out of the circle as fast as I can, fearing a bloody, broken stub. Instead, it's fine. The sharpknife is also fine, although shining dangerously, with tiny wine-scented tendrils coming off of it in a way that probably causes cancer in the state of California.

Even my jacket is fine.

I shove the sharpknife into my infinity pocket and inspect my arm more closely. The arm is fine. The jacket is fine. The long sleeve of my fancy dress? Not so much.

Beth, where are you? Answer me, goddamn it.

Max's thought in my head catches me off guard, and the surprise of it pulls me to my feet.

I'm here. I'm fine. Did that work?

Oh, Jesus. Thank God.

A thread of panic runs through my body.

Everything okay up there? I ask.

It's calmed down now. When the necrowizards started dropping dead one by one, shit went down. There were some spells loosed and maybe six wizards are dead. A ton more are injured, but they'll be fine. It looks like we did it.

Again, I wish I could get some sense of the tone he's saying that in. Relief? Pride that we pulled it off? Horror that the greatest living wizards were defeated so mercilessly? I feel like knowing how he is reacting to this in the moment it happens is important information that I need to know about him. But it's missing.

Oh, fuck, he thinks.

"Oh, fuck," I say out loud. The opening of the top of the cage around the Morrigan's heart is exploding with something that looks like blue vapor.

And here I had been, assuming that with the afterlife cut off from the Morrigan's heart everything would just fall into the void, or just cease to exist. But no, just when I thought I'd won, here come the ghosts.

I need a way to stop them.

No. I need a way to *hold* them.

In a few steps, I'm next to the Morrigan's heart. The stitches holding the infinity pouch into my fancy dress aren't hard to rip out. I'm not much of a seamstress to begin with, and I don't know what happens if I damage the pouch, so I didn't want to take chances. I hold the open end of the infinity pouch down over the floodgate. It does exactly as I'd hoped—the ghosts escaping the collapsing afterlife are instead disappearing into the pouch.

I don't know if that's better for them or worse. But I know it doesn't let them free into reality. Maybe they wouldn't be able to cling to the world of the living long without a circle, but I don't want to risk it.

Don't worry, I've got it, I think to Max. Though now that I'm processing it a little more, Max can't possibly have seen the spirits from where he is right now.

You've got a handle on the ghoul?

Oh, right. That. *Show me.*

I close my physical eyes when Max's current experience hits me. The ballroom is everything a little girl with princess fantasies could dream of, complete with monsters in disguise. Oh, and a bunch of dead bodies. It's hard to tell which ones are the necrowizards, and which ones are the modern wizards caught in the crossfire. Smoke hangs low in the air, as does a dizzying blend of scents I can't place and don't want to. After all that—after all that the necrowizards have threatened, they don't look like much of anything after they're dead. Just so much food for ghouls.

But no one is paying attention to the bodies. In the middle of the room, surrounded by angry wizards—not somewhere anyone should ever want to be—stands the ghoul. She's in her usual face but still wearing the dress she wore when she was the babysitter.

She just walked into the room when the fighting was dying down and took credit, Max thinks. His heart is beating as fast as mine is.

She said she was saving her species. I think back. *She must think this is how she could do it. Show up, take credit for whatever we do if we succeed. Or maybe turn us in if we don't. Either way, she gains favor with the wizards and can plead her case.*

Which is very much breaking the one rule of the arbitration. Which I'd be more annoyed about if I weren't such a corrupt judge in this specific case.

"I did what you couldn't do yourselves," the ghoul is saying in a voice that tells me she has far misjudged her circumstances.

That's a bad idea, Max thinks. I'd like to imagine he's sad about it, but I don't think he is.

Nothing but silence from the wizards. From the look on the ghoul's face, it seems to be dawning on her that she's overplayed her hand.

"And how did you do this?" A light-brown-skinned wizard with close-cropped gray hair who I don't recognize steps forward. "How *exactly?*"

The ghoul's ready for this. "I had a team to help me. We infiltrated the castle. Go down and get my lacky. She'll tell you."

She thinks I'm going to back her up. It takes me a second to recognize why that makes me feel good. And then I realize it's because she believes that even while I'm standing there, possibly about to pay with my life for getting captured, I'll help her leverage this situation into saving her species.

But what would the alternative be? Bringing her down with me out of spite? Outing Max? Maybe the threat is implicit that *she'll* out Max if I don't play along.

How sweet—she's staking the continued existence of her species on me sacrificing my life for Max. Don't know what to think of that.

It wouldn't help her, Max thinks at me. *Get out of here.*

I open my eyes, seeing the superimposition of both Max's vision and mine for a second. I have to tilt my head and peek down between the Morrigan's heart and the infinity pouch to be sure, but there's still a strong flow of ghosts.

I kind of can't right now. I'm busy with something.

Whatever it is doesn't matter. Beth. Get out. Now. Run.

"Oh, but we've already found your lackey."

My head whips around, searching the room for any guards that I'd managed to miss.

Beth?

Back in Max's vision, I see the wizard who was speaking turn his head toward the door. "Bring in the gate guardian," he calls out.

Well, fuck.

And that definitely *won't help her,* I think at Max.

Get out of here, Max thinks at me. *Whatever you're doing, drop it and go. Gigi can't lie for you.* Jesus, his pulse is pounding. I can feel it as though it's in my own chest, dwarfing mine.

I want to shoot back a "you think I don't know that?" but it'll only come off even ruder than I mean it. The crowd parts and in comes Gigi, her hands in handcuffs that must be enchanted if she can't just bust out of them. She has a proud, unshakable look on her face, and her chin is held high, but I know better. There aren't a lot of things that scare Gigi, but wizards are one of them. And she voluntarily came into a den of them. To save my dumb ass.

I check the flow of ghosts again and close my eyes to focus.

In a series of subtle, jerky movements and impossible to distinguish whispered words, the wizard who had been speaking forces Gigi to her knees. I can't see the mechanism, and I imagine that's intentional. No wizard in a ballroom of wizards wants to show what they can do. Too likely that their spell will get poached or they'll make themselves a target.

"Is what this ghoul is saying true?" the gray-haired wizard asks. "Did you help her to destroy our kin, hoping it would curry favor with us?"

And here it comes. She's about to doom both me and an entire species in a single breath.

"Well of course I did." Gigi's lovely, certain voice echoes through the over-height room. "She had a good plan, and I felt sorry for her. Told her as long as it was just the two of us, I was in. I don't trust allies, you see. She assured me it was, and I believed her, so I went along with it."

That's not Gigi, Max and I think at the same time. It's hard to read the wizard, but if I had to guess, I'd say his confidence is slightly shaken.

"Because you wanted to kill your creator?"

Not-Gigi laughs. It's so exactly like Gigi's laugh that it makes my heart hurt. "Oh, absolutely not. I loved my father. I'd never want to kill him. That was merely an unfortunate side effect. But the ghoul's cause was just, and I thought it right that she should save her species from extinction. Is that so hard to imagine?"

The wizard turns his attention back to the ghoul, who herself looks shaken. As surprised as me and Max are, I guess.

"And what is it you want to save your species from?"

I have to admit, the ghoul has a good pitch. She's had some practice and made some improvements since she explained the situation to me. Leaves the concept of arbitration out of her explanation, of course, which is a relief. She just says that the gravelings refused to break or bend the rules of the treaty, which Claude will like. When she's finished, there's a tiny part of me that almost thinks the wizards are going to buy it and reward her for saving their asses.

But that tiny part of me is dumb, and the hope on the ghoul's face is doomed.

The speaker wizard turns a wicked smile to the assembled monsters. "And how do we all think this creature should be rewarded for her actions? For sneaking into our event and trying to manipulate us?"

With no further encouragement needed, several spells take hold of the ghoul at once, no less effective in her destruction for warring with one another. Her bones and her flesh are ripped apart from one another. Her bones are turned to stone, her blood apparently evaporates, and her flesh turns a putrid shade of gray-green in a matter of seconds.

Max scans the assembly, but no one is giving away any sign that any of the spells used were theirs.

"Still, we should do something about the poisoning," a female voice from farther out in the crowd begins. For a second, I think this must be what Moira sounds like, but it turns out there are more than four wizards in existence, and the gorgeous, dark woman with luscious curls who emerges from the crowd to speak doesn't look familiar. "If this one went to all this trouble, they're desperate enough to cause problems if we don't act. We can revise the treaty to alter this one rule. I have a good working relationship with the gravelings in my domain. They'll happily accept a new duty if I give them one."

A good working relationship with a full-blown, non-apprentice wizard? What would that even look like? But though her suggestion is met with a few quibbles, the idea carries the day.

"And what do we do with this?" the wizard who spoke first asks, turning back to Not-Gigi. "I suppose I'll take her for my collection, though I've heard holding onto her can be trouble."

"I'll take her."

I've never heard Kristoff's voice before. It's higher and slightly more nasal than I would have expected, and it carries the slight Nordic accent that Max does so well when imitating him. But it has its own attractiveness to it, all the same. Their makeover spell wouldn't let it be otherwise, I imagine. He looks even better than he did the last two times I saw him, dressed as he is in a tuxedo and tails.

"Oh?" the speaker wizard says, the sheer weight of the implications loaded in that one word threatening to sink it.

Kristoff scans the room as though seeking to root out those who disagree for later targeting. The slight tightening of his eyes as they land on me—Max, really—makes my skin crawl. "Yes, I'll take her," he says. "I had a lovely estate in Haiti a few centuries ago. She interfered. I would like to repay her for that particular interlude."

Gigi's sister can't die any more than Gigi can. She also can't be wounded. But a knot still forms in the pit of my stomach as Kristoff, after leaving a moment to be certain no one's going to dare challenge him on this, steps forward. He pulls a single, thin green leaf from his pocket, releasing it to fall beside Not-Gigi. No sooner does it hit the stone than it begins to grow and twist into a thick, green vine that envelopes Not-Gigi. She struggles, but she doesn't stand a chance. The few tendrils of the vine she manages to snap only release a few drops of milky-white sap before healing themselves. The sap sizzles when it hits the stone floor.

"Much better," Kristoff says, and then addresses the room. "And now I think we all have better things to do, do we not?"

Wizards don't give other wizards of similar rank commands. It's very much A Whole Thing. But everyone must want to get out of there enough that no one argues. They all start moving. A few, I swear to God, disappear, though I know it can't be into the Crossroads. Kristoff, on the other hand, is laser focused in on me—or Max, rather.

He closes the distance between them and grabs Max by the front of his shirt. "You'll be catching a ride home with us," he says in a harsh whisper that brooks no argument. I feel Max nod and then relax as Kristoff eases away, heading back to Gigi's sister.

I'm dropping the connection now. Max thinks at me. *Kristoff and Moira will be able to sense it once we get away from everyone else. Get out of here, Beth. For real this time.*

His experience drops, and I'm once more only in one

place. It would be a relief if it didn't make me feel suddenly so alone.

I'll finish up what I'm doing and meander out when I'm ready, thank you very much, sir. Hopefully I went over the top enough that the joke comes through.

No, Beth, you'll get out now. They have to avoid suspicion. Which means…

Oh, fuck. I finish his thought for him. *They're going to destroy the place on their way out.*

THIRTY-ONE

A Lifeline

How long is it going to take the wizards to get out of here before they blow it up? Presumably, they'll bring their pets with them. At least, God, I hope so.

And how long is it going to take the ghosts to get out of the heart and into my bag?

I need to know both of these things in order to make a good decision, and I know neither. I try to reach out to think to Max again, but he's gone. I should feel abandoned—and to some extent, I do—but it's also good not to have anyone in my head right now.

Well, no one but the usual. I hope Aloysius knows I'm here. And wants to help me. Haven't I taken enough risks for him today? Aren't I due for a little divine intervention, Oh Powerful Crossroads Creator?

Nothing happens, and I don't expect it to. I try to rearrange the bag to hold it with one hand. If I can do that, I can pull out a stone in the wall and at least see if I'm underground or in the middle of the building or facing outward. If I'm facing outward, I can pull out enough stones to escape the building. Maybe I can even figure out how to get the heart out of the cage so I can just put the whole thing in the infinity pouch and be done with it.

But I can't get the bag to stay on one-handed, and it doesn't matter, because my sense of direction isn't good enough to know which side of the building I would be facing. If I pull out a stone to escape the falling rocks in front of a wizard, I'm not just going to die, I'm going to take everyone else down with me too. Drawing too much attention to myself will do the same thing. They're all going to be focused on the building. I need not to give them a reason to be focused on me. To hear something or feel something and choose to investigate. Max said they would be able to feel the communication spell if he kept it running, and I know from experience that wizards can sniff out magic. If I'm going to use one of the like three magic spells I know to get out of here, I need to do it when there's more magic going on that can cover it.

So I have to escape when the building is collapsing around me. Great plan. Just fantastic.

How long has it been? I try to crane my neck around to look at the watch Faisal gave me, but that doesn't tell me much. I know what time I got out of the Morrigan's afterlife, but not how long people spent talking upstairs. I hunch down, keeping my focus on the stream of ghosts. Some of them have already escaped. Maybe it's inevitable that more will. It makes sense to cut my losses, pull the bag off the cage, and prepare myself for my survival attempt. The only thing that stops me from doing so is the memory of the inn and the man with bone stumps instead of hands. To let some of them escape may be necessary. But I won't be able to live with myself if I let loose more than necessary, not knowing what might happen. Especially if the spirits of the necrowizards that I cut off their summoned bodies went back into the collapsing afterlife when I did. Without a physical form, they'll be more limited in what they can do—at least, I hope so. But that's not a theory I want to test.

A great shuddering crack from somewhere far above me rips through the building. It's starting. It's time. Has it been long enough for them to rescue the humans? It doesn't feel like it's been long enough.

I struggle with the infinity pouch. The flow of ghosts has slowed to a trickle. I won't get them all, but this is going to have to be good enough. All my attempts to get the pouch snug over the cage have backfired, and as I pull at it, a jagged metal nib on the cage snags the fabric. Before I realize what's happening and stop pulling, I've yanked a hole in the bag.

A great, deep crashing from all around me echoes my horror as the infinity pouch splits open. I catch a glimpse of blue, and for a long, horrified moment, I think it's going to spill out its entire contents. There's a horrible moment of expansion, as though everything I put inside the pouch is going to explode outward. But then it all collapses back in again, and I have to hurry to catch the resulting glass orb, about the same volume as the infinity pouch, but perfectly round and full of writhing blue.

Fuck. Okay. That's better than it could have been. Call it a failsafe, I guess, although there was nothing about this in the trove, and I have no idea what I'm going to do with it now.

Another round of stones falling on stones. These are closer. I'd guessed right—they aren't going to stop at destroying what the necrowizards had rebuilt upon their return. They know there's evidence of magic buried in the building, and with the necrowizards gone, the spells that must have kept it from discovery for the last millennia may not be intact. They're going to pull the entire castle apart stone by stone.

Well, I'm going to beat them to a few of the stones. Cradling the newly formed infinity globe in one arm, I reach a hand out to the wall. Like breathing, I shape my hand, get into Right Mind, and grip, calling one of the stones in the wall toward me, dropping the spell and stepping to the side to keep it from hitting me. Horror fills me at the sight of what is behind it—nothing but more dirt and stone.

I spin around to look at the other three walls. One of them leads to the hallway and, therefore, death. I'm sure the other one must just have another room on the other side, based on the way we came in. But the fourth wall...

On instinct or Aloysius's luck, I step forward just in time to miss a hunk of stone falling toward me from the ceiling. Not taking any time to count my blessings, I follow through with the motion, picking up speed, heading for the fourth wall as I ready my spell to make a pathway.

For one agonizing moment, I think the stone is pulling back to reveal another collapsing room. But then the fresh air hits me. I throw myself out of the building and toward my greatest chance of survival.

And find myself freefalling off the side of a cliff, losing hold on the smooth surface of the orb full of ghosts.

Castles weren't built for fun. Castles were built to be defensible. And what's more defensible than a sheer cliff face? If I were an attacker, I would not choose to be here voluntarily.

But I just did this—and this time, I'm at least on my normal plane of existence. I reach out for a crag of rock and latch onto it with my magic, readying myself for the way it'll wrench my arm just about out of its socket. Maybe one day I'll get used to that.

The second the shooting pain in my arm tells me I've made a connection, I look down for the infinity globe. If it weren't for the ghosts roiling inside it, it might be hard to spot, but as it is, I pick it out easily from the dark night. I latch onto it with my free hand and focus on nothing but maintaining my grip at a distance as my body swings to a hard rest against the cliff face.

Chunks of castle are still passing by me. I even imagine that I see a piece of what was once a necrowizard's circle, but I can't be sure. If one of them is going to hit me, it's going to hit me. There's nothing I can do about that now.

Finally, after a longer time than I think it really should take, the world around me is still. I don't see any wizards from my current vantage point, so hopefully that means none of them see me. And I have no intention of doing anything to call attention to myself until enough time has passed that they've all most likely left the area.

I want to pull the infinity orb, with its precious and dangerous cargo, up to my physical hand instead of just maintaining a magical grip on it at a distance. But I've never pulled an object to me with one hand while holding onto a different object with the other, and now seems like a terrible time to experiment.

I wait. For the wizards to be gone. For inspiration to strike. For my god to recognize that I'm not getting out of this one alive, and I'm no good to him dead, so now would be a great time to make an exception, please and help me the fuck out of this.

The wizards leave, probably. But no inspiration strikes. And Aloysius does not appear. I do, however, feel the cold settle into my bones.

I didn't know about very much danger in my life before I found magic. I knew the ordinary fears of riding with a bad driver or walking across campus at night alone. But I'd never had time to examine up close the difference between an acute, in-the-moment fear that makes you jump out of your skin, and the creeping fear that unless you do something, your own choices are going to do you in, and you have no idea what options you can even pursue to avoid that.

Climbing isn't a possibility. I guess I could fall and catch myself, the way I did when Max and I were falling out of the sky. Slide down the rock face in ten-foot segments, falling against my arm joints with every move. If I had two hands available for use, I could probably even do a decent job of it. It might not hurt that much. I'd be swinging like Tarzan from invisible vines. I've got the bare feet and everything. If only I had two available hands.

But the longer that takes, the colder I get. I'm not sure I'd be able to even make the next one down, numb as my hands are growing.

I've already left it too long, maybe. I had to be sure the wizards wouldn't see me when I moved. But if I start trying to descend now, I might find myself falling a lot farther than I intend.

Still, that's the right move. It's my only move. I take a deep breath in, trying to will myself to try. I should be able to, but I can't. If I were forced to, I could. But under the pressure of nothing but slow inevitability, I just can't.

And with every minute that I can't force myself to risk it, my death by cold, and by eventually losing my grip, becomes all the more assured. I blink tears out of my eyes. This is what you get for abandoning me, Aloysius. I become a shitty priest who literally can't take a gamble to save her life.

Before I can finish deciding whether I'm angrier at myself or my god, a movement in my lower hand surprises me. I look at it, but there's nothing close to me. It's not until I look down at the infinity orb and see a dark figure clinging to the cliff face that I put it together. It's too far away to make out what the figure is—let alone see facial expressions—but when the person down there gives the infinity orb a gentle, meaningful tug, I let it go.

Half of me expects to see the orb fall down the rest of the cliff, possibly to break and release its ghosts. What's the likelihood that I'm beginning to hallucinate, all things considered? But instead, I see the figure tuck it away, presumably in some kind of pocket or bag on its person.

This accomplished, the figure continues its climb up the side of the cliff with smooth, sure motions, neither hurried nor apparently worried. As it grows closer, and I can begin to judge its basic details—humanoid, bulky, probably about eleven feet tall—I begin to put it together. By the time the troll is close enough to me that I can make out his stocky, stunted-looking features, relief is already beginning to chip away at my despair.

"This yours?" the troll asks, pulling out the infinity orb as he comes to a rest alongside me, casually hanging off the cliff side like we've just run into each other on a seaside boardwalk.

"Yeah. I kinda dropped it. Thanks for bringing it to me."

It hits me that I haven't spent much time actually talking to trolls. I know Wilbur—and I like Wilbur a lot. But I also like Max, and I wouldn't be jazzed about a wizard coming up to me when I'm vulnerable. But I do know some things *about* trolls, and I can use that, at least.

With my one free, numb, shaking hand, I struggle to pull off one of Max's diamond and emerald earrings. A twinge of pain in my ear when I finally get it free isn't a good sign that I did that right, but whatever. "Payment for connecting me with my lost property," I say, holding the lone earring out to him.

The troll regards it with a thoughtful look on his face for about a hundred years before finally reaching out to take it, somehow maintaining his hold on the cliff with only his lower body. "I appreciate your manners, Arbiter."

He holds the infinity orb out to me, and I take it gratefully—if also very, very carefully. If he knows who I am, that's half the battle, hopefully.

"Did Wilbur send you?"

The troll examines the earring I gave him. "These are real," he says.

"Yeah, that seems right."

The troll eyes me suspiciously. "You paid me with property not yours?" His face leaves little doubt that this would not be considered acceptable.

To survive, I have to accept Max's over-generous Christmas present. Officially. Cool.

"They're mine. But they were a gift, so I didn't buy them."

That seems to satisfy the troll, as he tucks the earring away. "I don't know Wilbur. But this is near where I live, and he put the word out to look for you here. Said you get into trouble sometimes, but it would be worth anyone's while to get you out of it."

The troll's tone of voice when he says that makes me want to defend Wilbur's honor somehow. I know I'm always pushing him to help more than he wants to—to stray from a troll's traditional lane. I guess I always thought of that as personally difficult rather than potential reputational damage. Still, I think he'd agree that my life is worth his name getting dragged through a little mud.

"I wasn't going to come up here, but you paid my cousin to carry your gifts. And his wife, too. Twice, even."

Gifts? Oh, the meat. My somewhat useless troll-community outreach that was part of what inadvertently caused this whole mess is going to get me out of it? I could laugh if I weren't too cold and exhausted for the cause-and-effect levers in my emotions to work properly.

"Right, then," the troll says, reaching one giant, meaty hand out to me—to the hand that's been the only thing holding me up on this cliff. "Here we go."

I open my mouth to protest, but the sudden feeling of falling as the troll's hand closing over mine breaks the spell and steals the words from my mouth. I don't even have time to consciously think the words *I'm going to die* before the soft, grassy earth, smelling of melting snow and rich dirt, breaks my fall. I look up, the moon illuminating the troll from the cliff and another, slightly shorter, distinctly troll-like figure.

I cradle the infinity orb close to my body, reassuring myself that it's still there, as I watch the two mountains of flesh talk to each other in Trollish in the moonlight. Their words don't seem antagonistic to me, but it's hard to tell without speaking the language and with my contacts still in. After a short exchange, Wilbur pulls a thick disk from an inner pocket of one of his faded, layered jackets. I'd say it was a coin, but it looks wooden to me, and at something like four inches across, it's too large to be a coin—even taking into account trolls' different scale. A token, maybe. The troll from the cliff takes it and steps back into the Crossroads the way he came.

I have just enough time to wonder if the troll is having a hard time re-situating himself on the cliff face before Wilbur reaches down. With large, gentle hands, he helps me up.

"He was quite a climber," I say, instead of *thank you*.

Wilbur's broad, stubby features smile. No one would

ever confuse Wilbur with a handsome man, but the familiarity of his expression is beautiful to me in this moment. "We live under bridges. Be hard to do if we didn't know how to climb."

I let out a long, relieved laugh, and Wilbur joins me.

"Are you ready to head back to Springfield?" he asks, when we've calmed down enough to speak again.

"Soon," I answer. "There's somewhere I need you to take me first."

THIRTY-TWO

A Christmas Present

When we finally find the Casino, I'm wishing my jacket were a hell of a lot thicker than it is. The world around us is dark, desolate, and magical. It's covered in snow, which refracts the light from the Casino in a disorienting way.

The Casino always looks different. It always has onion domes, although the number and size of them vary as it grows or shrinks to accommodate the number of eligible gamblers in the catchment for its current Crossroads. Here, far north and isolated as we are, it's the smallest I've ever seen it—even smaller than the time I saw it outside Springfield. Its one dome is so small that I'm reminded of the Vegas version of the Eiffel Tower. It still towers up a few stories above me and Wilbur, but it's dwarfed by the snow-covered mountains around us. Behind us is an expanse too wide and flat to be anything but frozen-over water.

"Do you want to come in?" My words are almost carried away by the wind, but Wilbur must hear them because he looks at me like I'm crazy and shakes his head.

"It's pretty cold out here," I try, eyeing his insufficient clothing.

"Trolls don't get cold. I'm safer waiting in the snow than tangling with a demon."

"Suit yourself," I say and begin the arduous process of fighting my way through the thigh-high snow in bare feet and my ruined gown, only worse for the wear for this final leg of the journey. It helps that there's a trail from about where we're standing to the doors of the Casino, presumably formed by those poor unfortunate humans whom Aloysius has lured here to gamble with their souls, feeding him the worship he needs to keep going.

That is, the worship he needs above and beyond the worship I give him by taking massive gambits with my life while wearing his blessing. Gambits that, so far, have worked out.

My hands get coldest the fastest, and I have to tighten my grip and pay close attention to be sure the glass ball with a universe full of homeless ghosts doesn't slip from my grasp and fall to the ground. I doubt it would break on the snow, soft as it is, but I don't exactly want to risk it.

There are only three stairs leading up to the landing, and the Casino is so small this time that the usual double-height wooden entry doors that could stop an invading army are no bigger than your average supermarket doorway.

And, unfortunately, they're closed.

I spare a glance to the red pennant flags on either side of the doorway and am relieved to see that they are hanging limp and motionless, despite the breeze blowing my hair, carrying away my heat, and making flurries dance in the warm incandescent light shining from all around the entryway. From past observation, confirmed by Faisal, that means the Casino is running at the same speed as the world around it.

I'm already dreading how much knocking on the door will hurt my already-freezing hands when I realize I don't have the option. I don't trust the infinity orb to one hand, especially now that I'm standing on hard stone instead of soft snow.

Boy, gee willikers, I sure do hope that someone lets me into this here casino before I freeze to death.

Prayer is an unusual doorbell, but Aloysius is an unusual man. And if it works, don't knock it. The door swings open, and a blast of warm air and warm light hits me. I have to squint to see the familiar figure of Arjun standing in the doorway behind.

"Elizabeth. Come on in. You are cold?"

"Yes, thank you." I say, stepping inside, careful not to slip on the polished marble stone in my bare feet and trying to adjust to the warmth. The door closes behind me with a solid thud.

The Casino is mostly one big room this time, with a boxing ring set up in the center and nine folding tables with men clustered around them. Rather than slack-jawed and in a slots-induced trance, these men are volatile and engaged in their card games, shouting. The onion dome above us has tiny glow-worm-like pinpricks of light set in it, and every time one of the tables erupts in a Scandina-vian-sounding argument, the lights pulse brighter.

"Your feet," Arjun says in dismay, startling me from my reverie. I wince.

He raises a finger. "One moment," he says, and then slips away through a door a few feet away that I really should have noticed but didn't. When he returns only a few seconds later, he has a pair of brown fur-lined slippers and a green, fuzzy blanket.

I carefully set the infinity orb on the ground while I get into my gear. I'm not trusting it to the grasp of someone who isn't really there, even if he did seem capable of carrying the slippers and blanket. The slippers immediately do me a world of good, and with the blanket around my shoulders, I almost don't feel like I'm about to die of exposure.

"Himself is in his office," Arjun says, once I've settled into my new duds and have the infinity orb in my hands again. "I'll lead you."

I nod dumbly and pad along behind him, feeling ridiculous but something approaching comfortable as I take in my surroundings.

In addition to the boxing ring and tables, I now notice a variety of figures, all different versions of supernatural. If I didn't still have Max's contacts in, I wouldn't be able to tell. As it is, I give up on identifying them based on what I know from the trove. I don't have the energy right now to figure out how scared I'd have to be of them if I weren't standing in my god's domain.

Aloysius's office turns out to be behind a solid, nondescript door near the back of the Casino. Arjun knocks three times and pauses. He must hear something I don't, because after a minute, he nods his head twice, turns the elaborate brass knob to open the door for me, and then unobtrusively scurries away.

Still not willing to trust the infinity orb to one partially thawed hand, I nudge the door open, step inside, and then close it behind me with my hip.

Inside, Aloysius's office is more like I would expect. In the middle of the room is a great big boat of a desk, dark wood carved with skill, intricacy, and no sense of decorum regarding what types of images belong in an office. The walls of the round, windowless space are crowded with paintings and tapestries in various themes and from various times. I don't recognize the artists, but I admire the skills, and I admire the way the subjects in every scene seem happy to be where they are.

Aloysius himself is seated behind the desk in a chair that would make a king feel insecure, clad in a white silk shirt trimmed with white fur. His hair, perfect to a strand every time I've seen it, is attractively tousled. His sparkling eyes and generous smile are exactly as I remember them.

"Elizabeth," he says with evident delight, his voice deadened in the confined space with the soft walls and soft floor. "This is a surprise. What have you brought me? Does this contain the ghosts that no longer belong?"

I walk toward him, compelled. Aside from Aloysius's chair, there are none in the room, and nothing prevents me from stepping to the edge of the desk and placing the infinity orb in his waiting hand. "I didn't know what to do with it. I can't take it home. Some of the ghosts in there hate me. And there's no one I trust enough to give it to that I know won't just destroy it if they can find a way. Most of the ghosts in there deserve better than to be trapped like that."

He brings the glass orb up close, examining it with a care and fascination that convinces me he must see something in it that I don't. "So you decided you'd make of it an offering."

The simple act of rolling my eyes does me a world of good in feeling like myself again. "I didn't say that," I say flatly.

Aloysius doesn't take his eyes off the ball, but his fascinated expression turns back into a delighted smile. "You don't have to. I will."

I sigh and readjust the green blanket around my shoulders, more to help the way I feel exposed than for the warmth. It's plenty warm in here, which is thawing out both my body and my thoughts by the second.

"You should have warned me. You knew what I was doing, and that it would cause problems. And you shouldn't have refused to help me when I needed it."

Aloysius digs in a drawer I can't see and comes out with a little folding stand, somehow just the right size for the ball. He places it in the corner of his desk and settles the ball into its new home before he fixes me again with a radiant, playful look.

"If I had, you'd never have given me such a wonderful Christmas gift."

I stare in disbelief. "It's not a present. It's a problem."

"It's a beautiful and unique problem," he returns.

I shake my head, dumbfounded.

"You look lovely," he says, changing the subject with apparent sincerity in the face of my bloody dress, tangled hair, bumps, bruises, and scrapes. "If you wanted to stay for the fight, you wouldn't even be underdressed."

The warm feeling in my center cools. The fight. I suppose I knew what the boxing ring in the center of the Casino was for, and why those supernatural creatures were milling about, but I didn't want to think about it. "And watch a death or a dismemberment? No, thank you."

His smile comes the closest to fading as it has since I came in. "It's usually dismemberment, you know," he says. "And you'd be surprised at the ways people in our community have of reconstituting limbs. Or, at the very least, working around missing ones."

I clench my jaw. "Still, I don't get why they come. I mean, sure, they could be assuming you probably won't pick them to fight. But they know there's a chance."

He leans back into his chair, regarding me with a preciseness that rivals what he turned on the infinity orb moments ago. "They know they might be picked, but they never think they'll lose."

"Okay, but what do they have to gain? What if they win?"

Aloysius lets out a soft breath, as if in a silent laugh to a joke I don't get. "Glory, partially. And a favor from me. Subject to my approval, of course, but a valuable prize all the same."

The pieces click together into place, and I see the restless figures in a new light.

"Deciding if you approve?" Aloysius asks, bemused rather than offended.

"Something like that."

"Are you staying? There are a lot of interesting folk living up this side of the Arctic Circle. It promises to be quite a contest."

The warmth in my core rekindles a bit. It smells good in here—like spices and oranges and just the barest hint of incense. "*Interesting folk* like gnomes and dwarves and elves?"

Aloysius laughs, the sound again draining into the softness of the space around us. "No elves, luckily. There's one who lives nearby, but she wouldn't come in here."

I give an exaggerated shrug and sigh of disappointment. "Oh, well, that's too bad. It's elves or nothing for me, I'm afraid."

Aloysius's eyebrows shoot up, and his chin lands in his palm with his elbow on the desk—a posture far too modern for the ancient thing he is. "I do hope one day you meet an elf, so you can understand what I'm feeling right now, hearing you say that."

He could almost look human, sitting like that. Except for the depth of mysteries buried behind his eyes. A *knowing* expression—that's what he always has. My eyes shift involuntarily to the infinity orb sitting in the perfectly sized stand. "You couldn't *possibly* have known what was going to happen," I say, thinking over the events of the last week.

Aloysius shifts and stands, pulling my attention. "No," he says, coming around the desk to stand in front of me. "But I knew *something* was going to happen. And I want things to happen for you, Elizabeth." He puts his hands on the upper part of my arms, over the green blanket, rubbing gently as if to warm me. And then, like magic—maybe, in fact, *exactly* like magic—the last cold vestiges of my freezing trip around the frigid world and through the piles of arctic snow dissipate.

He wants things to happen for me. Why wouldn't he? The more shit that gets fucked up in glorious fashion, the more likely I'll have to take unreasonable, inadvisable gambles. It's all about the worship, in the end.

"The Morrigan died angry at you," I say into the small space between us.

His hands stop their motion, but they stay on me. "She was right to," he says.

"Did you help the necrowizards capture her?"

His hands fall to his sides, but he stays close. "People do things in war they wouldn't do otherwise. It's only after the dust has settled that they can set the world right."

"But you didn't set the world right," I say, feeling color rising in my cheeks.

"My priest did."

"That doesn't count."

"It counts a little."

His hands rise slightly, like he wants to put them back on my shoulders, but when I stiffen in response to his movement, he doesn't. "You never ask me what you really want to when you come visit me," he says.

I swallow. "The ghosts in the Morrigan's afterlife were

atemporal," I say, almost whispering. "They saw the future."

"Yes," Aloysius says patiently, matching my volume.

"Is the future they saw inevitable?"

Aloysius reaches up and smooths out my hair, then carefully removes my one remaining earring from my ear. "The future they knew was a future in which their afterlife remained. The future that would have happened if they had not intervened in the world." He pulls up my hand and sets the earring in my palm, closing my fingers over the precious object. "That was the Brotherhood of Eternal Life's great gamble: They could see the future if the ghosts they trapped did not interfere in it, and they knew that it would leave them victorious. But to get to that future, the veil would need to thin and rip. And when it did, the ghosts would spill over into the world as wraiths. And when they did, anything might happen to change the future they saw."

I lean back slightly, realization spreading through my body like black ink in cold water. "Their gamble, huh?"

Aloysius gives me a slow, meaningful nod. I feel unsettled and a little bit sick. I need to say it out loud, to be sure. "They dedicated the worship of that gamble to you in exchange for helping them trap the Morrigan."

"I wouldn't have survived the war, or the time after it, if I hadn't made that bargain."

More realization dawns. I stand up a little straighter. "Which is why you couldn't help me, even if you wanted to. It would have tainted not just my worship, but the worship you paid for with the Morrigan's life." It sounds more like an accusation than I mean it to. But hell, in for a penny. "Even a thousand years later, you still weren't willing to give up their worship to fix things."

Aloysius's eyes narrow. "I wish it were that simple. But

all of it is so tangled up with time. I can't say for sure that had I interrupted the gamble with my direct, intentional interference, it wouldn't have spoiled the worship retroactively. And without that worship, I would have been dead long ago. I don't like to think what paradoxes that might have introduced. I only know I wouldn't have been alive to see them."

He wouldn't have been alive. And if I hadn't met him, I wouldn't have survived either. But even so, my eyes trace back to the infinity orb. Aloysius follows them, walking over to the desk and picking the precious object up, peering inside it.

"Are you going to give them a new afterlife?" I ask.

Aloysius's face sets. "I am not a death god."

"Not born with the genes for it?" I'm trying to introduce some levity, but I'm not quite hitting the mark.

"Never developed that particular inclination toward cruelty."

I let out a harsh breath. "It wouldn't have to be a hell. You could make them a heaven. That wouldn't be cruel."

At those words, Aloysius slumps against the side of his desk. He gazes into the ball for a moment, at the ghosts churning within, before he sets it back in its stand and addresses me directly. "The shadow of life isn't life. And any lie that profound is cruelty."

I don't know what to say to disrupt the depths of his intense stare, but he saves me the trouble by coming out of it himself. "I do think you're right, though," Aloysius says, straightening, his tone brighter.

"Right about what?" I ask, trying to navigate my way back out of the dark place we'd jointly visited.

"With the right spell, your pet wizard should be able to use the graveling dagger to free your mother of her affliction." His smile is radiant.

My jaw drops, and my eyes shift to the infinity orb. Aloysius follows my gaze and lets out a low laugh.

"You got the dagger stuck in the ball, didn't you?"

"Yes," I say. "Yes, I did."

Eyes shining, he picks up the ball again and takes a step back toward me, making me pull in a hurried breath.

"That's why you're actually here." There's a brutal joy to his smile that terrifies me.

"I was hoping you could help with that."

"I think you were very carefully *not* hoping anything at all."

I shrug, aware that his smile is contagious enough to have spread to my face. "Last time I needed help, you stopped me from coming here. Didn't want that to happen again. Can you do it?"

He raises an eyebrow and holds the ball aloft between us. "Remove the dagger? Naturally. Remove it without spilling out all the ghosts? I can't be certain. Reaching into the orb carries with it a chance of breaking it. It's on you to decide. Will you risk it? Will you stake the unhaunted world for the hope that your mother may be healed?"

He fixes me in an unblinking, joyful gaze.

Oh, smug bastard. He can do it.

"Go ahead."

With two fingers, Aloysius reaches into the orb and pulls out the dagger with such ease that I'm tempted to ask him to go in again and get my phone as well. He reaches it out to me, hanging by the handle, and I take it gingerly.

"Merry Christmas, Elizabeth," he says when I have the dagger, all gentleness.

"Merry Christmas," I return in similar fashion. "Or Yule, or Saturnalia, or whatever you celebrate."

Aloysius's eyes sparkle like they did when I first walked in. "Oh, I'm always celebrating something. And right now,

I'm celebrating that you came to talk to me. I've had something to tell you for a while now."

My mouth drops. Not another emergency. It's *Christmas.*

"There's a vampire living in Springfield under the radar, as it were," he says. And then, to my unasked *what the fuck?* he leans in conspiratorially. "And *you*, my dear little priest, burned down his warehouse."

"What?" The word shoots out of me.

Aloysius smiles and taps the center of my forehead with one slim forefinger.

And then I'm standing in the snow again, right next to a very startled Wilbur.

"Did it go okay?" he asks as I clutch the green blanket close. It keeps me warmer than it has any right to.

I nod a few times, as if trying to convince myself. "Yeah, it went… great. Good chat. Wilbur?"

"Yes?"

I take his arm. "Let's go home."

Epilogue

In the days between Christmas Eve and New Year's, I look for evidence online of the ghosts that I missed escaping from the Morrigan's heart causing trouble. I don't find any. Faisal says Olivia told him that she found a few potential accounts of things that might be activity from them, but it's hard to tell for certain. After all of the wraith encounters over the weeks leading up to Christmas Eve, it's hard to separate the true stories from the people who are imagining things and/or just want to be included.

Besides, most of the conversation on the internet after I destroyed the Morrigan's afterlife had to do with conspiracy theories about why the ghosts had so suddenly disappeared. There were a variety of popular theories, none of which were accurate in fact, but a few of which were accurate in spirit, which seems fitting. And, at the end of the day, I brushed the supernatural up against the everyday world in a way that the wizards couldn't entirely block, and I did it without them even knowing it was me. The rumor going around the wizard community was that it was a long-game necromancer plan finally coming to fruition that caused both the ghoul poisoning issue and the veil breaking issue, and with the lack of a clear alternative, no one is investigating too much further.

That's what Max tells me when he finally calls, at least. I wait for him to contact me first, rather than reaching out to him, to be sure I don't call him when he's home with his masters. I make sure to post on social media so he can see I made it out alive if he cares to check. When he calls me on the twenty-seventh, he thanks me for that, although he asks me for his knife back almost in the same breath. I tell him I'll be happy to return it—but not while it has the graveling magic infused in it. And if he removed the graveling magic, then it could never be used to fix my mom.

"Is this a test? You playing games with me, Elizabeth?" he asks.

"I mean…" Okay, maybe I am.

"I can't use the damn thing, anyway," he grumbles. "I guess I'm in no hurry to get it back."

ON DECEMBER THIRTIETH, I gather up my courage and head to the Emporium to try to talk to Gigi. I go right when the shop opens at eight-thirty a.m., before she's likely to have a crowd. I'm hoping to catch her alone, without any customers in the store, and I do.

"Hey," I say as I step up to the counter, feeling awkward. I half expect her to ignore me, yell at me, anything.

"We don't do those trendy Christmas mixes," Gigi says, already grabbing the little espresso handle thingy to start making my drink, "but I can add a little cinnamon to your usual oat milk latte. That seems festive enough."

I slump forward in relief, folding my arms and resting them on the countertop.

"Your sister—" I start.

"Made her own choices," Gigi says, continuing with her work. "And even came out of her centuries-long obscurity to do so. I love my sister—in a way. But sisters are complicated, and the choices they choose to make are complicated, too. You ought to know that as much as anyone."

"You heard I ran into her, then."

Gigi nods, tamping down the grounds and putting the handle in the machine. "Olivia told me a few days ago, when she was warning me that Max was going to be coming and going upstairs, trying to figure out how to fix your mom's mind. Apparently, you've got a dagger now that might make it possible."

"Yeah, we do," I say. I want to say more—to get into the nitty-gritty details of the whole ordeal, starting with when I wouldn't let her take me away from the haunted battlefield in Scotland. But she doesn't look like she wants to hear it.

"I suppose it's a good reason to keep him around. A good reason to want to save him. If he's going to try to heal your mother."

It isn't an admission of being wrong. It isn't saying Max is intrinsically worth saving. And the fact that Max could be useful to me isn't why I wanted to save him, either—at least, not entirely. But it's something.

"You're going to have to apologize to him for leaving him, you know," I say, covering the same ground I had with her sister, when I had thought she was Gigi. "I didn't mean to tell you that you couldn't help with things anymore. I need you. I wouldn't have survived this time if it weren't for your sister. But whatever way I'm going to find to fix things with Max, it's going to take an apology from you."

Gigi smiles. "Oh, don't worry about that. I have a plan. You're not going to like it, but I have one."

Her smile worries me. "What is it?"

"Now, why would I tell you that? You'd only get in the way."

Just what I need. At least she gave me a warning in advance that she's going to do something I won't like. That's progress. The steam wand makes its loud foaming noise in the little metal carafe full of oat milk.

"You're still going to have to apologize, though. Apologies are important."

Gigi sprinkles cinnamon over my completed latte in its paper cup, puts on the lid, and sets it on the counter directly in front of me.

"Of course they are. They're not magic, but they can open doors. Want to know one reason I'm sure of that?"

"Why?" I ask, putting my hands around the warm cup.

"Because that latte was paid for when I talked to Olivia a few days ago."

I grip the cup tighter. It's a little too hot to hold without a sleeve or an extra cup right now, but I don't care.

"She can't forgive, so she needs to forget. That can take a little while, but it's worth the time."

The jingle of the front door jolts us from the moment and pulls my attention. A large family enters, complete with an excited young girl, a sullen teenage girl apparently annoyed to be dragged along, a college-age boy staring at his phone, and a couple of cheerful—if tired-looking— dads. They fall in behind me. Best not hold up the line.

"Happy New Year," I say to Gigi, heading to the door.

"Happy New Year!" she returns.

———

Faisal goes back to work, flying off to Dubai on January third. It feels unfair, somehow. Surprises me, even, which doesn't make sense.

Until I puzzle out that the dumb part of me that feels like the world should be fair has decided that for my good and great deeds, I had earned him staying at home. But it turns out that magic doesn't pay for his student loans, so off he goes.

So, on the sixth of January, when I come home after work, I'm surprised to feel as though the house isn't empty. I'm even more surprised to see a lanky figure sitting at my kitchen table with his back to me.

"Claude?" I say when I reach the dining room. "You're here."

Claude raises his eyebrows and purses his lips in an expression that could be mocking, affectionate, or a mixture of both. I'm not going to try to figure out which. "Your powers of observation are unmatched, Arbiter."

I set down my laptop bag and shuffle out of my winter coat, wishing that I had my leather jacket on. It's my supernatural uniform, after all. I go to slide into the chair across the table from him, but decide better of it, heading instead for the rarely used cupboard above the refrigerator. I'm not quite tall enough to open it, which I remember too late. But it opens on its own, presumably nudged by an invisible root. The bottle of red wine that I'd been going for—a gift from one of Faisal's coworkers last year when we invited her for dinner—likewise slides out of the cupboard and into my hand.

"Thanks," I say, though the gesture of surprising him with a treat feels a little undercut by his help. Hopefully it'll still moderate any potential anger he has over the arbitration not ending up the way he might have expected. I pour the wine into two actual wine glasses and set one in front of him.

He gestures to the chair across from him, and this time I take it. My cheeks are still red from coming into the warm house from the cold early evening.

Claude takes a sip of his wine, and I stifle the reflex to apologize for its likely poor quality, as well as for not airing it out. He can't taste it, after all.

"I didn't break my word with you," I say, after he's set the glass back down.

"I know. I am not here for that."

"What are you here for, then?"

Claude reaches into his illusory impeccably tailored sportscoat and pulls out a bottle that would look more at home in an eighteenth-century apothecary than in a twenty-first-century house. It's full of a thick, viscous, cheerful-cherry-red liquid.

He slides it across the table to me, and I'm inordinately proud of myself for neither missing it nor knocking over my wine glass to catch it.

"Ghoul blood?" I take a stab in the dark. I know it's not graveling blood.

Claude nods. "It's become an unwritten rule that the winner of your arbitrations gives you a vial of their blood, is it not?"

I give him a noncommittal shrug. Unwritten rule? Not really, but I can see how someone rules-obsessed might see it that way. Since the sirens gave me a vial of their blood, it happens more often than not in my bigger arbitrations. I don't have a ton of big arbitrations, but I have four vials of supernatural blood in the back of my freezer. Why? I have no clue. The Pacific Siren Queen seemed to think it would be useful to me for some reason, but we're not exactly on good enough terms for me to ask her why.

"I didn't rule in favor of the ghouls," I say.

"No, but they got what they wanted. I think for now it's close enough."

I let out a bitter laugh. I try not to think about the ghoul's body being mutilated in four different ways at the same time. I fail sometimes. "That wasn't me. That only happened because the ghoul we were talking to mis-played her hand."

Claude cocks his head and gives me a long, intent look. "Did she?" he asks.

The corner of my mouth twitches. I feel worse about the ghoul's fate every time I consider it might have been voluntary. That she went into that situation knowing she'd probably die a gruesome death, but that making a big enough nuisance of herself and getting in the middle of a big wizard conflict, one way or another, would convince the wizards to step in on her problem. Maybe she hoped that taking credit for my victory, if I came out victorious, would leave her alive. But she did seem smarter than that, and I have enough things to feel shitty about. I don't need to take on any more.

I flick my eyes meaningfully to the bottle of ghoul blood. "So you're enforcing my rules now? Does that mean you think I have power?"

Claude smiles. "It means you demonstrated a certain power one time. And I can tell no one about that time, remember? You insisted on that."

"I did."

Something's not fitting into place about Claude showing up here and giving me this. Something's not right. The blood payment is a rule, *maybe*, but only because he bent it to be one, and it's not like it would be enforced. We had a deal, and I maintained it, but that doesn't come out with him owing me something.

Maybe I look too much like I'm trying to puzzle it out, and Claude doesn't want me to get there before he leaves. Maybe he's just been sitting in my kitchen waiting for too long, and he's gotten bored. Either way, he downs the rest of the wine in his glass, and I get that subtle feeling of unseen motion around me of him preparing to leave.

It's not until he has the slider open and is standing in front of it that I put it together.

"Say, Claude," I remark, stopping him cold.

"Yes?"

"Do you think wielding that dagger you imbued would interfere with a protection spell? Like my amulet, for instance?"

Claude lets out a breath, sets his hand on the slider door handle, and faces me.

"I could imagine that might perhaps be the case," he says, his tone admitting a certainty his words don't.

"And you didn't tell me. Knowing how much I must rely on my amulet, and knowing that I was going to be running headlong into wizards who wanted me dead if they knew who I was." I no longer sound angry when I tell people I recognize they've done something that could harm me—just matter of fact. That's probably not a good thing.

"If I had told you, you would not have wanted the weapon. And I needed for you to want something only I could give you."

The air between us is alive with tension for a few seconds before I say, "And I killed two of you. And you're not supposed to die."

He gives me a deep, solemn nod, closing his eyes briefly

at the bottom. It's the least human thing I've seen him do through the wizard's illusion. "Yes."

I take a deep breath in and let it out slowly, while Claude stands still with his hand on the slider. Then I lean back into my chair, pick up my wine glass, and take a drink.

"Thanks for this," I say, nudging the bottle of ghoul blood.

"Yes, I thought it was appropriate that you should have ghoul blood of all kinds. It will be especially useful to you, I think."

My eyes shoot up at Claude, and the hunger in them for the information he apparently has makes him smile.

"You do not know why you are collecting the blood, but you do it anyway?"

"I don't know why I do a lot of things. Enlighten me?"

Claude steps backward out the door, the smile still on his face. "Blood is the essence of life. A wizard with the right spell can use blood to transform. They never do it. When they change back, they too often find all their power gone. But for you, with no power to begin with…"

Claude walks into the yard and toward a cellar door that has already appeared in the ground. I take a step onto the back porch to be sure I catch his final words before he disappears beneath the earth.

"That would be a useful spell for you to find, would it not be so?"

The End

About the Author

Amanda Creiglow lives in Rhode Island with her little pitfall and way too many projects. Sign up for her newsletter to find out more and be notified about her next book at author.amandacreiglow.com.

facebook.com/TroveArbitrations

twitter.com/amandacreiglow

instagram.com/amandacreiglow